D0499026

Few stories are as cherished—and as contested—as the lives of the saints: the joyful St. Francis of Assisi, the steadfast St. Joseph, the ascetic and visionary St. Catherine of Siena. In this unique volume, seventeen distinguished writers explore the deep and varying responses the saints inspire in us today.

Through these eloquent and moving essays, the saints emerge as fascinating paradoxes: like T. S. Eliot's Becket, they have felt "a tremor of bliss," but they must fight all-too-mortal battles with despair, social indifference, and hardness of heart. This provocative collection of contemporary writing poses spiritual questions with uncommon intelligence and grace.

"The mortal nature of the saints is here given a contemporary voice...a unique and personal perspective regarding the saints."
—*Library Journal*

A Tremor of Bliss will "connect the readers as surely with the writers as with the saints who are their subjects."
—*Booklist*

A Tremor *of* Bliss

Contemporary Writers on the Saints

Edited *by* PAUL ELIE

Introduction by ROBERT COLES

RIVERHEAD BOOKS, NEW YORK

Riverhead Books
Published by The Berkley Publishing Group
200 Madison Avenue
New York, New York 10016

Harcourt, Brace & Company edition published 1994
Riverhead edition: December 1995
Published simultaneously in Canada.

Library of Congress Cataloging-in-Publication Data

A tremor of bliss : contemporary writers on the saints / edited by
    Paul Elie ; introduction by Robert Coles.—Riverhead ed.
        p.   cm.
    Originally published: New York : Harcourt Brace, c1994.
    ISBN 1-57322-513-4
    1. Christian saints—Cult.   2. Christian life—Catholic authors.
    I. Elie, Paul.
    BX2325.T74   1995   95–22201
    282′.092′2—dc20   CIP
Printed in the United States of America

10 9 8 7 6 5 4 3 2 1

Acknowledgments

The editor thanks Alane Salierno Mason, Sue Young Wilson, Celia Wren, and Amanda Urban for their encouragement and support.

I have had a tremor of bliss, a wink of heaven, a whisper,
And I would no longer be denied; all things
Proceed to a joyful consummation.
> —Archbishop Thomas Becket,
> in *Murder in the Cathedral*,
> by T. S. Eliot

CONTENTS

Introduction

ROBERT COLES

THE ESSAYS in this book tell us that the idea and the ideal of sanctity, as it has been lived in certain lives over the centuries, persist in our significantly secular time for these American writers, among others. Not that most of us think of sharing in print our spiritual inclinations or preoccupations, as they find expression in this or that historical figure. Reflection, let alone reflection put forward and shared with others, is surely a privilege—though a curse, too, many authors would also say. In that regard, some who barely can read or write (because of their age, or the social circumstances of their life) would eagerly assent—it is a mixed blessing to try to find one's spiritual bearings. "I wish I wasn't sick," a boy afflicted with polio told me in 1958, amid a severe epidemic of that disease. I was then working on the pediatric ward of a Boston hospital, and was not surprised to hear those words—they had become a daily chant, spoken plaintively by child after child. But this youngster had something else in mind for me to hear, to contemplate: "Before I got this [illness] I didn't pray to all those people, that they should help me out with God." I wasn't sure what he meant, and I was quite busy, in a hurry. I was just curious enough, though, to risk a question: "Which people?" He smiled, volunteered: "All the saints." His mother, it turned out, had been urging him to seek help through those who "lived in Heaven," she put it, and thereby had the ear of God. The boy obliged; but he wasn't happy to do so: "I don't want to bother those folks, and besides, they must have so many kids to worry about." He paused, then added this: "I'd just as soon they forgot me; and I wish I could go back to my life before here." He more than implied his desire to forget *them*.

I had no time or inclination, back then, to pursue the matter with that boy—aim for a bedside colloquy on the saints as putative, intercessory agents in the lives of Christ's faithful ones. But many years later, while working as a volunteer teacher in a Boston elementary school that served a ghetto neighborhood, I found myself remembering that boy and his comments. I was teaching vocabulary and spelling to a fourth-grade class, nine- and ten-year-old boys and girls. A girl was spelling the word "angel," and she stumbled: she wrote "angle" on the blackboard. Sure she was right, she quickly put the chalk down and went back to her seat. I waited for objections, corrections, and soon enough realized that no one had noticed anything wrong. The children, actually, seemed bored, noisily indifferent to the entire exercise—no surprise at all. Yet again I prepared myself for a show of irritation, for an outburst meant to secure attention, interest, compliance. Yet again, I was dragging my feet, praying that somehow, through some miraculous intervention of luck, someone would say something that would spare me the necessity of behaving in that manner: raising my voice high to purchase a fleeting moment of obedience, silence—all of us, thereby, humiliated, and moments later all of us once more lost to one another as, inexorably, the sound level would rise and rise. Suddenly, a boy, a wise guy of a boy, snickered, laughed, and then spoke: "Hey, that's angle, not angel." Now, a quiet classroom—and then lots of whistling, hooting, slapping of rulers on desks, cheering. I got annoyed: *Come on*— enough, more than enough: an overreaction on my part that had to do, nevertheless, with how little respect for ordinary classroom civility could be assumed by a teacher, by any student oddly inclined to be serious.

But I am, too, suddenly moved to take stock. I decide I am too down on these youngsters. I have underestimated their capacity to move from evident playfulness (interpreted by me as the same old disorder and callousness of a failed ghetto school system) to sly, provocative thoughtfulness. Then, I hear: "Well, what's the angle the angels have, I want to know"—a girl musing out loud. Utter quiet, uninterrupted, this time, by any background noise. As if to prompt further introspection, she amplifies: "Everyone has an angle, don't you think?" Nods tell her that she is right on target. A girl sitting right in front of her turns around to offer a conjecture: "The angels are good friends to God, I think. They're good, real good, like God is. They don't go around messing up. They're the ones who are one hundred percent perfect: not like anyone who's here—not like any people, because even the best of people, they'll do wrong as well as good, so there's no one hundred percent from [among] them."

A boy sitting in the last seat of the last row, almost always without comment, though quite observant and quite smart, surprises everyone with his hand raised high, kept there until the teacher acknowledges him, whereupon he gives a pointed disquisition of sorts: "You don't have an angle if you're an angel; that's what I think. The reason is: an angel doesn't exist, the way we do. You see, an angel is a spirit; our priest told us. A saint, that's different. A saint is a person; so I agree, a saint can't be perfect. No one is. A saint will have an angle: he's trying to strike a home run, or she is, if it's a woman who's the saint. [There was Joan of Arc.] Saint Francis, he wanted people to be nicer—that was his angle. He was very nice, and wanted people to be like him, more like him. Our priest says he had 'ambition' for all of the people; and that was his angle, maybe. Do you see what I mean?"

A spell of absolute silence; *he* had hit a home run. Students who had been listening to him had turned to look at him, and continued to do so, while he looked down at his desk. Finally, as others began to stir (and, I speculate, ready themselves with things to say), he looks up, decides he has more to tell: "You could probably guess: a lot of those saints, they would have liked to be angels, but you can't be an angel unless God makes you one. If He makes you a person, then you'll just be here a little while, and you die. I think angels live forever. I'm not sure. That's a difference [between angels and saints]. But the big difference is that if you're a person, you make mistakes; you can't help it. We try to remember the saints because of the good they did; but they didn't always do good. You should remember that."

More of the unusual silence, and then a burst of remarks from other children, the gist of which is a confirmation of the spiritual (if not theological) exegesis just given us. One girl says a lot, summarizes a lot, when she comments upon the "big struggles those saints must have [had] when they were trying to be saints, but they couldn't be, not all the time, that's for sure. Who can be, even one of them?" We all realize, courtesy of this discussion, the real anguish and conflict involved for those men and women, posthumously declared saints by church officials, and by generations of believers, and nonbelievers. It is all too easy to forget the essential humanity of such individuals, as these children, in their charming so-called innocence, were not wont to do—a contrast: their earthy, blunt recognition of that humanity, opposed to the common presentations, in churches, in history books, of so many saints, certainly Saint Francis: a perfection rendered incarnate.

No question the great Danish theologian and essayist Kierkegaard was quite conversant with the point of view those children were proposing when he offered the few who would then be his readers "On the Difference Between a Genius and an Apostle." Again and again he insists that the "difference" has little to do with talent or intelligence; has everything to do with purpose, with a kind of commitment—in his terms, a moral rather than an aesthetic distinction. The apostle, the saint, is "called," but, in consequence, we ought to keep in mind (we who are ever tempted by idolatry of one kind or another) that he or she "does not become more intelligent, does not receive more imagination, a greater acuteness of mind and soul." Rather, the apostle, the saint, makes an appeal to "divine authority," aligns himself or

When I was a college student, I took a course, Classics of the Christian Tradition, offered by Perry Miller, who spent so much of his life trying to fathom the Puritan sensibility of the seventeenth and eighteenth centuries. He was the one who introduced us to Kierkegaard's powerfully affecting, sometimes stunning and haunting essays, to his dramatic virtuosity, his daring raids upon the accepted and the conventional, his moral brilliance, so unnerving and suggestive. We got into a discussion one day about saints (we were a class of about thirty). Miller listened, nodded, asked questions, provoked us to silent contemplation, interrupted, sometimes, by his own gruff, hearty, earthy but thought-laden comments, or, often enough, his outcries of the soul as much as of the head. That day, while names of saints came up, one after the other, as we tried to make sense of their diverse and not rarely difficult, even (seemingly) tormented lives, Miller sat before us in a kind of stoic bemusement, with not a word to say. Finally, we stopped fighting for his attention, stopped fighting with one another. We'd been eagerly, and competitively, offering various explanations and interpretations of sainthood, drawing, of course, on contemporary psychology and sociology, and on history and theology. Miller pushed back his chair, told us he didn't really have a definitive idea or definition of what constitutes sainthood, but he could offer us a "personal surmise." I recall, even now, writing down those two words—so characteristic of this extraordinary professor:

a deliberate tentativeness that certainly approached modesty. We were all ears, and we heard this: "A saint is a sinner, writ large, someone who struggles exceptionally hard to turn a bad thing into a good one." He went on to remind us that rather often such a person has no such explicit or conscious agenda in mind—the conversion of darkness into light, so to speak. Saints, he went on to speculate, are "driven by a moral nature, much in jeopardy," are "ready to take huge risks and chances," because they know well the "terror of hell," or "the loneliness that awaits them in hell."

As he kept leaning backward in his chair, we were all hunched, sitting forward, trying to digest a particular offering. Nor were we having an easy time. This was, after all, the second half of the twentieth century, and we were attending a more or less secular American university. We wanted some "psychodynamics," maybe, or some "cultural history," or, if we had to settle for it, some damned original, and of course subtle, theology: no thinly masked pieties from earlier, more "respectful" times in Christendom's past. Yet, we knew not how to spell out our needs, our interests—ourselves, really: who we had already become, what our assumptions were, and, yes, what we found unconvincing, if not utterly unacceptable. At last, one of us broke the spell of nervous quiet with a question: "You don't believe in hell, do you?" Miller laughed; he understood, right away, that as he had been trying to explain the way *saints* thought, *their*

reasons for being, for acting as they did, he had spoken
as if the hell they dreaded existed for him, too. We
wanted him, he realized, to distance himself from that
word, to use language, or a mere gesture, a facial expression, to indicate his awareness of ancient superstition! Instead, we were told this: "Hell has lived in minds, driven
souls to countless adventures and achievements, inspired
great deeds"—a pause, and then the briefest of explications: "Fear or dread as grace."

That last phrase landed on us just as we were sum-
moning what we regarded to be a clever, an adroit psychology, the contemporary mannerisms of the clinic: he
is dodging; he is telling us that he believes in the subjective reality of hell as it gets experienced, still, by some,
and even gets used "adaptively," that final word meant
to be a compliment, though one not without the risks of
condescension. But Miller had confused us, as well as
given us pause, with his use of the word "grace"—not
exactly a word one encounters in today's social-science
vocabulary. We wanted to ask about *that,* too: what in
the world did "grace" *really* mean? I now realize (I'm
sure Miller *then* realized) that we didn't even have the
vocabulary that would enable a reasonably polite consid-
eration of the subject matter. We were materialists at
heart, and in connection with this discussion we could
venture only so far away from our cultural and historical
roots—say, toward the metapsychology Freud had bestowed: hell as an assault of the Super-Ego on the Id,

and grace as some "equilibrium" (the "scientific" satis-
factions of such a word!) between Super-Ego and Ego.
Taking stock of us, and looking inward, too, I'm sure,
Miller tried yet again to be of assistance: "How can one
imagine a saint without imagining heaven and hell as utterly imaginable to them?" Once more, he held back
words, just as we craved them, ached for their familiar
solace, no matter their sometimes irritable, or upsetting
challenge. We had learned to wait, though, and did, until
he turned his attention decisively away from those saints,
toward us: "I think if we are to understand saints, we
have to try to follow their lead. Imagine the worlds they
never stopped imagining, reaching for, fleeing with all
their might."

In my notes, with their hurried capture of his remarks, I managed to assert myself with one word he
chose deliberately not to use: the desirability of "empa-
thy"—a caveat to myself, courtesy of the professor, or
so I earnestly believed to be the case. Now I think I
understand the desperation, if not (in the tradition of
Kierkegaard) the resignation, that informed that tutorial
effort. How to speak of angels and devils, of heaven and
hell, of saints and even sinners in such a setting—a reasonably humane (so we hoped) secularism at the peak of
its influence? A professor was both gently and fiercely
suggesting that to comprehend the assumptions of others, we had to give hard scrutiny, first, to our own—
rather than take it upon ourselves to walk, willy-nilly,

into anyone's life with our modern diagnostic strategies, formulations, shoptalk in the expectation that a discovery (always on our terms, in our terms) would be forthcoming. We who claim to understand human feeling more precisely than was possible ever before were being asked to test the range of that understanding, take a big leap into the shoes of others (a bit more, such an effort, I fear, than that of sounding the trumpet of "psycho-historical" theory).

So with these writers here: they try in their several ways to connect with certain saints; to leap across generations, centuries, entire eras, in order to bring alive men and women who are, finally, fellow human beings, at once tempted and tried, hugely given over to spiritual passions, insistently intent on realizing them in word, in deed, no matter the personal consequences. What follows in these essays is a chemistry of bonding, an anthropology of affiliation, of kinship, a psychology of moral imagination raised, given voice. These late-twentieth-century men and women of the industrial West attempt an intimacy of mind, heart, soul with chosen predecessors in the human parade, those who by dint of their daunting, sometimes desperate spirituality continue both to confound and to inspire us. Ordinary souls that we are, we respond to such lives, such lived moments, such brief spells amidst an infinity of time, such utterly transient locations of moral and spiritual struggle in an infinity of space, with what resources we can muster—the biographer's effort at an account, a chronicle; the writer's mix of memory and narrative cogency, urgency. Through these essayists, others long dead or not so long gone come to life yet again, and in turn, the tasks they attempted, the examples they sought to find for themselves and show to others, the passions of faith they tried to affirm, share, encourage, are given the life of a reader's attention, and maybe more, too: a celebration of the miracle of commitment, moment by moment tested and strained by the doubt that not rarely goes under that name of faith.

In their sum, too, these essays attest to the variousness of that faith: the many ways of getting down on one's knees, in the hope (the hope against hope) that there is in this cosmos the listening, the watching, and, not least, the judging, the sorting, which so many of us, for so long have sought, prayed for, spent lives wondering about, waiting for—God in all the mystery of the word, in all the perplexity and frustration that the word can evoke. The saints, maybe, have tried to give their lives over to that mystery, that perplexity and frustration: Here I went, stumbled, but plodded on, and here you are, fellow pilgrim; take my hand, therefore, and walk your given allotment of days with the effort of faith, even if the ending of both of our journeys is known to none of us—but we do pray, Lord, we pray to a world insubstantial, indeed, though real enough right now, right here, for us so tethered to human existence.

Il Poverello

BRUCE BAWER

FOR YEARS, the biggest annual draw at North America's largest cathedral has been a high mass commemorating the feast of Saint Francis. It's called the Missa Gaia, or Earth Mass, and if you show up early enough at New York's Cathedral of Saint John the Divine to squeeze into the teeming nave, you'll witness a procession of animals that includes parrots and turtles, cats and dogs, a horse, a camel, an elephant, even amoebae.

It's an unusual service, but then it honors an unusual saint—indeed, the most popular saint there is. Born late in 1181 or early in 1182, he was baptized Giovanni, for Saint John the Baptist, at the request of his mother, who was named Giovanna but was apparently known as Pica (which may mean that she came from Picardy). His father, Pietro di Bernardone, an Assisi clothing merchant who did business with the French, rejected the boy's baptismal name and replaced it with an unusual one: Francesco. It's tempting to see the contrast between the two appellations—the one Biblical and the other a Francophile neologism perhaps inspired by commercial considerations—as reflecting the tension between a mother who was a good Catholic and a father who was a good businessman. Certainly the history of Francis's early years suggests that the boy was no stranger either to the essence of the Christian message or to the worldview of the medieval mercantile class.

The volumes of saints' lives are crowded with stories of men and women who as children were noted for their piety, self-abnegation, and acts of contrition—and, in many cases, supernatural visions and visitations. Not so with Francis, whose "sudden conversion in the midst of a life of pleasure" H. G. Wells compared with Gautama Buddha's. A worldly youth, he spent his father's money on amusements; perhaps because Bernardone traded in cloth, moreover (Francis is said to have worked in his clothing store), the young man was something of a clotheshorse. He also dreamed of glory in battle. Yet when he was dispatched to the rival town of Perugia with a contingent of armed noblemen, he was promptly captured and imprisoned. Released after a year, he resolved to give war another chance; yet, setting out for the Fifth Crusade, he made it only to Spoleto before he heard a voice telling him to return home. He did.

Soon it was clear: Francis, at twenty-five, had changed. The clothier's son began to dress plainly and to give his good clothes—along with money—to beggars. When it developed that he was also handing out merchandise from his father's store, Bernardone dragged Francis home, beat him, and locked him up. Freed by Pica, he was hauled before the bishop. (Considering himself to be in God's service, Francis refused to face civil authorities.) Ordered to restore his father's possessions, Francis stripped, leaving nothing on his body but that popular medieval penitential aid, a hair shirt. The bishop, impressed by his respectful audacity, released him.

Had Francis stolen from his father? It would seem so. But Francis, stubbornly set on doing good with the wealth he'd been accustomed to spending on himself, may not have realized it. Then again, the Francis–Bernardone relationship does seem awfully like something out of Freudian case study. Whenever their paths crossed after Francis's trial, Bernardone cursed his son. In response, Francis hired an old beggar to follow him around Assisi; if Bernardone began hurling maledictions, the beggar would bless Francis, who would then rebuke his father for *not* blessing him. Was Francis being unfair, using his Heavenly Father as ammunition in an Oedipal rebellion? Or was he, a Biblical literalist, merely observing Christ's injunction that his followers must hate their parents? Was Christ, after all, being unfair to Mary when he refused to see her, saying, "My mother and my brothers are those who hear the word of God and act upon it"?

For that is what Francis was about: he sought to lead a Christlike life, and not to do it by halves. The first lesson of his story is that living like Christ is not just a matter of being vaguely nice and inoffensive; at times one may find it necessary to behave in ways that seem obstinate, self-righteous, even uncharitable. The second lesson is that the path to Christ can be bumpy and meandering. Before discovering how best to serve God with the gifts at one's disposal, one can make some terribly wrong turns and misguided choices. It's said, for instance, that when Francis first became a beggar he frankly sought glory as a "knight of God" in the same way he'd aspired to military glory—hardly an example of proper Christian humility. Did he continue to think this way, or did humility come gradually?

Whatever the case, Francis found his way to God's service by stages. The first stage involved a dilapidated San Damiano church. Convinced that God had commanded him to "repair my house," Francis—a literalist not only Biblically but also, apparently, in the matter of heavenly voices—set about restoring the structure. Presently, in a wood near Assisi, he discovered a small Benedictine chapel, Our Lady of the Angels, later Our Lady of the Portiuncula, which would become the hub of Franciscan activity; this, too, he repaired.

At first mocked and stoned in Assisi, Francis came to be tolerated, then esteemed. Like Christ, he began to draw disciples to his side, a development that wasn't part of his original intent. The Franciscan order just *happened.* Why? Part of the reason for it—and for Francis's popularity down to the present—lies in his simplicity of life, thought, and expression. His "Canticle of the Sun" (now considered the first great poem in Italian), his letters, and the rules he wrote for his order reflect a firm and uncomplicated conviction that human beings are put on earth to praise, serve, and rejoice. As Hans Küng has noted, Francis is of all medieval figures the one with whose view of Christ today's Christians can most readily identify. No intellectual giant, no maker of systematic doctrine, he appeals to most Christians' antipathy for abstruse formulations. His warning that knowledge could be self-destructive—a warning motivated by his belief that theological discourse had severed the clergy from God's pure message of love and from the laypeople they were called to serve—speaks loudly to the antiintellectualism of the average man or woman in the average pew. For scholars, this aspect of Francis can be troubling. Yet even bookish Christians will acknowledge that a simple hymn can help one to achieve a sense of spiritual communion that an entire theological library may not. That's the essence of Francis's ministry, then and now: his simple, perhaps overly literal, and (to some) even ingenuous obedience to Christ's charge to serve the poor—his willingness to be "God's fool"—confronts us all with the degree to which our own Christianity is a matter of speech more than of action, a belief intellectualized rather than passionately lived.

One aspect of Francis's simplicity was his strong sense of attachment to and brotherhood with animals—most famously, his preaching to birds. Yet, although this side of Francis may appeal to the sentimentally inclined and theologically shaky—those who dwell on such questions as "Will my dog go to heaven?"—one need not fall into that category to find positive meaning in Francis's avian homiletics. As a smart preacher once observed, the proper Christian question is not "Will my dog go to heaven?" but "Will I bring heaven to my dog?" In other words, "Does my faith manifest itself in such a way that not only my fellow human beings but animals as well can tell the difference?" This is the proper light, I think, in which to regard Francis's preaching to birds—as the manifestation of a love of God so powerful that he felt compelled to share it with all of God's creation.

Francis even saw the heathen as his brothers—a novel idea in thirteenth-century Europe, where high-profile Crusaders were routinely canonized for slaughtering infidels. Traveling in 1219 to Egypt, he determined to make a Christian of the Egyptian sultan, Malek el-Kamil, and bravely crossed the Crusaders' battle lines to meet him. The sultan proved to be a sophisticated man, far more interested in cultural and spiritual matters—and far more tolerant, too—than most European royals. After a friendly theological conversation with Francis, he reportedly said, "I would convert to your religion, which is a beautiful one, but I cannot: Both of us would be massacred." Remarkably, it is recorded that Francis accompanied the sultan's nephew to a mosque and prayed there, saying: "God is everywhere." Today, when stories about Francis meeting Christ don't convince, and when even the Roman Catholic Church recognizes the stigmata as psychosomatic, Francis's sojourn with the sultan stands out as the most impressive event of his life. As Julian Green writes, he "was and still remains the man who transcends our sad theological barriers," rising above the intense sectarian antagonisms of his time—and ours— as an emblem of religious tolerance, interfaith ventures, and ecumenical bridge-building.

For his contemporaries, Francis's simple existence— and his decision to call himself the Little Pauper (the "Poverello") and his society the Order of Friars Minor— contrasted strikingly with the lives of the many priests and monks who kept concubines and lived in luxury. His humility, to be sure, did not prevent him from preaching a sermon to the Pope and several cardinals chiding them for their vanity and dissipation. Yet this archetypal rebel remained a loyal, obedient Catholic. He was also, in some ways, much like other medieval saints. He recoiled from sex, for instance, avoiding women and enjoining his brothers to do the same; when forced into mixed company, he was taciturn, even rude. An early biographer notes that his antipathy for the opposite sex was so powerful that "one would have thought it was fear or disgust rather than prudence." "Don't canonize me too soon," Francis once said. "I am still perfectly capable of fathering children." He shared, then, the tendency often encouraged by the Roman Catholic Church to see physical intimacy, even in marriage, as inconsistent with virtue. Given this severe posture, the introduction into his life of a young woman named Clare seems almost like a plot device out of some old movie—a medieval version, say, of *The Bells of Saint Mary's*. A biographer of Francis has written that Saint Clare "brought to the Franciscan movement a consistency, a strength and a tenacious intuition of elemental issues which it might otherwise have lacked." She also brought women. Pressing herself on Francis, imploring him to allow her into his fold, Clare forced him to accept the fact of female spirituality and to permit her to form an associate order, the Poor Clares. Yet he continued to have misgivings, saying to one of his brothers that "it is the Lord who has preserved us from taking wives, but who knows whether it is not the Devil who has sent us sisters?"

Francis wasn't above the superstitions of his day. It had been decreed that those who died on the Crusades would go straight to Heaven; claiming that Christ had told him to make the request, Francis asked that those who confessed at La Portiuncula be accorded the same benefit. Pope Honorius III agreed, but stipulated that complete absolution would be granted only one day a year. That was enough for Francis, who proclaimed: "I shall send them all to paradise!" The apparent egoism of this remark can give one pause, as can Francis's eagerness to believe that souls might be purchased in such fashion—a view that militates against our sense of him as being, in many ways, our contemporary. And what of his stigmata? The Middle Ages loved them; they figure prominently in most paintings of him, and for centuries had their own feast day. Today, however, these once seemingly miraculous episodes serve only to underscore Francis's similarities to lesser, more ordinary saints.

It's not miracles that mark Francis as extraordinary; it's the fullness of his humanity. Some saints are celebrated for their lives in the world, their practical service to humankind; others are venerated for having been mystics, hermits, visionaries—people who renounced society to be closer to God. Most saints (martyrs aside) fall squarely into one category or the other. Francis straddled them; at once inner- and outer-directed, a man of contemplation as well as action, he adhered with equal ardor to Christ's commandments to love God and one's neighbor. Indeed, it's tempting to see a reflection of this mixture of spirituality and earthiness in his two names: Giovanni, for the Baptist, who marked people as citizens of Heaven, and Francis, for France, a portion of the earth.

This isn't to suggest that the most popular saint was necessarily the most saintly of men, any more than the most celebrated film star is the finest of actors. Like a film star, a great saint is someone whose life can be reduced to a strong, uncomplicated image. Francis's is such a life. Yet he remains, for us, very real. "I want to hear a saint converse," John Henry Newman wrote. "I am not content to look at him as a statue." Countless artists have depicted Francis, but to view their works is not only to be confronted with an image of holiness but also to be reminded of a singular life, to feel a personality's presence, and, yes, to hear a voice. There is no danger that those artworks will be rendered mute any time soon; all it takes is a glance at one of them for Francis to come alive in our minds as do few other Christian figures aside from Christ Himself.

Indeed, in a time when not only Protestants but more than a few Catholics rebel at the idea of sainthood, Francis speaks to us as few men or women of his time do— and as few saints do, medieval or otherwise. What, many Christians wonder with good reason, do hermits, cults of suffering, and supposed posthumous miracles have to do with the gospel message that lies at the heart of the faith?

Why, they ask, must we feel obliged to continue cele-brating certain historical figures for what may not, to our eyes, look like Christian virtue? Especially in an Age of Celebrity, how can we justify heaping additional praise onto a life already amply glorified when honor might in-stead be paid to a virtuous unknown?

The Church canonizes men and women so that they may be emulated, not prayed to. Yet people being what they are, canonization has always carried with it the dan-ger of replacing the ideal of a Christlike life with a fetish-ism about relics and a tendency to pray to saints rather than to God. Francis defies that sort of vulgarization: the plain, powerful story of his life keeps forcing us back to his earthly example even as it reveals to us the startling light of Christ, that breakthrough of the kingdom into the darkness of this world. Unlike many saints, who in medieval paintings look remote and severe, there's noth-ing forbidding about him. He reminds us that when we speak of the "communion of saints," we are talking not just about those famous figures enshrined in the pages of Alban Butler, but about "the Church in earth and heaven"—about the people who sit every week around us in church, and about unsung men and women who led ordinary lives with faith and goodness. Precisely be-cause the Christlike pattern of his life remains a potent fact in Christians' minds, Francis is in no danger of being reduced to a mere name invoked in prayer or an iconic image set up over an altar—and thus, paradoxically, in

no danger of being magnified beyond his remarkable hu-
manness into a substitute, in some minds, for God.

Time and again, in fact, Francis is paraded in order
to defend sainthood itself. When the Catholic Worker
founder Dorothy Day was posthumously proposed for
canonization, her friends and family protested because in
their view sainthood encourages veneration rather than
imitation (a fascinating commentary, by the way, on the
institution's present state in the Roman Catholic
Church). Observes Kenneth L. Woodward: "Who could
doubt that Day herself would prefer imitation to veneration? But then again St. Francis of Assisi, surely no lover
of pomp and puffery, had survived the rigors of official
sainthood; might not Dorothy Day do the same?"

Yet in the very potency of Francis's life there is also
a danger. For he's proven to be an easily secularized, or
least de-Christianized, saint. His biography and prayers
lend themselves to misinterpretation by New Age nature-
worshipers who in claiming him as one of their own
ignore the Christian context of his earth-love, and by
iconoclasts who see him as a comrade-in-arms without
recognizing his deep respect for the institutional Church,
his appreciation of the proper tension between continuity
and Christ's insistence on *dis*continuity. Some modern liturgical celebrations of Francis can be dismaying to serious Christians. Take the Earth Mass I've mentioned: in
addition to the parade of animals, it features recorded

whale and seal calls, leotard-clad dancers gyrating eroti-
cally in the pulpit, and reserved seating. During the service, many people take flash pictures and hold crystals
aloft in their open palms. The casual atmosphere is presumably a tribute to Francis's own spartan way of life;
but how to explain the incessant talking, the children
who are urged to shriek and scamper about, and the parents who hoist tots on their shoulders? Most of those in
attendance are content to honor Francis's radicalism, in
short, but have learned nothing from his piety and self-
discipline. John Andrew, rector of New York's Saint
Thomas Church, once noted in a sermon on Francis that
"the world's generation of hippies could have had him as
their special patron saint if only they could have appreciated what led him to do the things they thought they
were doing and to live the life they thought they were
living. But sadly few got it, and got it right."

That's the ultimate point about Francis's life: that he
got it, and got it right. He didn't accomplish everything
he set out to do, and may not always have made wise
choices; as Colin Morris has written, "It is hard to imagine any more improbable founder of an order, for Francis
had a talent for disorganization and was reluctant even
to produce a rule." Yet more than anyone else in his
time, Francis understood the gospel message and acted
on it, dedicating his work and wealth and wisdom to
living out Christ's commandments to love God and his

fellow human beings. Francis recognized the intercon-
nectedness of these two commandments—recognized
that they are, in reality, one. He was a mystic without
being a hermit (though he had periods of solitude), a
servant of his fellow human beings but not just a social
worker. More than any other saint, he continues in the
Age of the Information Highway to do what saints are
supposed to do—namely, to figure in countless lives as
an inspiration to the spiritually torpid and a rebuke to
the pietistic.

I've criticized the annual Earth Mass at Saint John the
Divine. Yet for all its misguidedness, there is in that service enough of Francis to speak powerfully to those who
have ears to hear. The friend (now my companion) who
first took me to the Earth Mass several years ago had
been raised as a Christian, and so had I—he as a Sev-
enth-day Adventist, I as a hybrid Protestant—but we
had long since lapsed. In retrospect, it's clear that the
example of Francis's lively faith and tireless service, as
communicated (however contortedly) in the cathedral's
commemoration of his feast, awakened something that
had been lying dormant in both of us; our attendance at
that service proved to be the first step along the road
to active Episcopal Church membership—though not
(it must be admitted) to a life of single-minded self-
abnegation.

This leads to what is, for all of us, the ultimate question about the Christian life: Does it make us irredeem-

able hypocrites that we honor Francis without even trying to live as he did? I don't think Francis would have said so. "In whatever way you think you will best please our Lord God and follow in His footprints and in His poverty," he wrote to one of his companions, "take that way with the Lord God's blessing." The lesson of Francis is not that one must feel obliged to live as radically abstemious a life as he did, but that one must listen as acutely as he did for the still, small voice in the windstorm and must strive conscientiously to commit one's gifts, whatever they may be, as selflessly to God.

Catherine Means Pure

KATHRYN HARRISON

for Janet

MY MOTHER DIED of breast cancer when I was twenty-four. I took care of her while she died. I gave her her morphine, her Halcion, her Darvocet, Percocet, Demerol, Zantac, and Prednisone. I bathed her and I dressed her bedsores. Though I had to force myself into such communion with disease, I kissed her each morning when she woke and each evening as she fell asleep. Then I went into the bathroom, took a cotton pad soaked with rubbing alcohol, and scrubbed my lips with it until they burned and bled. Sometimes as I did this I thought of

Saint Catherine of Siena, who, in 1373, collected into a bowl the pus from a woman's open breast cancer lesions. The woman was Andrea, an older member of the Mantellate lay order to which Catherine belonged. Previously, Andrea had caused Catherine much trouble and public censure when she had implied that the saint's infamous raptures and fasts were a pretense rather than any manifestation of holiness. The bowl's foul contents stank and made Catherine retch, and both in penance for her disgust and in determination to love her enemy, Catherine drank the old nun's pus. "Daughter! Daughter!" cried Andrea, tears of contrition wetting her cheeks. "Do not kill yourself!"

That night, Catherine had a vision of Christ. Her Holy Bridegroom bade her to his side, and she drank the blood of life that flowed from his wounds.

"You were named for saints and queens," my mother told me, when I was young enough that a halo and a crown seemed interchangeable. We were not Catholics yet. Judaism was our birthright, but we had early strayed and now we were members of the First Church of Christ, Scientist. Above my bed was a plaque bearing these words from its founder, Mary Baker Eddy: "Father-Mother Good, lovingly thee I seek, patient, meek. In the way thou hast, be it slow or fast, up to thee." The little prayer, which I was taught to recite as I fell asleep, worried me. I did not want to die fast. I had asthma, and each attack seemed capable of killing me, so when I was not thinking of my mother, whom I loved without measure, I thought of death and of God. They made my first trinity: Mother, Death, God.

I might have remained immune to the mind-over-matter doctrines of Mrs. Eddy, and to the subsequent seduction of the saints, had I not, when I was five, suffered an accident which occasioned a visit to a Christian Science "practitioner," or healer. The circumstances were these: My mother, divorced when I was not yet a year old, and when she was not yet twenty, had recently moved out of her parents' house in Los Angeles, a house where I continued to live, as an only child with my grandparents. It was the first of my mother's attempts to make a separate life for herself—a life which did not seem possible to her unless motherhood was left behind—and so now it was my grandfather who drove me to school each day. The egocentric logic of the small child damned me to a belief that my mother had left me with her parents because of my unworthiness. I knew already that my birth had interrupted her education; now I learned that my continued existence somehow distracted her from her paralegal job and, worse, chased off romantic prospects. The shiny, pink stretch marks which pregnancy had traced over her stomach seemed emblematic of the greater damage I had done, and each time my mother undressed before me, my eyes were drawn to this record of my first transgression. Each afternoon, I sat in the closet of her old room, inhaling her perfume from what dresses remained; each morning I woke newly disappointed at the sight of her empty bed in the room next to mine. So, despite my grandfather's determined cheer, it was a glum ride to school that was interrupted, dramatically, the day the old Lincoln's brakes failed.

Pumping the useless pedal, my grandfather turned off the road in order to avoid rear-ending the car ahead of us. We went down a short embankment, picked up speed, crossed a ditch, and hit one of the stately eucalyptus trees that form the boundary between Sunset Boulevard and the UCLA campus. On impact, the glove compartment popped open; and, not wearing my seat belt, I sailed forward and split my chin on its lock mechanism, cracking my jawbone.

My grandfather was not hurt. He got me out of the wrecked, smoking car and pressed a folded handkerchief to my face. Blood was pouring out of my mouth and chin, and I started to cry, from fear more than pain. I was struggling against the makeshift compress when, by a strange coincidence, my mother, en route to work, saw us from the street and pulled over. Her sudden materialization, the way she sprang nimbly out of her blue car, seemed to me angelic, magical, an impression enhanced by the dress she was wearing that morning, one with a tight bodice and a full crimson skirt embroidered all over with music notes. Whenever she wore this dress I was unable to resist touching the fabric of the skirt. I found the notes evocative, mysterious; and if she let me, I would trace my finger over the spiral of a treble clef or feel the stitched dots of the notes, as if they represented a different code, like that of Braille or Morse, a message that I might in time decipher.

My mother was unusually patient and gentle as she helped me into her car. We left my grandfather waiting for a tow truck and drove to UCLA's nearby medical center, where I was X-rayed and prepared for suturing. I lay under a light so bright that it almost forced me to close my eyes, while a blue, disposable cloth with a hole cut out for my chin descended over my face like a shroud, blocking my view of my mother. I held her hand tightly, too tightly perhaps, for after a moment she pried my fingers off and lay my hand on the side of the gurney. She had to make a phone call, she said; she had to explain why she hadn't shown up at work.

I tried to be brave, but when I heard my mother's heels clicking away from me on the floor, I succumbed to an animal terror and tried to kick and claw my way after her. All I had understood of what she said was that she was leaving me again—this time with strangers— and it took both the doctor and his nurse to restrain me. Once they had, I was tranquilized before I was stitched and then finally taken home asleep.

Later that afternoon, I woke up screaming, in a panic which had been interrupted, not assuaged, by the drug. My mother, soon exhausted by my relentless crying and clinging to her neck, her legs, her fingers—to whatever she would let me hold—took me to a practitioner, whose name she picked at random from the First Church of Christ, Scientist's directory.

The practitioner was a woman with gray hair and a woolly, nubby sweater which I touched as she prayed over me, my head in her lap and one of her hands on my forehead, the other over my heart. Under those hands, which I remember as cool and calm, even sparing in their movements, I felt my fear drain away. Then, the top of my skull seemed to be opened by a sudden, revelatory blow, and a searing light filled me. Mysteriously, unexpectedly, this stranger had ushered me into an experience of something I cannot help but call rapture. I felt myself separated from my flesh, and from all earthly things. I felt myself no more corporeal than the tremble in the air over a fire. I had no words for what happened—I have few now, almost thirty years later—and in astonishment I stopped crying. My mother sighed in relief; and I learned, at five, a truth dangerous to someone so young and lovelorn. I saw that transcendence was possible: that spirit could conquer matter, and that therefore I could overcome whatever obstacles prevented my mother's loving me. I could overcome myself.

In the years following the accident I became increasingly determined to return to whatever it was I had visited in the practitioner's lap, and I thought the path to this place might be discovered in Sunday school. Around the wood laminate table I was the only child who had done the previous week's assignment, who had marked my white vinyl-covered Bible with the special blue-chalk pencil and had read the corresponding snippet from Mary Baker Eddy's *Science and Health, with Key to the Scriptures.* The other children lolled and dozed in clip-on neckties and pastel sashed dresses while I sat up straight. The teacher had barely finished asking a question before my hand, in its white cotton glove buttoned tight at the wrist, shot up. Sometimes I would see the teacher looking at me with what seemed, even then, like consternation. The lassitude of the other children, their carelessly incorrect answers, which proceeded from lips still bearing traces of hastily consumed cold cereal, were clearly what she expected. What was disconcerting was my fierce recital of verses, my vigilant posture on the edge of the red plastic kindergarten chair.

The arena of faith was the only one in which I had a chance of securing my mother's attention. Since she was not around during the week to answer to more grubby requirements, and because she was always someone who preferred the choice morsel, it was to my mother rather than to my grandparents that the guidance of my soul had been entrusted. On Sundays, we went to church in Westwood and afterward to a nearby patio restaurant, where we sat in curlicued wrought-iron chairs and reviewed my Sunday-school lesson while eating club sandwiches held together with fancy toothpicks. The waiters flirted with my mother, and men at neighboring tables smiled in her direction. They looked at her left hand without any ring; they seemed to share my helpless longing. Through the awful calculus of mortal love, my mother—who already embodied for me the beauty of youth, who had the shiny-haired, smooth-cheeked vitality my grandparents did not, who could do backbends and cartwheels, and owned high-heeled shoes in fifteen colors—became ever more precious for her elusiveness, her withholding absence.

In order to reexperience the ecstatic rise that had for an instant made me an attractive child and that had come through the experience of pain, I began secretly—and long before I had the example of any saint—to practice the mortification of my flesh. At my grandfather's workbench I turned his vise on my finger joints. When my grandmother brought home ice cream from Baskin-Robbins and discarded the dry ice with which it was packed, I used the salad tongs to retrieve the small smoking slab from the trash can. In the privacy of the upstairs bathroom I touched my tongue to the dry ice's surface and left a little of its skin there. I looked in the mirror at the blood coming out of my mouth, at the same magic flow that had once summoned my mother from the impossibly wide world of grown-ups and traffic and delivered her to my side. Now I was fully ensnared in the wishful, initiating mistake that was to confuse and pervert my spiritual growth: from the beginning I viewed whatever power God represented as a means toward my mother's love. Through those transformations made possible by faith, I would become worthy of her loving me. Either that, or faith would make me feel no more pain from my mother's rejection than I had from my jaw while lying in the practitioner's lap. So I looked in the mirror at my tongue, I tasted my blood, and I practiced not hurting.

My mother converted to Catholicism when I was ten, and I followed in her wake, seeking her even as she sought whatever it was that she had not found in Christian Science. We had failed at even the most basic of Mrs. Eddy's tenets, for by then we routinely sought the care of medical doctors. At first we went only for emergencies like the accident to my chin, but then my mother developed an ulcer, and I, never inoculated, got tetanus from a scrape, physical collapses both stubbornly unaffected by our attempts to disbelieve in them.

In preparation for my first Communion, I was catechized by a priest named Father Dove. Despite this felicitous name, Father Dove was not the Holy Spirit incarnate: he chain-smoked and his face over his white collar had a worldly, sanguine hue. Worse, I suspected that my mother was in love with him. She fell in love easily. One Saturday, I made my first confession (that I had been rude to my grandmother and had taken three dollars from her purse), and the next day, I took Communion with eleven other little girls dressed in white; and from that time forward I attended church in a marble sanctuary filled with gilt angels, rather than in a gray-and-blue auditorium. Light came through the stained-glass windows and splashed colors over everything. A red circle fell on my mother's white throat. Incense roiled around us, and I looked down to compare the shiny toes of my black patent-leather shoes to those of hers. When we left, lining up to shake Father Dove's hand, I was able to study the faces around me and confirm that my mother's wide hazel eyes, her long nose, and high, white forehead indeed made hers more beautiful than anyone else's.

For Christmas the following year I received, in my stocking, a boxed set of four volumes of *Lives of the Saints,* intended for children. There were two volumes of male saints, which I read once, flipping through the onionskin pages, and then left in my dresser drawer, and two of female saints, which I studied and slept with. The books contained color plates, illustrations adapted from works of the masters. Blinded Lucy. Maimed Agatha, her breasts on a platter. Beheaded Agnes. Margaret pressed to death under a door piled high with stones. Perpetua and Felicity mauled by beasts. Well-born Clare, barefoot and wearing rags. Maria Maddalena de' Pazzi lying on the bed of splinters she made for herself in the wood-shed. Veronica washing the floors with her tongue, and

Angela drinking water used to bathe a leper's sores. I saw that there were those who were tortured, and those who needed no persecutors—they were enemies to their own flesh.

Saint Catherine of Siéna began by saying Hail Marys on every step she climbed. Soon she slept on a board, with a brick for a pillow. She did not like her hair shirt because it smelled, so she took to wearing a little belt of nails that bit into her waist. As Catherine's *Dialogues* (dictated years later, while she was in a sustained ecstasy, which lasted weeks, even months) make clear, she believed earthly suffering was the only way to correct the intrinsic baseness of mankind.

My mother, also, held forth an ideal of perfection, an ideal for which she would suffer, but hers was beauty. For beauty she endured the small tortures of plucking and peel-off face masks, of girdles and pinched toes, of sleep sacrificed to hair rollers and meals reduced to cottage cheese. I knew, from my mother's enthusiastic response to certain pictures in magazines, to particular waifs in the movies, that the child who would best complement her vanity was dark-haired and slender and balanced on point shoes. I was blond, robust, and given to tree-climbing. By the time I was thirteen, all of what was wrong with me—the very fact of me, my presence— settled in an unavoidably obvious issue between my mother and me: how much I weighed. How much there was of me. As my conception had been accidental, as I ought not to have been there at all, it must have struck my mother as an act of defiance that I was so large a child, taller and sturdier than any other girl in my class.

I wished myself smaller. I began to dream at night of Beyond-the-Looking-Glass potions, little bottles bearing draughts that shrank me to nothing; the bit of mushroom which let me disappear between grass blades. I began, too, to dread Sunday lunches taken with my mother, who fastidiously observed my fork in its ascension to my mouth.

Saint Catherine was fourteen when her older sister Bonaventura died in childbirth. Bonaventura was the only member of Catherine's family with whom she shared any real sympathy, and Catherine blamed herself for her sister's death. She believed God had punished her and Bonaventura because Catherine had let her big sister tempt her into using cosmetics and curling her hair. She had let Bonaventura's example convince her, briefly, that a woman could embrace both heavenly and earthly desires.

Whatever buoyancy, whatever youthful resilience Saint Catherine had had, disappeared when she lost her sister. She became uncompromising in turning away from all worldly things: from food, from sleep, from men. Their mother, Lapa, a volatile woman whose choleric screams were reputedly so loud that they frightened passersby on Siena's Via dei Tintori, redoubled her efforts to marry off her uncooperative twenty-fourth child.

Some accounts hold that Catherine's intended groom was Bonaventura's widowed husband, a foul-tongued and occasionally brutish man. Catherine refused; she had long ago promised herself to Christ. She cut off her hair and she fasted, eating only bread and uncooked vegetables. She began to experience ecstasies, and it is recorded that when she did, she suffered a tetanic rigor in her limbs. Then Lapa would take her daughter up from the floor where she'd fallen and almost break her bones as she tried to bend the girl's stiff arms and legs.

Though it had been ten years since my mother moved out, she had yet to find a place that suited her for any length of time, and so she received her mail at the more permanent address of her parents, and would stop by after work to pick it up. She came in the back door, cool and perfumed and impeccably dressed, and she drifted into the kitchen to find me in my rumpled school uniform, standing before the open refrigerator. One day, I turned around with a cold chicken leg in my hand. My mother had tossed her unopened bills on the counter and was slowly rereading the message inside a greeting card decorated with a drawing of two lovesick rabbits locked in a dizzy embrace. She smiled slightly—a small and self-consciously mysterious smile—and kept the content of the card averted from my eyes. When she had had her fill of it, she looked up at me. She said nothing but let her eyes rest for a moment on the meat in my hand; then she looked away, from it, from me. She did not need to speak to tell me of her disapproval, and by now my habitual response to my mother had become one of despair: muffled, mute, and stumbling. But in that moment when she looked away from me, hopelessness gave way before a sudden, visionary elation. I dropped the drumstick into the garbage can. The mouthful I had swallowed stopped in its descent, and I felt it, gelid and vile inside me as I washed the sheen of grease from my fingers. At dinnertime, after my mother had left for her apartment, I pleaded too much homework to allow time to eat at the table, and I took my plate from the kitchen to my bedroom and opened the window, dropping the food into the dark foliage of the bushes below.

Among saints, Catherine is remarkable for her will more than for her humility. One of the two women in all of history named a Doctor of the Church (the other is Saint Teresa of Ávila), she, too, confused crowns with halos, and presumed to direct the affairs of popes and kings. Even in her reports of self-flagellation, readers find the pride of the absolutist. No one believed more firmly in Catherine's baseness than did Catherine. Determined that she be the least among mortals, so also—by the topsy-turvy logic of Christian salvation—would she be assured of being the greatest. In her visions of Christ, it is Catherine alone who stands beside Him as His bride.

To earn that place was exhausting beyond mortal ability. Even as the saint tirelessly cared for plague vic-

tims, even as she exhorted thousands to convert and
lobbied effectively for the return of the papacy from
Avignon to Rome, she criticized, scourged, and starved
herself. She allowed herself not one mortal pleasure: not
food or rest, not beauty, not wealth, not marriage or children. Categorically, she rejected the very things that a
mother hopes a daughter's life will hold. And reading
accounts of her life, one senses how Catherine enjoyed
thwarting her mother, Lapa, enjoyed refusing the life her
mother gave her. Biographers record that Catherine tried
to eat—she wanted to do so in order to dispel accusations of demonic possession—but vomited if so much as
a mouthful remained in her stomach. "She lived for years
on one lettuce leaf!" was how my mother introduced me
to Saint Catherine, as if she were revealing the teachings
of a new diet guru.

Holiness. The idea of being consecrated, set apart.
And of being whole, pure, untainted by anything. There
are different kinds of purity, just as there are many reasons for rejecting life. But, no matter the motive, to the
ascetic the rejection always looks the same: like salvation. Catherine would guide me to the salvation I sought.
Inhumanly, she had triumphed over mortal limitations,
over hunger, fatigue, and despair. She had seen demons
and fought them off. And I would use her to fashion my
solitary and sinful faith. Sin. A term long ago borrowed
from archery: to miss the mark.

During the celebration of the Eucharist, the priest

would place the Communion wafer on my tongue. I withdrew it into my mouth carefully, making the sign of the cross over myself. Back in the pew I kneeled and lay my head in my arms in a semblance of devotion, stuck out my tongue, and pushed the damp wafer into my sleeve. I was a little afraid of going to hell, very afraid of swallowing bread. My rules had grown more inexorable than the Church's; they alone could save me. But the host was the host, and I could not bring myself to throw it away. So I kept it in my sock drawer with my other relics: a small fetish of my mother's hair, stolen strand by strand from the hairbrush she kept in her purse. An eye pencil from that same source. Two tiny cookies from a Christmas stocking long past, a gingerbread boy and girl, no taller than an inch. A red leather collar from my cat which had died. The trinity in my sock drawer: Mother, Death, and God in the form of weeks' worth of accumulated bits of the body of Christ which I would not eat. Despite Christian Science's early announcements to me, despite mind over matter, I remained enslaved to the material world. In my confused struggle with corporeality I clung to these bits of rubbish, a collection that would look more at home in a trash can than in a drawer, and resisted what might better save me: food.

I still had my little books of the female saints. I looked at them before bed some nights, stared at their little portraits, at bleeding hands and feet, at exultant faces tipped up to heaven. But I read longer hagiographies now, grown-up ones. When Catherine was twenty-four she experienced a mystical death. "My soul was loosed from the body for those four hours," she told her confessor, who recorded that her heart stopped beating for that long. Though she did not want to return to her flesh, Jesus bade her go back. But henceforth, she was not as other mortals; her flesh was changed and unfit for worldly living. From that time forward she swallowed nothing she did not vomit. Her happiness was so intense that she laughed in her fits of ecstasy, she wept and laughed at the same time.

As I lost weight I watched with exultation as my bones emerged, believing that what I saw would irresistibly lure my mother's love. By the time they had failed to do that—those unlovely angles and hollows—I had so thoroughly confused the sight of them with the happiness I had hoped they would bring that I had created a satisfying, if perverse, system of rewards, one that did not require my mother's participation. I had replaced her with the bait I had hoped would entice her. I loved my transformed self. I could not look at myself enough, and I never went into the bathroom that I did not find myself helplessly undressing before the mirror. I touched myself, too. At night I lay in bed and felt each jutting rib, felt sternum and hipbone, felt my sharp jaw, and with my finger traced the orbit of my eye. Like Catherine's, mine was not a happiness that others understood, for it was the joy of power, of a private, inhuman triumph. Of a universe—my body—utterly subjugated to my will.

My life was solitary, as befits a religious. Too much of human fellowship was dictated by hunger, by taking meals in company, and what I did and did not consume separated me from others. Since I had not yet weaned myself completely from human needs, I drank coffee, tea, and Tab. I ate raw vegetables, multivitamins, No-Doz, and, when I felt very weak, tuna canned in water. When I climbed stairs, I saw stars. And when forced to eat with my grandparents, I did so, but the mask of compliance was temporary, and upstairs in my bathroom, I vomited what I had eaten. Afterward, I would lift my shirt and examine my ribs in the mirror, wanting to be sure that there was no evidence of my brief defilement.

After meals, Catherine drank cold water and gagged herself with a stalk of fennel or a quill pen. It hurt her, and she was glad. She wanted to do all her suffering on earth so that she would be spared purgatory. *This will make you pure,* I used to think when I made myself throw up. I used ipecac, the emetic kept in first-aid kits, a poison to be taken against poisons. It was worse than using my finger, perhaps even worse than a quill; at least that had to have been quick in its mechanical approach. Ipecac was suffering; it seemed to take forever and caused a reeling, sweaty nausea that made me wish I were dead. The retching was violent, but then, I intended it to be punishment.

My grandmother and grandfather, sixty-two and seventy-one at my birth, were now so old that their failing senses granted me freedom unusual for a teenager. Going blind, they did not see my thinness. Deaf, they never heard me in my bathroom. By the time I was sixteen, they depended on my driver's license for their groceries; and en route to the supermarket, I would stop at the mall. "Where did you go, Kalamazoo?" my grandmother would ask when I returned, trying to understand why I was hours late. Sometimes she accused me of secretly meeting boys; she used the word "assignation." But I had always spent my time alone. In the department stores and I went from rack to rack, garment to garment: size two, size two, size two. Each like a rosary bead: another recitation, another confirmation of my size, one more turn of the key in the lock of safety.

Having conquered hunger, I began on sleep, and one night, in my room, very late, and in the delusional frenzy of having remained awake for nearly seventy-three hours, I began to weep with what I thought was joy. It seemed to me that I had almost gotten there: my flesh was almost utterly turned to spirit. Soon I would not be mortal, soon I would be as invulnerable as someone who could drink pus and see God. The next day, however, I fainted and suffered a seizure that left me unable for a day to move the fingers on my right hand. In the same hospital where I had long ago attacked the ER nurse with my fingernails, I had an electroencephalogram and a number of other tests which proved inconclusive. A different nurse, a different doctor, a different wing of the hospital. But nothing had changed: my mother was making a phone call in the corridor, and I lay on a table trying not to scream, far less able to articulate the danger I sensed than when I was five.

When college gave me the opportunity to leave home, I recovered partially. At heart, I wanted to believe in a different life, and I stopped going to mass and gained a little weight—not too much, because I began taking speed and still made myself throw up sometimes. I wore my mother's clothing, castoffs and whatever I could steal from her, articles that filled the reliquary of my peculiar faith. I zipped and buttoned myself into her garments as if they could cloak me with the love I wanted from her. Like miracle seekers who would tear hair, fingers— whatever they could—from a holy person's body, I was desperate, and one September I took my mother's favorite skirt from under the dry-cleaning bag hanging in the back seat of her car. It was purple, long and narrow. I packed it in my suitcase and took it to school with me. She called me on the phone a week later. "Send it back," she said. I denied having taken it. "You're lying," she said.

Lapa did not want Catherine to scourge herself, so, although her daughter was a grown woman, Lapa took away her private bedroom and forced Catherine to sleep in bed with her. Not to be denied the mortification of her flesh, the saint dragged a plank into the bed after Lapa had fallen asleep, and she laid it between her mother's body and her own. On Lapa's side was smooth wood; on Catherine's, spikes.

I wore the skirt twice, and when it fell from the hanger, I let it remain on the dark, dirty floor of my closet. When my mother called me again, I decided to return it, but there was a stain on the waistband that the dry cleaner could not remove. For an hour I sat on my dorm bed with the skirt in my lap, considering. Finally I washed it with Woolite, and ruined it. I returned the skirt to my mother's closet when invited, during spring break, for dinner at her apartment. *Please,* I begged silently, tucking it between two other skirts. *Please don't say anything more about it. Please.* When she called me late that night at my grandparents' house, I hung up on her. Then I went into the bathroom and I sat on the floor and wept: too late, too many hours past the dinner she had fed me to make myself throw up.

Kathryn, Katherine, Catherine. All the spellings proceed from the Greek, *Katharos,* or "pure one."

Did Lapa know who her daughter would be? Did my mother know me before she named me? Did we announce ourselves to our mothers in the intimacy of the womb, flesh whispering to flesh?

Or did they make us to fit our names?

I still believe in purity, and I believe that suffering

must at least prepare the way for redemption. I believe, too, in love's ability to conquer. I believe in every kiss I gave my mother, even those I scrubbed away in fear. At the end of her life, I waited for my mother to tell me how much she loved me and how good a daughter I had always been. I had faith that my mother was waiting until the end to tell me that all along she had known I had performed impossible feats of self-alchemy.

She did not, but, as faith admits no end, mine continued beyond her death. After the funeral, I packed up her apartment and looked through all her papers for a note, a letter left for me and sealed in an envelope. I closed my eyes and saw it: a meticulous, fountain-pen rendition of *Kathryn* on creamy stationery. When I didn't find that, I looked for clues to her affection. I read what correspondence she had saved. I reviewed check registers dating back ten years. I learned how much she had spent on dry cleaning her clothes, on her cats' flea baths, and on having her car radio repaired.

The death of my mother left me with a complex religious apparatus that now lacked its object, and I expected, then, to become an atheist. I frankly looked forward to the sterile sanity of it, to what relief it would bring. But I could not do it; I could not not believe. The habit of faith, though long focused misguidedly on a mortal object, persisted; and after a few years, I found myself returning to the Church. Sporadically, helplessly, I attended mass. Having relearned to eat earthly food, now I practiced swallowing the Eucharist. Often I found myself crying out of a happiness I did not understand and which mysteriously accompanied the sense that my heart was breaking.

Rapture, too, returned. Long after I had stopped expecting it, it overcame me on a number of otherwise unnoteworthy occasions. I excused this as a fancy born of longing, as an endorphin effect brought on by exercise or pain, as craziness, pure and simple. But none of these described the experience, that same searing, light-filled, ecstatic rise, neither pleasant nor unpleasant, for no human measure applied to what I felt: transcendence.

My prayers, too, were helpless. I mouthed them in spite of myself. *Make me good. Love me. Please make me good and please love me.* For the first time, I entrusted my spiritual evolution to some power outside my self and my will; I entrusted it to God's grace. If I were going to reach any new plane, my enlightenment, it would have to be God who transported me.

In the last months of her life, Catherine lost the use of her legs. Her biographers record that for years she had lived on little more than water and what sustenance she got from chewing, not swallowing, bitter herbs. In church one night, when she was too weak to approach the altar, the Communion bread came to her. Witnesses saw bread move through the air unassisted. Catherine saw it carried by the hand of Christ.

She died at thirty-three, the same age as her Bridegroom at his death. She died in Rome, and her body was venerated from behind an iron grille in a chapel of the Church of the Minerva, so that the throngs who came would not tear her to bits, each trying to secure a wonder-working relic.

All I have left of my mother are a box of books, a china dog, two cashmere sweaters with holes in the elbows, a few photographs, and her medical records. Among the last of these is her final chest X ray, and just over the shadow of her heart is the bright white circle cast by the saint's medal she wore on a thin gold chain. No matter how many times the technicians asked her to remove it, she would not. Not long ago, I unpacked the box of medical records, and retrieved the X ray. I held it before a light once more, trying to see the image more clearly, but of course I could make out nothing. Just a small, white circle of brightest light. A circle blocking the view of the chambers of her heart. A circle too bright to allow any vision.

I will never know, but I have decided that the medal, now with my mother in her coffin, bears a likeness of Saint Jude. I have given my mother to this saint—the patron of lost causes, the patron of last resort—just as long ago she gave me to the saint of her choosing.

A Friend to the Godless

P AUL W ATKINS

M Y GREAT-GRANDFATHER returned from the
Somme in the winter of 1916. He was an officer in a
Welsh Guards regiment. He had been gassed and shot
and had seen his platoon numerically wiped out and replaced more than three times since he first took command of it. He had used his side arm, a Webley revolver,
so much that the barrel was pitted into uselessness. I
heard a story about one of his advances across no-man's-
land in which he set out with a full company and by the

time he arrived at the German wire was one of only two men left alive.

Until that time, this branch of my family had been Calvinistic Methodists, teetotaling, high-minded, and convinced, as one member of my family phrased it, that everyone was going to hell except them.

But when he returned from the war, my great-grand-father had seen enough to change his mind. He gathered the family together and banned religion in his house. "Either God is a bastard," he said, "or God isn't there at all."

Since then, religious faith has crept back into my family, but to me it still feels burdened by my great-grandfather's pronouncement. Holidays are still celebrated—Christmas for example—but with more attention paid to the tree than to the birth of Jesus.

The one festival I do remember seeing celebrated without the aegis of my great-grandfather's proclamation to muffle it into insignificance is Saint David's day, March 1.

In writing about Saint David here, I have for the first time explored why the day of the saint, whose name (my middle name) has echoed through my family for genera-tions, survived untarnished, even after the war that cata-pulted my great-grandfather into the ranks of unbelievers.

The first mention of Saint David, and it is only a men-tion, comes in an Irish manuscript called the "Catalogue

of the Saints of Ireland," which was written in A.D. 730.
In it, David is acknowledged as a "Holy Man of Britain."
In fact, there is in existence only one original and reliable
document on Saint David. It was written, in Welsh, by a
man named Rhygyvarch, around the year 1090, shortly
after the Norman invasion of Britain. The best copy of
this document is in the British Museum in London, in a
dust-choked file marked "Vespasian A xiv" of the famous
Cottonian Codex.

Rhygyvarch, a local clergyman in the area, now
County Dyfed, where St. David's cathedral now stands,
may have written his account in order to draw the Welsh
together after the Norman invasion. The once powerful
rulers of the Cymri (the Welsh word for themselves) lay
either dead or defeated in the wake of William the Con-
queror. "Alas!" wrote Rhygyvarch in his *Lament of the
Times,* "that life hath led us to such a time as this,
wherein a cruel power threatens to oust from their rights
those who walk justly. Free necks submit to the yoke.
Nothing is too excellent that I may be compelled to surrender it. Things once lofty I despise. Both people and
priest are scorned by every motion of the French. They
increase our burdens and consume our goods. . . . Art
thou hated of God, O British nation, that thou darest not
bear the quiver, stretch the bow, carry the sword, vibrate
the spear?" Some see this, in conjunction with his *Life of
Saint David,* as a call to arms for the divided Welsh.

David, or Dewi to the Welsh, was perhaps the only
rallying point that Rhygyvarch could have chosen. David's life had been, by that time, converted almost entirely to myth. His coming was foretold to Saint Patrick
by a "truth-telling oracle of angels" thirty years before
David's birth. David's father, a local ruler by the name
of Sant, also received a vision, in which he was ordered
by an angelic voice to go hunting stag near the river
Teivi, on the banks of which he would find three gifts,
"namely the stag which thou pursuest, a fish and a
swarm of bees settled in a tree in the place which is
called Llyn Henllan. Of these three, reserve a honeycomb, a part of the fish and of the stag, which send to
be kept for a son, who shall be born to thee. . . . The
honeycomb shall proclaim his wisdom, for as honey in
wax, so shall he be spiritual in mind and body. And the
fish declares his aquatic life, for as a fish lives in the
water, so he, rejecting wine and beer and everything that
can intoxicate, shall lead a blessed life for God on bread
and water only. The stag signifies his power over the
Old Serpent." Bear in mind that to the Welsh, the Old
Serpent was as real a presence as anything else around
them. It was not, as psychologists have later palmed it
off to be, a symbol of the struggle with the self. It was,
the Welsh believed, a real dragon, with claws like scimi-
tars and armored scales and incendiary breath. Y Ddraig
Goch, the Welsh called it, and today it is the national

emblem of Wales. So to have the forecast of a man who would one day hold power over Y Ddraig Goch was no small prediction.

Even the land over which David was to rule was squared away for him in advance. On a visit to west Wales, Saint Patrick was informed by "an angel of the Lord that God hath not disposed this place for thee, but for a son who is not yet born, nor will he be born until thirty years are past." On hearing this, Patrick was so upset that he announced he would give up the faith "and submit no longer to such toil." The angel, however, quickly pacified him with promises of dominion over all of Ireland, which at that point had not yet been Christianized. "As proof of this," the angel said, "I will show thee the whole of Ireland. Let the mountains be bent; the sea made smooth, the eye bearing forth across all things." And at that moment, from the place where Patrick stood, the whole Emerald Isle unraveled before him from across the stormy Irish Sea. Patrick quickly rushed down to the shore, but unable to find a boatman to ferry him across, he raised from the dead a sailor who had lain buried beneath the beach for a dozen years, a man named Crumther, and the two of them left the Welsh to await the arrival of their saint.

Other portents were presented to the small fishing community of the place now called St. David's. When David's mother, Nonn, still pregnant with David, entered the local church, the preacher there was struck dumb and was unable to continue his sermon until Nonn had left the building. The priest then announced, "The son, who is in the womb of that nun, has grace and power and rank greater than I, because God has given him status and sole rule and primacy over all the saints of Britannia forever." Then, just as Patrick had done before him, the priest packed his bags and left town.

God's clearing of land for the arrival of David meant that the young saint had already attracted enemies by the time of his birth. The evening Nonn delivered was heralded by terrible storms, which ravaged the coastline and scattered cattle with bolts of well-aimed lightning. Through all of this, however, Nonn remained bathed in sunlight, long after nightfall had come. The stone on which she rested while she delivered became impressed with her handprints "as if on wax." This stone was later used as the foundation stone for David's church.

David was raised by a sage named Paulens, "in a manner pleasing to God." David "preserved his flesh pure from the embraces of a wife" and was taught the hymns of God by a bird with a golden beak who hovered around his head and sang to him.

David performed the first of many miracles attributed to him when Paulens was suddenly stricken with blindness. "Holy David," Paulens called to the boy, "examine my eyes, for they pain me greatly." But due to the manners of the day, it was forbidden for a pupil to meet a teacher's glance. Instead, David laid his hand upon the old man's face, at which point "the master received the light which had been removed."

Before his twentieth birthday, David had founded twelve monasteries around Britain. Among these were Glastonbury, Bath (where he first "caused the deadly water to become salutary," thus ensuring the survival of a thriving spa town), Croyland, Repton, Colva, and Glascwm, all of which are still in existence.

Close to his home in the Welsh county of Dyfed, his rise in power provoked the anger of a local warlord named Bywa. The chieftain set out with a band of warriors to kill David, but they were stricken with fever along the way, and by the time they arrived were able to do no more than "blaspheme the Lord and Holy David, for the wish to injure was not wanting, although the power to act was thwarted by the Eternal."

Ridiculing Bywa's failure, the warlord's own wife set out to finish off David. She brought with her a gaggle of handmaidens, who proceeded to parade naked in front of the holy settlement, "making shameless sport, simulating coition and displaying love's alluring embraces." This display, in fact, did considerably more damage than Bywa's own cursing, fever-sweating thugs. " 'Let us fly from this place,' " said David's disciples, " 'because we cannot dwell here owing to the molestation of these spiteful sluts.' " Rather than cajole his own supporters, it seems that David gave Bywa's wife such a tongue-lashing that she and all her naked, frolicking maidens ran off into the trees, "and no one under heaven knows by what death they ended their lives."

David wasn't yet finished with Bywa. It is here that Rhygyvarch's narrative grows cloudy, and becomes more of a sermon than a story. He seems reluctant to admit the truth, which was that David and his followers stormed Bywa's camp and butchered everyone in it. Rhygyvarch contents himself with a vague warning: "For it is meet that destruction should overtake him who threatens the death of a man of God, and he who is pitiless to the servants of God will suffer vengeance without pity."

Following the death of Bywa, David set about building the cathedral, parts of which can still be seen in the valley of St. David's town. The cathedral, the smallest in Britain, was built in a hollow to hide it from Viking raiders who patrolled the coast. They raided churches because in those days the church acted as a repository for all local wealth, safe against Christian attack. But to the Vikings, followers of Odin, some heavy crucifix held up by a monk to ward off evil was nothing more than a convenient weapon, with which to bludgeon the monk to death. Not only was St. David's attacked, but hundreds of other churches as well, until the British agreed to pay the Danes protection money (called Danegeld, literally

"Danish money") to stop them from ravaging the countryside.

In building the cathedral, David was a hard taskmas-
ter, withholding food from those he felt did not work
hard enough. Again, Rhygyvarch camouflages all brutality with the severity of the devoted: "For knowing that
untroubled rest was the fomenter and mother of vices,
David subjected the shoulders of the monks to Divine
Fatigues." At table, they were allowed to eat only bread,
"not however to excess, for too much, though it be bread
only, produces wantonness."

During this time, David increased his congregation,
not only due to his cathedral but also due to the need
for more labor. He was nothing if not choosy, however.
Anyone wishing to become a disciple was forced to wait
for ten days at the gates of the settlement "as one rejected, being subjected to reproachful words. But if he
stood his ground, duly exercising patience till the tenth
day, he was received. . . . And when he had toiled there
for a long time, many antipathies of his soul being broken, he was at length deemed worthy of entering the
society of the brethren."

Within the brotherhood, life was both spartan and
severe. "No superfluity was allowed, voluntary poverty
was loved . . . being received naked, as one escaping from
shipwreck, he might in no way extol or raise himself
above the brethren, or relying on his wealth fail to enter
upon equal toil with the brethren."

The miracles continued to surface as construction of the cathedral progressed. David never seemed to be at a loss for enemies, and an attempt to poison him was instigated by a former disciple. Having been informed of the plot, David used the occasion to further his stature by breaking the poisoned bread in three. The first piece he gave to a dog at the settlement gates; "as soon as it had tasted the bit it died a wretched death, for in the twinkling of an eye all its hair fell off, its entrails burst forth and all its skin split all over." Not surprisingly, "all the brethren who saw it were astonished." The second piece David gave to a raven, which was in its nest on one of the settlement gates. The poor creature fared no better and "fell lifeless from the tree as soon as the bread touched its beak." The third piece David ate himself, but he showed no signs of poisoning.

When one of the disciples began to rankle under the punishing work schedule, David scolded him. Overcome with rage, the disciple lifted an axe with which he had been working, determined to split David's skull. But the saint merely lifted his hand, and the disciple's arm withered away.

Once he had finished the cathedral, many reports, including Rhygyvarch's, claim David undertook a pilgrimage to the Holy Land. Although this is greatly disputed and has never been proved, Rhygyvarch and others have used the legend to increase the volume of miracles attributed to David. Predictably, the journey was begun when a holy angel appeared and said to David, "Gird thyself, put on thy shoes. Start to go to Jerusalem." His arrival in the Holy Land was foretold and a welcome prepared in Jerusalem before he had even left Wales.

Along the way, all language barriers were broken, not with Latin, the lingua franca of the day, but "with the gift of tongues bestowed upon David, so that he was never in need of an interpreter."

Rhygyvarch is very brief in his mention of this visit, perhaps because there is so little to back it up. With entire, massively armed crusading armies being thrashed to pieces by the likes of Saladin and Basil the Bulgar Slayer, who took ten thousand prisoners, blinded all but one, and then sent them wandering home, one wonders how much chance a small band of Welshmen reared on bread and water would have had.

By the time he supposedly returned, a new crisis had evolved in Britain. The Pelagian heresy was in full swing, moving through the country "like the venom of a poisonous serpent." Pelagius was a fifth-century monk who denied original sin and the need of grace for salvation. This was as a result of a visit he paid to Rome at the time of Pope Anastasius. He found the city so degenerated in moral fiber that the only escape, Pelagius felt, was to offer a doctrine of free will in which "a person is free if he does what he wishes and avoids what he wishes to avoid."

The British, David included, regarded this as the approach of anarchy, and conducted long debates about how to extinguish the movement. Three times David refused invitations to speak to a synod regarding the movement. "Depart ye in peace," he told them. "Let no one tempt me."

Finally he agreed to speak, and it was here, at the synod of Llandewi-Brefi, that David made a name for himself, not only in the realm of myth but also in substantiated fact. He was instrumental in dismantling the Pelagian movement and restoring the church to its original power over the country. The miracles that attended him at Llandewi are, if not the most dramatic, at least the most often recalled.

With David unable to address the masses because of the lack of a pulpit, his disciples began making a pile of clothing on which he could stand and preach. But while he was waiting, the ground rose up under him to offer him a natural podium. During his speech, a dove came to rest on his shoulder, and remained there until he had finished. As a result, depictions of Saint David in manuscripts or stained glass often show him standing on a mound with a dove perched on his shoulder.

Following this restoration of the faith, David retired to Dyfed, where, Rhygyvarch asserts, he lived to be 147 years old, perhaps his most miraculous feat of all. During those final years, David offered sanctuary to anyone who asked for it, "every ravisher and homicide and sinner and to every evil person flying from place to place."

As he weakened and his death approached, David found that he and his tiny cathedral had become objects of pilgrimage. Thousands of soon-to-be mourners crammed the town. They did not have long to wait. On the day of his death, disciples crowded around to hear his final words. "Take me," he said, "after thee."

Today St. David's is still a point of pilgrimage. The cathedral has been rebuilt several times. Some newer structures bear the scars of looting during the English civil war. There is a strange pair of footprints on a grave outside the windowless cathedral building. They are said to belong to the Devil, who appeared on the earth only to find himself face to face with the spirit of St. David, and vanished forever from the valley.

On Saint David's day, March 1, inevitably under a dreary northern winter sky, the Welsh wear the green and pungent leaves of leeks pinned to their lapels. This tradition dates from a hundred years after the death of Saint David, when a detachment of Welshmen at the Battle of Agincourt, finding themselves so plastered with mud that they could not tell friend from enemy, picked leeks growing in a nearby garden and wore them as insignia. Those translate now into the miniature gold leeks worn on the khaki berets of Welsh Guardsmen today, and by my great-grandfather in 1916.

Why would a man abandon God, but not the saint who proclaimed him? I can only guess, but what appears likely is that, although my great-grandfather became an unbeliever, he did not completely lose his faith. His faith merely shifted, and I believe what he chose to respect was not the God whom he blamed for sending his platoon three times into oblivion, but the men themselves, who carried on in full knowledge of that oblivion. They were just men persevering, and I think my great-grandfather thought of David as just a man persevering. I doubt he believed all the miracles. But the church itself is there as proof of David's other work and of the sanctuary that he offered.

I used to wonder about this idea of sanctuary each morning as I walked into the chapel at Eton, where I was a student for five years. The chapel is a vast, echoing building constructed around 1460. The pale stone steps leading up to its main door are worn concave from centuries of use.

Our names were checked off a list as we filed in, and we were punished if we failed to appear. It was always a hovering, uncertain time of day, with classes stretching ahead in a seemingly endless procession. While the hymns were being sung, you could sometimes look across the rows of singing boys and see a few chanting out their Latin grammar instead, in last-minute preparation for a test. Once, when the Thames had flooded, I heard coffins bumping into each other as they drifted around in the crypt below.

This church was no sanctuary for me. My heart did

not beat quickly when I walked under the arch of the titanic organ, with its pipes racked up like leg-thick javelins above me. It gave me no inspiration to stare up at the stained-glass window. I wasn't the only one who felt this way. I know of no one who was with me at the school who now goes to church more than twice a year. We could not be bullied into reverence.

Instead, we chose different Holy Ground. For some, it was the fields or roads or back alleys of home. For myself, not until I reached the windswept beaches of St. David's did I feel a reverence, which came from the knowledge that my ancestors had lived here for a thousand years. It came from the harsh beauty of the purple heather and yellow gorse, balanced at the edge of cliffs which dropped sheer into the sea, and from the fact that the saint himself must have walked here, gathering driftwood for fires, as people still do today.

For the longest time, I did not tell anyone that I thought of this place as sacred. When at last I did, some of the sacredness disappeared. So I think back to a time of greater innocence, when I would walk the beach with my great-grandfather.

I have a photo from this time of myself with him. It was taken one year before he died. We had just walked from the beach. I am staring at the camera, holding a long trail of seaweed. The seaweed is blurred because the wind was blowing. My great-grandfather is leaning on a walking stick and looking out to sea, as if his attention has been momentarily distracted. I think this was his Holy Ground, as well, although he never said so. It is the only picture I have ever seen of him in which he looks at peace.

Sources

The Black Book of Saint David, tr. J. W. Willis-Bund (1902).

Bonned Y Sant, twelfth-century Welsh document containing part of Rhygyvarch's *Life of Saint David* (Wales: Peniarth Library).

J. G. Evans, trans., *The Text of The Book of Llan Dav* (1893).

J. E. Lloyd, *A History of Wales* (1911).

A. W. Wade-Evans, trans., *Life of Saint David* (New York: Macmillan, 1923).

Hugh Williams, *Christianity in Early Britain* (Oxford: Oxford University Press, 1912).

Called by Name

Susan Bergman

Is it a fortunate or an unfortunate thing, to own a life that makes
you believe in the invisible? I still don't know. Faith can come to a
person slowly, like a gradual climb up a long stairs, or it can be
heady and dizzying. Or it can be strong as an iron bannister, never
reached for or thought of at all. But the propensity for faith is
inherent, like an organ or a sexual inclination. I always possessed
the place for religion.

—Mona Simpson, *The Lost Father*

I too have a propensity for faith. Mine was a childhood gift that hasn't left me but that I find wandering
from its object, which is God, to various ideas and images that I would inadvertently substitute for God. It's a
common meandering—from the unseen Creator to the
visible creature, or creed, or care—a fascination that becomes a distraction, or merely a mistaken hope. Whether
a detour draws me into the deep woods of hard work
(these spiritual exercises, readings of those martyrs' lives,
a pilgrimage into theology, self-sacrifice, self-discipline),

or across the plains of slackness, I am prone to lose clear sight and need to be reclaimed from a dark path.

So I cling to the promises that if we seek God we will find him, that if we knock the door will be opened. In these words lie powerful incentives to an active life of faith. By faith we can cross the threshold between this world and the unseen place where God dwells, though we must accomplish this faith now, in our bodies and encumbered by the hurts and limitations of our lives and those of the world around us. This is the supreme tension that we endure, believing in God: we live in two worlds, this world, which is no longer home and yet attracts and constrains us, and what Jesus calls the Kingdom of God, which we can't enter fully until death, and yet which has already entered those who believe in the form of God's Spirit.

St. Paul wrestles with this tension, which he put succinctly: "I have been crucified with Christ; and it is no longer I who live but Christ lives in me; and the life which I now live in the flesh I live by faith in the Son of God, who loved me, and delivered Himself up for me." [1] To live by faith, Paul suggests, is to enter a spiritual union with God, an existence that will be fully realized only through putting ourselves spiritually to death. To live is Christ, Paul says elsewhere, and to die is gain. The early Christian martyrs took up this cry, and in the first centuries after Christ's death tens of thousands willingly confessed Christ as Savior and lost their lives.

For early saints and for Christians today, faith sets
up a discontent, a longing for God's Kingdom not only
for personal but also for cultural reasons. The passage
above continues: "For all of you who were baptized into
Christ have clothed yourselves with Christ. There is neither Jew nor Greek, there is neither slave nor free man,
there is neither male nor female; for you are all one in
Christ Jesus."[2] Comparing the potentially radical social
promise of such a statement to actual social practice
makes clear the disparity between the life of the spirit
and the life of the flesh. Paul himself seems not to have
fully understood the implications this statement could
have had within his own culture. Yet he and others with
him had clearly undertaken that uneasy process by which
they began to live the Kingdom of God in their daily
lives. It is to the early Christians and those honored as
saints through history that we turn for a glimpse of the
life of faith of which Paul speaks.

Saints challenge us, writes Garry Wills in a compelling essay on Dorothy Day, by "escaping the boundaries
that hold the rest of us constrained by self-regard, con-
vention and fear."[3] We look to their devotion to stir
ours, to their example to strengthen our ardor so that we
may consecrate our lives to Christ. But there are boundaries of a present existence that even saints don't elude
until they finish living.

In the account of another early saint's life, we find
an inspiring and a troubling portrait of life in two worlds,

a story of a woman so compelling that it has been retold for centuries. In A.D. 202, Perpetua, a twenty-two-year-old woman, with her pregnant attendant, Felicity, is arrested by the Roman authorities because she is a Christian. While in prison she records her spiritual visions and gives an account of prison life. She describes her sorrowful conflict with her unbelieving father, whom she loves. An eyewitness records the events of her martyrdom when, after surviving exposure to wild heifers in the arena, she is killed by the sword of a Roman soldier whose hand she guides to her throat.

Saint Perpetua writes in her prison diary with a constant consciousness of the presence of God, which she feels certain she is about to enter more fully. She also writes with a well-tuned awareness of the physical realities that surround her and influence her well-being and that of her child and her father. Saints live, however exemplary their faith, within the same constraints of body and time and world that we all do. This is the consolation saints offer along with their challenge.

It is this kind of comfort I seek when I turn to the text of Perpetua's prison diary, which begins with these words:

> While I was still with the police authorities my father out of love for me tried to dissuade me from my resolution.

"Father," I said, "do you see here, for example this vase, or pitcher, or whatever it is?"

"I see it," he said.

"Can it be named anything else than what it really is?" I asked, and he said,

"No."

"So I also cannot be called anything else than what I am, a Christian."[4]

Her life displays a faith which, instead of wavering when opposed, strengthens her belief that God is ever present with her. "You may be sure," Perpetua says to her father, who worries for her, "that we are not left to ourselves but are all in his power."[5] She speaks of her faith, alive with the unseen world-to-come, in the vital, sensory detail of her experience, which allows us to feel her hardship and aspire to her fidelity.

Hers is the earliest record I have found of writing by a woman about spiritual experiences. Perpetua is one of four known Christian women of the late Roman Empire whose writing survives.[6] In vigorous language she recounts her capture and torture by Roman authorities in Northern Africa when she was a new convert to Christianity. Arrested in Carthage with six friends during the persecutions by Emperor Septimius Severus, she refuses to fear, defying her tormentors, though not escaping torture, and she records visions more vivid to her than her own body's pain. Tertullian, a contemporary of Perpetua's, is thought by some scholars to be the witness and redactor of her death, completing her story when she was unable to continue. The original manuscript's survival, paired with its verification by another prisoner and the testimony of an eyewitness to their deaths, makes it one of the more historically reliable documents within a body of works known for their embellishment.

Written in Latin, Perpetua's manuscript consists of twenty-one sections with four divisions. The unnamed eyewitness provides a simple theological context for what follows. As the narration begins we are told that the purpose of such a record is to honor God and encourage Christians, so that we may be reminded of the glory of God and through the narration "associate [ourselves] with the holy martyrs and, through them, with the Lord Jesus Christ." This account of two martyrs' visions and the deaths of several others manifests "God's continuing work among his people," the narrator tells us, and also signals the "last days," which promise the return of Christ.

Sections three through ten are Perpetua's prison diary, in which she briefly describes her trial, her life in captivity, and her visions while she is imprisoned. Following her diary, another captive, Saturus, depicts his vision, and the narrator concludes with an account of the actual killing of the captives.

In the opening passage of the diary, in which Perpetua asks her father to consider the reason for her public confession, we see that the basis for Perpetua's clear sense of her place, her identity, is her committed identification with Christ. She is a Christian. To claim to be something other than what she is will not change her condition, Perpetua tells her father, a wealthy provincial whose tranquility has been spoiled by his daughter's conversion, and whose sight does not extend with hers beyond his immediate cares. This is a young woman whose faith in Christ has altered the very core of her existence. She bears the name Christian as a testimony to that change. No longer is she merely a Roman citizen willing to offer sacrifice to the emperor as deity; she is now a citizen of Heaven who cannot recant despite the pleas of her aged father or even the pangs of motherhood when, because of her imprisonment, she must depend on others to care for the child to whom she has recently given birth.

Perpetua's spiritual identity causes her to break every cultural and ecclesial code of her day. Writing during the decline of the Roman Empire, in which women were rarely educated, she proclaims Christ the one true God and so contests the Romans' army of deities. When asked by the governing authority to offer a sacrifice for the emperor's welfare, Perpetua refuses, and at her father's plea, while her heart breaks to witness his hurt for her, she reiterates, "I am a Christian." Opposing both the power of Rome and the authority of her father, Perpetua asserts her submission to God alone and so is condemned to die.

Perpetua's faith, which she clearly enacted to comply with the teachings of those in authority in the early Christian community, implicitly amends the limited perceptions of women's value within that community. Among those who have committed themselves to following Christ, she lives within the constraints of an incomplete realization of God's Kingdom. Unable to love as Christ loved, to fully envision the liberation Christ offered, believers of any age will ache with the longing that results from discord between the promise of unity in Christ and our actual circumstances.

A few women are known to have served as deaconesses in the early Christian church, but they were not ordained as elders or priests. Valued as virgins and widows if they committed themselves to the service of the church, these women are the ones who have most often been canonized as saints. The act of martyrdom, however, granted an equality among those who gave their lives for their faith—laity or clergy, male or female. Martyrdom was thought to usher one immediately into Heaven, where communication with God was face to face. To die for Christ offered a distinction impossible for women to realize through any other service. And

perhaps, given women's position, the material world ten-
dered a lesser promise than it might have for a person
with property rights and social or religious standing.

But Perpetua's writing expresses no consciousness of
a desire to die in order to reform the church's governing
structures or to desert her present situation. Her martyrdom does not seem to be consciously political, or escap-
ist. The force of the defiance of her actions is balanced,
in her account, with her wish not to offend and with her
evident consternation when she sees the effects of her
testimony on others. She weights her decision to declare
her faith, despite the risk to her own life, with genuine
compassion for those who surround her, often expressing
more acute feelings for the suffering of others than for
herself.

> In my anxiety for the infant I spoke to my
> mother about him, tried to console my brother,
> and asked that they care for my son. I suffered
> intensely because I sensed their agony on my ac-
> count. These were the trials I had to endure for
> many days. Then I was granted the privilege of
> having my son remain with me in prison. Being
> relieved of my anxiety and concern for the infant,
> I immediately regained my strength. Suddenly
> the prison became my palace, and I loved being
> there rather than any other place.

Her personal woes are mitigated when she is able, from prison, to care for the needs of those she loves. Later, as Perpetua stands before the governor, Hilarion, and testifies that she is a Christian, her father's pleading with her to renounce her faith becomes so incessant that the governor throws him out of the hall and has him beaten with a rod.

> My father's injury hurt me as much as if I myself had been beaten, and I grieved because of his pathetic old age. Then the sentence was passed; all of us were condemned to the beasts. We were overjoyed as we went back to the prison cell. Since I was still nursing my child, who was ordinarily in the cell with me, I quickly sent the deacon Pomponius to my father's house to ask for the baby, but my father refused to give him up. Then God saw to it that my child no longer needed my nursing, nor were my breasts inflamed. After that I was no longer tortured by anxiety about my child or by pain in my breasts.

Overjoyed. The prisoners identify their present suffering with that of Christ and so find reason to celebrate their own earthly condemnation, mixed, again, with care for those who take no pleasure in these temporal losses.

As may be evident in these few passages, the prison

journal documents Perpetua's experience for the encouragement of others. Her private meditations and visions reveal a figure who is mentally preparing herself for whatever it is that her faith will require of her. Rich with anticipation of her imminent death and of a life to come, the prose melds visions of heavenly reward with images of physical endurance. In contrast to her apocalyptic visions, her description of her life as a prisoner is immediate and matter-of-fact. "Never before had I experienced such darkness," Perpetua writes. "What a terrible day!" Calm in crisis, she writes almost clinically about nursing her baby and the premature birth of her slave Felicity's child while in captivity, aspects of experience often passed over or nonexistent in the records of saints' lives.

Married women with children are not often regaled with their spiritual options. The early church fathers directed their writings concerning women to virgins and consecrated celibates, perhaps conscious of their unfamiliarity with a mother's lot, but in effect ignoring mothers. The contemporary church has consistently resisted the freedom for women that Jesus offered. Women's "wrestlings," it has been assumed, are less with aesthetic and spiritual fiends than with the quotidian fevers of necessity.

In Jesus' lifetime we see his loving release of one woman from the socially assigned role she had adopted, that of feeding and nurturing others. He does not criticize

her service, but the way her perception of her duty en-
croached on her ability to know Him. Jesus is staying at
the home of his friends, Mary and Martha, and Lazarus,
who has recently died. Luke gives an account of that
visit. "Martha was distracted with all her preparations;
and she came up to him, and said, 'Lord, do You not
care that my sister has left me to do all the serving alone?
Then tell her to help me.' " To which Jesus replied,
"Martha, Martha, you are worried and bothered about so
many things; but only a few things are necessary, really
only one, for Mary has chosen the good part, which shall
not be taken away from her." Jesus contrasts Martha's
activity, her domestic "preparations," to the quiet devotion of her sister to things eternal.

This invitation to become spiritually complete, to engage with him, which Jesus offers to all in the example
of Mary and Martha, is an opportunity that Perpetua
seems to grasp. Her understanding is shaped, however,
by the young institution of the church, which had not so
fully eluded social norms and restraints for women.
Though Perpetua studied Scripture with other men and
women under the tutelage of a more mature believer, the
teaching passed among early Christians was laced, as we
shall glimpse, with disregard for the character of women.

Because of Perpetua's clear sense of purpose she is
able to release her hold on this world with great joy,
setting her sights on the promise of Heaven. But, as
would be impossible for any person, she can never fully

release herself from the grasp of her culture's ideology. As she records her last vision the day before the games are to take place in the Roman arena, we again see her borrow from and transcend her culture's view of women. In her most poignant writing she describes the struggle she imagines will lead up to her death.

The day before the battle in the arena, in a vision I saw Pomponius the deacon coming to the prison door and knocking very loudly. I went to open the gate for him. He was dressed in a loosely fitting white robe, wearing richly decorated sandals. He said to me, "Perpetua, come. We're waiting for you!" He took my hand and we began to walk over extremely rocky and winding paths. When we finally arrived short of breath, at the arena, he led me to the center, saying, "Don't be frightened! I'll be here to help you." He left me and I stared out over a huge crowd which watched me with apprehension. Because I knew that I had to fight with the beasts, I wondered why they hadn't yet been turned loose in the arena. Coming towards me was some type of Egyptian, horrible to look at, accompanied by fighters who were to help defeat me. Some handsome young men came forward to help and encourage me. I was stripped of my clothing, and suddenly I was a man. My assistants began to rub me with oil as was the custom before a contest, while the Egyptian was on the opposite side rolling in the sand. Then a certain man appeared, so tall that he towered above the amphitheater. He wore a loose purple robe with two parallel stripes across the chest; his sandals were richly decorated with gold and silver. He carried a rod like that of an athletic trainer, and a green branch on which were golden apples. He motioned for silence and said, "If this Egyptian wins, he will kill her with the sword; but if she wins, she will receive this branch." Then he withdrew.

We both stepped forward and began to fight with our fists. My opponent kept trying to grab my feet but I repeatedly kicked his face with my heels. I felt myself being lifted up into the air and began to strike at him as one who was no longer earthbound. But when I saw that we were wasting time, I put my two hands together, linked my fingers, and put his head between them. As he fell on his face I stepped on his head. Then the people began to shout and my assistants started singing victory songs. I walked up to the trainer and accepted the branch. He kissed me and said, "Peace be with you, my daughter." And I triumphantly headed towards the Sanavivarian Gate. Then I woke up realizing that I would be contending not with wild animals but with the devil himself. I knew, however, that I would win.

In this striking transformation of Scripture into literary imagery we see a metamorphosing of genders, which Perpetua envisions as necessary to be able to defeat her opponents. Not only are her advisers and trainer and assistants male, as we might expect, but she herself takes on the form of a man as she removes her shirt and is oiled for battle. This is not an evasion of her femaleness for the sake of modesty, but an absorption of the teaching prevalent in the church of the first centuries. Clement of Rome, in his letter to the Corinthians, admonishes the virgins and widows to fulfill their duties to the church and, recognizing women who were prophets, praises "many women invested with power through the grace of God, [who] have accomplished many a manly deed."[7] This implied deprecation of women as women repeats a common strain of thought that virtue is the property of men but that women whom God favors with a certain manliness also may be recognized as having the capacity for valor. Given this climate, it is little wonder that an estimated seventy-five percent of martyrs in the early centuries were women.[8] The willing acceptance of a martyr's death was one of the few ways that women's service to God could be recognized within their spiritual communities. These figures' names and stories, with the exception of Perpetua and a few others, have long since been forgotten.

To attain victory over her assailant, Perpetua adopts a male form, and the needed characteristics thought to be reserved for men. But as she receives the reward of the golden apples (an image evidently drawn from local mythology) she refigures herself in the form of a woman. Her trainer kisses her and says, "Peace be with you, my daughter." With the incomplete vision offered by the material world, the enemy inside or out taunts that we cannot contribute unless we call ourselves by another name, another gender, unless we busy ourselves with "women's work." This is a trickery to which even Perpetua momentarily fell prey, and then, in her woman's body, in her own dignified way, at the very moment she was called to lose it, she reclaimed the prize of her own life, which belonged to Christ.

The narrator goes on to describe the events in the arena in great detail. Perpetua's tormentors had readied a mad cow to match the sex of the women to be tortured. They stripped Perpetua and Felicity and enmeshed them in nets. "How horrified the people were as they saw that one was a young girl and the other, her breasts dripping with milk, had just recently given birth to a child." So, the indelicacy of the torture being too much even for a bloodthirsty crowd, the women were recalled,

dressed in loosely fitted gowns, and led back into the
arena:

> Perpetua was tossed first and fell on her back.
> She sat up, and being more concerned with her
> sense of modesty than with her pain, covered her
> thighs with her gown which had been torn down
> one side. Then finding her hair-clip which had
> fallen out, she pinned back her loose hair think-
> ing it not proper [the redactor supposes] for a
> martyr to suffer with dishevelled hair; it might
> seem that she was mourning in her hour of
> triumph.

My sense is that she was neatening herself not for appearances' sake, at this point, but so that she could more
clearly see the world she was about to leave behind. This
last look was not her only hour of triumph. She had,
through faith, understood her worth as a person and so
been able to stand up to social force. She had recognized
the constant presence of Christ in her life and the way in
which her identification with him freed her from this
world's constraints. These victories, as I read of them,
are more significant to me than the triumph of the
moment when she finally guides the gladiator's hand
to her throat because he is trembling as he tries to
strike her. "Perhaps it was that so great a woman,
feared as she was by the unclean spirit, could not have

been slain had she not herself willed it," the narrator concludes.

Perpetua first promised her life, and then gave it to God. In her culture, that resulted in her martyrdom. Called to no less than the Kingdom of God, we understand that the human battle is not against flesh and blood alone but against spiritual powers, and coercive evil and death. But, as Perpetua's life reminds us, we are Christ's who made us and does not forsake us and calls us each by name into the unity and ultimate triumph of his presence.

NOTES

1. Galatians 2:20, New American Standard Bible.
2. Galatians, 3:27–28.
3. Garry Wills, "The Saint of Mott Street," *The New York Review of Books,* April 21, 1994, 36.
4. Patricia Wilson-Kastner, G. Ronald Kastner, Ann Millin, Rosemary Rader, Jeremiah Reedy, eds. *A Lost Tradition: Women Writers of the Early Church* (Lanham, Maryland: University Press of America, 1981). All quotations from Perpetua's account are taken from translations in this work.
5. Herbert Musurillo, trans., *The Acts of the Christian Martyrs* (Oxford, Oxford University Press, 1973), 106ff.
6. See also the *Cento* by Proba, Egeria's "Account of Her Pilgrimage," and Eudokia's "Life of St. Cyprian of Antioch," in Kastner et al., *A Lost Tradition.*
7. *A Lost Tradition,* ix.
8. Arthur F. Ide, *Martyrdom of Women* (Garland, Texas: Tangelwüld, 1985), introduction.

Nuns, Prophecies, Communists, the Bomb, the Dread of Angels, Reason, Faith, and the *Summa Theologica*

RICHARD BAUSCH

"WE PROCEED *thus to the first article: It seems that the existence of God is self-evident . . .*"

Since Time is a human invention, and since the psyche knows nothing of it, really, I am always at least partly living in the presence, among all the other presences, of two separate days, both sunny and cool, both taking place in late March, at the tag end of winter, when the ground is still mostly gray or winter brown, but when some early blossoms are out, and the air has that fresh, earthy new-grass fragrance of spring.

The first of these days is in 1959. A Saturday morning. I'm sitting in a CCD class—Confraternity of Christian Doctrine—for Catholic children who attend public schools. There's a wall of windows to my left, looking out on the world, the wide fallow field and budding trees of the land bordering the church grounds; the sky is as blue as the idea of blue, and it is impossible to think that the whole of it is threatened.

1959. People are building fallout shelters, and everybody is talking about the Communists, and the Bomb. New tests are being conducted on both sides of the world. We have seen the huge terrible blooms of "smoke" in the newsreels. Scientists are finding something called strontium 90 in the milk we drink. It filters down in the rain, settles in the grass the cows eat, and gets into their bones, into their milk. Thus, the very essence of health and life—so the frowning newsmen on our little General Electric black-and-white television have informed us—now carries this deadly poison in varying amounts. Recently, Father Russell, our pastor, delivered a sermon about the end of the world—we must, as individual souls on our very private separate journeys to God, worry more about the end of our individual worlds, which is certain, than the end of the whole world, which is out of our hands.

Yet it seems that everybody's thinking about the general conflagration. The Communists have recently frightened the country by putting a satellite into space. Sputnik is orbiting the Earth. It's out there somewhere in the blue, blue sky, and people have been talking about trying to shoot it down.

On television there are ads with musical jingles about ducking when you see the white flash. "Duck . . . and cover," the voices sing. And in my eighth-grade class someone has given me a yellow card with instructions on what to do in case of a nuclear attack: 1. Remove all sharp objects from your pocket; 2. Remove glasses and any jewelry; 3. Seat yourself in a hardback chair; 4. Put your head between your legs; and 5. Kiss your ass good-bye.

Regularly at my public school the teachers conduct drills, which have us all lined up in the halls, crouched with our hands over our heads. It's so much a part of everything that we think nothing of it. I pretend the white flash comes, though I'm unable to imagine what the following shock might really feel like. At an all-school assembly, our assistant principal, a World War II veteran, like all the adult men, talked about how in 1944 and 1945 it took thousands of bombs to cause the destruction of Berlin. "Nowadays," he said, pausing for dramatic effect, "it would take one bomb. Just one bomb." He spoke into a surprisingly long silence for a junior-high-school gymnasium full of teenagers. The

Bomb, the one Bomb, has taken on a mythical power, as if it were something alive, with a kind of random will.

Everything is tinged with uncertainty and fear.

My father leads us in the Rosary every night, and I have begun thinking, as most Catholic boys do at one time or another, of the priesthood. My own whispered prayers, during the cold predawn weekday mornings I walk to the six o'clock Mass and Communion, are addressed to the fading stars, as if I'm already traveling among them. I seem to lose the sense of my own body: I'm all spirit in these moments, and keeping the commandments is easy.

But such passages are brief.

Mostly, all each damned day—to paraphrase John Berryman—I have to fight the battles of the flesh, and, as everyone knows, those battles are always fought, for good or ill, in one's mind. Some buried paragraph of a newspaper article I came upon in the school library said that people who bite their nails or move their legs rhythmically when seated, or perform other unconscious nervous movements when supposedly idle—all of which I do to the point of irritating those around me—are giving off the signs of "a marked mental conflict." I can't believe that others are not subject to the same constant fight. It feels sometimes as if I am nothing less than the battleground between God and the devil, and the devil seems to be winning. Mostly, I feel as if nothing of the faith my family practices is quite possible or true. For all the prayers and rituals, the sacraments and devotions, I am having trouble believing in any of it.

At Christmas, when my mother read to us the account of the angels appearing to the shepherds, how the shepherds were "sore afraid," I couldn't understand the passage at all. Why afraid? To have such visible and undeniable proof of the divine presence, to have the necessity of faith removed by the blinding fact of the angels suspended in the air over our heads? I would have rejoiced at such a vision, would have leapt to my feet shouting, "Look! Look everybody! It's true! It's all true! You don't have to worry about it anymore!"

On this particular Saturday morning in 1959, I am gazing out at the perfect sky, and trying not to think about the satellite hurling through it. Over the past few days, I have been reading some of the more dramatic accounts of the lives of the saints, and there's been talk from the nuns we spend the CCD classes with, about the stigmata—with graphic details, of course. I am trying to imagine the stigmata when abruptly I hear my name called, and realize that my instructor, Sister Theresa, has asked me a question. Because I am half in a daze, I say, "What?"

Calmly, yet quite firmly, she asks everyone to leave the room but me. I watch everyone else file out, some of them glancing at me as they go. The last one to go out is asked to close the door. He does so. The door makes its little clicking sound, and then the room is quiet. I'm sitting there with my sleeves rolled up and my hair combed as much as I can make it like Ricky Nelson's, and for an aching long time it's just the two of us, Sister Theresa and me. She shuffles papers at her desk, and stares out the sunny window, her face perfectly serene, as though she's forgotten me entirely. She's not an attractive woman, Sister Theresa; there's just nothing at all appealing about her: not her face, not her voice, not her personality, not her mind or heart, even—certainly not her manner. "These girls in their sunsuits," she'd said only this morning, having got onto the subject of the approaching summer and what everyone would be wearing. "Well, they aren't sunsuits, they're *sin* suits." This through crooked teeth, with a kind of relishing hatred; it's something she's fed on a long time, apparently.

Now, she rises slowly and comes toward me. Maybe she's learned of my plans for the priesthood. (I have recently seen Gregory Peck in *Keys of the Kingdom,* and the plans include my standing on some hilltop with music in the background while I recite the Magnificat to the sun and wind.) She takes my hand and squeezes it. It hurts.

"Ow," I say.

"Do you know what color your soul is when you're born?"

"No," I tell her, though I think I do. And then I remember to say, "Sister."

"This color," she says, and puts my hand against her starched white wimple. "And do you know what color your soul is now?" she asks.

Before I can answer, she puts my hand against the black cloth of her habit. "This color," she says.

I am in full agreement with her. But I say nothing. I know better than to speak unless asked to. This is not the place for discussion, or anything like reason, and I know this without having a way to express it, quite. I just know that there is no appeal, and nothing to say.

The nuns have a story about something the Blessed Virgin gave to those children at Fátima—a letter, the contents of which are so momentous that the Pope wept upon reading it. And each succeeding Pope has wept to know its frightful contents. These contents are to be revealed to the world in 1960. At Fátima, the nuns have told us, the Virgin prophesied that a country called Russia would rise up and cause trouble in the world, and we know this is all connected to the famous letter, which is stored in some secret vault in the Vatican.

It has been said that during the time of Paul, Christians ever expected the second coming. I expect it because I'm fourteen years old and adults are talking about it. The Russians are playing with their bomb and their space toys on the other side of the world. There are bigger and bigger explosions. Last week, in this same CCD class, we were shown slides depicting, in lurid color and graphic detail, people falling into a flaming canyon. A voice intoned, "Listen to the cries of the damned, falling into the everlasting fires of Hell." And we heard the tumult of a thousand voices, the screams of the punished— mostly, it seemed to me, the screams of women. Then the little dull, echoless bell dinged, and the picture of Hell was obliterated in the small mechanical clatter of the slide changing, and we saw the drawn throne of God, with an Egyptian-stiff Jesus seated at the right hand (our left) all in glorious light. The light, we were told, of Heaven.

I have no hope of Heaven, sitting in that small room with the nun holding my hand against the black cloth of her habit and staring at me with the eyes of an angry Godliness.

I never think of my religion in terms of reason.

"Now, get out of here," she says, letting go of me at last.

Later, in the evening, remembering the cries of the damned, and worried about falling into Hell, I kneel in the dark of my room, feeling that the end is indeed close at hand—it will be 1960 next year—and I begin to pray, thinking about the stigmata, the miracles and signs, all the hoped-for proofs. Perhaps such a thing might happen to me. I am devout; my soul is troubled if it is not black as a nun's habit; I am the battleground; I invite the moment, in a way, with that part of my mind that seems always to be idly speculating. The room is quiet, and quite dark; and abruptly I have the sense of something hovering near. There is an imminence, it seems, a deep pause in the darkness around me. I have stopped breathing. But it's more than that. Any second, it will happen—some gesture from the power and majesty. I can feel it along my spine; it is here. Here!

I have never moved more swiftly in my life.

I bolt out of the room as though it is on fire, or as if, to paraphrase poor old proscribed Boccaccio, ten thousand devils are after me. I almost collide with my mother, walking through the hallway of the house with a basket of laundry. "What's the matter with you?" she says.

"Nothing," I say.

"Well, look where you're going, honey. Will you?"

"We proceed to the second article: It seems that God is not altogether simple . . ."

The second of my two days takes place more than two decades later, though it is no more present or vivid than the first, since it occupies a place in that same wide, quiet province, the lived life that is behind me. It is another sunny March day, 1982, and I am being honored at a gathering of writers in Charlottesville, Virginia, the second annual PEN/Faulkner Awards. My second novel, *Take Me Back,* is one of the six nominees that year, and my wife, Karen, and I have been spending a lot of time with one of the judges, Walker Percy, and his wife, Bunt. We have toured Monticello, and spent hours walking around the city of Charlottesville. It is Walker who nominated me for the award, and who wrote the citation for it. He says that some time after reading the copy the PEN/Faulkner people sent him, he discovered a complimentary copy *I* had had my publisher send him, back when the book was published.

"Somehow it got in under some papers on my desk," he says. "There's always a lot of stuff piled up there. Some of it has been there for years."

I had the book sent to him because he is one of the writers I admire most in this world. The fact that he likes my book means more than I can adequately say, and I know enough not to embarrass him by saying this out loud. It is implied.

The night before, we stayed up late, with all the other writers, drinking bourbon and talking, though Walker did very little talking. He rattled the ice in his glass, leaning against the back of a sofa, in this crowded room with dim paintings of nineteenth-century faces on the walls, and debating voices going on around him. He sipped the bourbon, attending to everything. I sensed that some of the other writers were trying to outdo themselves in his presence, performing for him. I could feel it in myself when it was my turn to talk. There was an argument about whether a historical novelist has a responsibility not to alter the facts as he knows them in order to tell his story or make his metaphor about history. Walker seemed amused by this. He smiled, sipped the bourbon, and rattled the ice in the glass.

"Telling the truth used to be a pledge of the whole self, of the very soul," one of the other writers said. "A bargain with God. Telling an intentional lie in a circumstance of such an implied pledge was considered a violation of divine law. A sure ticket to Hell." This was spoken in the tone of someone explaining the use of an antique tool.

Walker yawned, and excused himself. I did, too. Out in the hallway, he asked what I was working on, and I told him that I was having trouble writing anything at all. I couldn't convince myself that the problems of the characters I'd made up mattered.

"You might listen to a lot less of that stuff in there," he said. "It doesn't pay to think too much about that end of it. Sometimes I think it's a little silly. To be an aging man, still making up stories. You shouldn't worry too much about the theoretical end of it, though." He smiled, then headed off to his room.

This bright Sunday, the four of us are off to find a place to go to Mass. I am driving. Walker and I are in the front seat, Karen and Bunt in back. Bunt sees a beautiful blanket of nasturtiums in a field we pass, and she calls our attention to it. Walker points out another splash of color on the other side of the road—a bed of tulips.

It seems to me that both of them notice the natural world more than other people; certainly more than I have tended to over the years. Karen points out a prodigious drooping wall of a weeping willow, which seems to dwarf the mansion whose front lawn it shades. We all remark on the fine weather, the mountains in the near distance, the blooms of forsythia bordering one fenced lawn. Walker and I talk briefly about writers we like to read. We talk about Henry James.

"I have a complete set of the New York Edition of James," he tells me. "But I haven't looked in them much."

I tell him that I've been reading all the short stories.

"I had a student years ago who got interested in James in a big way," Walker says. "She wanted to read everything he wrote." He looks out the window of the car, pausing, letting out a small sigh. "She disappeared into Henry James without a trace."

We laugh. It is getting late, and we haven't been by any churches yet. I vaguely remember a street with several, though I'm not certain any of them are Catholic. I do not know this city very well, and I am driving aimlessly around, looking for anything that looks like a church. At last, we come over a rise and find a gray edifice with spires and stained-glass windows, and ivy climbing the tall sides. We stop at the crest of the hill across from it, in the striped shade of trees that are about to bloom. Walker and I get out to investigate. As we approach the building, he says, "This one has an Episcopal look about it."

I laugh.

"It's too much like a real church," he says.

We make our way along the shaded walk to the front. Two men are standing outside, and we see from the big stone plaque at the entrance that this is indeed an Episcopal church.

"Excuse me," I say to one of the men. "Is there a Catholic church nearby?"

"Why, yes," the taller of the two says, squinting at us in the sunlight. "You go on down this road and take your first right, then take the next right, and it's on the left as you go up the hill. Look for a big aluminum statue."

Walker looks at me, and we both laugh. We are for the moment in that state of wordless understanding that nourishes the spirit, even if the object of that understanding is a sort of mutual dismay.

"It's Saint Thomas Aquinas," the young man says. "You can't miss it. Big statue of Saint Thomas right out front."

"Thanks," Walker says to them, and we walk back down to the car, still laughing, quietly. We pile in, and I take us to the church. We see it on the left, coming up still another hill, just as the man said we would—an enormous shining sculpture, flanked by the church, which is oddly suspended on many thin white columns over a deep declension in the ground. It looks a little like a flying saucer on props. And then it reminds me of houses near the ocean, built to withstand high water. A catwalk leads to the door, and to the left of the entrance to the catwalk, sits the big statue of Saint Thomas. He's wearing what I suppose are the robes of a monk, and is indeed made out of something like aluminum—bright metal, at any rate. He resembles no image I've ever seen of a saint. He's sitting or squatting, and the tin folds of the robe fall about him as if they have been arrested in the process of melting. He holds books on one massive arm, and he looks jowly, well-fed, faintly disgruntled, almost goofy. No stigmata for this portly gentleman, and no battles with himself about faith, either.

No, Thomas battled with his family when they tried to keep him from the priesthood, and he battled the ignorance and superstitions of his time, battled them reasonably, with that amazing document, the *Summa Theologica*. I cannot imagine him having any arguments with himself over the matters of ultimate concern. Certainly there are no wavering moments in his famous book.

I began reading it, understanding little, when I was eighteen, and still thinking about entering the priesthood. Having run away in abject terror from the intimation of some more visceral proofs, and having come to the knowledge of how superstitious and atavistic most of my training had been, I found the Aquinas as a form of

searching, though I was mostly unaware of its deeper
meanings, for some final intellectual explanation of the
matters on which my tottering faith might rest.

I was destined to fail in this, of course.

And through the years of my journey away from the
superstition and fright of the first day I've described—
which consequently became a journey away from my
church—the memory of the calm, reasonable, teacherly
passages of Aquinas remained, an anomaly in my experience. And Aquinas himself remained, a voice from the
distance, disputing in the pages of his book, which I had
kept. The great serene intellectual acumen of those marvelous propositions, with their clearly stated purposes
and precisely countered objections, gave me an inex-
pressible sense of some sure knowledge beyond faith,
which I had come to see as a form of superstition. But I
never stopped to think about it at all. I went through the
book, and then went on to the next. In my late teens, I
was finding a kind of nourishment provided by the
printed word alone. I hoarded everything, traveling in-
discriminately in the world's literature—reading mostly
philosophy and history. But I kept going back to
Thomas—this medieval saint, who had attempted an explanation of the whole matter of divinity.

And as I entered my twenties, and my concerns were
far from anything religious, I kept him in my mind as a
hedge, somehow, against all the desperate ravings of the
world I moved in, with its assassinations and its hopeless

little various wars near and far, its riots and body counts and burning villages and atrocities; its glass littered streets, and broken houses, its many innocent slaughtered—the wages of all those suppurating hatreds and appalling cowardices, and bigotry of every stripe and kind—the world I was trying to make my way in.

To this day, I know less about him than about his book. I have learned that after he took the habit of the Dominicans, who had recently put together a school of theology at the University of Naples, where he had been a student, he was seized by members of his own family, and it took special pleas from the Pope and from the Dominican order, along with his own resoluteness about his future, to obtain his release. I know that he spent his days, as I am spending mine, teaching and writing, and I know that along with the great *Summa,* he wrote hymns, composed a work attempting to reconcile the Greek and Roman Catholic churches, crafted explications of several works of Aristotle; and produced many, many treatises, on everything from Boethius to Scripture.

For me, over the two decades, drifting far from the church, yet still carrying the two sides of it—the atavistic and the reasonable—inside, still praying out of something like superstition, and still fighting the urge to give in to all on those terms, wanting to come to my religion without fear, if I could, and without all the hysterical and narrow voodoo of the nuns—I still thought of Thomas, with his questions, articles, objections, and replies.

Thomas stood in my mind as a principle of sorts: the one who reasoned his way to God.

And so on this particular early spring day in 1982, kneeling beside Walker Percy in the discouragingly modernistic building that is the Church of St. Thomas Aquinas in Charlottesville, Virginia, I find that I am aware of this terrible modernism as against the monk perched on his bench outside, and, as happens often when I am at Mass, I'm vaguely troubled, unpleasantly and somehow reprehensibly detached—feeling that perhaps I ought to be elsewhere, that my doubts and my old angers about the ignorance and folly of the earlier time, not to mention my lapsed state, make me an intruder here. I probably would not have come, were it not for Mr. Percy. And there he is, kneeling next to me, that consummate artist and philosopher, a deeply learned man with a scientist's knowledge (Percy, as most people know, was a trained physician), there he is, saying his prayers, head bowed, eyes closed, simply believing. Or, at any rate, believing first, before the complexities. And in that one moment, still thinking about the heavy scholarly figure depicted in the ugly metal statue on the lawn, I have a kind of revelation: for perhaps the first time in my life I think of Thomas not in terms of his great intellect, not in terms of reason at all, but of the faith that could drive an enormous undertaking like the *Summa*. Abruptly, with a shiver, deep, I realize something everyone else must already know: that it all has finally to stop there, in faith.

At faith. That what I have always felt was the tremendous reasonableness of Aquinas's book is not so much the product of intellect, as it is the most powerful manifestation of his faith. And I remember hearing that the year before he died, he stopped writing or dictating, claiming that what had been revealed to him in a revelation while saying Mass made everything he had written in his life seem "as straw."

Reason wedded to faith, then. But faith is first. The end and the beginning—or, in the exact words of the old prayer: as it *was* in the beginning, is now, and ever shall be, world without end.

Amen.

A Moderate in a Disputatious Age

AVERY DULLES, S.J.

I FIRST came across Robert Bellarmine in the late 1930s, when I was an undergraduate at Harvard, studying the history and literature of the Italian Renaissance. I remember him particularly because of the respectful presentation of his work in Charles H. McIlwain's course on the history of political thought in the West. About the time that I became a Catholic, in my first semester of Harvard Law School, I devoured James Brodrick's two-volume life of Bellarmine and came to admire the saint's many-sided personality and his manifold accomplishments.

Several months later, in the spring of 1941, when I received the sacrament of confirmation at the hands of Bishop Richard J. Cushing (who later became cardinal-archbishop of Boston), I was asked to choose a confirmation name, and I selected without hesitation "Robert." On that occasion the bishop presented me with a fine illustrated volume on Francis of Assisi, one of the saints that Bellarmine most admired. Born on the feast of Saint Francis, October 4, 1542, Bellarmine had been given "Francis" as his second name. He died on September 17, 1622, the feast of the stigmatization of Saint Francis, a feast that he had helped to insert into the calendar. When that feast was suppressed in the reform of the liturgical calendar after Vatican II, the feast of Saint Robert Bellarmine was transferred from May 13 to September 17, where it now stands.

When I entered the Society of Jesus in 1946, after a stint with the Navy in World War II, I was delighted to find that Bellarmine was one of the two Jesuit doctors of the Church and was the patron of all Jesuit theologians. I made him in a special way the patron of my own studies. When I went to Rome to get my doctorate at the Gregorian University, my associations with Bellarmine increased. I said Mass daily in the Church of Sant' Ignazio, where Bellarmine lies buried, as he requested, at the feet of his former penitent, Aloysius Gonzaga, whose marble tomb is a masterpiece of Baroque sculpture.

Since 1973 I have taught three times as a visiting

professor at the Gregorian University. The last time, in the fall of 1993, coincided with the fourth centenary of Bellarmine's rectorship of the university, known in his day as the Roman College (1592–1594). It was here that Bellarmine had studied philosophy (1560–1563), taught theology (1576–1588), and served as spiritual director (1590–1592). The college received its present name in honor of its "second founder," Pope Gregory XIII (1572–1585), who built the new Roman College, with its imposing classical façade, during Bellarmine's tenure.

There is every reason, then, why I should look back to Bellarmine as representing the finest traditions and perhaps the most glorious period of my own Jesuit theological heritage. He was a major actor in one of the most dramatic periods of Church history—the reorganization of the Catholic Church in response to the challenges of the modern age. The sixteenth century had witnessed, in many respects, the birth of modernity. Capitalism was edging out the medieval agrarian economy. Europe was becoming divided into rival principalities or nation-states, often governed by Machiavellian rulers who claimed absolute powers over their subjects. The Holy Roman Empire survived in theory, but it ceased to be a true empire (not to mention its failure to be either holy or Roman, as Voltaire once quipped).

This period also witnessed intellectual and cultural revolutions. Medieval manuscript communication rapidly yielded to the new print culture. Pamphlets and books, including the Bible, were widely circulated in affordable editions, frequently in the vernacular. Under the impetus of classical humanism, scholars were producing new and critical editions of ancient texts, both classical and religious, and were questioning many venerable legends about Christian origins. Critical reason was beginning to assume the upper hand over traditional faith. Dramatic scientific discoveries were being made, including the Copernican theory, which situated the sun rather than the earth at the center of the universe. It was also the great age of discovery, when Europe suddenly became conscious that it was only a fraction of a much larger world, in many parts of which Christianity was still unknown. Thus the medieval world picture, so glowingly immortalized in Dante's *Divine Comedy,* was in many respects superseded.

It was into this volatile situation that Luther, in 1518, issued his urgent call for ecclesiastical reform. His appeal hit upon receptive ears, because everyone recognized that corruptions and abuses were rampant in the Church. Luther's personal doctrines, however, were another question. Pope Leo X wrote him off as simply another German heretic, but he proved to be much more. With the support of several German princes, and the backing of German national feeling, he obtained a large constituency, so that his excommunication by Rome resulted in a major schism. Soon afterward, several other parts of Europe followed suit in seceding from the Catholic allegiance.

By the time Bellarmine reached adulthood, Europe was a checkerboard of different denominations—Lutheran, Calvinist, Zwinglian, Anglican, Anabaptist, and even Unitarian (Socinian). In many cases the religious affiliation of the people depended on that of their sovereigns. Catholics and Protestants therefore vied with one another in seeking to win the patronage of secular princes. Not infrequently the patronage became so vigorous that members of other denominations were tortured and executed. The principle of religious toleration was practically unknown.

The Jesuit order, founded by Saint Ignatius of Loyola in 1540, was immediately caught up in this religious ferment. While Ignatius governed his new Society from his headquarters in Rome, his companions fanned out to all parts of the world. They labored, often at the price of martyrdom, in India, China, Japan, Africa, and the Americas, seeking to spread Catholic Christianity all over the globe. In Western Europe they were involved in the inner reform of the Church, in the education of the clergy, and in turning back the advancing tide of heresy. At the Council of Trent the pope chose several of Ignatius's most brilliant companions to be his personal theologians. That council issued what still stands as the authoritative statement of Catholic doctrine in response to the Reformers. It set the agenda for Bellarmine's generation in much the same way as Vatican II has set the agenda for the late twentieth century.

Bellarmine, like other Jesuit theologians of his day, was first of all a servant of the Church, a defender of orthodoxy in an age when the foundations of Catholicism were being assailed. He taught, preached, and wrote in the Jesuit style, according to the rules laid down by Saint Ignatius. The early Jesuits were Christian humanists, well educated in classical languages and literature, with a high esteem for human nature, reason, and freedom. They kept abreast of the latest developments in scholarship and the sciences. Without being a scientist himself, Bellarmine kept himself informed through friends such as his colleague the great Clavius (Christoph Klau, S. J.), with whom Galileo often exchanged ideas. Clavius is best known as the principal author of the Gregorian Calendar and is also remembered by the "sea" on the moon that bears his name.

Although Bellarmine was by temperament a peaceful and friendly person, his career took him into a series of battles. In 1570, as a young professor at Louvain (in modern Belgium), he began his six-year struggle against Baius (Michel de Bay), whose pessimistic views concerning man's fallen condition resembled those of Calvin. Bellarmine, as a champion of human freedom and dignity, threw himself into the combat with alacrity.

When recalled by superiors to teach at the Roman

College, Bellarmine produced his magnum opus, the *Disputationes de Controversiis Fidei Catholicae adversus huius temporis haereticos,* published in three large folios in 1586, 1588, and 1593. Although never translated as a whole into vernacular languages, this work remained for centuries the standard Catholic response to the Reformation. It also established the main lines of Catholic ecclesiology until the middle of our own century. Many of the Latin apologetics manuals and textbooks published in the intervening years were little more than simplified versions of Bellarmine's masterpiece. While writing overtly as a controversialist, Bellarmine was exceptionally fair and moderate toward his adversaries, at least by the standards of his day. In order to meet the real difficulties, he took pains to state the opponents' arguments at their strongest. On occasion he even defended Protestants against unfair charges, such as Calvin's alleged deviations from the orthodox doctrine of the Trinity. Some Catholics distrusted Bellarmine on the ground that Protestants were using his account of them to find ammunition in their own defense.

Bellarmine's ecclesiology differed in several respects from that of his medieval predecessors. He portrayed the Church not primarily as a mystical communion but rather as a visible society, no less visible, he said, than the Republic of Venice. This society was, moreover, monarchical in structure, governed by a pope who could on occasion speak with infallibility. When the First Vatican

Council was preparing to define the doctrine of papal infallibility in 1869 and 1870, many speakers referred to Bellarmine as an authority.

Bellarmine taught that membership in the Church was absolutely necessary for salvation, but he made an important distinction between belonging to the "body" of the Church and to its "soul." Non-Catholics and non-Christians, if they erred in good faith, could belong to the "soul" of the Church. This distinction was widely accepted among Catholics until the middle of the present century, when different terminology came into use. Vatican II, for example, distinguishes between Catholics, who are "fully incorporated" in the Church, and others who, when separated from the Catholic communion without personal fault, may be secretly "conjoined" or "ordered" to the Church in various ways.

Bellarmine's work is still a valuable resource for ascertaining and criticizing the positions of Reformation thinkers. I experienced this a decade ago, when engaged in a dialogue with Lutheran theologians about the role of the saints in the Christian life. The Catholics and Lutherans managed to achieve a large measure of agreement on several issues: that the saints are to be honored for what God's grace had wrought in them, that their lives inspire us with gratitude and confidence toward God, and that they provide examples for us to imitate. With some hesitation the Lutherans conceded that the saints probably intercede for the Church on earth.

But at one point our ways parted. Was it proper for Christians to invoke the saints in prayer? The Lutherans contended that there was no biblical example or precept for so doing, that we have no way of knowing whether the saints in glory can hear us (even supposing them to be in glory), that consequently the invocation of saints introduces an element of doubt and uncertainty into Christian prayer, and, finally, that prayer to the saints derogates from the trust that should be placed in Christ as the sole and sufficient mediator of all grace.

Hard-pressed by these formidable objections, I made an expedition to the subterranean stacks of Fordham University, located the appropriate passage in Bellarmine's *Controversies,* and found to my delight that he had given an exceptionally lucid exposition of the Catholic doctrine of honoring the saints, in the course of which he dealt with ten objections culled from the Reformers, including all the objections I have listed. A central point in his argument was that, whether we pray to God directly or invoke the intercession of saints, nothing is asked or granted that does not come from God through the mediation of Christ. In the last analysis every prayer is directed to God, the giver of all perfect gifts. From this perspective it may be said that we do not so much pray *to the saints* as seek their solidarity with us as we pray *to God.* Prayer to the saints can never be played off in competition with prayer to God, nor can the intercession of the saints be regarded as detracting from the redemptive mediatorship of Christ alone.

From this example, which I have chosen in view of the theme of the present collection, it should be evident that Bellarmine's old volumes can still be uncommonly useful for theologians today. They should not be allowed to accumulate dust in deserted library stacks.

The Bible, of course, was a major point of contention between Protestants and Catholics, both of whom wanted to prove that their doctrines were consonant with the written word of God. Jesuits such as Bellarmine became expert in the biblical languages. As a young professor he wrote a very popular Hebrew grammar. In 1579, during his Roman professorate, he was called upon to assist Alonso Salmerón, an elderly survivor from Ignatius's original band of companions, in editing his sixteen folio volumes of commentaries on the New Testament. Later Bellarmine composed a large commentary on the Psalms (1611), a piece that is devotional rather than scholarly in character.

More significant for posterity is Bellarmine's role in the revision of the Latin Vulgate. Carrying out a decree of the Council of Trent, Pope Gregory XIII appointed a commission, with Bellarmine as a member, to produce a reliable edition of the ancient Vulgate translation. The commission did its work with great care, and in 1588 presented the results to the temperamental Sixtus V. To general astonishment, he rejected the commission's work and took the revision into his own hands. In 1590, just as his very faulty edition was emerging from the press, the pope suddenly died. Bellarmine was again called in to assist in correcting the errors. A new text was published in 1592 under the name of Pope Sixtus V, although Clement VIII was then reigning. In a preface Bellarmine tried to protect the reputation of the earlier pope by dwelling on the printer's errors in the edition that had begun to be published. The Sixto-Clementine Vulgate (as it is usually called) remained the standard Catholic Bible until the mid-twentieth century, when fresh translations from the original biblical languages were encouraged.

Another debt that the Church of later centuries owes to Bellarmine is for his contribution to the reform of the Breviary. Because of his mastery of ecclesiastical history, he was asked by Clement VIII to serve on a commission for this purpose. He argued for excluding various improbable legends concerning James the Greater, Denis the Areopagite, and Catherine of Alexandria, but his opinions did not always prevail. He composed a beautiful Latin hymn to Mary Magdalen that was included in the office for July 21, at the vespers of her feast.

In the 1590s, under Clement VIII, Bellarmine became heavily involved in a truly epochal struggle within Catholic theology—the controversy between the Dominicans and the Jesuits on the relations between efficacious grace and free will. Bellarmine, as a Jesuit, was inclined to favor the "Molinist" position (devised by Luis de Molina, S. J.) to the effect that God's salvific decree depends upon his eternal knowledge of the use that human beings make of their freedom in response to God's grace. While he did not fully accept Molina's theory, he resisted the opinion of Domingo Bañez, O. P., that God determines human acts by giving an infallible "physical premotion" *(praemotio physica)* to the will. Clement himself was inclined to support the Dominican view and, perhaps for that reason, removed Bellarmine from Rome in 1602, appointing him archbishop of Capua. But after Clement's death, Bellarmine was recalled to Rome, where he labored as a cardinal of the Roman curia. Following Bellarmine's recommendation, Paul V decreed in 1607 that both opinions were to be tolerated. Neither party was to impugn the positions of the other as heretical or temerarious. This decree illustrates the way in which the hierarchical magisterium can on occasion serve to protect the freedom of theologians and their immunity from unjust accusations.

In an age when popes were much given to deposing temporal sovereigns (as Pius V deposed Queen Elizabeth), Bellarmine was required to speak to the question of the pope's temporal power. Some theologians still held to the extreme position that Christ had given Peter "two swords," the spiritual and the temporal, thereby bestowing on the popes universal sovereignty in both spheres. Bellarmine held for the autonomy of the temporal power in secular matters, but he made provision in his theory for the pope to intervene in secular politics where the good of souls was at stake. Bellarmine's moderate doctrine of the "indirect power" of the Holy See did not satisfy the impetuous Sixtus V, who took steps to place the *Controversies* on the Index of Prohibited Books. But here again the death of the pope intervened, preventing him from promulgating this edition of the Index.

The most vehement objections to the theory of the indirect power came not from popes but from secularists who attributed absolute powers to kings. They rejected Bellarmine's contention that the temporal sovereign should be bound by international law to abide by moral principles and respect the human rights of all subjects, including the aborigines in the colonies.

Bellarmine's bad reputation in the English-speaking world is largely due to his polemical exchanges with King James I, undertaken at the direction of Paul V (1605–1621). Against the King of England, Bellarmine defended his doctrine of the pope's "indirect power," and attacked the idea that kings rule with absolute power by divine right. Bellarmine held that civil power comes to the ruler not directly from God but through the people, who may set up any kind of regime that serves the common good. Regalists such as William Barclay and Robert Filmer, responding to Bellarmine, characterized him as the ablest defender of the doctrine they were opposing.

John Locke, Thomas Jefferson, and James Madison seem to have been acquainted with Bellarmine, especially through the writings of his adversaries. It has been plausibly argued that in this way Bellarmine exercised an indirect influence upon the American system of government. In any case he belonged to the general movement of thought that favored popular sovereignty.

Yet another of the controversies in which Bellarmine was engaged is the trial of Galileo. As a member of the Holy Office he was asked in 1616 to be a judge when charges were made against the orthodoxy of the new astronomy. Like the other judges, he concluded, after consulting leading experts in the field, that Galileo had not proved his case, and that his theory stood in contradiction to the apparent meaning of several passages in Scripture. He advised Galileo to propose his theory simply as a hypothesis, which would seem to have been a reasonable solution. When Galileo refused, Bellarmine was party to a declaration that the Copernican theory, as received by Galileo, ought not to be held. But at that trial no condemnation was issued, no punishment imposed, nor was Galileo ordered to make any retraction. For the results of the second trial of Galileo, which occurred in 1633, Bellarmine cannot be held responsible, for by that time he had been dead for eleven years.

The Galileo case long continued to be a point of friction between the Church and the scientific community. In 1981 Pope John Paul II set up a papal commission to study the case anew. This commission, in its report of October 31, 1992, gave high praise to Bellarmine for having declared that if it were really demonstrated that the earth revolves about the sun, it would be necessary to reinterpret the biblical passages which seem to say the contrary. The commission also faulted Galileo's judges, who in the trial of 1633 judged that the Copernican theory, not yet definitively proven, was contrary to the teaching of Scripture and Catholic tradition. Pope John Paul II, addressing the Pontifical Academy of Sciences on the same occasion, repeated the commission's praise for Bellarmine. He agreed with its findings that the sentence of 1633 was "not irreformable" and was based on a misconception of the relations between biblical revelation and physical science.

Central though controversies were to the life of Bellarmine, as a theologian in a disputatious age, they do not make up his total achievement. A more positive element of his legacy may be found in the two catechisms he composed in Italian, the first for children (1597), the other for adults (1598). These catechisms, modeled on the Roman Catechism of 1566, remained popular for several centuries. Translated into various languages, they inspired other manuals, such as the famous Baltimore Catechism, widely used in this country until Vatican II. But unlike the Baltimore Catechism, Bellarmine's did not begin by having the child ask the metaphysical questions "Who made us?" and "Who is God?" The first question is, rather, "Are you a Christian?" to which the child replies, "By the grace of God, I am." Then the catechism goes on to inquire into the principal mysteries of the Christian faith, the Trinity, and the Incarnation.

At the First Vatican Council, in 1869, Pius IX announced his intention, with the fathers' approval, to have a new catechism drawn up on the pattern of Bellarmine's. Because the council was disrupted by war, it never arrived at a vote on this proposal. The Church had to wait another century before it would have a new universal catechism. The new *Catechism of the Catholic Church,* like Bellarmine's, is based on the Roman Catechism and uses as its four "pillars" the Apostles' Creed, the Our Father, the Ten Commandments, and the Seven Sacraments. Like Bellarmine's, again, it treats the Trinity and the Incarnation as the central mysteries of faith.

I have focused here on Bellarmine's theological writings rather than on his personality and his qualities as a pastor, spiritual director, and saint. His biographers tell us that he was serene, joyful, and optimistic. He had a playful sense of humor and was much addicted to puns. In spite of his exceptional talents he was always content to be given the smallest rooms, to wear the oldest clothes, and eat the poorest fare. As an archbishop and a cardinal he put his revenues at the disposal of needy families and drew multitudes of beggars to his doorstep.

One of my favorite stories about Bellarmine captures at once his self-mortification and his theological wit. In

the Roman summers he was pestered, like others, by
flies. His companions asked him why he did not brush
these nuisances away. He explained with a smile that it
would not be fair to trouble the little creatures, since his
nose was their Paradise.

In the entire corpus of Bellarmine's writings the spiritual works of his final years are the most accessible in
vernacular translations. Although the style of these
works reflects the mentality of an earlier age, they vividly illustrate how the piety of the saint can permeate the
reflections of the theologian.

The most popular of these spiritual works, *The
Mind's Ascent to God* (1614), is comparable in content and
structure to Saint Bonaventure's *Journey of the Mind to
God,* but in place of Bonaventure's flights of mysticism,
Bellarmine pursues a more logical and moralistic course.
Yet his prose is not devoid of eloquence. In examining,
in the first pages, how we are created in the image of
God, he delights in explaining that the mind, as a principle of reason and freedom, distinguishes us from the animals and makes us similar to God. The final chapters
celebrate the mercy and justice of God.

The series of small spiritual classics ends with Bellarmine's last work, appropriately named *The Art of Dying
Well* (1620). He maintains that "death, as the offspring
of sin, is evil, but that by the grace of Christ, who
deigned to undergo death for us, it has been rendered for

us in many ways useful and salutary, lovable and desirable."

Bellarmine was not remarkable for his originality or speculative genius. He was a practical man, concerned with serving the universal Church as it responded to the crises of the age. By his own intention he stood in firm continuity with the past, confident that the tradition of the Church was sound and valid. Yet, almost in spite of himself, he absorbed the spirit of the new age. As compared with Saint Thomas Aquinas and the medieval Scholastics, he was far more careful in scrutinizing the written sources and ascertaining the history of the questions he treated. Faithful to the precepts of Saint Ignatius, he brought positive and speculative theology into partnership. Breathing the spirit of Renaissance humanism, he adamantly opposed the assaults of neo-Augustinian pessimism.

The stature of Bellarmine is indicated by the enduring influence of his writings. They continued to be a major, even a dominant, source for Catholic doctrine during the next three centuries. Ours, however, is an age with different questions, different assumptions, and a radically changed context. We have passed from a print-dominated culture to one that is electronic. We have passed from a Eurocentric consciousness to one that is global and is verging on the galactic. Catholics are no longer arrayed in battle against Reformation Protestantism. They are seeking ecumenical rapprochement, and are in dialogue with other world religions. In short, theologians are called to do again, in a vastly changed context, something analogous to what Bellarmine did, with remarkable success, for early modern times.

What endures in Bellarmine is his example of loyal service to the Church in a time of confusion and crisis. He is a model of moderation and rationality, open to new developments but deeply attached to the Catholic heritage. He undertook almost nothing on his own initiative, and was content to labor at uncongenial tasks where duty seemed to require. He never raised a finger for the sake of his personal advancement, and perhaps for that reason was generally trusted by his religious and ecclesiastical superiors. Among his many virtues I would single out loyalty as perhaps the greatest. He did what was asked of him; he spoke frankly when consulted, but he never urged his own opinions to the detriment of the Church itself. He was loyal to his religious order, loyal to the Holy See, loyal to the Church, and loyal especially to God, in whom he placed all his trust and confidence.

The Pilgrim

RON HANSEN

MORE THAN two hundred miracles were attributed to Ignatius of Loyola when the judges for the cause of his canonization, the Rota, assembled their sixteen hundred witness statements in 1622.[1] A surgeon held a signature of Ignatius to his head and his headaches and sight problems ended. A Franciscan nun's broken femur was healed when a Spanish priest applied a patch of Ignatius's clothing to her thigh. A Spanish woman held a picture of Ignatius to her hugely swollen stomach and was soon cured of dropsy. Juana Clar, of Manresa, was gradually losing her sight until she got down on her knees and permitted a fragment of Ignatius's bones to be touched to her eyelids. She felt at once such pleasure that it was as if, she said, she'd seen fresh roses. Within a day her pain went away and her vision was perfectly restored. And so on.

Even though I presume those stories are true, I find myself oddly unaffected by them; it's as if I heard that Saint Ignatius, like Cool Hand Luke, could eat fifty eggs. I have read every major biography and book about Ignatius, I have held his shoes in my hands, I have walked through his freshly restored rooms in the house next to what is now the Church of the Gesù, and I have next to me as I write this a nail that was in one of the walls. Supernatural prodigies have nothing to do with my rapt and consuming interest in him. I have simply been trying to figure out how to live my life magnificently, as Ignatius did, who sought in all his works and activities the greater glory of God.

Iñigo López de Loyola was born in the Loyola castle in 1491, the last son of thirteen children born to a wealthy and highly esteemed family in Azpeitia, in the Basque province of Guipúzcoa.[2] His father, Beltrán de Loyola, died in 1507, but we do not know when his mother, Marina Sánchez de Licona, died, only that she predeceased her husband; it's highly probable she died in the child's infancy, for Iñigo was nursed by María de Garín, a neighboring blacksmith's wife, who later taught him his prayers and with whose children he played.[3]

Guipúzcoa means "to terrify the enemy"[4] and there was a huge, legendary emphasis on fearlessness and aggressiveness among the region's men. Juan Pérez, the oldest of Iñigo's brothers, joined a ship's escort for Christopher Columbus and finally died heroically in the Spanish conquest of Naples, and another brother, Hernando, gave up his inheritance in order to go to the Americas, where he disappeared in 1510. In fact, of Iñigo's seven older brothers, only one was not a conquistador or fighting man. That brother, Pero López, took holy orders and became rector of the Church of San Sebastián at Azpeitia; and his father may have sought holy orders for Iñigo as well, for he was enrolled in preseminary studies in the arts of reading and writing before he was sent, at the age of thirteen and probably at his own behest, to acquire the skills and manners of a courtier in the household of his father's friend, the chief treasurer of King Ferdinand of Castile.[5]

His fantasies became those of intrigue and gallantry and knightly romance. Of him in his twenties it was written: "He is in the habit of going round in cuirass and coat of mail, wears his hair long to the shoulder, and walks around in a two-colored, slashed doublet with a bright cap."[6] We have evidence that he was cited in court for brawling, and he himself confessed that "he was a man given over to the vanities of the world; with a

great and vain desire to win fame he delighted especially
in the exercise of arms."[7] We have no evidence from him
of his affairs of the heart beyond his furtive confession
that he was "fairly free in the love of women" and, later,
that he often spent hours "fancying what he would have
to do in the service of a certain lady, of the means he
would take to reach the country where she was living, of
the verses, the promises he would make to her, the deeds
of gallantry he would do in her service. He was so enam-
ored with all this that he did not see how impossible it
would all be, because the lady was of no ordinary rank";[8]
indeed, she seems to have been Doña Catalina, the glam-
orous sister of Emperor Charles V and future queen of
John III of Portugal.[9]

When his employer, the king's treasurer-general,
died in 1517, the twenty-six-year-old Iñigo found another
friend and benefactor in the Viceroy of Navarre, who
hired him as his "gentleman," a kind of factotum or
right-hand man. Iñigo de Loyola was a finished hidalgo
by then, a haughty Lothario and swashbuckler, famous
for his flair and charm and machismo, his fastidiousness
and fondness for clothes, his highly educated politeness
and chivalry and hot temper, his ferocity of will, his fortitude and loyalty—his Basqueness, as the Spanish would
say—and also his acuity and craft in negotiations, his
penetrating stare, his photographic memory, his fine pen-
manship, his reticence and precaution in speech, his love
of singing and dancing. Like his Spanish friends, he was

religiously naive, and Catholicism seems to have been
rather perfunctory for him—high-table rituals without
flourish or kisses. "Although very much attached to the
faith," a friend and biographer wrote, "he did not live in
keeping with his belief, or guard himself from sin: he
was particularly careless about gambling, affairs with
women, and duelling." [10]

Iñigo was not a professional soldier then, as he'd fancied he'd be, but a public administrator, "a man of great
ingenuity and prudence in worldly affairs and very skill-
ful in the handling of men, especially in composing difficulties and discord." [11] But in May 1521, his skillfulness
in the handling of men put Iñigo alongside the magistrate
of Pamplona in Navarre, defending its fortress in the
midst of a huge French offensive in the region along the
Pyrenees that the Spanish king had annexed five years
earlier. We have no idea how many citizens were with
Iñigo, but there could not have been more than a handful
holding out against a highly trained French force of three
hundred. [12] Late in the nine-hour siege of the fortress, an
artillery shot crashed between Iñigo's legs, shattering the
right and harming the other. After he fell, the fortress
surrendered, and the French made it a point of chivalry
to treat Iñigo with such exemplary kindness that it may
have seemed a form of sarcasm. Their finest physicians
operated on him and graciously hospitalized him for a
fortnight in his own Pamplona residence before hauling
him forty miles northwest to Azpeitia on a litter.

In his family's castle Iñigo's fever and illness grew worse, and village surgeons decided the skewed bones of his leg would have to be broken again and reset—without anesthetic. Even thirty years later he would describe that agony as "butchery," but he was fiercely determined to give no "sign of pain other than to clench his fists."[13] When finally his right leg healed, Iñigo realized that it was foreshortened and that the fibula had knitted jaggedly so that an ugly jutting was just under his knee. Still thinking of finding fame in royal courts and of striding forth in fashionably tight leggings and knee-high boots, he made himself "a martyr to his own pleasure"[14] and underwent the horrific ordeal of having the offending bone chiseled and shaved away.

And then a change began to occur in him. While lying about and suffering further treatments that failed to lengthen his brutalized leg, he sought books of Medieval chivalry to read. Surprisingly, the only books available in the Loyola house were a four-volume *Vita Jesu Christi* by Ludolph of Saxony and a kind of dictionary of saints called *Flos Sanctorum* by Jacopo da Varazze.[15] With a sigh. he read even those. A confidant later overstated the situation by writing of Iñigo that "he had no thought then either of religion or piety,"[16] but it can be fairly said that his simple, unreflective, folk Christianity had not forced him to take his life here seriously nor to compare himself to the holy men of the past, whom Ludolph of Saxony called knightly followers of Christ—*caballeros imita-*

dores.[17] Speaking of himself in the third person in his autobiography, Ignatius put it this way:

> As he read [the books] over many times, he became rather fond of what he found written there. Putting his reading aside, he sometimes stopped to think about the things he had read and at other times about the things of the world that he used to think about before. . . . Our Lord assisted him, causing other thoughts that arose from the things he read to follow these. While reading the life of Our Lord and of the saints, he stopped to think, reasoning within himself, "What if I should do what St. Francis did, what St. Dominic did?" So he pondered over many things that he found to be good, always proposing to himself what was difficult and serious, and as he proposed them, they seemed to him easy to accomplish.[18]

We are challenged by Ignatius in much the same way that he was challenged by Francis and Dominic. And that may be the best purpose for books of saints: to have our complacency and mediocrity goaded, and to highlight our lame urge to go forward with the familiar rather than the difficult and serious. We often find tension and unease with the holy lives we read about because there is always an implicit criticism of our habits and weaknesses in greatness and achievement. We know God wants us to be happy, but what is happiness? What is enough? What is the difference between that which is hard to do and that which ought not be done by me? Women are often put off or mystified by this highly masculine saint, but I find so many points of intersection with Iñigo's life that I feel compelled to ask, What if I should do what Ignatius did? And it does not seem to me easy to accomplish.

Iñigo was thirty years old, which was far older then, and yet he found himself wrought up by questions about his purpose on earth that his friends had put a halt to as teenagers. But he was helped in his religious crisis by his discovery of affective patterns to his inner experience, a discovery that would later form the basis for the "Rules for Discernment of Spirits" in his *Spiritual Exercises.*

When he was thinking about the things of the world, he took much delight in them, but afterwards, when he was tired and put them aside, he found that he was dry and discontented. But when he thought of going to Jerusalem, barefoot and eating nothing but herbs and undergoing all the other rigors that he saw the saints had endured, not only was he consoled when he had these thoughts, but even after putting them aside, he remained content and happy.... Little by little he came to recognize the difference between the spirits that agitated him, one from the demon, the other from God.[19]

Concluding that he ought to change radically, Iñigo chose to give up his former interests and pursuits, and, on a pilgrimage to Jerusalem, undergo the hard penances for his sins that "a generous soul, inflamed by God, usually wants to do."[20] Confirmation of that choice came one August night in his sickroom when he was graced with a clear and tremendously consoling image of Our Lady with the Infant Jesus, "and he was left with such loathing for his whole past life and especially for the things of the flesh, that it seemed that all the fantasies he had previously pictured in his mind were driven from it."[21] Even his family noted the difference in him and, far from thinking him crazy, seemed inspired by his faith and good example. Seeing that Iñigo wanted to go even farther in his religious life, however, Martín García de Loyola took his limping brother from room to room in the grand old house, pointing out the jasper and furnishings and fine tapestries, and appealing to him to "consider what hopes had been placed in him and what he should become . . . all with the purpose of dissuading him from his good intention."[22]

But Iñigo was not budged. He filled three hundred pages of a blank account book with extracts from the

Gospels and his readings, found a picture of Our Lady of Sorrows and a book of hours of Our Lady, fitted himself out like a knight-errant, and finally left the Loyola house in late February 1522. Offering farewells to his sister Magdalena at Anzuola and to his former employer, the Viceroy of Navarre, in Navarrete, he went eastward on his mule another two hundred miles to the Benedictine monastery of Montserrat in Catalonia. After a full, general confession of his past life in writing, which took three days, Iñigo gave up his fine clothes to a tramp, put on a penitential sackcloth tunic and rope-soled sandals, and on the eve of the Annunciation of Our Lady observed a knightly vigil-at-arms at the feet of the Black Madonna, where he vowed perpetual chastity and left his flashing sword and dagger in the shrine. Effectively, his former life was over.

Barcelona was the port of embarkation for Rome where, through agreement with the Turks, pilgrims were given permission to go to the Holy Land by the pope himself at Easter. But Adrian of Utrecht, the new pope-elect, was himself in Spain and on his slow way to the port, and Iñigo was at pains to avoid his old friends in the Navarrese nobility, whom he rightly presumed would be part of Adrian's retinue.[23] So he went from Montserrat to Manresa, a few miles north, with the intention of staying perhaps three days, but the affective experience of God he felt there was so powerful that he stayed in

Manresa almost a year, a period he later thought of as "my primitive Church."

To vanquish his vanity there, Iñigo let his nails go untrimmed and his hair and beard grow full and wild as nests, and as he tilted from door to door for food and alms in his prickly tunic, he found joy and sweetness in the jeering of children who called him *El hombre saco*— Old Man Sack.[24] He helped with the poor and sick in the hospital of Santa Lucia, finding no task offensive, and primarily resided in a Dominican friary, though he often withdrew to a hermit's cave in the hillsides above the river Cardoner. Eating no meat and drinking no wine, fasting until he was little more than skin and skeleton, ill and sleepless much of the time, flagellating himself for his sins, Iñigo was still an Olympian at prayer, attending Matins with the Dominicans, and Mass, Vespers, and Compline in the cathedral where the canons regular chanted the office in Latin, of which he knew not a word. Exhausting as that regimen might have been, he gave a full seven hours more to kneeling at prayer and, if he found a peseta of free time, read to the point of memorization *The Imitation of Christ* by Thomas à Kempis, a book he would later call "the partridge among spiritual books."[25] And yet, as he says in his autobiography,

> Sometimes he found himself so disagreeable that
> he took no joy in prayer or in hearing mass or

in any other prayer he said. At other times exactly the opposite of this came over him so suddenly that he seemed to have thrown off sadness and desolation just as one snatches a cape from another's shoulders. Here he began to be astounded by these changes that he had never experienced before, and he said to himself, "What new life is this that we are now beginning?" [26]

Compared to his former life as a grand hidalgo, it seemed to have no purpose, and he was so further anguished by his infirmities, fasts, mortifications, and scruples that he found it hard to imagine going on as he had and was assailed with the urge to kill himself, fear of offending God being the one thing that held him back. But gradually Iñigo figured out—possibly with the help of his Benedictine confessor—that he'd simply gone too far, and he gently tempered his penances in obedience, he thought, to the promptings of a Holy Being who was treating him, as he said, "just as a schoolmaster treats a child whom he is teaching." [27]

Enlightenment came to him on the foremost aspects of Catholic orthodoxy, of the Holy Trinity functioning like three harmonious notes in a musical chord, of how God created the world from white-hot nothing, of how Christ was really present in the Eucharist; and frequently over the next few years he saw the humanity of Christ and Our Lady, giving him "such strength in his faith that he often thought to himself: if there were no Scriptures to teach us these matters of the faith, he would be resolved to die for them, only because of what he had seen."[28] And one famous day on the banks of the Cardoner, the pilgrim, as he habitually called himself, was graced with an illumination of such great clarity and insight about "spiritual things and matters of faith and learning"[29] that "he seemed to himself to be another person and had an intellect other than he had before."[30] Testimony to the great learning Iñigo seemed to have acquired, as he said, *de arriba,* from above, was provided later by Martial Mazurier, a professor of theology at the Sorbonne, who asserted "that never had he heard any man speak of theological matters with such mastery and power."[31]

Because he often referred to his Cardoner illumination as the foundation of all that he would later do, it has been argued that Iñigo was given foreknowledge then and there of the Society of Jesus that would be formally instituted in 1540, but far more likely was it the origin of Iñigo's shift from a worried, isolated, flesh-despising penitent to a far more tranquil and outgoing man who was less concerned with harsh penances than he was with Christ-like services to others.

Essential elements of his *Spiritual Exercises*—finally

published in 1548—were probably composed in Manresa about this time. Influenced in part by Ludolph of Saxony's *Vita Jesu Christi,* the Abbot of Montserrat's *Ejercitatorio de la vida espiritual,* and *Meditationes vitae Christi* by a fourteen-century Franciscan, the *Spiritual Exercises* fashioned for the first time what is now popularly known as a retreat.[32] The handbook offered spiritual directors a practical and systematic method of having retreatants meditate, in silence and solitude over an intensive four-week span, on God's plan in the creation of human beings, humanity's fall from grace through sin, the gifts of humility and poverty, and the glory of the life, passion, and resurrection of Jesus.[33] Each psychologically astute meditation gently guided a retreatant to choose a fuller Christian life and, as the author himself had done, "to overcome oneself, and to order one's life, without reaching a decision through some disordered affection."[34]

Early in the *Spiritual Exercises* practitioners are told to reflect on themselves and ask: "What have I done for Christ? What am I doing for Christ? What ought I to do for Christ?"[35] Iñigo's own reply to that final question was to complete his long-delayed pilgrimage to Jerusalem. *El hombre saco* was by then affectionately being called *El hombre sancto,* the Holy Man, and when in the hard winter he forsook his tunic and sandals for a family's gift of shoes and beret and two brown doublets, the family preserved his sackcloth as a holy relic.[36] Refusing alms that were offered by friends—possibly because they themselves were in such great want—Iñigo left Manresa on foot in late February 1523, and stayed in Barcelona twenty days, going from door to door to beg for food and provisions for his journey and so impressing Isabel Roser with his talk of God and religion that she paid for his sea passage to Rome and remained his principal benefactor throughout his life.

Whoever met him seems to have liked him; he found no trouble getting an apostolic blessing for his pilgrimage in Rome from Adrian VI, formerly Spain's prime minister, nor finding free passage on ships in Venice and Cyprus, and on September 4, Iñigo walked into the Holy City in the midst of a huge procession of Christians and Egyptian Jews. He hoped never to leave.

Palestine was then fiercely held by Turkish Muslims, whose Christian go-betweens were Franciscan friars. After following a highly regulated program of pilgrimages to the Holy Sepulcher, Bethany, Bethlehem, and the Jordan, Iñigo's fervor was such that he approached a friar and told of his plan to stay on in the city where Jesus had walked, continually venerating the holy sites and helping souls. But he was forbidden that option by the friar's superior, who feared the Spanish crusader would be killed by the Turks. In fact, five hundred Turkish cavalrymen freshly arrived from Damascus were truculently prowling the city, and the panicked governor of Jerusalem was urging pilgrims to leave.[37] After hurried last looks at Christ's footprints on the Mount of Olives, for which he paid the Turkish guards a penknife and scissors, Iñigo obediently left with other pilgrims for Europe, hoping to find his way to Jerusalem again, but preferring, for the time being, to immerse himself in philosophical and theological studies.

To do that he would need Latin. Hence he withstood the hazards of four months of shipboard travel to go back to Spain, where Isabel Roser furnished the little that Iñigo needed while he was taught, gratis, by a professor of Latin grammar at the University of Barcelona. His life there was full of self-imposed hardships: he slept on the plank floor of a friend's garret room, walked about in shoes that had no soles, and begged food for the poor while subsisting himself on plain bread and water.

I feel furthest from Iñigo when he seems to ignore his needs and inflict miseries upon himself. A healthy discipline, chastity, and solidarity with the poor are all honorable desires, of course, but so often he seems to go over the top, to hate and scourge what is wholly natural and, in essence, pure gift. God finds us where we are, however, and God found Iñigo with one foot in the Middle Ages, believing, as the faithful did then, that flesh and spirit were at war and fearing that pleasure was a kind of death to the holy. There was little integration of flesh and spirit then, only rivalry and argument. We have not completely shaken those notions to this day.

After two years in Barcelona, his Latin tutor gave Iñigo permission to go to the University of Alcalá, just

Dominican friars, who heard hints of the Dutch humanism of Desiderius Erasmus in his talk and held him in their chapel until an inquisitor from Toledo could get there. Iñigo was again jailed. After twenty-two days of being shackled to a post in a foul upper room, he was interrogated by four judges, who found no great error in his teaching and ruled that he could catechize again, but only insofar as he did not try to define what were mortal and what were venial sins. Ethical distinctions in conscience and conduct were so at the heart of his public talks that Iñigo may have felt that they'd told him to teach geometry without azimuths. Hamstrung by that sentence, he thought it was high time to get out of Spain.

After hiking seven hundred miles north, he arrived in Paris on February 2, 1528, and went to the Sorbonne, a consortium of fifty colleges that was the greatest international center of learning in Europe. Even in peculiar times, he was a peculiar student, a frail mystic who knew no French, was less than fluent in Latin, and was then in his thirty-seventh year. Because his hasty studies at Barcelona and Alcalá had left him deficient in fundamentals, Iñigo enrolled in humanities at the Collège de Montaigu and studied Latin with boys of nine and ten.[42] Habitually heedless of money, he asked a Spanish friend at Montaigu to hold for safekeeping the princely sum he had been given for his education, but the friend frittered it away on wild living, and by Easter Iñigo was forced to find horrible lodging far away at the hospice of Saint-

Jacques and to go begging again, first among the wealthy
Spanish merchants in Bruges and Antwerp in Flanders,
and finally in England, garnering enough to enable him
to be a magnanimous almsgiver back in France.

In the fall of 1529, Iñigo transferred to the Collège
de Sainte-Barbe, "a kind of Portuguese dependency in
the University of Paris,"[43] and shared housing with his
professor and two highly regarded scholars whose lives
he was to change significantly. The first was Pierre Favre
of Savoy, a gentle, intelligent, psychologically intuitive
twenty-three-year-old whose intent was the Catholic
priesthood and who'd recently passed examinations for
the licentiate in philosophy. Francisco de Javier—or
Francis Xavier, as we know him—was also twenty-
three, and a handsome, jubilant, outgoing grandee and
fellow Basque from Navarre who wanted to be a famous
professor or counselor to princes, as his father had been,
and was already a regent in philosophy in the Collège
de Beauvais.[44] Each finally fell to Iñigo's flattery and im-
precations and agreed to go through a full month of his
Spiritual Exercises. Upon finishing them, Favre and Xavier were inflamed "friends in the Lord"[45] with Iñigo,
filling their hours with theological studies, religious practices and conversations, and in thinking about a future
that still had no firm goal. Allied with them were the
Portuguese student Simâo Rodrigues, who was at Sainte-
Barbe on a royal burse from King John III; Diego Laínez
and Alfonso Salmerón, both Spaniards and former

students at Alcalá; and Nicolás de Bobadilla, a philosopher at Alcalá and theologian at Valladolid before becoming a regent in the Collège de Calvi.

Ignatius de Loyola was given the title Master of Arts
at Easter ceremonies in 1534. We have no certainty
about his change of name. It may be that he mistakenly
thought the far more familiar name Ignacio was a variant
of Iñigo,[46] but it's also possible that in the age of reformation he was inspired by the Syrian prelate Ignatius
of Antioch, who faced the persecutions and theological
disputes of second-century Christianity and whom Emperor Trajan threw to the lions in Rome.

We do know that Ignatius was seeking priesthood
by Easter of 1534, and in preparation for holy orders he
was studying the *Summa Theologica* of Thomas Aquinas
with the highly esteemed Dominican faculty of the Collège de Saint-Jacques.[47] But Pierre Favre was the first
companion ordained, and on August 15, 1534, the feast
of the Assumption of Mary, he celebrated Mass for his
friends on the heights of Montmartre in the shrine of
the martyrdom of Saint Denis and his companions. At
Communion, Ignatius, Xavier, Rodrigues, Laínez, Salmerón, and Bobadilla professed vows to a life of poverty
and to undertake a pilgrimage to Jerusalem or, failing
that, to offer themselves to the Vicar of Christ, the pope,
for whatever mission he wished. Chastity was not vowed
but presumed, for they all intended to receive holy orders. Even Ignatius seems not to have thought that their

profession was the origin of a new religious order, but in hindsight it was.

Within a year, Claude le Jay, a Savoyard friend of Pierre Favre, had completed the Spiritual Exercises and made the same vows, and a year after that, again on August 15, the group was increased by Paschase Broet of Picardy and Jean Codure of Dauphiné. Ignatius missed those ceremonies. Chronic stomach pains that were prompted by gallstones forced him in 1535 to go on horseback to Azpeitia for the familiar weather and air of home that was thought then to heal a host of ills. After some time in Spain, giving news to their families of his "friends in the Lord," he went ahead of them to Venice, where they hoped to find a ship to the Holy Land. While waiting for them to get there, Ignatius studied theology, taught catechism, and helped a Spanish priest named Diego Hoces through the Spiritual Exercises and later welcomed him as another companion. And, it would seem, Ignatius was thinking a good deal about how a religious foundation ought to be organized, for with chagrin and humility he wrote a chiding letter to Gian Pietro Caraffa, a founder of the first order of clerks regular, called the Theatines:

When a man of rank and exalted dignity wears a habit more ornate and lives in a room better furnished than the other religious of his order, I am neither scandalized nor disedified. However, it would do well to consider how the saints have conducted themselves, St. Dominic and St. Francis, for example; and it would be good to have recourse to light from on high; for, after all, a thing may be licit without being expedient.[48]

Of the Theatines in Venice, who shut themselves in their houses of prayer and passively filled their needs with gifts from the faithful, Ignatius wrote that people "will say that they do not see the purpose of this Order; and that the saints, without failing in confidence in God, acted otherwise."[49]

Caraffa, the Italian bishop of Chieti, was a good but impatient and tempestuous Neapolitan who in December would be created a cardinal, and he did not take kindly to faultfinding from a Spaniard, an unfinished theologian, and a forty-five-year-old mendicant who was not yet even a priest. We have lost his reply to Ignatius, but we know his hostility was such that when the companions from the Sorbonne finally got to Italy in 1537, Ignatius sent them on to Rome without him so that Cardinal Caraffa would have no punitive reason to foil their Easter presentation to Pope Paul III.

At that papal audience in Castel Sant' Angelo, the highly impressive companions told the pope of their project to go to Jerusalem and begin an apostolate to the infidel there, and of their further wish to receive holy orders. Knowing the Turkish fleet was belligerently plying the Mediterranean, Paul III quietly put it that "I do not think you will reach Jerusalem."[50] And yet not only were their requests granted by the pontiff, but they also were given close to three hundred escudos for the voyage.

In Venice on the feast of Saint John the Baptist, June 24, 1537, Vincenzo Nigusanti, Bishop of Arbe, ordained Ignatius, Bobadilla, Codure, Xavier, Laínez, and Rodrigues under the title of poverty, *ad titulum paupertatis.*[51] Bishop Nigusanti "frequently repeated, later, that no ordination had ever given his soul such pure consolation."[52] In humility, Ignatius put off presiding at his first Mass for a year and a half, so he would be the last of the ten to do so, and so he could perhaps celebrate it at a shrine in Bethlehem. When that proved impossible, he chose to celebrate his first Mass in Rome on Christmas, 1538, at the church of Santa Maria Maggiore, which Christians believed held the true crib of the child Jesus— a worthy substitute, he thought, for Christ's birthplace.

While waiting for a ship to Palestine in the fall of 1537, the new priests preached in the streets and performed works of mercy in hospitals throughout the Republic of Venice, but for the first time in nearly forty years however, hot rumors of war and piracy kept any ship from sailing to the east. Gathering together again in Vicenza that winter, the priests chose to be patient in their hopes of sea passage and to concentrate their preaching in cities with universities, where they might find high-minded students to join them. If anyone asked who they were, they agreed, "it seemed to them most fitting that they should take the name of him whom they had as their head, by calling themselves the 'company of Jesus.'"[53]

Acknowledging at last that their hoped-for pilgrimage to Jerusalem was improbable, Ignatius, Favre, and Laínez walked two hundred and fifty miles south to Rome in order to offer their services to the pope in fulfillment of the vow they had professed on Montmartre. Stopping in the outskirts of Rome, at a place called La Storta, Ignatius and Laínez went into a chapel, where Ignatius prayed that Mary hold him in her heart as she did her son. Then he felt a change in his soul, and later told Laínez that he beheld "Christ with the cross on his shoulder, and next to Him the eternal Father, who said to Him: 'I want you to take this man as your servant,' and Jesus thus took him and said: 'I want you to serve us.'"[54] Ignatius also told Laínez "that it seemed to him as if God the Father had imprinted the following words in his heart: *Ego ero vobis Romae propitius.*"[55] I will be favorable to you in Rome.[56]

Uplifted by the La Storta illumination, Ignatius and his friends went into the city in late November 1537, and were again graciously received by the pontiff. Hearing their offer of service, Paul III gladly assigned Diego Laínez to teach scholastic theology at La Sapienza, a palace that housed the University of Rome. Pierre Favre was to fill an office in positive theology there, giving commentaries on Sacred Scripture. With those surprising papal assignments, the Italian Compagnia di Gesù ever so gradually became a company of teachers, but Ignatius sought to forgo the classroom in favor of giving the Spiritual Exercises in Rome, first to the ambassador of Emperor Charles V, and then to the president of the pontifical commission for reform of the Church, to the ambassador of Siena, to a Spanish physician, and to Francesco de Estrada, a Spanish priest who'd worked for the formidable Cardinal Caraffa in Rome and been fired. Upon completion of the Exercises, Estrada too joined the Company of Jesus, and late in life he would be named the Jesuit provincial of Aragón in Spain.[57]

Rome became Ignatius's and the companions' Jerusalem. After Easter 1538, all of them gathered there and, through the skills of Pietro Codacio, a papal chamberlain and the first Italian companion, got title to the Church of Santa Maria della Strada, Our Lady of the Wayside, chosen by Ignatius because it was on a high-traffic piazza that was handily near the papal court, government offices, a significant Jewish community, palaces of the upper class, houses of prostitutes, and hovels of the poor.[58] Santa Maria della Strada was the first foundation in the Eternal City for a host of what Ignatius called "works of piety"[59]: the Catechumens, a house for the religious instruction of Jewish converts; the Casa Santa Marta, a house of refuge for former prostitutes; the Conservatorio delle Vergini Miserabili, a house for girls who might be attracted to prostitution; homes for children that were supported by the Confraternity of Saint Mary of the Visitation of Orphans; and the Collegio Romano, a high school for grammar, humanities, and Christian doctrine that was free to boys in Rome.[60]

But the foundation of the greatest importance was, of course, that of the Society of Jesus—*societas* being the Latin for company—which was confirmed by Paul III in the papal bull *Regimini Militantis Ecclesiae* on September 27, 1540. Ignatius sketched the "formula" for the institute in five brief chapters that he introduced in this way:

> Whoever desires to serve as a soldier of God beneath the banner of the cross in our Society, which we desire to be designated by the name of Jesus, and in it to serve the Lord alone and his vicar on earth, should, after a solemn vow of chastity, keep what follows in mind. He is a member of a community founded chiefly to strive for the progress of souls in Christian life and doctrine, and for the propagation of the faith by means of the ministry of the word, the Spiritual Exercises, and works of charity. . . .[61]

Upon hearing the "formula" read to him, the aged Paul III had orally given his approval and added, "*Digitus Dei est hic*—" "The finger of God is here."[62] Ignatius and

Jean Codure later expanded "A First Sketch of the Institute of the Society of Jesus" into *Constitutions* of forty-nine points regulating frugality, governance, admission and formation of novices, and housing and other practical matters, but generally offering Jesuits flexibility in their ways of proceeding in order to give room to, as Ignatius put it, "the internal guidance of the Holy Spirit."[63]

In fulfillment of their rules on governance, on April 8, 1541, Ignatius was elected the first superior general of the Society of Jesus, the only ballot against him being his own. Xavier's ballot was probably typical of the others; he voted for "our old leader and true father, Don Ignacio, who, since he brought us together with no little effort, will also with similar effort know how to preserve, govern, and help us advance from good to better."[64]

Ignatius was then fifty and far different from the man he'd fantasized he'd be when he was a page to Spanish royalty, or a pilgrim to the Holy Land, or a philosopher at the Sorbonne. Ever seeking the greater glory of God and the good of souls, Ignatius surely imagined a grander fate than that of fifteen years of grinding office and managerial work in the house for forty professed fathers that he built on Via Aracoeli, or that of having as one of his prime contributions to history his hand-cramping composition of more than seven thousand letters to his scattered Jesuit sons—twelve full volumes in the *Monumenta Historica Societatis Jesu*. We hear no regret in his letters, however, no aching to be elsewhere, only geniality and hunger for news as he writes to the Jesuit *periti* at the Council of Trent; gentle hints as to how a homosexual scholastic could preserve his chastity; tenderness for the many Spanish women for whom he was a spiritual director; sympathy for a priest in Sicily afflicted by scruples, as he had been; fatherly chiding as he orders a house in Portugal to curb its hard penances; affection for his friend Xavier in Japan: "We have rejoiced in the Lord that you have arrived with health and that doors have opened to have the Gospel preached in that region." [65]

His holiness was unmistakable; he practiced self-mastery until there seemed to be no difference between God's will and his own. *"Eres en tu casa"* was his wide-armed greeting to anyone who visited him—You are at home—and all who talked with him left with the impression that he was kindliness itself: Michelangelo was so affected by Ignatius that he offered to build the Church of the Gesù for nothing. Ever a mystic, there were times in the midst of an official transaction when the saint's thoughts would lift up to God and hang there, and his witnesses would shyly shuffle their shoes until he got back to his papers again. But there were also stories of him surprising a melancholic with a jig in order to cheer him up, and his happiness was such that he said he could no longer apply his own rules for discernment of spirits, because he was finding consolation in all things: he once said he saw the Holy Trinity in the leaf of an orange tree.[66] Although children threw apples at him when he first preached in the streets of Rome—probably because of his horrible Italian—he soon was as genuinely beloved as the pope. In fact, he was so highly thought of by prelates that in the 1550 conclave at which Julius III was elected pontiff, Ignatius de Loyola received five votes. And we can get a feeling for the high esteem in which he was held by his fellow Jesuits when we read letters such as this from Frans de Costere, S.J., of Cologne:

> The day before yesterday I saw for the first time, with indescribable joy and eagerness, Reverend Father Ignatius. I could not see enough of him. For his countenance is such that one cannot look upon it long enough. The old man was walking in the garden, leaning on a cane. His face shone with godliness. He is mild, friendly, and amiable so that he speaks with the learned and the unlearned, with important people and little people, all in the same way: a man worthy of all praise and reverence. No one can deny that a great reward is prepared for him in heaven. . . .[67]

But Gian Pietro Caraffa, whom Ignatius insulted in his frank letter about the Theatines, thought of him as a tyrant and a false idol. In fact, the friction between Caraffa and Ignatius was such that when, in 1555, Ignatius heard

that Caraffa had been elected pontiff, as Paul IV, Ignatius's face went white, and he falteringly limped into a
chapel to pray. But after a while he appeared again and
happily said the new pope would be good to them, which
he was only to a degree, for after Ignatius died he tried
to merge his Theatines with the Jesuits, and briefly
forced them to sing the Divine Office in choir and to
limit the superior general's term to three years.[68]

Even some of his early companions had difficulties
with Ignatius, though. Nicolás de Bobadilla angrily called
him "a rascally sophist and a Basque spoiled by flattery,"[69] and Simâo Rodrigues, whose contrariness
prompted Ignatius to recall him from Portugal, claimed
that the superior general did so out of passion and hate,
and with slight regard for his reputation. Juan de Polanco
supposedly received hardly one compliment during his
nine years as Ignatius's secretary; Jerónimo Nadal was
often so harshly criticized that he couldn't hold back his
tears; and Diego Laínez, a favorite of his, once objected,
"What have I done against the Society that this saint
treats me this way?"[70]

An affectionate man who was wary of his *affectus,*
Ignatius was probably hard on his friends in accordance
with his fundamental principle of *agere contra,* that is, to
go against or contradict one's own inclinations if they
are not for the honor and glory of God or for the good
of others. We see hints of this in the sixteenth annotation
to his *Spiritual Exercises,* in which Ignatius wrote: "If by

chance the exercitant feels an affection or inclination to something in a disordered way, it is profitable for that person to strive with all possible effort to come over to the opposite of that to which he or she is wrongly attached."[71]

He was harder on himself than on his friends, punishing himself for his sins, getting to bed late and waking up at half past four, hardly ever going outside the house or strolling in the gardens, which he insisted on for his sons, dining on food that he called a penance, holding his gaze on the ground when he did walk in Rome, loving plainchant but forbidding choir for the order.

All of that took its toll. By 1556 his health was failing to such a degree that to his chronic stomach pains were added a hardening of the liver, high fevers, and general exhaustion. He was rarely seen outside his room and ate little more than fish scraps and broths and lettuce prepared with oil.[72] Spells of illness had troubled him so frequently in the past, however, and he'd shown such resilience in healing, that no one was especially upset by his confinement, and physicians often failed even to visit him as they ministered to others in the house who were thought to be far worse off, among them his friend Diego Laínez. But Ignatius knew how far he'd sunk and on the afternoon of July 30, he thought it would be fitting if Juan de Polanco, the secretary of the Society, would go and inform Paul IV that Ignatius "was near the end and almost without hope of temporal life, and that he humbly begged from His Holiness his blessing for himself and for Master Laínez, who was also in danger."[73] Misprizing his superior's condition, Polanco asked if he could put off the walk, because he was trying to finish some letters for Spain before a ship sailed. Ignatius told him, "The sooner you go, the more satisfied I shall be; however, do as you wish."[74]

Brother Tommaso Cannicari, the infirmarian, slept in a cell next to the superior general's quarters, and off and on heard Ignatius praying until, after midnight, he heard only, over and over again, the Spanish sigh *Ay, Dios!*[75] At sunrise the fathers in the house saw that Ignatius was dying, and Cannicari hurried to find the superior general's confessor while Polanco hurried to the papal residence to request the Holy Father's blessing. But it was too late. Two hours after sunrise on Friday morning, July 31, 1556, Ignatius of Loyola died, without having received the quite unnecessary graces of Extreme Unction or Viaticum or papal blessing.

In the first week of the *Spiritual Exercises,* Ignatius had offered this as the "Principle and Foundation" for all the meditations that would follow:

Human beings are created to praise, reverence, and serve God our Lord, and by means of doing this to save their souls.

The other things on the face of the earth are

created for the human beings, to help them in the pursuit of the end for which they are created.

From this it follows that we ought to use these things to the extent that they help us toward our end, and free ourselves from them to the extent that they hinder us from it.

To attain this it is necessary to make ourselves indifferent to all created things, in regard to everything which is left to our free will and is not forbidden. Consequently, on our own part we ought not to seek health rather than sickness, wealth rather than poverty, honor rather than dishonor, a long life rather than a short one, and so on in all other matters.

Rather, we ought to desire and choose only that which is more conducive to the end for which we are created.[76]

Saint Irenaeus said that the glory of God is a human being fully alive. But what is it to be fully alive? We are apt to look at Ignatius's life as one of harsh discipline and privation, and find only loss in his giving up family, inheritance, financial security, prestige, luxury, sexual pleasure. But he looked at his life as an offering to the God he called *liberalidad,* freedom,[77] and God blessed that gift a hundredfold in the Society of Jesus. The house of Loyola ended when Doña Magdalena de Loyola y Borgia died childless in 1626,[78] but in that same year there were 15,535 Jesuits in 36 provinces, with 56 seminaries, 44 novitiates, 254 houses, and 443 colleges in Europe and the Baltic States, Japan, India, Macao, the Philippines, and the Americas.[79]

NOTES

1. Paul Dudon, S.J., *St. Ignatius of Loyola,* trans. by William J. Young, S.J. (Milwaukee: The Bruce Publishing Co., 1949), 439.
2. Dudon, 17.
3. W. W. Meissner, S.J., M.D., *Ignatius of Loyola: The Psychology of a Saint* (New Haven: Yale University Press, 1992), 9.
4. Dudon, 13.
5. John W. O'Malley, S.J., *The First Jesuits* (Cambridge, MA: Harvard University Press, 1993), 23.
6. Meissner, 24.
7. Luis Gonçalves da Câmara, S.J., *The Autobiography of St. Ignatius Loyola,* trans. by Joseph F. O'Callaghan, S.J. (New York: Harper & Row, 1974), 21.
8. Meissner, 241.
9. Meissner, 240.
10. Juan de Polanco, S.J., *Chronicon,* quoted in Dudon, 37.
11. Cándido de Dalmases, S.J., *Ignatius of Loyola, Founder of the Jesuits: His Life and Work,* trans. by Jerome Aixalá, S.J. (St. Louis: The Institute of Jesuit Sources, 1985), 38.
12. Dudon, 36.   14. Câmara, 22.
13. Câmara, 22.   15. Dalmases, 43.
16. Jerónimo Nadal, S.J., quoted in Dudon, 37.
17. Hans Wolter, S.J., "Elements of Crusade Spirituality in St. Ignatius," in *Ignatius of Loyola: His Personality and Spiritual Heri-*

tage, 1556–1956, ed. by Friedrich Wulf, S.J. (St. Louis: The Institute of Jesuit Sources, 1977), 126.

18. Câmara, 23.   25. Dudon, 57.
19. Câmara, 24.   26. Câmara, 34.
20. Câmara, 24.   27. Câmara, 37.
21. Câmara, 24.   28. Câmara, 39.
22. Câmara, 26.   29. Câmara, 39.
23. Dalmases, 55.
24. Dudon, 59.
30. Dalmases, 62.
31. Hugo Rahner, S.J., *Ignatius the Theologian,* trans. by Michael Barry (New York: Herder and Herder, 1968), 1.
32. O'Malley, 46, 47.
33. George E. Ganss, S.J., *The Spiritual Exercises of Saint Ignatius* (Chicago: Loyola University Press, 1992), 1–3.
34. Ganss, 31.   37. Dudon, 83.
35. Ganss, 42.   38. Câmara, 61.
36. Dudon, 67.
39. Calixtio de Sa, Lope de Cáceres, Juan de Arteaga, and Juan Reynalde.
40. Dalmases, 97.   43. Dudon, 138.
41. Dudon, 113.   44. Meissner, 151.
42. Meissner, 142.   45. O'Malley, 32.
46. Gabriel María Verd, "De Iñigo a Ignacio: El cambio de nombre en San Ignacio de Loyola," *Archivum Historicum Societatis Jesu* 60 (1991), 113–60, in O'Malley, 29.
47. Dudon, 144.   50. Dudon, 249.
48. Dudon, 234.   51. Câmara, 87.
49. Dudon, 234.   52. Dudon, 238.
53. Juan de Polanco, S.J., *Fontes narrativi de S. Ignatio de Loyola et de Societatis Jesu initiis,* I, 204, quoted in Dalmases, 149.
54. Hugo Rahner, S.J., *The Vision of St. Ignatius in the Chapel of La Storta* (Rome: Centrum Ignatianum Spiritualitatis, 1979), 46.
55. Rahner, 46.
56. The La Storta experience probably inspired the conclusions to

the meditations of the second week of the Spiritual Exercises, wherein practitioners are asked to make a threefold colloquy, first with Mary, then with Christ, and finally with God the Father.

57. Dalmases, 154–55.

58. Thomas M. Lucas, S.J., *Saint, Site, and Sacred Strategy: Ignatius, Rome, and Jesuit Urbanism* (Rome: Biblioteca Apostolica Vaticana, 1990), 30.

59. Câmara, 92.

60. Tuition was free because of a magnificent gift from Francisco Borgia, the Duke of Gandía in Spain, the great-grandson of Pope Alexander VI and King Ferdinand V of Aragón, a father of eight, and, after the death of his wife, a Jesuit and the third superior general. See Dalmases, 186.

61. Lucas, 121.   62. Dalmases, 170.

63. Peter Hebblethwaite, "The Society of Jesus," in *Modern Catholicism: Vatican II and After,* ed. by Adrian Hastings (New York: Oxford University Press, 1991), 256.

64. O'Malley, 375.   66. Dalmases, 273.

65. Lucas, 8.

67. Hubert Becher, S.J., "Ignatius as Seen by His Contemporaries," in Wulf, 86.

68. Dalmases, 286.   74. Dudon, 428.

69. Wulf, 84.   75. Dalmases, 295.

70. Wulf, 87.   76. Ganss, 32.

71. Ganss, 26.   77. Rahner, *Ignatius the Theologian,* 4.

72. Dudon, 426.

73. Dalmases, 294.   78. Dudon, 421.

                                        79. Lucas, 35.

The Ironic Doctor

FRANCINE PROSE

IRONY IS NOT the quality we associate first with the saints.

Seen from this distance, and with the modernist's double vision, their lives appear to us to have been rich in ironic and playful incident and detail. Consider the vegetarian Nicholas of Tolentino, who, on being forced to eat a pigeon stew, caused the cooked birds' feathers to regrow, the sauce to flow like blood in their veins, until the revivified pigeons fluttered their wings and flew out the window; or Saint Datius, who exorcised a haunted house by mocking the devil for making the sounds of ghostly animals in the night. Let us think of Saint Ansovinus, who embarrassed a stingy innkeeper with a miraculous lesson about the ethics of watering the wine, or the gravity-defying Joseph of Cupertino, expelled from a series of monasteries for being unable to stop himself from frightening his brethren by levitating at mealtime or in the midst of saying Mass. Or let us contemplate the famous—and famously ironic—prayer of Saint Augustine, begging God to send him the gift of chastity . . . but not yet.

Even so, the character of the saint and the nature of sainthood may strike us profoundly incompatible with the ironist's perspective. Saints, we feel, are, by definition, impassioned and single-minded, tormented by unruly desires and devious temptations, by demons and doubt—but not by alienation and contradiction. Their apprehension of the world and of God is immediate and cohesive, not fragmented and conflicted. The saint's experience is that of proximity, of presence, of the imminence of grace, not of the world seen through a glass darkly: through the cloudy, fingerprinted lens of ironic distance.

As a Jewish child growing up in New York, I quite naturally longed to be a saint. Like many little girls (and many saints, one imagines), I intuited at a young age that early martyrdom would preemptively circumvent the problems and pressures of adulthood. Perhaps enough

has been written (some of it by myself) about the allure
of a perfect Bridegroom who promises that He will ask
nothing of us but absolute devotion and (in the case of
St. Thérèse of Lisieux) a fairly daunting amount of
housework. And much has also been said about the appeal of the promise of glory, of an eternity to be spent
in a paradise that our imaginations may endow with the
pink light and verdant heavenly landscapes of a Sienese
religious painting.

For the would-be and future saint, the lives of the
saints and martyrs can function as a kind of how-to man-
ual, listing the various obstacles posed and overcome: the
pagan background, the stubborn and often violent opposition of parents and of society, one's own troublesome
fondness for the pleasures and comforts of the material
world. But nowhere in the saints' lives that I devoured
with such avidity did I find a single example of a saint
who had triumphed over what I sensed early on to be
the main stumbling block in my path.

I have heard adults with no knowledge of children
claim that irony is an acquired trait, a quality belonging
to a later stage of development, like a taste for olives,
caviar, or champagne. But some children are born iro-
nists; I know because I was one. Almost from the cradle,
I watched the world from a certain remove and with the
consciousness of watching; everything seemed to me to
have several possible (or opposite) meanings and explanations, and that disjuncture, that ambiguity, struck me,

more often than not, as at once disturbing, comforting, marvelous—and funny.

Much of the *Autobiography* of Saint Teresa of Ávila— which I first read in my twenties during the early 1970s—is permeated by that same familiar, ironic, and (to me) intensely sympathetic sensibility. She is funny, edgy, self-mocking, and extremely sympathetic toward the excesses and self-dramatization that goes along with being young.

Who knows how different my life might have been had her book come into my possession earlier.

The opening sentence of Saint Teresa's account of her life is not only one of the great beginnings in religious or secular literature, but it may be one of the most barbed, ironic, and double- (or triple-) edged sentences ever written: "Had I not been so wicked, it would have been a help to me to have such virtuous and pious parents . . ."

So begins the narrative of the complicated, extraordinary life that began in March 1515 in an aristocratic household in Ávila, the walled city that rose out of the harsh, arid landscape of Central Spain. Teresa's father, Don Alonso Sanchez de Cepeda, was a charitable man who taught his daughter to read in an era when literacy was generally not numbered among the requisite feminine virtues, and despite his own disapproval of the distractions of frivolous literature—the chivalric romances that Teresa so loved. ("So completely was I mastered by this passion that I thought I could never be happy without a book.")

The little girl's fascination with courtly romances was shared by her mother, Dona Beatriz, who married at fourteen, bore nine children and, perhaps as a consequence, remained a lifelong invalid until her early death. ("Though extremely beautiful, she was never known to give any reason for supposing that she made the slightest account of her beauty; and, though she died at thirty-three, her dress was already that of a person advanced in years.")

In this large, chaotic household, Teresa's closest ally was her brother Rodrigo, and the most celebrated anecdote of her childhood—clearly the one she most delights in telling—involves their frustrated attempt to run away from home in search of instant martyrdom. Her description of their escapade typifies her irony, her humor, and the compassion—in this case, for her younger self—that (as the paragraph turns and turns) forms a sort of bridge between her gentle, forgiving self-mockery and the deep seriousness of her moral and devotional purpose:

We used to read the lives of the saints together; and, when I read of the martyrdoms suffered by saintly women for God's sake, I used to think they had purchased the fruition of God very cheaply; and I had a keen desire to die as they

had done, not out of any love for God ... but in
order to attain as quickly as possible ... the
great blessings which, as I read, were laid up in
heaven. I used to discuss with this brother of
mine how we could become martyrs. We agreed
to go off to the country of the Moors, begging
our bread for the love of God, so that they might
behead us there; and, even at so tender an age, I
believe that the Lord had given us sufficient
courage for this ... but out greatest hindrance
seemed to be that we had a father and mother. It
used to cause us great astonishment when we
were told that both pain and glory would last for
ever. We would spend long periods talking about
this and we liked to repeat again and again, 'For
ever—ever—ever!' Through our frequent repetition of these words, it pleased the Lord that in
my earliest years I should receive a lasting impression of the way of the truth.

Recognized by an uncle as they were leaving Ávila, the
two runaway children were promptly returned home,
where, in time, Teresa grew into a handsome, vain,
strong-willed and talkative young woman. ("I began to
deck myself out and try to attract others by my appear-
ance, taking great troubles with my hands and hair, using
perfumes and all the vanities I could get—and there
were a good many of them, for I was very fastidious. . . .

I always had the facet of making myself understood only with a torrent of words.")

Then with the onset of early adolescence came a series of personal and health crises that conspired (or, as Teresa would have said, manifested the will of God) to lead and then impel her toward the cloister. The most intriguing and mysterious of these involved a cousin from whom "I learned every kind of evil. . . . The result of my intercourse with this woman was to change me so much that I lost all my soul's natural inclination to virtue, and was greatly influenced by her, and by another person who indulged in the same kinds of pastime." The normally forthright, ironic Teresa is uncharacteristically elusive, vague, and portentous about the nature of this pastime, but much about her tone inclines one to agree with Vita Sackville-West's rather delicate and tactful assessment of her in *The Eagle and the Dove:* "Since few things are more distasteful than veiled hints, it may also be outspokenly noted that in her own country the name of Teresa has been associated with that of Sappho. . . . Nobody in their senses . . . would dream of comparing the organised orgies of Lesbos with the rudimentary experimental dabblings of adolescent girls. . . . The point is in any case perhaps not of very much interest, except in so far as every point concerning so complex a character . . . is of interest. . . . Above all, it is not introduced here in any spirit of scandalous disrespect to a wise woman and a great saint."

In flight from the guilts and terrors that this incident evoked in her, Teresa was, at sixteen, at once distressed and greatly relieved to find herself enrolled as a student at the convent of Our Lady of Grace. Her confusion about the religious life (and perhaps about her sexuality) may have led to the first of the many terrifying and near-fatal illnesses that would plague her for the rest of her life. (Like any number of historical figures—Van Gogh and El Greco, among others—Saint Teresa has had the benefit of better diagnostic and medical care after her death than she had during her lifetime: her condition has been variously diagnosed as hyperthyroidism, consumption, epilepsy, and, perhaps needless to add, psychosexual hysteria.)

After a recuperative stay at her sister's house, she stopped for a brief visit at the home of an uncle, to whom she read aloud from holy books. In the process, she began to understand "the truth ... that all things are nothing, and that the world is vanity and will soon pass away. I began to fear that, if I had died of my illness, I should have gone to hell; and though, even then, I could not incline my will to being a nun, I saw that this was the best and safest state, and so, little by little, I was determined to force myself to embrace it. This conflict lasted for three months. I used to try to convince myself by using the following argument. The trials and distresses of being a nun could not be greater than those of purgatory and I had fully deserved to be in hell. It would not be a great matter to spend my life as though I were in purgatory if afterwards I were to go straight to heaven, which was what I desired. *This decision, then, to enter the religious life seems to have been inspired by servile fear more than by love.*"

The italics are my own, and the reason I've been quoting at such length from Teresa's own version of these critical events is in the hope of conveying a sense of her unsparing honesty, her plainspoken urgency, her self-critical humorous sympathy, and, most strikingly, her immense tolerance for ambivalence and ironic contradiction—a tolerance that would seem unusual in anyone, during any era, but that strikes us as all the more stunning in a not-terribly-well-educated Spanish Catholic woman living at a time when the Inquisition had done so much to advance the cause of the vengeful, exquisitely cruel, and fanatically literal-minded.

This tolerance for conflict and for the apparently irreconcilable would not only serve Teresa well, but also prove to be a psychic necessity, since so much of her adult life appears to have been a nest of roiling, insoluble contradictions. ("When I was in the midst of worldly pleasures, I was distressed by the remembrance of what I owed to God; when I was with God, I grew restless because of worldly affections.")

What's most amazing—and most appealing—about her is the fact that she was such a creature of opposites. She describes herself as weak-willed, vain, shallow, fond of pleasures and comforts, easily seduced and distracted ("Anyone who gave me so much as a sardine could obtain anything from me"). And yet she possessed the courage and steely determination to accomplish (more or less singlehandedly) the strenuous and controversial reform of the Carmelite Order, which, as Sackville-West describes it, had become little more than an ongoing tea party:

> Friends and relations, both feminine and masculine, might be received there. . . . Little presents changed hands, sweetmeats and oranges, jam, scent. . . . Many a sister had her little private store of provisions in reserve. . . . Gossip and the latest news circulated freely in that agreeable circle . . . and the fashionable topics of culture, philosophy, music, literature, and even, more dangerously, Platonic love, came under lively discussion during the long afternoons.

That was the situation when Teresa became a novice, and for the next quarter century or so, until, in her late forties, she undertook the task of reforming her order. Under Teresa's direction, these pleasant amusements came to an end, and the seventeen convents that she helped establish throughout Spain were rededicated to the principles of poverty, purity, obedience, and contemplation. Though nearly always in ill health, she spent the last twenty years of her life (she died at sixty-seven) traveling constantly to oversee the foundation and operation of those seventeen convents — which represented nothing less than a reproof and challenge to the laxity and self-indulgence of the sixteenth-century Spanish clergy. (Nor did she accomplish these reforms without, as one might expect, overcoming a great deal of potentially perilous intrigue and strong opposition from the clerical establishment.)

Teresa claimed to hate writing, to be unable to write; her work is full of self-doubt, of protestations that she is unequal to the task before her, of excuses for procrastination and apologies for the repetitions resulting from her lack of time to read over what she'd written. (Why is she not — for these reasons alone — the patron saint of writers?) Yet she wrote voluminously, quickly (*The Interior Castle* was written in the space of four weeks) and under impossible circumstances — in freezing cold, cramped cells, without even a table or chair. She worked while desperately ill, frequently interrupted by uncontrollable, unbidden visions and by pressing problems within her order.

She was the most practical, down-to-earth, shrewd, and sensible of souls, persuasive and skilled at dealing with the clerical hierarchy and with the political forces of her day — and at the same time a celebrated mystic, famous for the (often racking and paralyzing) transports that removed her from quotidian reality, and from

ordinary consciousness. Certainly, the most striking contradiction in her life involved the disjuncture between her
commitment to the active life (to the reform of her order
and to the nuns in her charge) and to the more contemplative, meditative, quietist—and visionary—aspects of
religious experience.

Her mystical experiences ranged from comforting in-
timations of the nearness of God ("I used unexpectedly
to experience a consciousness of the presence of God, of
such a kind that I could not doubt that He was within,
or that I was wholly engulfed in him. This was in no
sense a vision; I believe it is called mystical theology, the
soul is suspended completely outside itself. The will
loves; the memory, I think, is almost lost . . .") to horri-
fying visions of the devil:

"Out of his body there seemed to be coming a great
flame, which was intensely bright and cast no shadow.
He told me in a horrible way that I had indeed escaped
out of his hands but he would get hold of me still. . . .
The Lord evidently meant me to realize that this was the
work of the devil, for I saw beside me the most hideous
little negro, snarling as if he was in despair at having lost
what he was trying to gain. . . . I have learned there is
nothing like holy water to put devils to flight and prevent them from coming back again." On another occasion, God appeared to her with the gift of a jeweled
rosary, which no one else could see.

No doubt the most famous of her visions was that of

the angel who pierced her heart with his burning lance "several times so that it penetrated to my entrails. When he drew it out, I thought he was drawing them out with it, and he left me completely afire with a great love for God. The pain was so sharp that it made me utter several moans; and so excessive was the sweetness caused by this intense pain that one can never wish to lose it, nor will one's soul be content with anything less than God."

It was this visitation—and her description, with its undeniably and almost comically sexual overtones—that was to inspire Richard Crashaw's overwrought verse and Bernini's graceful and equally over-the-top sculpture. Ironically, we can thank Bernini and Crashaw for the version of Teresa that has survived in the popular imagination: the swooning, hysterical female visionary, brought to the spiritual equivalent of orgasm by the overwhelming force of her religious fervor.

The reality was extremely different. Teresa was profoundly private about, and distrustful of, her visions. She tried desperately to hide her transports, which frightened and embarrassed her:

> I have lain on the ground and the sisters have come and held me down, but none the less the rapture has been observed. I besought the Lord earnestly not to grant me any more favours which had visible and exterior signs; for I was exhausted by having to endure such worries and

after all (I said) His Majesty could grant me that
favour without its becoming known.

Though she believed that her visions were coming from
God, she distrusted them, and feared that they might be
the work of the devil. Partly to ease these fears, her confessor "commanded me to make the sign of the Cross
whenever I had a vision, and to snap my fingers at it so
as to convince myself that it came from the devil. . . .
This caused me great distress."

Even her approach to prayer could hardly have been
less ecstatically passive than that of the semicomatose
woman we see in Bernini's masterpiece. What's striking
(and, in a way, hardest for the modern reader to comprehend) about her devotional writing is the cool precision
with which she outlines the steps, stages, and techniques
for "those who are determined to pursue this blessing
and succeed in this enterprise": "Beginners must accus-
tom themselves to pay no heed to what they see or hear,
and they must practise this during hours of prayer; they
must be alone and in their solitude think over their past
life—all of us, indeed, whether beginners or proficients,
must do this frequently."

And really, it should come as no great surprise: the
distance between the pretty, swooning saint we find in
Bernini and Crashaw and the plucky, resilient, practical,
and extremely capable middle-aged nun who braved the
Inquisition, reformed an entire order and, despite a life

of illness and hardship, somehow found the time and energy to write several of the great classics of contemplative literature. One image fits—and feeds—every reductive cliché about the nature of female religiosity. The other, the historical reality, defies and expands our conventional notions of what it means to be a woman (and a sixteenth-century Spanish woman, at that) as well as a great writer, and a great saint: a soul capable of embracing a dizzying range of contradictions, of keeping an unwavering focus on the nearness and grace of God without losing her humor, her common sense—and her ironic double vision.

Proceed in Darkness

DAVID PLANTE

SOME TIME AGO, I felt that everything was going wrong for me, and especially with my writing in the world. I was alone in Italy, and, after my supper, I would sit in the garden where fireflies flashed among the dark cypresses, and suddenly one evening all my senses—sight, hearing, smell, taste, touch—became engaged, and for at least a moment I felt my anxiety go. After that moment, I realized just how anxious I had been. My senses, engaged with what was all outside me and had nothing to do with my anxiety, had taken me out of myself, and that had been a relief to me. I wanted, I told myself, to be taken more and more out of myself.

Because I have always gone to books as perhaps my greatest recourse, I looked for a book in the library of the house where I was staying. Thumbing through novels and volumes of poems, I remembered having been told by my religious teachers when I was a devout adolescent that devotional books took one out of oneself, and this was what I wanted from a book now. (Though I am no longer a believer, my past faith comes back to me in profound echoes at moments, and after the fact I realized that, in a state of acute anxiety, I did not once tell myself that I must enter into myself to find out and act on the personal reasons for my anxiety, did not tell myself that I really must seek psychological help, but, instead, told myself that I *had* to get out of myself, and could find consolation only in what was all outside myself, and this, I am sure, has everything to do with Catholicism.) With, perhaps, the sentimentality that anxiety can cause, I searched for religious devotional books, but found none.

Then I thought how, as devout as I had been when young, I had never, ever experienced what had been promised me, by my religious teachers, in my devotion. Never had my prayers to God taken me out of myself and made me, by my union with Him, indifferent to myself in the world, but they had always brought me back, as if, finally, it was my fault that I couldn't rise above myself and the world, to myself in the world. And yet, I had the inculcated *idea* of the happiness I could have if I really and truly loved God, and with that idea came the greatest longing I have ever had or will ever have. It is a longing I now believe cannot be realized in religion, not least because I do not believe in God.

In the Italian house, unable to find a book that would console me and unable to sleep, I went to a desk and wrote in my diary. I wrote, not to account for my state, but simply to describe, as accurately as I could, how, that afternoon, out in the garden, I had looked through one of the glass doors into a room and had seen, reflected on the glass but as if projected into the room, a bank of white and red roses in which the furniture—a chaise longue and chairs and bookshelves—appeared to stand. And during a pause in my writing it occurred to me that exactly what I had once expected of my religion, but which had not happened, had happened while I was writing. I realized that there is an essential difference between a person as a self-regarding ego and that same person as a writer, and that writing does *not* refer oneself as a writer back to oneself, but out to something greater. The conviction came to me, as a small revelation, that whatever it is that makes one a writer has, in the end, very little to do with oneself, but rather with something beyond oneself. All writers of worth I have spoken to about this agree with me, even those in whose work there is not the least suspicion of otherworldliness. But what *is* this something beyond one?

Before going to bed, I went, late, from room to room

to make sure the shutters were closed, and in a guest bedroom at the top of a flight of stone stairs I saw a small bookcase, and there I found the works of Saint John of the Cross in the E. Allison Peers edition of 1934.

Saint John of the Cross did not even consider himself a writer. What he wrote was incidental to his main work in the world, which was the reform of the Carmelite Order he belonged to. Yet, what he wrote—poems and long exegeses on some of the poems—is equal in mastery, in beauty and glory, in spiritual power, to anything else ever written by anyone; and one does not read it for what it says about Saint John of the Cross, but for its devotion to the highest possible level of universal love.

Saint John's father, Gonzalo de Yepes, was a minor nobleman who married an orphan, Catalina Alvarez, and for this was ostracized by his family. He died shortly after the birth of his third son, Juan (or John) de Yepes, in 1542 at Fontiveros, near Ávila, in Spain. Juan and his two older brothers, Francisco and Luis, were brought up in poverty by their widowed mother. Seeking support for her family from her dead husband's brothers, one a priest and the other a doctor, Catalina traveled from town to town, but the relatives were no help. Luis died of starvation. Catalina and Francisco and Juan, just old enough, found work weaving in the commercial city of Medina del Campo, but this didn't provide enough. Juan was sent to a boarding school for poor children, most often orphans, where he was taught Christian doctrine. He worked as a sacristan in a church, and also as a nurse in a hospital. He chose to become a novice in the Carmelite Order and went to study in Salamanca, where, in 1564, he gave a student's discourse on contemplation. Ordained a priest in 1567, he returned to Medina del Campo.

Saint Teresa of Ávila arrived in Medina del Campo at the same time. She was fifty-two, devoted to reform in the Carmelite Order, and had come to the town to found a convent of what were known as discalced nuns, as opposed to the calced, who were against reform. The calced Carmelites wore sandals—*calzos* in sixteenth-century Spanish—and the discalced did not, but went barefoot. Teresa was determined to bring the order back to what she believed to be the ancient rigor of its twelfth-century rules, not only among the nuns but also among the friars. The prior at Medina del Campo suggested John to her as a helper. They met, immediately became close, and Teresa fired John's devotion to reform. Until 1574, he worked to found reformed convents, even paving the cells, and acted as confessor and resident priest to the nuns.

Fighting to suppress the reforms, a group of calced Carmelites went so far as to arrest the discalced John and imprison him in one of their own monasteries in Medina del Campo. But the papal nuncio, in favor of the reforms, pressed for his release. (Both the discalced and calced factions of the Carmelites were appealing to the Pope,

Gregory XIII, for ratification of the one against the other.) The papal nuncio favorable to the reforms died, and, certain of the support of the next one, John was again captured by the antireformists, in 1577, and taken as a prisoner to their monastery of Carmel in Ávila. He was beaten and locked up, but managed to escape and returned to where he had lived to destroy papers that included plans for the reforms. He was yet again captured by the calced, and taken to the Carmelite monastery in Toledo.

He was locked in a small, dark cell, so cold he developed frostbite. The food he was given was bad, he was not allowed to change his clothes, he was beaten every day, and he was denied all communication with the world outside. John was told by monks speaking to him through the door that the reforms had been suppressed, and that his pretensions at being a saint had been vanity. Here, alone, he began to write his poems in his head.

After six months, his old, harsh guard was changed to a younger, gentler one, who brought him paper and quill and ink, and there, it is thought, he wrote down "The Dark Night of the Soul."

After three more months, John, with the help of his guard, escaped, and took refuge with Carmelite nuns. But even when, in 1580, the Pope ratified the separation of the calced and discalced factions, so they in effect became independent orders, John, though still active in founding monasteries and convents, and doing masonry work, was treated with disdain by many discalced in power for always taking a moderate point of view on issues of their reform. He accepted his removal from every office of influence and asked to be sent to Mexico. This was denied him, and when, instead, he was offered the appointment of superior at Segovia, he asked to go as an ordinary monk to La Penuela in Andalusia. There, he was accused of having had sexual relations with Carmelite nuns. Ill with an infection, John went on to Ubeda, where he assumed no one would know of him. But there the prior did know of him and, intolerant of his reputation for saintliness, humiliated him by assigning him to the meanest cell and by objecting to the cost of caring for him, now an invalid. He died on December 14, 1591, during the night.

Everyone who had met him said he appeared always to be in a state of delight. He was canonized in 1726.

Though it was not central to his life, what remains for us most powerfully of Saint John of the Cross is his writing. The best known of his poems is "The Dark Night of the Soul," on which he commented at length in the exegeses *The Ascent of Mount Carmel* and *The Dark Night of the Soul.* On his poem "Songs Between the Soul and the Bridegroom," he wrote the exegesis *The Spiritual Canticle.* And *The Living Flame of Love* is a commentary on a poem by the same name. But the poem that appears at the center of his work, as a gold cross suspended in the

darkness of an apse is often the center of a church, is
"The Dark Night of the Soul."

Here it is in Spanish:

> En una noche oscura,
> Con ansias en amores inflamada,
> ¡Oh dichosa ventura!
> Sali sin ser notada,
> Estando ya mi casa sosegada.

> A oscuras, y segura,
> Por la secreta escala disfrazada,
> ¡Oh dichosa ventura!
> A oscuras, y en celada,
> Estando ya mi casa sosegada.

> En la noche dichosa,
> En secreto, que nadie me veia,
> Ni yo miraba cosa,
> Sin otra luz y guia,
> Sino la que en el corazon arida.

> Aquesta me guiaba
> Mas cierto que la luz de mediodia,
> A donde me esperaba
> Que yo bien me sabia,
> En parte donde nadie parecia.

¡Oh noche, que guiaste,
Oh noche amable mas que el alborada,
Oh noche que juntaste
Amado con amada,
Amada en el Amado transformada!

En mi pecho florido,
Que entero para el solo se guardaba,
Alli quedo dormido,
Y yo le regalaba,
Y el ventalle de cerdros aire daba.

El aire de la almena,
Cuando yo sus cabellos esparcia,
Con su mano serena
En mi cuello heria,
Y todos mis sentidos suspendia.

Quedeme, y olvideme,
El rosto recline sobre el Amado,
Ceso todo, y dejeme,
Dejando mi cuidado
Entre las azucenas olvidado.

I will dare to give my own translation, which makes no
attempt to follow the rhythms and rhymes of the
original.

On a dark night,
Bright with longing—
Oh, the thrill of risk!—
I left, no one saw me,
My house now still.

Safe in dark,
Down the secret stairs, disguised—
Oh, the thrill of risk!—
Concealed in dark,
My house now still.

On that thrilling night,
In secret, no one to see me,
Seeing nothing,
No light guiding me
But the light that burned in me.

That light led me
More surely than noonlight
Where he waited for me—
How well I knew him—
Where no others came.

O guiding night,
O night more loved than dawn,
O night that joined
Loved one and lover,
Lover transformed into loved one.

On my blossoming breast,
All his,
He slept,
I caressed him.
The air about the cedars stirred.

In the breeze from the ramparts,
I parted his locks.
He wounded my neck
With his gentle hand,
My senses suspended.

There I remained, lost to myself.
I pressed my face to the one I loved.
All stopped, and I
Gave myself up,
My pain no longer pain
Among the lilies.

Saint John considered his commentaries inseparable from
the poems, so a poem and the explanation of it were, to
him, one. The commentaries *The Ascent of Mount Carmel*
and *The Dark Night of the Soul* leave no doubt that this
poem has to do with the soul—the poem is written from
the point of view of the soul, which in Spanish is feminine—and the soul's longing to be united with God;
and, moreover, that the fulfillment of its longing depends
on a total denial of the body and all its senses.

When reading the commentaries, I reached a point where, I realized, I had to make a choice—to read to understand what Saint John intended or to read for what his words inspired. In my Catholic youth, I believed that if devotional work was to mean anything, its meaning had to come through the Holy Ghost to me, and the Holy Ghost assured me that I could not misunderstand because my understanding came through Him. Saint John no doubt felt the same when he was writing, but his Holy Ghost and my Holy Ghost, I saw more and more as I read, were different, and what had inspired Saint John did not, for a large part of what he wrote, inspire me. Instead, I found myself disagreeing with, even objecting to, the way the writing, so much of which read as nothing more than justification of the poem's intentions. I did not want to read the poem for what it intended, but for what it inspired, and what the poem intended and what it inspired seemed to me opposed.

To see a saint merely in terms of history is, I think, to deny him his sainthood, which is transhistorical. And yet the contradictions I found between his poem and his commentaries seemed to place Saint John at a distance from me that was explained by our belonging to different times. Not that the distance was so very great. What he wrote in his commentaries was as true to the Church in which I was born and grew up as it was of his Church of the sixteenth century. But something happened in my maturity that put the Church of my youth at the same

distance as Saint John's Church. That a poem of such
sensuality should be explained as a spiritual experience
that demands the denial of everything that is sensual, demands the *mortification* of the senses, raised in me all the
resentment I, as a youthful believer, felt when the nuns
in the parochial school and the parish priest told us, as
an article of our faith, that our union with God, which
must be our greatest desire, required our denying ourselves the desires of our bodies. We were told that the
desires of the body would lead us only to defeat and
disconsolateness and despair. One of the reasons why I
ceased to believe was that I found, more and more, that
my senses were a source to me of great happiness, the
very happiness so sensually evoked in "The Dark Night
of the Soul," the very happiness that is such a consolation in the poem, the very happiness that takes one out
of oneself. The split between Saint John's poem and his
commentaries on the poem reminded me of the Christian
split between body and soul, a wound which I, over my
adult years as a nonbeliever, have healed in myself—a
wound I now see as historical and in no way a condition
of sainthood.

Still, I persisted in my reading of Saint John's commentaries to find the transhistorical saint, as all true
saints must be, and the inspiration I wanted from him.
And it occurred to me that there is at least one desire
that has always left writers feeling defeated, disconsolate,
despairing, and this has to do with their worldly ambi-

tions as writers. Worldly ambitions have never, ever brought writers happiness. But then, why does one write?

This is what Saint John can teach us:

That as the love for God cannot be achieved through reason, but through going out into the unknown, so, too, it is with writing.

That as the striving to love God often leaves one feeling arid, even abandoned by God, so, too, does one often feel arid, even abandoned, struggling to fulfill what one is drawn to fulfill when one writes.

That as the love for God requires a dedication, and, too, a renunciation of oneself to what is immeasurably greater than oneself, so does writing, and this something greater is, like God, not subjective but entirely objective, as vast in its objectivity as all of space.

And, most important, that as God, ultimately and sublimely, can only be seen as darkness in which the soul goes out to meet the one she loves, so, too, does one write in darkness, not because one has, in one's writing, nothing to say, but because everything there is to say is as great as all of that infinitely dark space which Saint John says God is.

In his commentaries, Saint John could have had writing in mind when composing this passage:

"One who is learning further details concerning any office or art always proceeds in darkness, and receives no guidance from his early knowledge, for if he left not that behind he would get no further nor make any progress; and in the same way, when the soul is making most progress, it is traveling in darkness, knowing naught."

But a writer not only writes in darkness, trusting the darkness to know more than he can know; the writer is aware that the final object of this work is always beyond him, and the closer he is drawn to that object, to try to write about it, the more he is blinded by it.

"For the nearer the soul approaches Him, the blacker is the darkness which it feels. . . . So immense is the spiritual light of God, and so greatly does it transcend our natural understanding, that the nearer we approach it, the more it blinds and darkens us."

To write about a saint is to invoke him, and the most important reason for invoking a saint is to pray to him to intercede between oneself and God. I, as a writer, pray to Saint John of the Cross to intercede with God on my behalf for the grace to write, not about what has to do with me, but about what has to do with the great and the brilliant darkness of God.

SOURCES

The Complete Works of Saint John of the Cross, 3 vols., trans. and ed. by E. Allison Peers (London: Burns Oates & Washbourne, 1934), 452, 453.

Alain Cugno, *St. John of the Cross,* trans. by Barbara Wall (London, Burns & Oates, 1982).

Second Thoughts on Certainty: Saint Jean de Brébeuf among the Hurons

TOBIAS WOLFF

THOUGH I WAS baptized a Catholic, I did not live among practicing Catholics, or go to Catholic schools, and therefore grew up knowing very little about the lives of the saints. I'd never heard of Saint Jean de Brébeuf until I came upon him in Francis Parkman's book *The Jesuits in North America.* His life was so astonishing and so dire in its conclusion that I couldn't get it out of my head, and even appropriated part of it for a short story, "In the Garden of the North American Martyrs." That was some fifteen years ago, and I still think of Brébeuf, but as I've learned more about him my admiration has become more complicated.

First, the bare bones of the man's life. He was born in 1593 to an aristocratic family in Normandy, and arrived in what is now the province of Quebec in 1625 as a Jesuit missionary to the Huron Indians. The English forced him out in 1629, but he returned to the Hurons in 1634 and remained with them until he was killed fifteen years later.

His death came about in this way. As the Huron confederacy grew stronger, or appeared to grow stronger through its alliance with the French, the Iroquois came to regard it as an unacceptable threat to their own prosperity and set about to annihilate the Hurons. This they did, in a series of assaults and massacres culminating in the destruction of the fortified villages of St. Ignace, St. Louis, and St. Marie in 1649. Jean de Brébeuf and his fellow missionary Gabriel Lalemant knew of the impending Iroquois attack and were urged to flee, but they remained in St. Louis to minister to eighty Huron warriors who were fighting a rearguard action to cover the retreat of their people. The Hurons put up a fierce resistance but were finally overwhelmed. Those who hadn't been killed in battle were afterward, according to the custom of both sides, tortured to death. Brébeuf and Lalemant were among them.

Brébeuf was led out first. They tied him to a stake and went to work. He showed no sign of pain, but called out encouragement to his fellow captives and threatened the Iroquois with hellfire for their wickedness. They applied their own fire to him, and when that didn't shut him up they cut off his lips and stuck a hot iron down his throat. They poured boiling water over his head in mock baptism, hung a necklace of burning hatchets around his neck. They made him witness the torture of Lalemant. Nothing broke him. His stoicism provoked them to greater and greater outrages. They stripped off his flesh and ate it in front of him. Finally, in a fury, they cut his heart out and ate that too. By his calm fortitude he inspired them to kill him much sooner than they'd intended. They tortured him for less than four hours before impatiently taking his life. Lalemant's agony was more evident, and therefore more satisfying, and they carefully spun it out for seventeen hours.

It would be presumptuous to describe such men with words like "faith" and "courage"; what they endured cannot be accounted for in words. It can hardly be imagined. But what strikes deepest in me is their concern for the Huron warriors whom they stayed behind to serve. They laid down their lives for their friends. That is something I can imagine. And it happened here, on ground familiar to me, not in some distant desert. Brébeuf, especially, is an American figure—no miracle-working monk or haloed cave dweller but a pioneer, an explorer, at home on wild rivers and murky forest paths, at the council fires of painted men who ate their enemies and were not always clear as to who their enemies were. Think of it: the young heir of a proud name raised to receive the best the world had to offer, refusing it all for a life of famine and disease, solitude, arctic winters, and unrelenting danger among people whose suspicions could never be allayed, whose friendship could never be relied on, whose motives and intentions must always remain a mortal mystery.

Brébeuf did all this, and more. Through ceaseless study he became an eloquent speaker of the Huron language, and created a grammar and lexicon to help other missionaries master the tongue. As a matter of course, and regardless of personal risk, he visited the sick and dying to preach and baptize. He kept a record of his life among the Hurons that is remarkable for its anthropological detail and, at times, its poetry. Here is Brébeuf on the subject of dreams, and their importance to the Hurons:

> They hold nothing so precious that they would not readily deprive themselves of it for the sake of a dream. If they have been successful in hunting, if they bring back their canoes laden with fish, all this is at the discretion of a dream. A dream will take away from them sometimes their whole year's provisions. It prescribes their feasts, their dances, their songs, their games—in a word, the dream does everything and is in truth the principal God of the Hurons.

Every glimpse we have of Brébeuf shows us a man of unshakable certainty. Not even in his last and darkest hour does he cry out, "Father, why hast Thou forsaken me?" This certainty is the source of all that I find chastening and stirring in his life, and all that troubles me as well. His mission was to bring unbelievers to the Church, to harvest souls, and he allowed no scruple or doubt or courtesy to stand in his way. When he couldn't persuade, he threatened. His sermons were hectoring and endlessly repetitious, so much so that ridiculing him came to be a sport among the Hurons, who had to be bribed with tobacco to listen to him at all. He hoarded food, and during times of starvation rationed it out to those who made the best show of piety. He was capricious in his use of baptism; at one time he withheld it from dying children for fear of being blamed for their deaths, at another he forced it on them even against their parents' wishes.

Brébeuf had come to speak, not to hear. He offended the Hurons by treating their own beliefs with scorn. He heaped contempt on their shamans and healers, and ignored the advice they gave him concerning the medicinal properties of native plants. He made fun of their ceremonial attempts to influence nature, but did not hesitate to play the wizard himself with magnets and clocks and magnifying glasses, and with self-designed rain-making rituals; at one point he was tried for sorcery before a tribal council and barely escaped with his life. He thus gave legitimacy to Huron suspicions that Christianity was, at best, a healing society of the kind they already had, or, at worst, a bag of tricks. Baffled by his failures, he tried to persuade the Huron chieftains to coerce their people to convert, and helped institute the practice of sending children away from their parents to be educated by French priests and nuns in Quebec. (The children kept running away, and the experiment was abandoned.)

For all his transcendent purposes, Brébeuf was help-lessly a creature of his own time and culture. The Jesuits depended on support from the French government and business enterprises, and had no choice but to serve their interests; in fact, they were tolerated by the Hurons only because the French had declared the acceptance of the Jesuit missions a condition for trade. The missionaries used this arrangement for their own ends. They allowed only converts to buy muskets, and at one point threat-ened to break off all commerce unless the entire Huron nation became Christian. These policies led to many ex-pedient baptisms, and created hard feelings between Hu-ron traditionalists and those who were willing to take up the cross for the sake of trade. Brébeuf himself made mis-chief between the Hurons and their allies the Neutrals, ham-fistedly playing them off against each other until he was nearly killed for his pains.

When Brébeuf first arrived among the Hurons they were a strong and numerous people. Twenty-five years later their nation was extinct, reduced to a few starving bands seeking adoption by other tribes. The Jesuit missionaries had much to answer for in this sorry end. They'd given the Iroquois plenty of reason to suspect that their presence among the Hurons was less a revelation of apostolic zeal than of French territorial and mercantile ambitions. In promoting their faith, the same missionaries tirelessly attacked Huron rituals and beliefs and traditions of tolerance that held this diffuse people together, and thereby divided them at the moment of their greatest danger. Brébeuf, especially, was relentless in his scorn for the spirituality that gave Huron life its meaning and coherence. In the end, he helped destroy the people he had come to save.

I do not mean to judge Jean de Brébeuf. He put all his gifts on the altar. He was loyal and resolute and courageous to his last breath. He lived the faith he professed. He was willing to accept any duty, any danger, any hardship, not for his own sake but for the sake of the people he hoped to serve. Everything he did, he did with the best of intentions. And yet this is exactly what disturbs me when I consider his life among the Hurons: that with complete purity of motive and satisfaction of conscience he was able to injure their deepest beliefs, their pride, their social structure, their very humanity, by treating them as crude and expendable vessels of the souls it was his business to save. He did these things not to please himself, but in accordance with the common understandings of devout, civilized men of his time and place. He had no idea of the limits placed on those understandings by the conditions of his upbringing and nationality and language. Who does? The perspectives from which we see Brébeuf were not available to him, as the perspectives from which we will one day be seen are not available to us.

Here is the problem. Is it possible to live a life of authentic faith without the kind of headlong conviction shown by Brébeuf? What else could have sustained him in his solitude and frustration and suffering? I envy him his certainty, until I think of the arrogance and blindness that came with it. We have learned to suspect such ardor. As I write these words, men of unbending principle and purity of motive are righteously herding people into camps and planting bombs on airplanes and firing artillery shells into crowded marketplaces. Our greatest murderers have been True Believers. And so, mindful of the evils done in faith's name, we have learned to be wary of faith itself, and of the voice that speaks for any single faith. We've taught ourselves to listen for the truth in each competing voice, to extend recognition to every contender.

But how much of this tolerance can we stand, without losing our way? If all things are true, then what particular thing is worth living for, let alone worth dying for? How unsatisfactory it is to be forever open to discussion, to see the other side of every argument, to give respect in so many directions at once. I know I am not alone in my disgust with the flaccidity of spirit that comes upon us as the consequence of trying always to accommodate the justice in each claim on our sympathy and understanding. I believe that this disgust is the greatest spiritual problem of our time. In its grip we long for certainty as for the clear streams and lush fields of a childhood home we never really had. How dangerous this longing is, what terrible things it makes us do for those who promise to satisfy it.

And still I confess that I feel rebuked by such assurance as Brébeuf's, Brébeuf who never hesitated, who went to his death without a second thought. The Lord Himself didn't do that. He prayed for the cup to pass Him by. Even at the end, He doubted, for which I give thanks. His doubts are blessings. They pardon us for ours. I'd be lost without them.

Sources

Denys Delâge, *Bitter Feast,* tr. by Jane Brierly (Vancouver: University of British Columbia Press, 1993).

Francis Parkman, *The Jesuits in North America* (Boston: Little Brown and Co., 1900).

Reuben G. Thwaites, ed. and trans., *Jesuit Relations and Allied Documents* (Cleveland: Burrows Bros. 1886–1901).

Bruce G. Trigger, *The Children of Aataentsic: A History of the Huron People to 1660* (Kingston and Montreal: McGill-Queen's University Press, 1976).

My Left Feet

ENRIQUE FERNÁNDEZ

I'M THE PERSON you want to be lost in the desert with. Follow me and you will not die of thirst. How will I find us water? By stepping on it. You will sense we are safe from the eternal drought of the eternal sands when you notice that on my feet I am not wearing Clark's desert boots but Timberland's waterproof brogans. For I know that even in the desert there must be one puddle and that it is my fate to step on it.

Even when it hasn't rained, I step on a puddle caused

by a backed-up street sewer or splashed by an open fire hydrant or fed by the hose of a Central American refugee who is washing the curb of a Korean greengrocer. One night, one tropical night when like all tropical nights it had rained, I walked with a friend in the darkness of a Miami nightclub parking lot toward our car. Splash! He stared at me in disbelief. "It's true what they say. You step on puddles."

I also step on feet. In a nightclub parking lot I have only the shame of my wet shoes—until I discovered the waterproof brogans—but inside the club I walk with the tread of a golem in a German Expressionist movie, ruining the gloss of polished Italian loafers, destroying toes in open sandals, provoking contempt and ire. Living dangerously. My work as a Latin music journalist has taken me to salsa clubs where a) unlike, say, a hardcore scene, inflicting pain on your fellow clubgoers is not a sign of solidarity; b) being light on your feet, deft, smooth, sharp, suave is highly regarded; c) many of the patrons are tough customers, gun-packing machos who practice rough trades in the mean streets and who don't find the ruining of their Italian loafers or the destruction of their lady friends' toes simpatico.

It's a miracle I'm still alive.

When I was in college I worked as a waiter in a very small, trendy, charming Spanish restaurant. After a week of enduring toe-crushing pain, my fellow workers, who included the owner's wife, agreed I should be exempted from the dress code and allowed to, nay, ordered to, wear sneakers instead of hard-soled dress shoes.

I didn't play sports as a kid. The few times I did, one of my ankles would twist and I would be out of the game. My parents took me to a bone surgeon, who diagnosed something or other and prescribed orthopedic shoes. They hurt. Also, they did no good.

I'm feet dyslexic. I'm faultily wired. I'm clumsy.

"You better go get yourself fixed by Saint Lazarus," a fellow Cuban American told me after observing how often I tripped, stumbled, and stepped on puddles. He was a musician, conversant with the religious practices that have come out of our native country, what is known in Spanish as *santería*, the worship of saints.

Santería mixes African religion with Roman Catholicism. It was first practiced by slaves from the Yoruba nation brought in the eighteenth and nineteenth centuries from what is Nigeria today to work in Cuba's sugar plantations. The Yoruba were and are a highly sophisticated people, and they found a way of holding on to their religion without alarming their white masters. They looked for affinities between their own deities, the *orichas*, and the representations of Catholic saints. For example, a saint holding a sword, like Saint Barbara, stood in for Changó, the fierce warrior god.

In the Spanish and Portuguese colonies of the New

World, the Africans were not forbidden to play drums, as they were in the American South. When the slaves played to their gods, the masters assumed they were paying homage to the Christian saints, albeit in a very rhythmic way.

Because of its association with saints, this cultural sleight of hand was called *santería*. With time, *santería* became more than a disguise for African rites, as true elements of Christian belief and practices seeped into the mix. And with time, the new mixed religion—syncretism is the academic name for this process of cultural fusion—spread beyond Cuba's African subculture. *Santería* became so widespread everyone came to believe in it, at least enough to fear its powers. *"Con los santos no se juega,"* Cubans of all races say. "You don't mess with the saints." And *santería* kept on spreading.

The Cuban exodus prompted by the radical changes of Castro's revolution brought *santería* to the United States on a massive scale. Many other Latinos embraced it with the same enthusiasm with which they embraced Afro-Cuban music, baptized in the American barrios as "salsa." And even non-Latinos got into *santería*.

Walk into a *santero*'s house and you will find altars to the saints. Many are familiar Catholic images, like the Virgin Mary or the Baby Jesus. One popular image is that of a bearded man on crutches, wearing little more than a loincloth and exposing a body covered with sores.

He is Saint Lazarus, and the African deity he represents is Babalú-Ayé. Remember Desi Arnaz banging on drums and chanting, "Babaloo"? That's who he was calling.

The lame Saint Lazarus, aka Babalú-Ayé, is the patron saint of feet. Thus my compatriot's prescription to cure my chronic stumbling, ankle-twisting, and stepping on puddles. Like most Cubans I respect *santería*, but I have never really practiced it. My forays into this wonderful, magical, and yet very practical and earthy religion have been intellectual. It plays such an important part in my home country's culture and in the culture of U.S. Latinos that I have felt obliged to understand its basics. I have even written articles about it, and have researched them by going to drum ceremonies and interviewing practicing *santeros*. But I am not an initiate. There is no altar in my home; nor do I light candles, sacrifice chickens—animal sacrifice is *santería*'s most controversial feature—or consult a *babalao* to help me order my life. So when it was suggested that I seek Saint Lazarus's help, I thought, Why not? But I did nothing about it. Until . . .

I was in Havana two years ago, writing a magazine piece on what life was like in my home country these days. Another Cuban-American journalist, also there on assignment, suggested I go to the shrine of Saint Lazarus during the week of his feast day: "It's a freak show." And then I remembered how in my childhood I had seen a photo essay in a Cuban magazine about the Saint Lazarus parade—if that's what it can be called. Like other

Catholic countries, Cuba has had a tradition of making "promises" to the saints. That is, you ask the appropriate saint to help you with some problem, like getting over an illness, and you offer to visit the saint's shrine in repayment.

Every year believers who have made promises to Saint Lazarus walk miles to his shrine. On the last stretch, about a mile and a half of a semirural road a few miles outside Havana, the march to the shrine becomes more dramatic as those who have made serious promises walk it on their knees, praying for their sins' forgiveness. At least, that's how I remembered it from the magazine article.

All of this was standard folk Catholicism. But the Cuban twist was *santería,* since, as I said, the Catholic saint and the African god were fused into one. In fact, the Catholic saint was not the guy with the crutches and the sores—along with Saint Christopher, the patron saint of travelers, and Saint George, who slew the dragon, *that* Saint Lazarus was declared pure fable many years ago by the Catholic church and banished from the company of legitimate saints. This Saint Lazarus was some early Christian bishop who stood squarely on two feet and wore proper bishop's vestments. But never mind; his name was Saint Lazarus also, and as far as *santeros* were concerned, he was Babalú-Ayé, patron saint of the lame and of those who have problems with their feet.

I went there to ask him to cure mine from their em-
barrassing ineptitude with puddles and the toes of gangsters' molls.

It was December, the day before the feast of Saint
Lazarus, and I could see pilgrims walking alongside the
road that led to the small town where the shrine was
located. The shrine was outside the town, at the end of
a smaller road, which was blocked to traffic so the believers could do their thing. And the things they did!

Sure enough, there were folk who walked that last
mile and a half on their knees. But the ones who had
made really intense promises went down on their bellies
and crawled. In most cases the connection with the crip-
pled saint was obvious. One severely disabled man, in
filthy rags which had become bloodied from his crawling,
had big chunks of cinder block tied to each twisted leg—
an extreme form of fulfilling his promise. His body zig-
zagged up the road like a sidewinder's. Two young men
from the town, used to this yearly procession and to
seeing this one penitent every year, cheerfully announced, "*La culebra* is here!" The snake. Caribbean humor is merciless and tough. But no tougher than another
crawling believer, who insisted on his macho privilege
to suffer.

In front of this penitent, another man brushed away
the pebbles on the road with a palm frond. It was a *santería* practice of *abrir camino*, opening the road, which usually has metaphorical and spiritual meaning, but here was

carried out quite literally. The road-opener would encourage the crawler and give him instructions, acting like
his spiritual personal trainer. When the tough crawler,
who was not tied down by stones and showed no signs
of physical disability, reached a strip of metal laid at the
churchyard's gate, his road-opener told him to "kiss Oggún," that is, to kiss the metal in honor of Oggún, god
of iron, and he kept on brushing away the pebbles.

The crawler did not kiss Oggún; instead, he looked
up at the other man with fierce bloodshot eyes and told
him to stop his road-clearing work. He wanted to feel
the pebbles. He wanted to feel the pain. He wanted to
bleed. The other man kept brushing until the crawler
stopped, looked up again, and said, "If you don't stop,
I'm going to stand up and fuck you up." The other man
stopped. The crawler went inside the church, which was
filling with pilgrims. He crawled up to the altar, received
a priest's blessing, and then stood up, lean, muscular,
able-bodied. Observing the fierceness of his promise and
his obvious lack of physical handicap, a man in the
church commented, "He must have done something terribly evil to feel he must pay for it like this!"

A woman I assumed to be a nun—no one wears
religious habits in today's Cuba—was leading the crowd
in prayer and giving them advice on religious protocol.
Most of it had to do with observing Catholic instead
of *santería* rites. She asked for the silence required in
church—characteristically Caribbean, *santería* ceremonies

can be social and informal even while being intense; that is, someone can be going into a spiritual trance at one end of a room while at the other end someone else is eating and talking. And she asked people not to give the saints anything to smoke; it's a common practice to offer a lit cigar to the images of certain saints. "This is a Catholic church," she said, "and we have rituals different from those of other religions. Please observe our rules."

I stood to one side of the procession of crawlers and walkers and genuflectors and looked at the statue of Saint Lazarus. He seemed overly dressed and overly healthy, unlike the folk of Saint Lazarus, whose life-size, sore-infested, leaning-on-crutches statues can be seen on display in the windows of religious stores on Bergenline Avenue in Union City, New Jersey, and, of course, on Miami's Little Havana strip, Calle Ocho. But if people will crawl to pray for this Saint Lazarus's help, he must be the right saint. So I prayed. Something like: *Saint Lazarus, Babalú-Ayé, please help me walk straight without tripping, stumbling, twisting my ankle, stepping on feet, or splashing on puddles.* And then, I turned around and went back up the road to the car. It was getting dark.

Along the way I noticed that police officers were frisking men who had just arrived on the scene. I asked one of the cops what this was about, and he replied that some people took advantage of the crowd and the darkness to settle old scores. Some of these guys certainly looked like they should be searched. One was a virtual

folk caricature of a Cuban tough guy, a *guapo*. He was a
light-skinned mulatto with a thin mustache and a hard,
handsome face. He wore perfectly creased jeans and a
tight-fitting undershirt. He was built like a motherfucker.
And by his side stood his son, no more than ten years
old, dressed exactly like his father, also built like a motherfucker, staring hard and mean; absolutely frightening.
He also got searched.

Others who were frisked appeared quite harmless:
hippiesque student types slinging bookbags. No women
were frisked. And no one—it hurts to admit it—frisked
me. Too old, perhaps, too soft, too unlikely to flash a
blade on the night of Saint Lazarus.

By the time I got back to my hotel it was nighttime.
I stepped out of the car.

Splash.

Havana, I remembered, always had a water-drainage
problem: too much rain. It also had a water-supply problem. I know all this because many years ago my father
worked for the city's water department. He got to drive
a white station wagon with the city's coat of arms and
the words ACUEDUCTO DE LA HABANA on it, but after a few
days of having rocks thrown at it when he cruised
through neighborhoods where there were water short-
ages and/or flooded streets, he gave it back to the city.
Water problems. Puddles. Splash! Saint Lazarus had not
worked his magic on my feet.

———

I told all this to the Cuban-American musician as soon
as I was back in New York. I felt betrayed by the saint.
I had gone to his shrine, albeit not crawling. I had
prayed. I was still a clumsy idiot.

"Did you believe in the saint's power?" he asked.

"Well, I prayed, didn't I?"

"But did you believe?"

"I don't know. Yes. No. I prayed."

"If you don't believe, it doesn't work."

So that was it. The problem was not my physical
clumsiness. I was, I am, a spiritual klutz. I prayed without believing. "Words without thought do not to heaven
go." Even Claudius, that vile, incestuous, usurping murderer knew this, while Hamlet, my fellow klutz, thought
Claudius was praying, so he didn't kill him for fear of
dispatching him to heaven. Spirituality has its rules. *Con
los santos no se juega.*

Anyway, what was the big deal? The Timberland
company had already solved half my problem. And by
now the gangsters and their molls were used to seeing
me stumbling around the clubs, so they just moved their
nimble feet out of my way.

I saw something else that late afternoon on the
pebble-strewn road to the shrine of Saint Lazarus. There
was a man who was crawling for the sake of his son, a
two-year old boy with a clubfoot. The man was big and
ebony-skinned, as perfectly muscled as a classical sculpture. His knees and feet and elbows were bleeding badly.

In front of him a light-skinned *santero,* dressed in white from his shoes to his hat, opened the road with a fresh palm frond, while by his side the man's wife walked, holding their son's hand. She was a high-toned mulatto, gracefully shaped in a tight satin dress and she walked on high heels. On the man's back rode his son, naked and beautiful, so beautiful his clubfoot seemed like no imperfection at all. I couldn't help but think he would grow up to be a Caribbean Lord Byron.

The man was powerful, but he had been crawling for some time and occasionally he would stop. Then, someone would come out from a neighborhood house and offer him water to drink. Thus revived he would resume his pilgrimage. The boy bounced on his father's broad back, having the time of his life, the ride of his life, smiling to the passersby; absolutely, perfectly happy. I didn't stay with them, but went on ahead toward the church, and when I walked back I missed them in the crowd.

When I later wrote about this visit to Cuba, I left out the pilgrimage to the shrine of Saint Lazarus/Babalú-Ayé. The article I eventually published was infused with politics, as have been all recent articles on Cuba. I had thought I would find politics on the road to Saint Lazarus, people praying for the fall of Fidel or for his endurance. But I found—and lost—something else instead: grace.

The image of that family fulfilling a promise was so

overpowering that it confused me. Everything was too meaningful, too symbolic: the Holy Family, the Passion of Christ, the white-clad *santero* with a palm frond moving with the grace of an Alvin Ailey dancer, the crawler built like a titan, the child with the clubfoot hanging loosely on his father's back like a Greek boy on a dolphin, the mother walking with the sass of a *mulata* in the old Cuban folk theater. Too much.

And there was my failure with the saint, which seemed like an entirely different agenda. Only now do I realize my blindness. Just as I had prayed without believing, I had seen without praying. Visions are spiritual gifts and I had seen this one with secular eyes.

That *was* Saint Lazarus. That *was* Babalú-Ayé. Who else could command so much iconography? I left him crawling, bleeding, sore-infested. What I should have done was pray right there and then for a cure for his son's disability, to give him a spiritual power charge. Maybe then the deity brought in chains to the New World, reincarnated as a false saint, surviving as a real one, summoned a thousand times in the foolish rituals of an old American TV show, crawling along a road full of penitents that December afternoon, would have shown mercy on my petty pilgrimage and blessed away the clumsiness of my two left feet.

A Family Man

PAUL BAUMANN

WE WERE LYING IN BED discussing our children, as married people sometimes do just before turning off the light and just after tossing aside in bitter and covetous disgust the real-estate transactions in the local newspaper. How can there be peace with justice if one's neighbors' property values ascend heavenward while yours languish in purgatorial suspension? But to whom does the beleaguered and undervalued property owner, fantasizing a killing on the real estate market and early retirement to pursue pious works, cry? To Saint Joseph,

another overanxious father? To Saint Joseph, the patron
saint of petit-bourgeois dutifulness and uxorious discipline ("When Joseph woke from sleep, he did as the
angel of the Lord commanded him; he took his wife, but
knew her not until she had borne a son; and he called
his name Jesus")? To Saint Joseph, the obedient taxpayer
("In those days a decree went out from Caesar Augustus
that all the world should be enrolled")? To the church's
patron of social justice (". . . Joseph, being a just man
and unwilling to put her to shame, resolved to divorce
her quietly"), harried fathers of families ("And he rose
up and took the child and his mother by night, and de-
parted to Egypt, and remained there until the death of
Herod"), and working men ("Is this not the son of the
woodworker?")? What satisfaction can one expect from
the heavenly solicitor for such notoriously undervalued
properties as Peru, Belgium, Canada, and China? Or
should I petition "Joseph the Joiner," as James Joyce im-
piously described the world's most famous carpenter,
cuckold, and foster father, "patron of the happy demise
of all unhappy marriages"?

More on that soon. But about our children, those
mites of God's clay, the fruit of our lawful embraces
(Joyce again; he was, after all, a family man if not a
property owner, and, as it turns out, a keen ruminator
on Saint Joseph's travail). Would our eldest, heir apparent and apparent visitor from Mars, ever learn to pay
attention and stop tormenting his sister? we asked each

other. Would she ever stop tormenting him—not that he
didn't deserve it? Why does he act like that, anyway? It
can't be sex; he's only ten. Maybe it is sex. Jesus! When
will the two-year-old stop throwing her dinner dishes
across the kitchen and taking off her soiled diaper in the
living room? But she's only two. When will he stop spill-
ing food on the floor? Will he learn how to pour milk?
How is it that she, the eight-year-old, so delicate of com-
plexion and ankle, so sneaky with a rabbit punch, never
spills anything? Where did they come from? Is someone
crying? How would Saint Joseph—spouse of the Queen
of Heaven, reputed father of the King of Kings—handle
this? Patiently, I know.

Ah, family life. If it didn't have a patron saint, someone would have to invent one. How did my wife and I,
once vowed to perpetual procrastination, get in so deep
among the pacifiers, Legos, and dollies? How did we end
up back at Caldor, where once our own parents led us in
solemn procession down the evil-smelling aisles and
where we swore never to return? How did we come to a
reconciliation with plastic and polyester, with Pampers
and the color pink? How did my life end up looking
more like Saint Joseph's than like that of my original role
model, James Bond?

It is in the nature of things, I suppose. Turning to
my overworked and underpaid, overwrought and under-
Catholicized (read Jewish) wife, I put a respectful hand
on her deflated belly, that omphalos of our little world.

Each of our children had kicked but more often fluttered about in utero, and I warmly remembered how uncanny and unnerving it had been to feel such palpable life inside my wife's familiar body. ("And when Elizabeth heard the greeting of Mary, the babe leaped in her womb; and Elizabeth was filled with the Holy Spirit. . . .") My wife, too, thought of that sovereign and mysterious liquid universe in which her children leapt and tumbled as numinous and as achingly wondrous as first love. An unexpected, unearned, incalculable visitation. "Yes," she said, "yes," in the manner of Joyce's expansive Molly Bloom but in shorter sentences. "For he has done great things for me," she might have said in the manner of Mary, according to Luke. What could I do but stand by at a discreet distance, seeming to tend the livestock somewhat in the manner of Saint Joseph—he who was entrusted, as tradition tells us, with the sublime secret of the Incarnation and, more prosaically, the care and guardianship of Virgin and Son?

I want to get at the curiously diffident figure of Joseph by way of Joyce, and by aligning him with the equally self-effacing figure of Leopold Bloom, the cuckolded hero of *Ulysses*. The truths of fiction and the truths of biblical religion are not unrelated. Certain aspects of reality can be captured only in narrative. Paradox and parable must in this sense be enacted or witnessed to, not analyzed away. Like liturgy, literature uses language and drama to immerse us in a re-created and revivified world.

Karl Rahner, the late German theologian, writes of the lives of saints that "the events of this earthly life are not simply gone and past, over and done with forever, but they are preparatory steps that belong to us for eternity, that belong to us as our living future."

That is not a bad way to describe what happens in Joyce's novel. In *Ulysses,* Joyce employs a variety of narrative techniques, especially parody and stream of consciousness, to present the events of one day, June 16, 1904, in Dublin. Stephen Dedalus, an aspiring writer, and Leopold Bloom and his wife, Molly, are the central characters. Mimicking the mythic structure of Homer's *Odyssey,* Joyce follows Stephen and Bloom, his Telemachus and Odysseus, or Ulysses, as they wander the city on their mundane rounds, unknowingly in search of each other. Every act, gesture, and emotion of Joyce's characters takes on an imperishable quality thanks to the intensity of his writing and the manifold allusions of the novel's plot. Joyce wants to pull back the veil before the quotidian to reveal the mythic or transcendent quality of human existence. In this regard, I think the tribute to that "insignificant man" Joseph in Rahner's collection of sermons, *The Great Church Year,* can aptly be applied to the inconspicuous Leopold Bloom: "The life of this insignificant man did have significance; it had one meaning that, in the long run, counts in each person's life: God and his incarnate grace. . . . Who can doubt that this man is a good patron for us? This man of humble, everyday routine, this man of silent performance of duty, of honest righteousness and of manly piety, this man who was charged with protecting the grace of God in its embodied life?"

Joyce, as is well known, imbued his fiction with the kind of spiritual revelations or "epiphanies" he no longer found compelling in Irish Catholicism. He created the kind of mysteries, enigmas, and signs in his fiction that he had initially found in Catholic doctrine and ritual, and he borrowed freely from Catholicism in doing so. As Malcolm Bradbury has written, Joyce's work retains the church's redemptive imagery as well as its message of love. *Ulysses'* elaborate documentation of one day in Leopold Bloom's life challenges any merely material or naturalistic accounting of human existence. "Bloomsday," as Joyce's admirers have labeled the events of *Ulysses,* is something like what Rahner calls the "one today of eternity" God has promised for those who love him.

For Joyce, artistic creativity mimics and even partakes of the mystery of creation itself. In her famous stream-of-consciousness rumination at the end of the novel, Molly Bloom, Leopold's unfaithful wife and the novel's Penelope, puts the riddle of the world this way: "... as for them saying theres no God I wouldn't give a snap of my two fingers for all their learning why don't they go and create something I often asked him atheists or whatever they call themselves go and wash the cobbles off themselves first then they go howling for a priest

and they dying ... ah yes I know them well who was
the first person in the universe before there was anybody
that made it all who ah that they dont know neither do I
so there you are they might as well try to stop the sun
from rising tomorrow. . . ."

Fatherhood, or the "mystery of paternity," in the
phrase of the Joycean critic Stuart Gilbert, is emblematic
of the power and paradoxes of creation. In this sense,
Bloom's famous cuckoldry seems to be a sign of the essential ambiguity of all human longing and attachment.
As Richard Ellmann has written, Joyce used sexual betrayal as "a parable of the dilemma of all creators,
whether of books or of worlds." There is something
"sado-masochistic," as Ellmann characterizes it in his essay "Becoming Exiles," in the very nature of our passions. Without desire we can achieve nothing, yet there
is no desire without jealousy, no valuing one thing without spurning something or someone else. Worse, "to delight in possession is to allow the conceivability of
dispossession, to rely on constancy is impossible because
it can only exist as a relation to inconstancy; what is
absent calls attention to what is present." Human happiness is fleeting because the desires that ignite our passions in the same motion undermine our certainty.

Who is a father and who a son is not at all easy to
unravel, Joyce suggests. Stephen Dedalus, a spiritual orphan, must find his way to the childless
Leopold Bloom, his mystical foster father. In the

maternity-hospital scene where Stephen finally meets
Bloom ("now sir Leopold that had of his body no man-
child for an heir"), Joyce celebrates the mystery of new
life in his commendation of a new father. "By heaven,
Theodore Purefoy, thou has done a doughty deed and
no botch!" Joyce rejoices. "Thou art, I vow, the remark-
ablest progenitor barring none in this chaffering allin-
cluding most farraginous chronicle. Astounding! In her
lay a Godframed Godgiven preformed possibility which
thou has fructified with thy modicum of man's work.
Cleave to her! Serve! Toil on, labour like a very bandog
and let scholarment and all Malthusiasts go hang. Thou
art all their daddies, Theodore. Art drooping under thy
load, bemoiled with butcher's bills at home and ingots
(not thine!) in the countinghouse? Head up!"

Maybe it takes a Joyce to evoke without cliché the
joy and nagging mystery of fatherhood—its uncertain-
ties so easily distorted by the language of "family values." Bemoiled with bills and drooping under a freely
willed load puts the right gleeful spin on the mock-epic
adventure of fatherhood and husbanding. Conceivably
the angel's real words to Joseph were, "Cleave to her!
Serve! Toil on, labour like a very bandog." At least that's
what Joseph appears to have done.

Understanding what fatherhood's "modicum of
man's work" entails is not a straightforward proposition.
Joseph's fate, like Leopold Bloom's, is especially suggestive. You have to be given one of those heedless God-

framed Godgiven preformed possibilities to appreciate
how onerous and liberating custodianship can be. That
paradox is compounded by the constant and eerie discovery of oneself in one's offspring. "I'm becoming my father," moans one exasperated son after another as he
raises his own children. In this regard Joyce reminds us
that the Virgin Mary in fact gives birth to a son who is
also her own father. "Paternity may be a legal fiction,"
Stephen Dedalus further speculates. "Who is the father
of any son that any son should love him or he any son.
. . . Fatherhood . . . is a necessary evil. . . . Fatherhood in
the sense of conscious begetting is unknown to man. It
is a mystical estate, an apostolic succession, from only
begetter to only begotten. On that mystery and not on
the madonna which the cunning Italian intellect flung to
the mob of Europe the church is founded and founded
irremovably because founded, like the world, macro- and
microcosm, upon the void."

Stephen Dedalus finds that mystical estate, that spiritual legacy, in the advertising canvasser Leopold Bloom,
the uncommon common man Joyce makes the unlikely
hero of his novel. In this sense, Bloom can be seen as a
kind of Joseph—and perhaps Joseph as a kind of Bloom.
Every new creation needs a foster father, Joyce contends.
Even the incarnated God needed one.

But to return, for the moment, to my wife and me in
our bourgeois bedroom. The metaphysical connotations
of fatherhood alluded to above had more or less banished

comparative real-estate values from my mind. So I contemplated further how those mites of God's clay had forged a bond between my wife and me that was deeper than the word "domesticity" suggests. A bond that is, in fact, as deep as the world itself—which is what I take Joyce to mean when he describes human life as "soaring imperishable impalable being." Like a good many couples, we knew each other for many years before marrying and having children. We knew the macro- and microcosm and the void, so to speak. For those years our lives revolved around—ourselves. We were, after all, urged on to self-fulfillment as a generational, even constitutional duty. But now there are (gulp) three more very Godpossibled and equally grasping souls in the picture. We somehow let scholarment and all Malthusiasts go hang. But while our world has become more crowded, I would argue that it also has become larger. "For sirs," Stephen Dedalus puts it, sounding uncannily like Pope John Paul II, ". . . our lust is brief. We are means to those small creatures within us and nature has other ends than we."

I ventured to express these aboriginal feelings to my less mystically inclined roommate.

"Children are a real bond, don't you think," I said dreamily.

"Yes, they are," she replied with a slyness of tone that should have alerted me to the banana peel ahead. "So where, exactly, do you fit in?"

My wife laughed. ("But as he considered this, behold, an angel of the Lord appeared to him in a dream, saying, 'Joseph, son of David, do not fear. . . .' ") Not a wicked or unfriendly laugh. More a knowing laugh. I took this teasing in the spirit in which it was intended. At least I think I took it in the spirit in which it was intended. It was, in part, a legitimate complaint about the dishes I had left unwashed in the sink. But it was more. Saint Joseph, I vaguely remember, appeared before me at that moment.

Well, maybe he didn't exactly appear. But Joseph's notorious marital forbearance did cross my mind. It was not so much that my wife was about to reveal the until then unsuspected real paternity of my children. At least I have received no hint of such a complication. No, it was rather that Saint Joseph's unique circumstances exemplify those ambiguities surrounding paternity.

My wife was asserting, in her whimsical way, a certain primacy of place in regard to our offspring. I took no offense. While I don't think biology is destiny, I do think that it is, well, biology. In *Ulysses*, for example, Joyce devotes each episode to an oblique discussion of a different bodily organ. "My book is among other things the epic of the human body," he said. And the procreative body obviously takes center stage. The ties that bind mothers to children are physiologically irrefutable, emotionally unmistakable, and, I realize, culturally highly suspect. Nevertheless, I confess that I think motherhood is closer to the center of things, if by the center we mean the source of life. "They all write about some woman," Molly Bloom observes. Mothers and babies are literally knitted together. The attachments are multiple and unmediated, and that solidarity transcends the womb. We are linked navel to navel to Eve, not Adam.

Motherhood is an irrevocable umbilical connection. Women carry life within them as well as nurturing it with the substance of their own bodies. (That's transubstantiation for you!) Fathers, however, are physically detached, apart. Connection must be forged. Fatherhood is an artifice in a way motherhood never can be. In some sense it really is a matter of apostolic succession, a leap of faith—is that why we call God the Father Almighty? Mommy seems to come first in myth, fairy tale, and popular prejudice. *Mother* is often the last word on the lips of the dying. "Mamafesta" is what Joyce called *Finnegans Wake*. So it is not surprising that a mother comes first, at least from the human side of things, in the Christian story of redemption. Or that the man—Joseph, that is— is conspicuously shunted to the side. So Joseph's status as foster father may be worth thinking more about. Compared to the intimacy, risks, and rewards of motherhood, all fatherhood is, Joyce suggests, a kind of foster fatherhood. And if read broadly, Joseph's consternation over Mary's seeming procreative autonomy is the consternation of every man over a woman's procreative near self-sufficiency. From the only begetter to the countless begotten, every human father is a stand-in.

In this context, it is a pleasing paradox that patriarchal religion should single out as a model of fatherly duty a man who is denied any biological connection to the son for whom he is remembered, and in whose name he is venerated. Joseph, as Joyce might say, seems utterly superfluous, a necessary evil, in the central drama of the Incarnation. How we make sense of this paragon of fatherhood who yet is not a father in the strict definition of the word tells us something about the nature of God as well as that of our own destiny.

Of course Joseph was not above worldly or stereotypical masculine concerns. Scripture is determined to provide answers of a sort to the delicate questions about Joseph's and Mary's conjugal life. Learning of Mary's condition, Joseph is perplexed—as perplexed as the most incredulous New Testament reader. Understandably, he "resolved to divorce her quietly." He may have been concerned about Mary's safety, for the penalty for adultery was stoning. Happily, the problem is resolved by the intervention of an angel, to this day the most practical solution to the problem of suspected adultery. "Do not fear to take Mary your wife, for that which is conceived in her is of the Holy Spirit," goes history's most famous reassurance of a suspicious husband. Joseph is obedient. Very much like Bloom's return to the adulterous Molly, Joseph turns away from any attempt to control things. Dependency is somehow equated with humanity in both instances. In choosing faith and constancy over doubt and separation, Joseph establishes himself as the guardian of the saviour of the world and subsequently as a protector of children and virgins down through the ages. To be sure, Joseph's willingness to believe what the Holy Spirit tells him in his dreams also established him as the butt of a million jokes. As a befuddled cuckold, he became a stock figure of ridicule in story, legend, and song. Indeed, the popular imagination finds it hard to separate Joseph from the idea of cuckoldry, even if he has been cuckolded by the Progenitor of us all. In the traditional English Cherry Tree carol, Joseph emerges as a very human figure indeed.

> Joseph was an old man,
>   And an old man was he,
> When he wedded Mary
>   In the land of Galilee.
>
> Joseph and Mary walked
>   Through an orchard good,
> Where were cherries and berries
>   So red as any blood. . . .
>
> O then bespoke Mary,
>   With words so meek and mild
> 'Pluck me one cherry, Joseph,
>   For I am with child.'

more plausible Mary's perpetual virginity. As a heavenly patron, Joseph—Mary's chaste and holy spouse and Jesus' father—was thought to be particularly well situated to intercede on behalf of his earthly clients. Saint Francis de Sales (1567–1621) put his analogical imagination to work in suggesting that the threesome of the Holy Family was a kind of earthly counterpart to the Trinity. Mother, Father, and progeny do, after all, form the primeval triangle. The Christian story has been described as a family drama. But to a large extent, any cult of Saint Joseph lay dormant through the first millennium of Christianity. This is attributed to the problems Joseph's status as husband present to the ideas of Mary's virginal conception and her perpetual virginity. Once those doctrines were firmly established, Joseph could emerge as a more substantial figure in his own right.

A French religious writer, Jean Gerson (1363–1429), is reputed to have been the most effective early promoter of Joseph's cult. Gerson's efforts resulted in Pope Sixtus IV's promulgation, in 1480, of March 19 as Saint Joseph's feast day. Saint Teresa of Ávila was another advocate. She attributed to Joseph the successful financial management of her burgeoning order. The Jesuits also promoted Joseph as a model of Christian fatherhood. In more recent years the "chaste spouse" shouldered significant ecclesiastical and even political responsibilities. Pius IX proclaimed him Patron of the Universal Church in 1870. Pius XI commissioned him into the church's battle against atheistic communism in 1937. In that capacity, the Catholic church established a second feast day, the Feast of Saint Joseph the Worker, on May 1, 1955. Given the subsequent demise of dialectical materialism and the collapse of the Soviet Union, Joseph's spiritual potency appears not to have diminished in the time since his fiduciary exploits among the Carmelites.

Asking what we know about the "real" Joseph is a bit like asking what we know about real sightings of Elvis. Obviously there is little we can know. Scripture, as usual, contradicts itself on many of the relevant facts. In Matthew, for example, it is Joseph, not Mary, who receives the annunciation of Jesus' birth. Joseph's gospel appearances are confined to the birth narratives in Matthew and Luke, although his status as Jesus' foster father is referred to briefly elsewhere. No actual word of Joseph's is recorded in the New Testament. Matthew tells the story of the Incarnation from Joseph's perspective. Regarded as the most "Jewish" of the evangelists, Matthew emphasizes the importance of Joseph's Davidic lineage. "Matthew's major concern," writes Biblical scholar John P. Meier in *A Marginal Jew: Rethinking the Historical Jesus,* "[is] Jesus' Davidic sonship through Joseph. We might almost sum up the message of 1:18–25 with a paradox: although Jesus is virginally conceived, nevertheless he is the Son of David through Joseph, his legal father."

According to Meier, Joseph was most likely a native

of Nazareth and an observant Jew. As such, he would have taken a special interest in his firstborn son, and probably passed on his occupation to him. What Joseph's occupation was, except that he worked as a craftsman, is uncertain. What seems certain, at least according to scholarly consensus, is that Joseph's conspicuous absence from the accounts of Jesus' ministry in all likelihood indicates that he died before Jesus began his public life. Joseph is not with Mary at the foot of the cross.

Questions about the virgin birth and Mary's and Joseph's chaste marriage are outside the competence of scholarly investigation, Meier winningly notes. Obviously, the virginal conception of Jesus lies at the heart of the Christian incarnational message and of any real understanding of Joseph. As the historian Peter Brown writes in his seminal study, *The Body and Society: Men Women, and Sexual Renunciation in Early Christianity,* "the cult of the Virgin offered the luminous inversion of the dark myth of shared fallen flesh." Mary's motherhood of Jesus redeems "the physical bonds created between human beings by their bodies." Through Mary, Christians have been able to embrace the full humanity of Jesus, for in looking at Christ they "looked on the flesh of a kinsman, taken from the tranquil human substance of the Virgin's womb."

Alongside the mystery of Mary's "yes" to God stands the curious figure of Joseph, who was as obedient and faithful in his way as Mary was in hers. Under the circumstances, you might say Joseph's chaste fidelity was a miracle in its own right. "Let him pluck thee a cherry/ That brought thee now with child," the Joseph of popular imagination says, confronting his wife's apparent betrayal. Yet the Joseph of tradition miraculously soldiers on, laboring like a very bandog, searching for shelter where Mary can give birth, fleeing to Egypt to protect his young foster son, traveling to Jerusalem to have his firstborn dedicated at the Temple, returning to the Temple courtyard in search of Jesus when he was left behind as a twelve-year-old. "Son, why have you treated us so? Behold, your father and I have been looking for you anxiously," Mary reprimands her son, only to be told a mystery. "How is it that you sought me?" Jesus replies. "Did you not know that I must be in my Father's house?"

In such riddles, we are vividly reminded of Joseph's surrogate status. Yet his fidelity did not waver; not much, anyway. Doubtless that is the obvious and yet difficult point. All human constancy seems miraculous given the transitory nature of things. The faithful are vulnerable to the mockery of the world. As Joseph is. As Leopold Bloom is in his essentially chaste marriage to the adulterous Molly. Joyce even plays these two cuckolds off against each other. "Qui vous a mis dans cette fichue position?" Stephen Dedalus idly remembers a French joke. "C'est le pigeon, Joseph." Similarly, Buck Mulligan, Stephen's blaspheming companion, put the implausibility of Jesus' origins into the "Ballad of the Joking Jesus."

I'm the queerest young fellow that ever you heard.
My mother's a jew, my father's a bird.
With Joseph the joiner I cannot agree,
So here's to disciples and Calvary.

Ulysses is notoriously the chronicle of the exceedingly ordinary events of that June day in 1904 (the actual day
Joyce met his wife, Nora). Joyce's mock-epic gives to the
humblest of human activities and the humblest of lives
the solemnity of ritual. In both the novel and the story
of Joseph, what is most characteristically human depends
on memory and the tangible presence of the past. That
depth of time and experience finally depends on simple,
or not so simple, human constancy and love. In *Ulysses,*
that love is manifest in the life Bloom and Molly have
shared, and which now, despite every betrayal, is an in-
expungable part of who they are individually. Constancy,
for which Joseph is rightly remembered, is the essential
virtue. Without it—without daily human promise-
making and -keeping—we cannot hope to see ourselves
or life whole. Promise-keeping connects the past to the
future—it gives structure to the disconnected flux of
events and experience. Leopold Bloom's transcendent
virtue is this sort of dogged constancy. His dead father
and son, for example, live vividly in his memory, shaping
his every living expectation and feeling. His unfaithful
wife is still his wife. This humane steadfastness prepares
him in turn to become Stephen Dedalus's spiritual father.

Like Joseph, Bloom is a practical family man, a Jew, a provider and protector. Like Joseph, he is a prosaic figure yet "a just man." It is said of Joseph that into his hands was entrusted the saviour of the world, the incarnate Word. Bloom is also entrusted with the incarnate word in the form of Stephen Dedalus, future author of *Ulysses,* the word made flesh on the page. As Karl Rahner wrote of Joseph, Bloom is very much a protector of the grace of God in its embodied life when he allows himself to become the lost and betrayed Stephen's guardian.

Like Joseph, Bloom is a cuckold who yet demonstrates a larger and truer loyalty, and in doing so reveals a redemptive sense of human possibility. If Joseph must call upon angels to assuage his doubts over Mary's miraculous conception, Bloom calls upon the angels of his better nature to accept his wife's waywardness with loving equanimity. "By what reflections did he, a conscious reactor against the void incertitude, justify to himself his sentiments?" Bloom answers: ". . . the futility of triumph or protest or vindication: the inanity of extolled virtue: the lethargy of nescient matter: the apathy of the stars." In other words, Bloom will trust his heart against the logic of the calculating world. Life's betrayals cannot be remedied through human mastery and manipulation. Bloom, the doting family man, knows that self-sufficiency is an illusion. Love puts an end to self-sufficiency. According to Anthony Burgess's wonderfully engaging study *Rejoyce,* Bloom is also entrusted with the word, for in becoming Stephen Dedalus's guardian Bloom gives shelter to the future author of *Ulysses.* In a typical Joycean paradox, Bloom is foster father to his own creator.

Fatherhood is one way in which men live that need, and is perhaps the most seductive way in which we try to extend our imagined control over life. But for Joyce, paternity is a sign of the limited nature of our control. Bloom is the truest father because he is the least vain of men. Paternity, like any good and truly human thing, is something given to us, not something we can claim authorship of. From the only begetter to the countless begotten—from Joseph the carpenter to Leopold Bloom the advertising man—human fathers are but intermediaries.

Bloom is also, of course, married to another Mary— the famous Molly—a Mary who is very much a second Eve, an earth mother, a sign of creation and renewal, and of life itself. In *Ulysses,* Molly is the center of things, and like the Virgin Mary she sanctifies in Joyce's scheme the bonds created between human beings by their bodies. In the famous litany of affirmation with which she concludes the novel, the adulterous Molly Bloom is understood to be just as much the handmaiden of creation as her virgin prototype. Mary and Joseph, Molly and Leopold, I want to say, are two of a kind.

For Joyce, fatherhood is a powerful sign of the paradoxical nature of reality. Similarly, Karl Barth, the Protestant theologian, saw in the mystery of Jesus' birth a sign of the ultimate nature of God. What was the meaning, Barth asked in his explication of the Creed, of "the miracle of the procreation of Jesus Christ without a father"? Mary's virginal conception of Jesus was not a sexual but a pneumatological act, an act of the Holy Spirit. As in Genesis, God's breath—"the pigeon," as Joyce notes—impregnates Mary. "God himself takes the stage as the Creator and not as a partner to this Virgin," Barth writes. Yet it is within a woman's body that this new creation and ultimate self-revelation of God takes form. Joseph, as said earlier, is pointedly "excluded." What then are we to make of the "powerless figure of Joseph"?

Barth regards Joseph's exclusion as a judgment. To the extent that "the male [is understood] as the specific agent of human action and history," such perishable human accomplishment is subordinated to God's power as creator and redeemer. Joseph as representative man is a symbol of all human vanity, of "the sovereignty of human will and power and activity generally." In this sense, perhaps it is as fathers—as worldly creators—that men are most tempted to imagine themselves self-sufficient and self-perpetuating. Both Joyce and the Bible suggest that such hubris is less a temptation for women, who in giving birth to all new life have a more realistic understanding of our connection and dependence on the source of life itself. (Barth does not argue that men are innately more creative or women immune to sin.) "In this sovereignty"—in this human longing for mastery and autonomy—"man is not free for God's Word." Only "when his sovereignty is excluded, he is able to believe in the Word of God."

Or the words of Joyce. Saint Joseph, like Leopold Bloom, remains a compelling figure because of the way he relinquishes sovereignty where we expect him to demand it most. In looking to either man, it is possible to see that what we pride ourselves on giving to others— our trust, fidelity, and love—is not ours to withhold; that what we receive in return is not ours to keep. Where at first we feel most excluded—"So where, exactly, do you fit in?" asked my wife—we are ultimately most at home. For, finally, we cannot make ourselves happy. Fulfillment must come from outside—it must come as a gift. That is the multifaceted paradox embodied in these two figures. Joseph and Bloom participate in the transcendent by the measure of their self-abnegation; they find reconciliation not in retribution or even justice, but through faith and love; they embrace human finitude as an affirmation of mystery, not its denial. They are most fully themselves, and their stories most open to a transcendent reality, when they are least self-regarding. Bloom asleep alongside Molly and Joseph alongside Mary are icons of hopefulness. That, at least, is what this husband and father takes away from their strikingly similar stories.

SAINT THOMAS
APOSTLE

Seen and Not Seen

PAUL ELIE

IN THE SUMMER of 1993 the Metropolitan Museum of
Art exhibited a pair of bronze sculptures by the Renaissance master Andrea del Verrocchio. Since 1483 the two
figures had stood in a cupola outside the Orsanmichele
in Florence, exposed to sun and moon, wind and rain,
chimney smoke and car exhaust, until their surfaces
were hardly visible under layers of grime. In 1988 they
were removed for restoration, and five years later they
were put on view at the Metropolitan, flanked by exhibits

that showed how they had been restored and how they had been cast in the first place, five centuries ago.

"Verrocchio's Christ and St. Thomas" was the sort of modest, unsung, scholarly exhibition that even the most ardent museum patron can miss without knowing the difference. I almost missed it myself. I had come to the museum intending to see the Magritte retrospective, but the line was a Sunday afternoon long, so I wandered into the cool dark rooms of medieval art, just looking. Here were works I knew well, shorn of wonder by their familiarity. I paid my respects and moved on. Farther in, the Lehman wing was brightly lit, and there the two figures loomed up like some medieval prophet's vision of the Renaissance beyond—Christ and Saint Thomas, a pas de deux in shining bronze. Christ's right hand was raised in blessing; his left one pulled his cloak away from his side so that Thomas, leaning toward him, might see the wound there, and touch it, and know him as the risen Lord.

I wasn't just looking anymore. Something majestic was being enacted in the next room. I went closer to see for myself—and I had an insight there, as Thomas had had in Jerusalem two thousand years before, and I remembered how he had become my patron saint when I was confirmed as a Christian once upon a time. But I am getting ahead of my story, and Saint Thomas's.

Thomas's encounter with Christ is one of the more familiar episodes in the New Testament. We have an account in chapter 20 of John's gospel. Over the centuries scholars have conjectured a great deal about the authorship of this gospel. Because it is thick with concepts from neo-Platonic philosophy, for centuries it was thought to be the gospel written last and embellished most—the gospel most remote from the experience of the apostles. But more recent scholars have argued that its idiosyncracies mark it as "authentic Jesus material." And no one has successfully dislodged the tradition that its first author was John the apostle, an eyewitness who recounts what he saw.

John tells us that on the evening of the day when Jesus rose from the dead—the first Easter Sunday—the apostles assembled in a room and barred the doors, afraid they would be persecuted. Yet Jesus came and stood among them. "Peace be with you," he said. Then he showed them his wounds. He breathed on them, and bid them receive the Holy Spirit (the Greek word *pneuma* means both "breath" and "spirit"). As the Father had sent him, he declared, so now he was sending them, and with power: as they forgave sins so sins would be forgiven, and as they retained sins so sins would be retained.

Here enters the apostle who will be known till the end of time as Doubting Thomas. We have seen him before. He appears in all four gospels, and in John's account he emerges as ardent but hesitant, like Peter but without the keys to any kingdom. When Lazarus died

and Jesus made plans to go to see Lazarus's sisters in
Judea even though he might be stoned there, Thomas
said: " 'Let us also go, that we may die with him.' "
Later, when Jesus tried to explain his destiny to the apostles, Thomas didn't understand, so he pressed the point,
prompting Jesus' boldest declaration about himself.
" 'You know the way I am going,' " Jesus said. But
Thomas didn't know, and he said so. " 'Lord, we do not
know where you are going; how can we know the
way?' " To which Jesus replied, " 'I am the way, the
truth, and the life.' "

This Thomas, John tells us, was absent from the
group on the evening after Jesus rose from the dead.
"Now Thomas, one of the twelve, called the Twin, was
not with them when Jesus came." In the days afterward,
the disciples told him they'd seen Jesus. But Thomas had
his doubts, and he knew what it would take to dispel
them. " 'Unless I see in his hands the print of the nails,
and place my finger in the mark of the nails, and place
my hand in his side,' " he told them, " 'I will not believe.'

"Eight days later," John continues, "his disciples
were again in the house, and Thomas was with them."
Again the doors were shut, yet again Jesus came and
stood among them and offered them peace. Now Jesus'
arrival might itself be a sign that he really had risen from
the dead. Remember, there were bars on the doors. But
Thomas still had his doubts, and rightly so, because if
what he doubted (and this is what John suggests) was

that the Jesus the others had seen was flesh and blood, a man walking and talking, he would hardly be persuaded by a figure who was able to pass through locked doors.

Prove it to me, this Thomas insisted. Show us what you're made of.

Jesus turned to him and said, " 'Put your finger here, and see my hands; and put out your hand, and place it in my side; do not be faithless, but believing.' "

We don't know whether Thomas reached out then, whether he pressed his finger in Christ's wounded hands and felt the gash over his ribs. All we have is his reply, and it is enough.

" 'My Lord and my God,' " Thomas said.

" 'Have you believed because you have seen me?' " Christ asked Thomas. " 'Blessed are those who have not seen and yet believe.' "

In the moment Christ speaks as if to all time: his words rise from the text to address us directly, a line cast in a long high arc across the centuries to fall at our end of the pond. *Blessed are you, dear reader, you who have not seen me and yet believe.* But it is the visual image of the encounter, not the words, that hooks the mind and sinks in and doesn't let go. Christ reveals himself. Thomas reaches out. The other disciples look on.

John's account of Christ and Saint Thomas is read at services in the days after Easter, and in the Catholic parishes I know, it is often presented as a footnote to the Resurrection—a story on a human scale, easier for the ordinary churchgoer to understand and identify with than the astonishing and theologically packed accounts of Jesus' passion, death, and rising from the dead. The priest will note that Thomas is also called Didymus, "twin" in Greek, and he'll make this the moral of the story: Doubting Thomas is the most ordinary of believers, a twin to us all.

In Verrocchio's "Christ and St. Thomas," though, the encounter is rendered literally larger than life. Christ and Saint Thomas crowd out of the cupola that would enclose them. They are giants, with broad shoulders and deep chests, draped in cloaks that fall over them fold upon bronze fold. Thomas is the proverbial innocent of antiquity, all apple cheeks and flowing hair. And Christ—well, he looks the way a man who has died and come back to life might look: his face is lined, his eyes are hooded, his hairline has receded, and there are jagged gouges in his hands where the sculptor who created him, like the men who crucified him, must have hammered spikes through.

Seeing "Christ and St. Thomas," one can understand why Verrocchio was a favorite of the Medicis and the teacher of Leonardo and Botticelli. And yet the grandeur of the two figures seems to derive from something other than Verrocchio's way with bronze. Other artists have depicted the episode's natural climax, and shown Thomas touching Christ's wounds. Verrocchio has presented instead the moment just prior to that one, when Christ shows his wounds to Thomas. This arrangement is known in Christian iconography as "The Incredulity of St. Thomas," and it is a subtle and profound approach to the story. The moment of truth comes not when truth is confirmed, but when truth is revealed. It is open-ended, undecided, still in progress.

In Verrocchio's work this moment of truth is made incarnate with power, and the notion that Thomas is our twin is given body and soul. That day at the Met, I was struck by the way Thomas's experience of revelation resembles the experience of the person who looks at Verrocchio's sculptures. Thomas has come to see something; in a different way, so has the museum patron. As if to stress this kinship, Verrocchio has shown Thomas leaning in from the lip of the cupola, keeping a foothold in the world outside it—our world—with the huge toes of his right foot.

You don't have to be an art historian to feel that kinship in your bones. And you don't have to be a believing Christian to suppose that it finally has to do with religious experience. Thomas leans close to examine Christ, and meets his God. The art lover steps up to see the work, and encounters Christ. Christ invited Thomas to see and believe, and so has Verrocchio, in a work packed full of the implications of seeing and revealing.

I spent nearly an hour with the two figures that Sunday afternoon at the Metropolitan. I looked at them from every conceivable angle, now straight on, now from one side, now the other, now up close, now from afar, as though I hoped to make the work's solidly classical proportions fragmented and cubist. And I looked at the other people clustered around the sculptures. Most of them considered the work itself for a few moments and then moved on to the ancillary exhibits arrayed around it. In time I joined them. Glass cases displayed models of Christ and Saint Thomas—the size of G.I. Joe dolls—to demonstrate the "lost-wax" casting process. A series of photographs showed the two sculptures in their original cupola outside the Orsanmichele, their surfaces a rheumy green, and then at various stages of the restoration— hung on winches, laid on worktables, attended to by experts in lab coats and protective eyeglasses. A documentary film played over and over on a television in a far corner, filling the gallery with the narrator's coolly authoritative voice.

The side exhibits were very interesting. There was something comforting in the way the models and photographs reduced the two figures to the scale of our own time, presented them as the subjects of chemical analysis and curatorial know-how. And yet I kept returning to the figures themselves. They held their poses in the cupola, caught forever in the act of encounter. Christ pulled his cloak away from his side. Thomas leaned toward him. So did I. I was in the mood to wonder.

Thomas struggled to see Christ with his own eyes—as flesh and blood, and as Lord and God. For this, the church has recognized him as the patron saint of people who suffer from blindness. That is wonderfully paradoxical. I would like to go further, though. I think we can recognize Thomas as a patron or type of all those who would reckon with Christ, and I think we can see his encounter with Christ as a definitive example of how that reckoning might come about.

No one today can see Christ the way Thomas did. We cannot be present in a locked room in Jerusalem in the first century, eating and praying and going over the events of the past week when Christ comes by. We cannot put our finger into the wounds in Christ's hands, or place our hand in his side. We cannot look him in the eye and say, "My Lord and my God." Christ himself seems to have acknowledged this when he called blessed those who have not seen and yet believe, and the New Testament is full of warnings to those who would see the divine. Thus Paul, who was blinded by lightning during his conversion, called faith "the substance of things hoped for, the evidence of things not seen," and observed that Christians must live by faith and not by sight.

Yet those who would believe in Christ must see him,

somehow, and must see him for who he is. Arguably this is the point of the Doubting Thomas story. If anyone is going to believe in Christ, he has got to reckon with him personally—see him with his own eyes. John, whose gospel is an account of what he has seen, tells how Thomas reckoned with Christ so that other would-be believers might be led to reckon with him themselves.

In itself that doesn't tell us much. For practically every passage in the gospels is a record of somebody's reckoning with Christ—as a son, a teacher, a healer, a feeder of multitudes; as a religious rebel, a threat to public order, and a convicted criminal; as a stranger on the Emmaus road, and as risen Lord and God, ascending to heaven but promising to return when the time is right.

Thomas's encounter with Christ occupies a special place in the gospels, though. Scripture scholars have proposed that John's gospel, traditionally placed last when the four are grouped, originally concluded with chapter 20, the account of Thomas and Christ being followed only by a brief coda: "Now Jesus did many other signs in the presence of the disciples, which are not written in this book; but these are written so that you may believe that Jesus is the Christ, the Son of God, and that believing you may have life in his name." Presented at the end of the gospel accounts, Christ's revelation of himself to Thomas at once sums up those signs and wonders we've read about and points toward those we can only imagine. And Thomas's response can be seen as a précis of the shape conversion might take in those who would see Christ with their own eyes. Doubt yields to faith; sight leads to insight, and then, God willing, to vision. Thomas seeks God, and in the risen Christ he finds him.

If we are latter-day twins of Doubting Thomas — as the priests tell us in church on the Sunday after Easter — we've got to wonder just how a person today might see Christ. And some of us must wonder just how we might see Christ ourselves, with our own eyes. How, how? Tell us. Show us. Let us know. Twenty centuries is a long time, and wayward history has accumulated on the figure of Christ like grime on a bronze giant; we look around us, and don't see signs and wonders but a broken world, a fractious people, and no end in sight, just length of days unfolding further and further away from the moment of truth. With Ivan Karamazov, we say: Sure, we would believe, if only we too could know Christ personally, as the apostles did, if only we could see for ourselves the miracles we're told he performed.

What must we see in order to believe? Where do we stand in relation to Christ and his contemporaries, such as Saint Thomas? Kierkegaard dwelt on these questions at length in *Philosophical Fragments,* weighing what he called "The Case of the Contemporary Disciple" against that of "The Disciple at Second Hand." As Kierkegaard saw it, the disciple who was a contemporary of Jesus (called "the God" in his text) had the great advantage of seeing him with his own eyes. "But may he also believe

that this makes him a disciple? By no means. If he believes his eyes, he is deceived, for the God is not immediately knowable." For Christ is knowable only through
faith, which is granted by God. Given this, the disciple
who had actually seen Christ probably found it *harder* to
believe as a result. "He is constantly reminded that he
did not see or hear the God immediately, but merely a
humble human being who said of himself that he was
the God."

For the disciple at second hand, things are harder in
some ways—but easier in others. Distant in time from
the events in Jerusalem, he must sift through all the
"gossip, chatter, rumors" and the like that have come to
surround Christ, and he is insulated from the shock of
Christ's appearing, which would make clear just how
radical a proposition faith in Christ is. To his advantage,
the notion that God walked the earth has been "natural-
ized" over time, and so in some ways has become easier
to believe. More important, this disciple's distance from
Christ in time reminds him that his stance toward Christ
is founded upon faith and not mere historical evidence.
Kierkegaard found a characteristically brilliant metaphor
for this: "Is not Venice built over the sea, even if it became so solidly built up that a generation finally came
upon the scene that did not notice it; and would it not be
a sad misunderstanding if this last generation made the
mistake of permitting the piles to rot and the city to
sink?"

Kierkegaard's point is that "all disciples are essentially equal." The contemporary disciple and the disciple of the last generation—our generation—stand in the same relation to Christ. We become his disciples—and his contemporaries—through faith.

Kierkegaard was a Lutheran and deeply iconoclastic, and these aspects of his character help to explain his insistence that Christ can be known through faith alone. In declaring his own contemporaries equals of Christ's through their faith, he could more or less take for granted that Christ had been made known to them through the churches and through a vigorous Christian culture—art, music, liturgy, philosophy—present in Denmark and the rest of Europe at that time.

This can no longer be taken for granted. Christ is still present in our culture, but even in the churches there is doubt about whether he ought to be, and even those who would see Christ are reluctant to be seen as Christians, to make him known. And much of Christian culture today seems to dispel faith rather than call it forth.

Someone once wrote that the church is Christ made visible. Here and now such a thought seems smug and dishonest, an echo from a presumptuous age. Yet if it can't be said that the church is Christ made visible, it can't be denied that the church should make Christ visible. That is its work in the world. And in these circumstances, the Doubting Thomas story makes clear that the act of seeing Christ is intimately connected with the act of making him visible. Witnessing and bearing witness are two parts of the same encounter, and one encounter with Christ gives rise to another.

That's the way it was in the church's beginning, with Christ's first disciples. Once they had seen Christ, they were compelled to make him visible to others. John explained this in the opening passage of his first letter, in words that call to mind Thomas's encounter with Christ: "That which was from the beginning, which we have heard, which we have seen with our eyes, which we have looked upon and touched with our hands, concerning the word of life—the life was made manifest, and we saw it, and testify to it ... that which we have seen and heard, we proclaim also to you." John made Christ visible by telling about him in his gospel, and through his account, Thomas's struggle to see Christ has become a way for others to see Christ for themselves.

We can see this in the Doubting Thomas story. After his rising Christ came by. The apostles saw him. They told Thomas. Thomas doubted. Then he came and saw him too. John was there. He saw it. And he let the world know.

Thomas himself went on to make Christ known to others as a missionary, according to the Christian tradition. He is said to have brought the gospel to parts of Persia, Syria, and India, where Christians on the Malabar coast have long called themselves "Christians of Saint Thomas." Tradition has it that he was martyred there, speared to death by an enemy of the gospel. His relics, according to Butler's *Lives of the Saints* (1759), have had a complicated journey: they were brought from Malabar to Edessa in Mesopotamia to the Aegean isle of Khios to Ortona, in the Abruzzi region of Italy, where they were still venerated in Butler's time.

The legends told of Saint Thomas are collected in works such as the third-century *Acts of Thomas,* which Saint Augustine dismissed as apocryphal, and *The Golden Legend,* a medieval collection of readings on the saints. In these legends, as in John's gospel, Thomas is ardent but hesitant. One tells how the apostles divided up the parts of the known world as destinations for their missionary work. India fell to Thomas, but he was reluctant to go there even after Christ appeared to him in a vision. "Send me anywhere but India," Thomas begged. Christ then appeared to an Indian king, Gundafor, and sold Thomas to him as a slave. (Christ as a slave trader? Clearly Thomas was to be a slave to the gospel.) When Thomas arrived in India the king asked him his trade, and learning that he was a carpenter, commissioned him to build a new palace. But while the king was away Thomas preached and taught instead, and gave the building funds to the poor.

From this point Butler's telling cannot be improved upon. "On his return Gundafor asked to be shown his

new palace. 'You cannot see it now, but only when you
have left this world,' replied Thomas. Whereupon the
king cast him into prison and purposed to flay him alive.
But just then Gundafor's brother died, and being shown
in heaven the palace that Thomas's good works had prepared for Gundafor, he was allowed to come back to
earth and offer to buy it from the king for himself. Gundafor declined to sell, and in admiration released Thomas
and received baptism together with his brother and many
of his subjects."

Here we have Thomas seen through the eyes of medieval Christendom. He balks about his work in the
world, but in his faith he is sure. Once, he had to see for
himself before believing; now, his eyes are on heaven,
his claim in things not seen.

Thomas appears more characteristically in a legend
of the Virgin Mary's Assumption. It is believed that upon
her death Mary was assumed into heaven, body and soul.
As the story goes, Thomas wasn't present at the bedside
when Mary died, and when the other apostles told him
what had happened to her, how she had gone, he
doubted it. But an angel appeared to him and dropped
into his hands the girdle Mary had worn; then, and only
then, did he believe.

It seems obvious that this legend is the Doubting
Thomas story adapted to suit a different miracle. Even
so, the legend suggests a religious truth: that even after

he had seen the risen Christ, Thomas had fits of unbelief. At the Cloisters one afternoon I came upon a fifteenth-century German wood carving of the legend which presents his predicament in splendid miniature. The other apostles—dressed like burghers—are shown gathered around Mary's deathbed, and through an open door the absent Thomas is seen scrambling up a rock precipice to where the angel dangles Mary's girdle above him. For Thomas, faith is an uphill climb; the signs are before his eyes but just out of reach.

Apocryphal, incredible, contrived to support a point of Marian doctrine, with Christ absent and an angel appearing at the moment of truth, the legend of Thomas and the girdle displays all the qualities that made the Protestant reformers suspicious of the saints, and that make us suspicious of them today. But the biblical account on which it is based suggests why the saints are vital to Christian belief in any age. Thomas's experience one Sunday in a locked room in Jerusalem presents in bold relief the would-be Christian's encounter with Christ. Thomas doubts, yes, but he seeks. He sees Christ for himself. He recognizes him as God. And once he has seen Christ, he makes Him known to others.

These are the essentials of the life of a saint, really any one. For whatever else they are, the lives of the saints are records of personal encounters with Christ

from his time down to ours. In them we can see the great
variety of ways people have seen Christ with their own
eyes, then gone on to make him known.

How unfortunate, then, that in an effort to emphasize
the need for a personal encounter with Christ the church
has come to doubt the usefulness of the saints. John Paul
II has canonized prolifically, but the church in North
America is unsure and even embarrassed about the
saints. Saints are present to us as statues or the occasion
for feast days, as symbols of ethnic solidarity or the stuff
of theological quandaries, but they generally are not seen
as people who sought God and in Christ found him
made known.

So it was that when it came time for me to be confirmed as a Catholic Christian a dozen years ago, I knew
almost nothing about the saints. I was sixteen, and my
family belonged to a suburban parish that seemed determined to symbolize American Catholics' emancipation
from the urban, ethnic, tradition-soaked enclaves typical
of the church earlier in the century. The parish church,
dedicated in 1963, was named not for a saint but for a
doctrine—the Assumption, which had been promulgated
only in 1950 (five hundred years after that German artist
depicted Saint Thomas scrambling up a rock face for
Mary's veil). It was (and is) built of red brick and shaped
like a seashell, the pews fanned out around the altar; in
the windows, pieces of stained glass had been cut into
triangles and diamonds and trapezoids and then com-

bined to form abstracted figures of Christ and the apostles. The pastor and his associates were decent, genial,
no-nonsense men who made the effort to make the gospel relevant to the parishioners' lives, and to leave out
the sticky accretions of history and culture, of Latin and
plainchant and scholastic theology—all the bars of the
cage from which, due to the Second Vatican Council, the
church and its people had just been sprung.

One priest who had worked in the parish was now
the bishop of the diocese, and he would return in the
spring to confirm several dozen of us in our faith. During
the winter we prepared for confirmation in weekly
classes organized around a workbook called *Making
Moral Decisions,* and in a retreat during which we were
asked to lie in the pews and pray. Then, one evening a
month before the date of the rite, we were told to return
the next week having picked a confirmation name, that
of the saint who would be the patron of our adult lives
in faith.

My father was waiting in the parking lot in his green
'74 Valiant, and as we drove home I explained the assignment. There was a problem, I told him. I didn't know
about any saints.

"Well," he said. "There's Saint Francis of Assisi, and
Saint Francis Xavier, the missionary, and Saint Bonaventure, the medieval theologian—the college in Buffalo is
named for him. There's Saint John, and there's Paul—but
you already have his name. And there's Saint Thomas—

Thomas Aquinas, the philosopher, and Thomas More, he was a martyr, and the apostle Thomas. Doubting Thomas."

"Right, right." He was naming the greatest saints, the most intellectual ones, I could tell, appealing to my exalted sense of myself. I appreciated the effort. He was missing the point, though, and I told him so. Here I was, supposedly ready to be confirmed, and I didn't know anything about those saints except what he told me. Wasn't it wrong to be confirmed in a faith I really didn't understand or even know much about? Wasn't that shallow and hypocritical, exactly what Jesus wouldn't want?

We were almost home. He turned down our road. The headlights flashed on the siding of the house on the corner.

"Maybe you're right," he said. "Maybe you're not ready to be confirmed after all." And then: "Maybe you don't believe."

"Maybe not," I said. "Maybe I never will."

"May be."

He pulled the car into the driveway and we went inside, and right away I called Eileen. She was my best friend, and I was in love with her—in love with the way she abandoned chemistry-lab procedures in favor of spontaneous public readings from *Look Homeward, Angel* and the *Norton Anthology of Poetry*.

I asked her if she knew what her confirmation name would be.

"Thomas," she said. "For Thomas Wolfe, because he's my saint, isn't he? It's supposed to be meaningful, the name is supposed to mean something to you. I don't care what they say. I'm going to be confirmed and my patron is going to be Thomas."

It was decided. I was going to be confirmed and my patron was going to be Thomas.

We were confirmed in our seashell church a month later, dozens of us, all with new names of obscure provenance. Eileen delivered the first reading, I, the second. After the gospel, the bishop performed the rite itself. He sat in a chair in front of the altar. We stepped up, one at a time. Eileen had learned that he disliked the prospect of confirming a girl in the name of Thomas, but she went right ahead, and so did he, etching the sign of the cross on our foreheads with his right hand.

What about the crisis of faith that had struck me as my father and I rode home from church in the green Valiant that evening? I hadn't resolved it. In a sense I never have, and don't fully expect to. But my father had told me what I needed to know. While he couldn't give me a crash course in the lives of the saints, he made clear that confirmation was an authentic sounding of my experience of Christ as I surged toward adulthood. My doubts were my own. My faith was my own. I was free to see Christ for myself, and it was up to me to reckon with him in the encounter. Thomas the apostle was my patron saint after all.

And what a patron. He is the patron saint of doubt-
ers, of those of us who find that belief and disbelief trade
places in the soul like watchmen taking shifts; he is the
patron saint of those who suffer from blindness, who try
as we might can't see as we ought. I want to go further,
though, to claim more. Thomas is the patron of all of us
who would try to see Christ for ourselves, who would
dare to draw close, to reach out and touch him and know
him as Lord. Thomas is our twin, yes—but more than
that he is Christ's twin, the human person Christ came
to make himself known for. One is of God, the other is
one of us, yet they are figures cast from the same bronze,
forever joined in an encounter, the end of the story still
waiting to be told.

Between "Point Vierge" and the "Usual Spring"

KATHLEEN NORRIS

For the birds there is not a time that they tell, but the *point vierge* between darkness and light, between nonbeing and being. You can tell yourself the time by their waking, if you are experienced. But that is your folly, not theirs.

—Thomas Merton, *Conjectures of a Guilty Bystander*

I FIRST CAME TO the virgin martyrs as an adult, and from a thoroughly Protestant background, which may explain why I have little trouble taking them seriously. I find them relevant, even important, but many Catholics I know so resent the way they were taught about these saints that they've shoved them to the back of the closet. "Why are you writing about the virgin martyrs?" one Benedictine sister asked me, incredulous and angry: "They set women back! As if in order to be holy, you had to be a virgin, preferably a martyr. And that's not

where most women are." Another friend relates, "In parochial school, we were taught things like, 'She sacrificed
her life to preserve her virginity,' and we thought, well,
why didn't she just give it to him—like a handbag? The
nuns never explained to us what virginity *was.* They
didn't want you to know exactly *what* you weren't supposed to give up, so you were regularly confused by
these cryptic narratives."

The women who provoke such irritation and puzzle-
ment, identified in the church's liturgical calendar as "virgin and martyr," were among the first women revered
by Christians as saints. Most date from the persecution
of Christians under the Roman Emperors Decius and Di-
ocletian in the third and fourth centuries, but they range
from second-century Rome to sixth-century Persia,
where Christians were persecuted by both Persian emperors and Jewish kings. They were a source of inspiration to Christians through the Middle Ages, but today
they are maddeningly elusive. There is no entry for "virgin martyr" in *The Catholic Encyclopedia,* and one can
search entries there, and in *The Encyclopedia of Early Christianity,* on both "virginity" and "martyrdom" without
getting a picture of these women or their importance in
church history. A secular reference, the *Women's Studies
Encyclopedia,* reveals that while the tales of early women
saints and martyrs (some of them virgins) have largely
been dismissed as legendary, historical sources do exist,
notably the *Ecclesiastical History* of Eusebius, written early

in the fourth century, and the third-century *Passion of Perpetua and Felicitas,* which is especially valuable because Perpetua's diary—our main source for the episode—is also one of the only examples of women's writing to come down to us from antiquity.

Growing up a Methodist, I envied Catholic girls their name days, holy cards, medals, and stories of women saints. I had few female images of holiness, except for the silent Mary of the crèche, and "girls of the Bible" stories sanitized for middle-class consumption. It was a far less textured and ambiguous world than that of a Benedictine sister I know who recalls two virgin martyrs among the many images of women in the windows of her childhood church. "There was Barbara, and Catherine, my namesake," she says, "which made me enormously proud. I found it inspiring that women could be saints. I also remember that my mother used to pray to Saint Barbara 'for a happy death,' which seemed a powerful thing." Like many girls of the 1950s, she was also invigorated by Ingrid Bergman in the film *Joan of Arc.* "After I saw that movie," she said, "I had my hair cut short, and walked around *being* Joan. I had no armor, of course. My uniform, all that summer, was a faded blue sweatshirt."

But for all their power to inspire a young girl, the virgin martyrs convey an uneasy message of power and powerlessness. They die, horribly, at the hands of imperial authorities. They are sanctified by church authorities, who eventually betray them by turning their struggle and witness into pious cliché, and even by lying about the causes of their martyrdom. It's enough to make one wonder if the virgin martyrs merely witness to a sad truth: Whatever they do, or don't do, girls can't win. A book published in the early 1960s, *My Nameday—Come for Dessert,* is a perfect expression of this heady ambiguity. Offering both recipes and religious folklore, the book defines virgin martyrs as young women "who battled to maintain their integrity and faith." But the radical nature of this assertion—that girls could have such integrity as to suffer and be canonized for it—is lost in Betty Crocker land: "St. Dorothy was racked, scourged, and beheaded in Cappadocia. Her symbols are a basket of fruit and flowers, which may be incorporated in a copper mold for her nameday dessert."

A girl named Dorothy, reading such prose, might conclude that the world (or a part of it called Cappadocia) is a very dangerous place. At least until dessert. Eventually she might discover that, more than most saints, the virgin martyrs expose a nerve, a central paradox of Christian history: While the religion has often justified the restricting of women to subservient roles, it has also inspired women to break through such restrictions, often in astonishingly radical ways. And the church, typically, has emphasized the former at the expense of the latter.

The story of Dorothy is beautiful, in a way. A young

woman who has refused a lawyer's proposal of marriage
is mocked by him as she is being led away to her execution. Her crime, as with most of the virgin martyrs, is
being a committed Christian who refuses to marry or to
worship idols as required under Roman law. The young
man calls out to Dorothy, asking her to send him fruits
from the garden of paradise. This she agrees to do.
When, after her death, an angel delivers three apples and
three roses, the young man converts to Christianity and
is also martyred. Dorothy, then, is a dangerous young
rebel, a woman with the power to change a man and to
subvert the Roman state, in which, as Gilbert Marcus has
noted in *The Radical Tradition,* "marriage and the family
were the basis of *imperium* . . . the guarantee of the gods
that Rome would continue."

Although the names of many of the young women
martyrs of the early church are known to us (Agatha,
Agnes, Barbara, Catherine, Cecilia, Dorothy, Lucy, Margaret), the political nature of their martyrdom has been
obscured by the passage of time and by church teaching
that glorifies their virginity, which we erroneously conceive of as a passive condition. For them, virginity was
anything but passive; it was a state of being, of powerful
potential, a *point vierge* from which they could act in radical resistance to authority.

The vigorous virginity of these martyrs has also been
muted by the language Church Fathers have used to describe them. Contrast an account of the sixth-century

slave Mahya—who ran through the streets of her south Arabian town of Najran, after her owners and family have been put to death, shouting: "Men and women, Christians, now is the moment to pay back to Christ what you owe him. Come out and die for Christ, just as he died for you.... This is the time of battle!"—with the words of Methodius of Sicily, in a passage still found in the Roman Breviary for the feast of Saint Agatha: "She wore the glow of a pure conscience and the crimson of the Lamb's blood for her cosmetics." While this imagery may have impressed Agatha's bravery upon Methodius's original ninth-century congregation, to us it just seems sick.

We live at the end of a century sickened by violence. Any claim we make to an enlightened modernity must be weighed against the fact that child prostitution is big business on a global scale; that most marriages in the world are arranged, as they were in ancient Rome, for economic and/or social advantage (the most advantageous being the selling of a young daughter to an older, wealthier man); that female infanticide and genital mutilation are still commonly practiced in many cultures; that in more civilized countries, the stalking, rape and often the murder of young women are staples not only of the nightly news but of dramatic entertainment. Maybe it's time to reclaim a *point vierge,* and try to hear what the virgin martyrs are saying.

The most recent virgin martyr to be officially sanctified by the church is Maria Goretti, a twelve-year-old who was stabbed to death during an attempted rape in 1902 by a man we would now term a "stalker." Maria Goretti was an Italian peasant from a town near Anzio, a girl in a vulnerable position, both economically and socially. Her father had died when she was ten, and, reading between the lines of the Roman Breviary ("she spent a difficult childhood assisting her mother in domestic duties"), we can assume that both child and mother were at the extreme margins of a marginal culture. For a young man to take advantage of such a situation is not unusual, nor is his resorting to violence when he is rebuffed. We understand these facts all too well, from similar events in our own day.

Maria Goretti, canonized in 1950, was the first virgin martyr declared such by the church for defending her chastity rather than her faith, and it's easy to see this development in a cynical light: a perfect expression of a sexually uptight era. Indeed, a popular pamphlet of the time, written by an American priest, dubbed her "the Cinderella Saint." But our cynicism blinds us to a deeper truth: A martyr is not a model to be imitated, but a witness, one who testifies to a new reality. And our own era's obsession with sexual "liberation" blinds us still further, making it difficult to see the true nature of Maria Goretti's witness, what it might mean for a peasant girl to "prefer death to dishonor." We may make fun of someone so foolish—a male friend recalls with shame

how he and his schoolmates snickered over Maria Goretti in the playground of his parochial school, not long
after she was canonized—but such joking is a middle-
class luxury.

For Maria Goretti, the issue was not a roll in the
hay. The loss of her virginity in a rigidly patriarchal
peasant culture could have had economic and social consequences so dire that it might well have seemed a choice
between being and nonbeing. And is it foolish for a girl
to have such a strong sense of her self that she resists its
violation, resists being asked to do, in the private spaces
of her body, what she does not want to do? When I was
fifteen, and extremely naive, I was attacked by a young
man, a college student, who I'm sure remembers the evening as a failed attempt at seduction. What I remember
is my anger, the ferocity of my determination to fight
him off. I know now that I'm lucky that I was able to
simply wear him out; another man might have beat me
unconscious and then raped me. It happens more than
we like to think, even to middle-class girls like me. But
the poor are far more vulnerable; perhaps the scandal of
Maria Goretti is the recognition that there can be bodily
integrity, honor, and even holiness among the poorest of
the poor—that even a peasant girl can claim an inner
self that no man can touch.

What we resist seeing in late-twentieth-century
America—where we are conditioned, relentlessly, by images of girls' and women's bodies as *available*—is how

fierce a young girl's sense of bodily integrity can be. Pre-pubescent and adolescent girls often express, as Robert Bolt writes of Saint Thomas More in his preface to *A Man for All Seasons,* "an adamantine sense of self." This is not necessarily a sure sense of who they are—in girls, this is still developing—but, rather, a solid respect for their physical boundaries. In the early Christian martyrs, this expressed itself as an unshakable faith in Jesus Christ, which enabled them to defy worldly authority. And, as Andrea Dworkin observes in a chapter on virgin-ity in her book *Intercourse,* each of the virgin martyrs "viewed the integrity of her physical body as synony-mous with the purity of her faith, her purpose, her self-determination, her honor."

The virgin martyrs make me wonder if the very idea of girls *having* honor is a scandal, and if this is a key to the power that their stories still have to shock us, and, even more important, to subvert authority, which now, as in the ancient world, rests largely in the hands of males. The genocidal excesses of our century have not dulled our capacity to be appalled by the brutality of the tortures inflicted on these young women. If anything, our era has made us more fully aware of the psychological dynamic of sexual violence against women that these sto-ries express so unconsciously, in raw form.

The story of the fourth-century martyr Saint Lucy of Syracuse is typical of the genre. At the age of fourteen (the median age for marriage in a culture that expected women to bear five children on average and die young, often in childbirth), Lucy was betrothed to a young pagan nobleman. Inspired by an earlier virgin martyr, Saint Agatha, Lucy refused him and gave her goods to the poor. Both acts marked her as a Christian, and as Agnes Dunbar's *A Dictionary of Saintly Women* (1904) recounts: "The young man to whom she was betrothed denounced her as a Christian before the governor, Pascasius, who spoke insultingly to her. As she openly defied him, he ordered her to be dragged away" to a brothel, that she might be raped there, "but it was found that neither strong men with ropes nor magicians with their spells could move her an inch; so Pascasius had a fire lighted to burn her where she stood; but as the flames had no power against her, one of the servants killed her by plunging a dagger into her throat."

Other versions of Lucy's story, like so many of these tales, provide detailed accounts of the verbal give-and-take between the martyr and the governing authorities, who are both enraged and frightened by the claim of the martyrs to an inviolable, divinely grounded sense of self. Saints Barbara, Catherine, Irene, and Margaret, among others, give speeches so replete with scriptural allusions that they amount to a form of preaching. Here is Mahya again, as Sebastian Brock and Susan Ashbrook Harvey describe her in *Holy Women of the Syrian Orient,* "castigating her torturers with a mighty freedom in the Spirit. . . . Publically stripped naked at the orders of the king,

Mahya yet holds to her dignity, boldly stating, 'It is to your shame . . . that you have done this; I am not ashamed myself . . . for I am a woman—such as created by God.' Had she finished her scriptural allusion," the authors note, "Mahya would have added, 'created by God in his own image,'" both male and female. Typically, such speech angers male rulers; an account of the Syrian martyr Euphemia states that "Priscus the Proconsul was troubled in his mind that he was overcome by a woman." And typically, the more the martyrs talk back, the more they mock those in power by their allegiance to Christ and his invincible power, the more frenzied is the male response, and the more the violence escalates. It's not pleasant reading, but it is good psychology.

It should come as no surprise that the virgin martyrs are both admired and feared for their intelligence, and for their articulate tongues; Catherine of Alexandria, for example, is the patron saint of philosophers because she converted the fifty philosophers who were sent to explain to her the error of her ways. No surprise, either, that they are often tortured by having their tongues torn out; it's one way to silence a woman. But a theme of many of the stories is the martyr's miraculous ability to remain lucid, even eloquent, throughout her tortures; to retain even the capacity for worship (expressed best in these memorable words: "plunged into a cauldron of burning pitch, she lived for three days, singing praises"). While this outrages the modern consciousness, it also demonstrates that the silencing of holy women is not easily accomplished.

Accounts of virgin martyrs are so full of what one critic has termed "imaginative chaff" that they've typically been dismissed by church historians, labeled "dubious," "spurious," "a farrago of impossibilities." To appreciate the relevance of the virgin martyrs for our own time, we need to ask not whether or not the saint existed, but why it might have been necessary to invent her; we need not to get hung up on determining to what extent her story has been embellished by hagiographers, but to ask why the stories were so popular in the early church, and also to contemplate what we have lost in denigrating them. A case in point is Thecla, a virgin and, by some accounts, a martyr of the second century. Her cult was officially suppressed by the Catholic Church in 1969—she is thought never to have existed—and few people other than scholars are aware of her today. But, as Englebert's *Lives of the Saints* informs us, "there was no more famous name in Christian antiquity."

One can easily see how Thecla's story would have appealed to women in a church that had begun to consolidate power in its male clergy. Converted to Christianity by the apostle Paul, she becomes an apostle herself. When Paul refuses to baptize her, fearing that because of her youth and beauty she will not remain celibate, Thecla baptizes herself. Paul, having learned his lesson, later commissions her to preach. Thecla is one of several miracle-working women mentioned in apocryphal acts of the apostles, and as scholar Gail Paterson Corrington writes in *Women in Early Christianity,* "the equality of the female convert to the male apostle is frequently demonstrated both by her assumption of his role and functions (teaching, baptizing, preaching) and by the continuity of her apostolic work without his assistance." In studying the relevance of the virgin martyrs for our own time, we might also note that belief in their power still shows up in surprising ways. As a Benedictine historian wrote to me, "I have always been struck by the inverse ratio of historical knowledge about a saint and the oral tradition. We know nothing about Agatha other than the tradition of her death during Decius' persecution in the East coast of Sicily." The monk continues, "But when I ran across a statue of Agatha in a Chicago fire station and a year later saw people in Catania, Sicily, invoking Agatha's intercession to keep Mt. Etna's lava at bay, I had to admit to an incredibly deep and broad current of tradition at work."

Ironically, it is by taking the virgin martyr stories at face value that we can best see the kernel of meaning that they contain, their wealth of possibility. Surely it is significant that the "acts" of these young women, based on the acts of the apostles, those in turn based on the actions of Jesus in the gospels, incorporated the hopes of an embattled and vulnerable Christian minority. Their stories often strike me as Christianity of the most radical sort; these seemingly powerless girls were able to do what Jesus did, and change the world around them. Irene, for example, a first-century martyr, raises her father from the dead after his attempt to kill her (by having her dragged by wild horses—a typical grotesquerie) results in his own death. She brings back a child from the dead, and later raises *herself* from the dead, an event which results in the conversion to Christianity of many thousands.

What may be most valuable for modern people in the accounts of virgin martyrs is the depth of psychological truth they contain. An account of Saint Barbara states that her father, a wealthy man, built "a strong, two-windowed tower in which he did keep and close her so that no man should see her great beauty." When Barbara escapes his control—surreptitiously baptized a Christian, she convinces the workmen to add a third window, so that she may meditate on the Trinity—her father's rage is without bounds. It is he who betrays her to government authorities for refusing to worship pagan gods. When their tortures, including a scourging and burning, do not work, but seem only to strengthen Barbara's resolve to pray, the men beat her with hammers and lop off her breasts. Finally, it is her father who drags her up a mountain by her hair and beheads her. He is then struck dead by lightning. A dysfunctional relationship, to say the least. In our day, Barbara and her dad might end up on the front pages, fodder for the true-crime market.

And where is Barbara's power in all this? The oddly satisfying logic of hagiographical construction makes her the patron saint not only of stonemasons, architects, and prisoners, but of electricians and artillery gunners—of anyone, in fact, in danger of sudden death. Here the depth of Barbara's radical subversion is made clear. While she is most commonly depicted holding her tower, she is also one of the very few women saints who is sometimes pictured holding the eucharistic elements, a chalice and host. A person in danger of dying without receiving the last rites from a priest may pray to Barbara, and it's taken care of; she replaces the priest, and the sacrament.

One would think that Barbara's priestly attributes, or those of Petronilla, a first-century martyr, whose "usual emblem," according to the *Oxford Dictionary of Saints,* is "a set of keys, presumably borrowed from St. Peter," would make them favorites of Catholic feminists; instead, like the other virgin martyrs, they are largely forgotten, considered an embarrassment by women still smarting from the prayers of the old Roman Missal, which managed to be both sappy and insulting in giving thanks that God "didst bestow the victory of martyrdom on the weaker sex." But to forget a martyr is to put her through another martyrdom. Eric Partridge's *Origins* gives as the

origins of our English word "martyr" both the Latin
memor (mindfulness) and the Greek *martus* (witness);
which suggests that when we are no longer mindful of
a martyr, we lose her witness, we render her suffering
meaningless.

I believe that the meaning, and the relevance, of the
virgin martyrs rests in what one scholar of the early
church, Francine Cardman, terms their "defiance of the
conventions of female behavior," a defiance that their belief in Christ made possible. Knowing that they were
loved by Christ gave them the strength to risk a way of
life that was punishable by death (under Roman law,
both a soldier's refusal to fight and a woman's refusal to
marry and breed for the Empire were treasonous of-
fenses). That the virgin martyrs have been betrayed by
the very church that sanctified them may be clearly seen
in the fact that, although they were executed for rejecting
marriage, by the Victorian age, when Christianity had
long been the dominant religion in the West, a scholar
translating stories of the virgin martyrs could label as
"unchristian" that which had made them Christian martyrs in the first place.

In a classic case of blame-the-victim, Agnes Smith
Lewis, writing in 1900 on the subject of Syrian martyrs,
seems shocked by their unladylike behavior, stating that
they "made themselves unduly obnoxious to the heathen,
and brought upon themselves and their friends a bitter
persecution, not only by their steadfastness in the faith

of the Christ, but also by their *unchristian* renunciation of the marriage bond; a teaching which, if successful, would have upset all respectable society, and put an end to civilization." (Italics mine.) This was exactly what the Romans had feared; what most offended their sense of family values. Lewis does express some sympathy for the martyrs, recognizing that "their alternative was to have been forced into loveless marriages with unsympathetic, and perhaps godless men."

In their stories, the virgin martyrs are usually betrayed by those closest to them: fathers, suitors, mothers. Over the centuries they have been betrayed, even sneered at, by their biographers, who turn the loveliest of their symbols into objects of derision. Take the tale of Juthwara, an English virgin martyr listed in *The Oxford Dictionary of Saints.* A young girl becomes gravely ill when her beloved father dies; she is duped by a conniving stepmother, who offers a remedy (for some no doubt thoroughly English reason, cheeses applied to the breasts) and then suggests to her son that Juthwara is pregnant. In the telescoped drama typical of these tales, when the young man finds Juthwara's underclothes moist, he immediately beheads her, and, the narrator notes, dryly, "The usual spring of water then appeared."

Juthwara patiently carries her head back to the church—the virgin martyrs are nothing if not persistent—shocking the young man into repentance. He eventually founds a monastery on a former battleground.

The narrator reports, saucily, that Juthwara's "usual emblem is a cream cheese or a sword." Once our laughter subsides, we might ask what message this tale carried to its original audience. We might look beyond the fairy-tale elements to a story of betrayal transformed into love, of a witness given that has the power to change lives, to transform a battlefield into a house of prayer.

Once again (or, as usual), a virgin martyr gives witness to a wild power in women that disrupts the power of male authority, of business as usual. Is this a *point vierge?* Do we need to speak now about the power of virginity? Current dictionary definitions of "virginity" are of little use in helping us to discover why, in legends of the Christian West, virginity has so consistently been associated with the power to heal, why the virgin spring is a place of healing.

The 1992 *American Heritage Dictionary* defines a virgin in terms of incompleteness, as "a person who has not experienced sexual intercourse." The adjective *virgin* is defined in a more revealing way, as a "pure, natural, unsullied state, unused, uncultivated, unexplored, as in virgin territory," a definition that allows for, and anticipates, use, exploration, exploitation. In *Intercourse,* Andrea Dworkin correctly sees such definitions as coming from a male frame of reference, in which "virginity is a state of passive waiting or vulnerability; it precedes and is antithetical to wholeness." But "in the woman's frame," she writes, "virginity is a fuller experience of selfhood and identity. In the male frame, virginity is virtually synonymous with ignorance; in the woman's frame, it is recovery of the capacity to know by direct experience of the world."

We so seldom hear virginity defined from a woman's point of view that it is shocking, and difficult for us to fathom. Here are the words of a Benedictine sister, startled to be asked about the power of virginity. This is "something I carry very deep within," she writes, "that I carry very secretly . . . virginity is centered in the heart and could be named 'singleness of heart.'" Now we are far indeed from our dictionary definition, and hearing virginity described not in terms of physicality but as a state of being. The sister continues, "Virginity is a state that returns to God in wholeness. This wholeness is not that of having experienced all experiences, but of something reserved, preserved or reclaimed for what it was made for. Virginity is the ability to stay centered, with oneness of purpose."

And now I am doing what I've often longed to do, what my education and cultural conditioning have trained me *not* to do: to bring the virgin and the whore together, only to find that they agree. The designation might seem brutal: Andrea Dworkin is not a whore, nor am I. But we were both formed sexually in the maelstrom of the 1960s, at Bennington College, and the point I am making is that the great lie (or lay) of sexual liberation expected us, conditioned us, to play the whore. This is not an idle metaphor. I knew a Williams boy—no doubt destined for great things in the corporate world— who regularly solicited at Bennington for his thriving business as a pimp. And a few years ago, when the movie *Pretty Woman* was a hit, an exceptionally bright and gifted fifteen-year-old girl I know attended a school Halloween party as the "pretty woman" character—a prostitute—and her parents, teachers, and friends considered it cute, not worthy of discussion.

I am grieving now for the girl I was back in the 1960s, who struggled with cultural definitions of a woman as someone attached to a man; who had to contend with a newly "liberated" definition of sexual freedom as that which made me more available to men. My response was to fear my own sexuality: mostly, I kept to myself and read books. Other girls expressed their fear by throwing themselves at men, often throwing themselves away. I grieve for the suicides, and for the girl I knew who survived, but with badly mutilated genitals. She had cut herself with a razor blade in a desperate attempt to rid herself of an exceptionally cruel and manipulative boyfriend. It took me a long time to see that with the peculiar logic of the mad, she had done something powerful (from the Latin "to be able to do things," to achieve a desired end). By damaging the only part of herself that was valuable to her boyfriend, she managed to get rid of him, and also received the psychiatric help she needed to become her own person.

I think of this girl as a virgin martyr, though she was neither a virgin nor a martyr by the dictionary's definitions. She may represent another kind of virginity, what Dworkin has termed "the new virginity, a twentieth-century nightmare," based on the belief that "sex is freedom." Now, Dworkin writes, the blood demanded of us is "not the blood of the first time [but] the blood of every time," expressed in increasingly violent images in both pornography and the fashion industry, and in bodily mutilation as fashion.

What might it mean for a girl today to be like the early virgin martyrs, to defy the conventions of female behavior? She would presume to have a life, a body, an identity apart from male definitions of what constitutes her femininity, or her humanity. Her life would articulate the love of the community (be it a family, a religious tradition, Christian or otherwise) that had formed her, and would continue to strengthen her. And she would be virgin, in the strongest possible sense, the sense Methodius had in mind when he said of Saint Agatha: "She was a virgin, for she was born of the divine word."

What about the virgin martyrs? Do they set women back? Do they make room for the majority of women, who are not virgins but mothers? The Benedictine sister spoke of virginity as something "reserved, preserved or reclaimed for what it was made for." In reclaiming our virginity, we women can reclaim our first selves. We can allow the fierce, holy little girls we were to cast judgment

on the ways our adult lives do and do not reflect what
we were made for. If the Catholic Church chose, for its
own purposes, to suggest that a holy woman need be a
virgin, preferably a martyr, that is not our problem. As
Thomas Merton observed, birds do not tell the time.

We can reclaim our own saints—Wilgefortis (or
Uncumber), for example, a virgin martyr who just may
be an example of earthy, feminist humor. To avoid an
arranged marriage, she grew a beard (a crime for which
her father had her crucified), and since then she has
served to help married women become unencumbered of
evil husbands. All you need is a prayer and a peck of
oats. And there is Saint Perpetua, that martyr of early-
third-century Carthage, breast-feeding her child in prison
before being fed to the lions; and the aged deaconess
Apollonia, seized by a crowd that beats her, breaks her
jaw, and tears out her teeth. The issue here is not physical virginity, but the status of unprotected women whose
outrageous claim—to have been made in the image of
God—was greatly feared by governing authorities and
punished to the full extent of the law.

We can use these stories to remember the extent to
which women have always been feared by male authorities, to better recognize the ways that this fear translates
into violence against women. We can remember that no
woman is safe, or respectable, once she claims for herself
the full psychic power of virginity. The noblewoman
Ruhm responds to news of the massacre of her husband

and other Christians in her town by walking bareheaded with her daughter and granddaughter into a public square: "She, a woman whose face no one had ever seen outside the gate of her house," gives a speech so powerful that the king is shaken by it. He wants to execute all the townspeople "for letting her go on at such length and thus lead the town astray." When Ruhm refuses to deny Christ, the king has her put to death, but not before he has killed her daughter and granddaughter and poured their blood into her mouth.

That story comes from sixth-century Syria; a witness to a horror closer to us may be found in a *New Yorker* article by Mark Danner about a massacre that occurred in December of 1981 in El Salvador, in the hamlet of El Mozote. Most of the peasants killed were evangelical Christians, and among the stories the soldiers told, years later, was that of a young girl, a story remarkably similar to accounts of the virgin martyrs:

> There was one in particular the soldiers talked about that evening (she is mentioned in the Tutela Legal report as well), a girl on La Cruz whom they had raped many times during the course of the afternoon, and through it all, while the other women of El Mozote had screamed and cried ... this girl had sung hymns, strange evangelical songs, and she had kept right on singing, even after they had done what had to be done,

and shot her in the chest. She had lain there on La Cruz with the blood flowing from her chest, and had kept on singing—a bit weaker than before, but still singing. And the soldiers, stupefied, had watched and pointed. Then they had grown tired of the game and shot her again, and she sang still, and their wonder began to turn to fear—until finally they had unsheathed their machetes and hacked through her neck, and at last the singing stopped.

One wonders: will the "usual spring" appear on the site where she died? Will this strange story of a powerless young girl who has the power to make soldiers afraid be embellished over the years, as the soldiers try to live with the horror of what they have done? This nameless girl has made her witness: it began when the soldiers' wonder began to turn to fear; and continued as they argued afterwards about her death. She had brought them to the *point vierge,* where conversion begins in the human heart.

"Some declared that the girl's strange power proved that God existed," Danner writes. "And that brought them back to the killing of the children. There were a lot of differences among the soldiers about whether this had been a good thing or whether they shouldn't have done it." Sometimes it takes a death to make us see the obvious. Sometimes it is a fierce little girl who is hard to kill, who gives witness to a mystery beyond our understanding and control. And in the wild center of that young girl's heart, we glimpse love stronger than death, a love that shames us all.

Good Friday, 1994

SOURCES

Brock, Sebastian P. and Susan Ashbrook Harvey, *Holy Women of the Syrian Orient* (Berkeley: University of California Press, 1987).

Brown, Peter, *The Body and Society: Men, Women and Sexual Renunciation in Early Christianity* (New York: Columbia University Press, 1988).

Cardman, Francine, "Acts of the Women Martyrs," Gail Paterson Corrington, "The Divine Woman," and other essays by JoAnn McNamara, Elizabeth Clark, Ross Kraemer in Everett Ferguson, David M. Scholer, and Paul Corby Finney, *Studies in Early Christianity* (New York: Garland Publishing Co., 1993).

Clark, Elizabeth A., *Women in the Early Church* (Wilmington, DE: Michael Glazier, 1983).

Danner, Mark, "A Reporter at Large: The Truth of El Mozote," *The New Yorker,* December 6, 1993.

Dunbar, Agnes B. C., *A Dictionary of Saintly Women* (London: George Bell & Sons, 1904).

Dworkin, Andrea, *Intercourse* (New York: Free Press, 1987).

Englebert, Omer, *The Lives of the Saints* (New York: Collier Books, 1964).

Farmer, David Hugh, *The Oxford Dictionary of Saints* (Oxford: Oxford University Press, 1982).

Ferguson, Everett, ed., *Encyclopedia of Early Christianity* (New York: Garland, 1991).

Grubbs, Susan Evans, "Saints and Martyrs (Women) in Early Christianity," in *Women's Studies Encyclopedia,* vol. III, *History, Philosophy, Religion* (New York: Greenwood Press, 1991).

Lewis, Agnes Smith, trans., *Studia Sinaitica No. X: Select Narratives of Holy Women from the Syro-Antiochene or Sinai Palimpsest* (London: C. J. Clay and Sons, 1900).

McLoughlin, Helen, *My Nameday—Come for Dessert* (Collegeville, MN: The Liturgical Press, 1962).

McNamara, Jo Ann, *A New Song: Celibate Women in the First Three Christian Centuries* (Binghamton, NY: Harrington Park Press, 1985).

Marcus, Gilbert, *The Radical Tradition: Revolutionary Saints in the Battle for Justice and Human Rights* (New York: Doubleday, 1993).

New Catholic Encyclopedia (Washington, D.C.: Catholic University, 1967).

Our Patron Saints. With Prayers and Indulgences (New York: John Crawley & Co., 1963).

The Roman Martyrology (Baltimore: John Murphy Co., 1916).

Our Lady of Guadalupe and the Soup

NANCY MAIRS

TAKING AN UNFAMILIAR SHORTCUT through a residential neighborhood on Tucson's west side, my husband screeches to a halt and throws the van into reverse, bobbing me around like one of those dashboard puppies in my wheelchair in the back. "Look at that!" George cries, pulling up beside a mural depicting La Virgen de Guadalupe painted on a hole-in-the-wall grocery, La Tiendita, at the corner of two empty streets. "Isn't that wonderful!" Such wall art is common here, especially in the barrios, and it often features La Guadalupana, as do

jewelry, scarves, and other articles of clothing, and even
the hoods of automobiles. This is a relatively crude pro-
duction, not signed: the figure faces the wrong direction,
and most of the significant details are missing. But she
stands upon the head of a truly glorious fanged serpent,
painted a violet so intense that it shivers in the opales-
cent light of an overcast winter day in the desert, surrounded by scowling brown pre-Colombian heads. The
overall effect is exuberant and, indeed, wonderful, a treasure stumbled upon in haste.

Perhaps because we're in a hurry, it doesn't occur to
me until hours later, as I settle in to begin this essay, that
I am, both aesthetically and spiritually, not the woman I
used to be. I was certainly brought up to know that the
colors in that mural clashed. Except the brown, of
course—but oh! those hideous lowering profiles with
their huge noses and pendulous lips! And besides, images
of saints, even those painted in the most delicate pastels,
though marginally tolerable in museums, simply weren't
to be put on display in the everyday world. The Mary
on the Half Shell decorating a front lawn, the pale plastic
statue on a dashboard ("I don't care if it rains or freezes,
'long as I got my plastic Jesus . . ."), the Saint Christopher medal around a traveler's neck: revolting! And now
here I am admiring a garish Virgin painted on a public
wall. I guess that shows what Catholicism—even a relatively late conversion—can do to you.

On the whole, I do not regret my Protestant girlhood. With advancing age and accelerating physical debility, I have gotten out of the habit of regret. The alternative, I am afraid, would drive me mad, and I no longer wish to go mad, a state I endured with horror during my Protestant youth, not ever again. And anyway, the memories of Catholic girlhood I've read and listened to suggest that although I missed a great deal, most of it wasn't the sort of experience to be coveted. I've known woman after woman of my generation who still seethes about some elements of her religious upbringing: obtuse and even abusive nuns and priests who wielded church doctrine along with yardsticks or birch switches to intimidate their young charge, inculcating superstition and self-hatred so poisonous that, even after decades at a safe distance, she still can't speak of those dreary years without a frisson of revulsion. In the long run, Congregationalism left me a little flat, all the mystery scrubbed out of it by a vigorous and slightly vinegary reason, but hardly furious.

All the same, I do wish (and in this I may be more curious than rueful) that it had offered me the Blessed Virgin Mary. Or any feminine figure, for that matter. It may not have been altogether wholesome for a girl to grow up venerating women who leaped out of coffins and soared to the rafters to escape the stench of human flesh, like Saint Christina the Astonishing, or in response to compliments on their beauty rubbed pepper on their faces and lime on their hands, like Saint Rose of Lima.

But another kind of soul-sickness, even more enervating in its way, arises in those deprived of any sense of identity with the divine. In Congregationalism I encountered a rather abstract but unequivocally masculine God and, of course, His Son, as well as a Holy Ghost, suitably attenuated and untainted by any association with Sophia. No saints, except the guys who composed the Christian Scriptures. And no holy representatives on earth, except maybe the minister, who was invariably—and without question—a man.

Prayer, within such a structure, was always to an Other, who could be counted on to judge but not always to understand, if you had your period, say, and needed the cramps to stop, or if you were crazy in love with your boyfriend and wanted more than life itself to go all the way and had no idea where you were going to find the strength to say no. This latter situation was especially troublesome, since in Congregationalism the loss of one's virginity was strictly prohibited without any notably spiritual point being put upon the matter. Since the King James Version, like others, reproduced the mis-translation *parthenos,* "virgin," for the Semitic term for a young unmarried woman, we referred to Jesus' mother as the Virgin Mary when we referred to her at all, which wasn't all that often, but no one ever suggested to me that I should preserve my virginity in order to emulate her chastity and obedience to God. No, mine was being "saved" for the husband I would inevitably have (though it wasn't until I discovered feminist theory twenty years later that I figured out why society thought it important enough to save). Not just her virginity, however, but also her motherhood would have provided a valuable model, in my struggles as a daughter and, not many years later, a mother myself.

Because I sensed a mysterious element here for which the utter virility of the Congregationalist godhead failed to account, from early adolescence onward I coveted the saints, what little I could gather about them from books and films, having no Catholic friends, and especially Mary, whose multiplicity—maiden and mother intertwined—authenticated the personal mysteries I was destined to experience yet feared to endure without guidance. Her presence, if I could make it real in my life, could create spiritual space not for the encounter of God and man but for the bond between the holy and me.

Sometimes when alone I'd cross myself and murmur a Hail Mary, which I must have learned young from hearing the Rosary prayed as I twiddled the radio dial, and this habit persisted as I grew older. I did not pray to the Madonnas I studied in art class in college, but I contemplated their images—the severe dark skinny Byzantines, the luminous Italians—until they became a permanent part of my interior furnishings. Although I later named my daughter for my mother, I knew that the name Anne had belonged to Mary's mother, too. At last, I began to walk boldly into Catholic churches, forbidden

me in my youth, staring—amused, awed, appalled—at
painted statues got up in silk and stiff lace with browning
bridal bouquets at their feet. In these ways, I suppose, I
was preparing myself for the conversion I would eventually choose, whereby I claimed her for my own.

I don't know whether I'd have become a Roman
Catholic had I remained in New England. But if I had, I
feel certain that I would never have developed a devotion
to Our Lady of Guadalupe. In fact, I'd probably never
even have heard of her. In the area around Boston where
I grew up, Catholic parishes tended to be identified eth-
nically. The Irish who went to St. Jude's would never
have strayed into the Italian—or Portuguese or Polish
or French-Canadian—Sacred Heart across town. Even
though Pope Pius XII designated Our Lady of Guadalupe "Empress of the Americas"—from Eagle, Alaska,
to Tierra del Fuego, North, Central, and South—in
1945, only a church attended by Mexicans or Mexican
Americans would likely be dedicated to her. And certainly none would be in Enon, Massachusetts. (Of the
106 such churches in the United States as of 1980,[1] I
doubt that any are in Massachusetts.) To find her, I really
did have to move to the Southwest.

This matter of ethnicity has been a tangled one, right
from the moment of her first apparition, on December 9,
1531, a decade or so after the Spanish conquistadores
came to this continent, a long enough span for the native

people who had greeted them as gods to figure out that they were human beings, and rapacious ones at that. In this bitter context, on Tepeyac Hill, at the edge of what is now Mexico City (a site already sacred to Tonantzin, snake woman and mother of gods[2]), an early convert to Catholicism, a Nahua named Juan Diego, was waylaid on his way to Mass by the sound of sublime music, perhaps birdsong. A young woman appeared and addressed him, using the affectionate diminutive "Juanito," little John. She was, she told him, the Virgin Mary, Mother of the True God, and she wanted a sanctuary to be built on that spot. He must take her message to the bishop of Mexico, Fray Juan de Zumárraga.

The bishop was polite enough, but skeptical, Juan Diego reported back to the Virgin, begging her to replace him with someone more eminent, and therefore more credible, than a peasant; but she wouldn't hear of it, and so he dutifully trudged back the next day to try again. This time Fray Zumárraga, still polite, asked for a sign, which the Lady promised to give Juan Diego the following day. Juan Diego's uncle fell ill, however, and Juan Diego stayed at home to care for him. On December 12, as he set out to fetch a priest to administer the last rites to his uncle, now dying, he was so chagrined to have missed his appointment that he tried to sneak around another way, but the Lady appeared nevertheless. Promising that his uncle would live (and indeed she appeared to the sick man and raised him from his death-bed), she sent Juan Diego up the barren hill to pick roses. These he bundled into his tilma, a cloak woven of fiber from the maguey plant, and carried to the bishop. When he unfolded the tilma, letting the roses tumble at Fray Zumárraga's feet, imprinted on it was an image, four feet eight inches high, of the Lady whom Juan Diego and his uncle had seen. The astonished bishop did as he'd been asked.

Despite the fragility of cactus fiber, the tilma still exists—preserved after 1647 under glass, though it hung open to candle smoke and the lips and fingers of worshipers until then—in the Basilica of Our Lady of Guadalupe, second only to Rome as a center of pilgrimage in the Catholic world,[3] in northern Mexico City. The image it bears has been associated with miracles, beginning with the healing of Juan Diego's uncle and including the end of a flood in 1629 and of a plague in 1736.[4] In modern times, the artifact has received scientific scrutiny. Infrared photography, one biophysicist claims, reveals an original and quite simple image that is, in terms of the media used, "unexplainable as a human work,"[5] overlaid by later additions, perhaps to repair damage from the 1629 flood. Five ophthalmologists signed a certificate stating that, on examining the portrait's eyes with their instruments, they found themselves "looking into a human eye."[6] Even more astounding, those eyes have been found to contain the reflected images of Juan Diego, as he appears in a contemporary painting, together with his interpreter and an unidentified third person.[7]

Thanks perhaps to a persistent Protestant intractability, I have an uneasy relationship with the miraculous. In fact, the notion of a miracle as an act of God for my benefit, which seems to underlie the use of the word by the devout, embarrasses the hell out of me. When a woman tells me that she has just escaped death because, at the last moment, God deflected an onrushing car off the road and into the desert, I wonder how she accounts for all the collisions that do take place. Does God find those people unworthy of rescue? Or does God blink? Even though my joyous life is made possible by a miracle, George having survived metastatic melanoma for some years now, and even though the wailing infant in me petitions constantly *Dear God please please don't ever let him die and leave me,* I prefer not to look on his good health as a special favor from the Almighty lest I should, at remission's end, be forced to believe myself personally abandoned.

And so my mind scuttles away from flood and pestilence and La Guadalupana's mysterious eyes. With the political features of her manifestation, however, I can engage quite comfortably. In *indigenista* terms, her image and message clearly inform the issues of social justice that first drew me into Catholic practice and, against all

odds, sustain me there. The figure, according to this in-
terpretation, encodes the concepts necessary to effect the
conversion of eight million Indians in the seven years
following the apparition.[8] (The desirability of becoming
a Catholic is a moot point, I recognize, today as four
centuries ago, but I won't get into it here. What's done
is done.) To begin with, "Guadalupe" is probably a mis-
translation, influenced by the shrine in Spain, of the
name she spoke when she appeared to Juan Diego's uncle; she might more accurately be referred to as Our
Lady of Tepeyac. Several Náhuatl alternatives have been
suggested, the most widely accepted being "Coatlaxopeuh," that is, "she who crushed the serpent's head"[9]
which suggests the overpowering of the native gods by
Christianity.

The icon itself reinforces this idea. It represents a
woman with dark skin and hair (La Morenita, she is
therefore sometimes called), her eyes downcast, in contrast to the straightforward gaze of Indian gods, and her
hands raised before her in an Indian offertory gesture.
She wears a rose-colored shift filigreed in gold, and over
it a cloak of blue-green, a color reserved for the chief
god Omecihuatl, or Ome-Téotl, scattered with gold stars
auguring a new age. The black maternity band at her
waist signifies someone yet to come, and below it, over
her womb, may appear the powerful Mesoamerican cross
to suggest just how mighty that Someone will be. The
rays surrounding her form show her eclipsing the Sun

Lord Tonatiuh; and the blackened crescent beneath her feet may be a phase of Venus, associated with Quetzalcóatl, the sacred Plumed Serpent. Hence the appropriateness of the name Coatlaxopeuh. She is borne by an intermediary "angel," the carrier of time and thus of a new era.[10]

Some of these signs seem hardly less fanciful than do miraculous remedies and mysterious ocular reflections, but that's not really their point. Their power lies in the suggestion that the Virgin appeared, long before the establishment of political boundaries in the "New World," to indigenous people whose old world had begun to crumble even before the Spanish invasion; she may thus signify both the "liberation and salvation" their prophets had predicted and the new spirit early Christian missionaries hoped to find here.[11] In this sense, she is a thoroughly American[12] saint, and her relegation by U.S. Catholics to Mexico and the Southwest, identifying her dark-skinned image with "an economically and socially unsuccessful and, hence, unacceptable ethnic group,"[13] probably does reflect bias against a minority woefully underrepresented among the clergy.

Ironically, however, this possibility strengthens her appeal for those of us, whether of Mexican heritage or not, who believe, as Virgilio Elizondo puts it, that "the role of the powerless is to evangelize the powerful."[14] A reviewer of one of my books once took me to task for accepting the tenets of feminist and liberation theology merely on faith, as though one could not possibly, after long contemplation and appraisal, continue to affirm them. But God's preferential option for the poor—expressed at least as far back as Isaiah's cry for the protection of widows and fatherless children—rings true to my understanding of the Christian ethos. I must accept it, both on faith and on reflection, and act upon it if I am to carry out God's will. And in the tale of a dark-skinned peasant carrying to the conquistadores for their veneration the image of a dark-skinned Lady who promised her compassion to all humanity (even, I must suppose, the conquistadores) lies a model of the care I am, I believe, required to give.

She entered our urban, white, middle-class lives slowly. George and I had converted to Catholicism not for its saints but in spite of them; and not knowing quite what to do with them, we politely ignored them, the way you might some atavistic eccentricity in an otherwise sophisticated friend. This is rather hard to do if, every week of your life, you ask Blessed Mary Ever Virgin, all the angels and saints, and your brothers and sisters to pray for you to God. Clearly these holy figures were integral to spiritual health in a way we didn't quite fathom. Still don't, I might add, and probably never will. When I hear my elderly friends talk about Our Blessed Mother, I suspect you may have to be brought up Catholic to fully apprehend the role of an intercessor in devotional life. I

still tend to talk to God directly, a habit fixed by the time
I was thirteen, and probably nowhere near as courteously
as Our Blessed Mother would do for me.

Rather than a repository of prayer, Our Lady of
Guadalupe was initially for me an exhorter to social action. In order to avoid being shut down by resentful
neighbors, Casa María, the Catholic Worker house of
hospitality in Tucson, was consecrated to her. The
kitchen there is known as Our Lady of Guadalupe
Chapel and Free Kitchen, and any tramp in the city can
probably direct you to "Guadalupe's," identifiable by a
brilliant painting of her on the wall beside the front door,
where a sack lunch with soup is offered every day and
Mass on Monday mornings. As George and I became increasingly involved in the community there, we began to
think of her as the guardian of the thousand and more
pobrecitos who lined up each day to be fed. And so it
seemed natural, when our daughter left us to live in Africa, to light a candle in the lady chapel of our church
after Mass each week and ask her to watch over Anne as
her human parents could no longer do.

For my birthday one year George gave me a framed
poster of her image. "What on earth will Mother say?" I
wondered as we hung this icon on the bedroom wall.
"Next thing you know, we'll be getting statues!" Sure
enough. Above me as a write, in a niche formed by an
old cooler duct, stands a porcelain Virgen (too white, but

I was politically ignorant all those years ago when I bought her) surrounded by two garish plastic flowers made at a local senior center and the likenesses of the Dalai Lama, Dorothy Day, and the deep-blue Medicine Buddha. Now she is everywhere in our lives: on the painted tiles outside the front door; on a plaque enameled by Salvadoran refugees in Guatemala, where the hill she stands on is dotted with animals, including a fat armadillo; as a crude little figure carved out of wood, the rays around her formed out of yellow toothpicks. I even have her likeness hand-painted on a T-shirt by a Casa María worker, holding a soup ladle and a white Styrofoam cup. Nuestra Señora del Caldo, I call her. Our Lady of the Soup. Glimpses of these images each day as I move from task to task serve to remind me to be grateful for the gift of roses in midwinter and to pray for the protection of us all.

Now I wonder how I can locate the painter of that Lady and her resplendent serpent outside La Tiendita. I have this wide blank cream-colored wall to the right of my studio door. . . .

Notes

1. Philip E. Lampe, "Our Lady of Guadalupe: Victim of Prejudice or Ignorance?," *Listening: Journal of Religion and Culture* 21 (1): 9.
2. James E. Fiedler, reprint from the *Denver Catholic Register*, December 7, 1977.

3. J. T. Meehan, S.J., *Guadalupe Our Mother* (Washington, NJ: Blue Army of Our Lady, 1970), 5.

4. Robert Feeney, *Mary, Mother of the Americas* (Ligouri, MO: Liguori Publications, 1984), 19.

5. Ibid., 21.

6. Harold J. Rahm, S.J., "Our Lady of Guadalupe," pamphlet, no publishing information.

7. Meehan, 7–11.

8. According to Rahm's pamphlet.

9. Miguel Leatham, "*Indigenista* Hermeneutics and the Historical Meaning of Our Lady of Guadalupe of Mexico," *Folklore Forum* 22 (1/2), 30.

10. I have extracted these details from Fiedler and Leatham.

11. Fiedler.

12. A term only residents of the United States would arrogate exclusively to themselves.

13. Lampe, 11, 12.

14. Quoted by Fiedler.

The Exemplar

MARTIN E. MARTY

"SAINT DOROTHY, hear our prayer and pray for us!" One might expect to hear such an utterance in a largely African-American parish church on South Eberhart Avenue in Chicago. One expects to hear saints evoked by name at parishes named after them, and this one is Saint Dorothy's. Yet Saint Dorothy is not a household name, and may not even be at the church named for her. In this case, as so often, Catholics have a teaching opportunity when someone asks a question. So we picture a child in that church asking "Who is Saint Dorothy?"

A teacher, priest, nun, or informed parent could answer: Dorothy lived long ago—sixteen hundred years—and far away from Africa or America, in Cappadocia. Her legend says that she would not bring an offering to the gods. The governor therefore had her tortured and sent her off to be executed.

On the way to her death Dorothy, "gift of God," met Theophilus, "friend of God," who made fun of her. She had said she was going to a beautiful garden. Scornfully he asked if she would send him some fruit from it. Dorothy did: while she was kneeling to be killed, she prayed. An angel brought three roses and three apples. The martyr-to-be sent these to Theophilus, saying she would meet him in the garden. He was converted. Wouldn't anyone have been? And she was canonized and received her day, February 6.

The child hears of Dorothy through a story that even the keepers of the books on saints call "apocryphal." She stores it in her mind along with all the other fairy tales and goes back to play, entertained, unmoved, ready figuratively to cross her fingers when she next prays. No roses, no apples for her.

Try another Dorothy. "Saint" Dorothy Day. Picture a church named after her in a poor section of any city. New York or Chicago, Detroit or Los Angeles would do. Tell the child that this Dorothy has a day, November 8, her birthday. She also comes from long ago, having been born in 1897. Day died in 1980, which in the mind

of the historyless urban young might as well have been
303, the presumed death date for the other Dorothy.

All saints are "other," and we tend to like them and
stories about them because of their difference from our
world and ways. Saints always come from far away, usually in time and space but also in their achievements. The
African-American child, or any child of today for that
matter, would need to use one kind of imagination to
grasp the world of the old Saint Dorothy, the kind children use when television presents them with stories of
wonder and fantasy. The new Saint Dorothy, were she
to be canonized, belongs almost to our time and lived in
cities like our own, but she also is "other," different, and
in many ways distant.

The legend of the new Dorothy needs no roses and
apples, though Miss Day helped plenty of hungry people
who stood in lines selling apples during the Depression,
or waiting for soup at one of the Houses of Hospitality
she helped set up and run. This legend needs no miraculous angels, though the survival of her Houses suggests
that some must have been near. The odds were always
against all of Dorothy Day's projects.

The modern Dorothy never had to kneel for execution, though she was capable of making good enemies.
She was a prophet—she would have cringed at the word
"prophetess," and abhorred prophetic tags—but nowadays, as they say, we do not stone the prophets. We
invite them to dinner, and dull their rough edges to do-

mesticate them. We try to make them like us, or likable to us. We even do see some of them canonized as saints. No martyr, our new Dorothy died peacefully in her sleep, her fifty-three-year-old daughter, Tamar Teresa, mother of six, at her side. If Miss Day had a grief at her hour of death, it resulted, says the new legend, from the fact that her Catholic faith meant little to her descendants. Whether she converted any Theophiluses, to compensate for their drift away, is known only to her God.

Back to the urban child who is being given an answer to her question "Who is Saint Dorothy Day?" We could answer in very flat prose or in a somewhat more oblique way, a way she would have found congenial.

First, the flat and straight way. The answer would be: Saint Dorothy Day, aka Miss Day, started her career as a journalist and never stopped publishing, particularly in the paper she founded in 1933, *The Catholic Worker*. After a wayward young life, she converted to Catholicism in 1927 and never stopped putting her Catholic faith to work. She helped invent Houses of Hospitality in her chosen New York and in many other cities, and got involved in direct action for and advocacy of the poor, the homeless, the victims of the Depression. In World War II and ever after she supported pacifism, a move that made her unpopular with many who admired her other positions and actions.

By this point, the child's eyes would be glazing over, and we would try a second answer to the question "Who

is Saint Dorothy Day?" This time we could say: Dorothy
Day is very different, she is "other," as saints are supposed to be. But she knew your world, child. The people
not far from your neighborhood did not choose to be
poor, but she chose poverty, at least of a relative sort.
She lived in cities, and could write of a Depression day
in New York:

> It was a beautiful clear summer in 1932. . . . I was
> able to walk home and savor the beauty of the
> city and of the day. For there is a beauty of the
> city, of the wide avenues, of the clean houses on
> orderly streets, of trees and little porches, and
> there were streets I loved and walks I loved . . .[1]

Such a city, to the child in a Catholic school not far from
the ghetto, would seem as remote as Cappadocia. But the
listening child would hear the rest of the sentence that
Day set in motion with the phrase "there were streets I
loved and walks I loved"; she ended it with "that were
not in the slums where I was living." As she hears this,
the child at St. Dorothy's has new reasons for identifying
with the Dorothy of this century. Dorothy Day can set
her to dreaming, to envisioning the future:

> One can conceive of a city with art and culture
> and music and architecture, and the flowering of
> all good things, as the image of the heavenly

city. Heaven is pictured as a city, the heavenly Jerusalem.

"Saint Dorothy, hear our prayer and pray for us and send us roses and apples from such a dreamed-of city!" Still, no roses, no apples: only a story of Dorothy Day sustains the listening child in an area Chicagoans call Chatham, where this noted African-American parish— never built beyond basement height, thanks to Depression-era financial setbacks—is an attraction in the ordinary neighborhood. This child, like millions of others around the nation and the world, lives in the mixed pattern of shadow and sunshine described by poet Rainer Maria Rilke the city, "is beguiling to beasts and infants alike." The child knows the beasts. She hears of an almost infantlike simplicity in her Dorothy Day, who chose the city, the slum, the poor places, and the poor. Day had to leave behind some of her love of "art and culture and music and architecture."

Dorothy Day, we would tell the urban child, dreamed of and worked for governable cities with economies that were fair. Call that Utopian, so foolish does it seem even thus to conceive of futures today. Day, we would further tell the child, was a pacifist, inconveniently for her legend—she might as well have offered her head on the block during "the last good war," in the 1940s, as to protest it—but conveniently for those who in more recent wars needed her kind of signals for peace. The

world of which she dreamed and for which she worked
would not experience shattered Sarajevos and Belfasts.
The cities would not be bombed and the children need
not be terrified. Call that paradisiacal, which means in-
sanely remote today. Still, the story of a search for justice
and peace might move the child as the story of apples
and roses would not.

A new Saint Dorothy? No one should count on it.
To be a fully registered saint one has to be canonized. A
whole sequence of bureaucrats have to busy themselves
going over the records and collecting the money. They
have to look past surface piety to find the flaws in a
potential saint's character and career. Day would have
snorted disdainfully to throw such employed advocates
off: simply ask her enemies, ask her friends, and they
will tell you how "difficult" she could be. Or simply ask
her, by consulting her autobiographical writings, for she
never hid her way of life in her younger days. From the
details Day herself provided, one has no trouble deduc-
ing that because of her bohemianism and her early ideology, many of the sanitized saints of old would shrug off
her story or even blush and refuse to listen. And if she
sometimes seemed saintly to those who allied with her
in an enterprise called the Catholic Worker, she did not
find them sanctified. Her holiness must not have rubbed
off. As Stanley Vishnewski, who looked in on the
Houses, put it: "The Catholic Worker consists of saints
and martyrs, and the martyrs are those who have to live

with the saints."[2] The saints appear as "other" and "different" and have to be kept at some distance if we are to paint them on icons, light candles at their shrines, or put them on pedestals.

Pedestals are precisely not the places for the likes of Day. She knew that, and so do her grandchildren, most of whom do not answer mail when the folks at *Salt* magazine, who would like to see her canonized, ask them about it. According to Kenneth L. Woodward, who knows and tells as much as anyone from the outside can about the cost and claptrap of canonization, of making saints, granddaughter Maggie Hennessy, then age thirty-four, wrote to *Salt*'s editors, who would have understood and anticipated her critique:

> I am one of Dorothy's granddaughters and I wanted to let you know how sick your canonization movement is. You have completely missed her beliefs and what she lived for if you are trying to stick her on a pedestal. She was a humble person, living as she felt the best way to improve on the world's ills. Take all your monies and energies that are being put into her canonization and give it to the poor. That is how you would show your love and respect to her.[3]

"Don't dismiss me so easily," Day is reported to have said, according to Woodward, when someone once

mentioned her sanctity. Equally discouraging to cam-
paigners for canonization was one of her better and bet-
ter-known friends, Father Daniel Berrigan, S.J., who
offered mass and suffered scrapes with her in the days of
protest against the Vietnam War. He spoke of the "wonderful suggestion about canonizing Dorothy":

> Abandon all thought of this expensive, overly ju-
> ridical process. Let those so minded keep a photo
> of Dorothy some place given to prayer or wor-
> ship. In such a place, implore her intercession for
> peace in the world, and bread for the multitudes.
> ... Dorothy is a people's saint, she was careful
> and proud of her dignity as layperson. Her pov-
> erty of spirit, a great gift to our age, would for-
> bid the expensive puffing of baroque sainthood.
> Today her spirit haunts us in the violated faces
> of the homeless of New York. Can you imagine
> her portrait, all gussied up, unfurled from above
> the high altar of St. Peter's? I say, let them go
> on canonizing canons and such. We have here a
> saint whose soul ought not be stolen from her
> people—the wretched of the earth.[4]

So, dear urban child, if you can still be listening, canonization and sainthood have come to this: sickness, pedes-
taling, easy dismissal, juridicism, gussied-upness, and

stealing from you. People who care may work for canonization, but immediately Dorothy Day must be yours.

This your Protestant friend, who does not pray to or
through or for or around saints, can cut a way past all
the canons and canonizations and is able to predict that
tomorrow we shall be less sure than once people were
about what a canon is and whether it is to be treasured
and how one canonizes. The lines between saints and
nonsaints become ever more blurred. The papal endorse-
ment does not mean enough in a divided Catholic church
and an ecumenical world, wherein the Catholic Day may
be closer to many Protestants and non-Christians (both
of which Day had been—baptized as a Christian by
Episcopalians, tutored in college years by skeptics, and
attracted soon after by leftists who were attracted to
Communism) than to many of those who put canonized
saints on Catholic pedestals. With all the rights and priv-
ileges given any human in general and a baptized Christian in particular, I hereby authorize you at Saint
Dorothy's to have *two* Dorothys in mind. Take your
choice between their legends, and we know which you
will choose.

What, then, does a modern saint mean to people in
canonizing and noncanonizing traditions alike? While
prayers to and through saints go on in some cases, in
others we seek exemplars and examples. The mazes of
contemporary life confuse all thoughtful people, beguiled

as we are in both our beastly cunning and our infantlike innocence. A Dorothy Day, for all the appearances of otherness and signs of difference that separate her ordinary life from our ordinary lives, is an example.

The medieval dictionaries related the word *exemplum,* something "cut out," to a clearing in the woods. Those who think about the *exemplum* say that it gives definition to the woods. Without it, there is no beginning and end to the thickness of the thicket, the darkness of its plotless, pathless ways. One cannot see the forest for the forest, so someone cuts out some trees and creates a clearing. Here the woods momentarily end and thus we define them; they become "*the* woods." Further, a clearing is the place where light falls, cultivation occurs, a cabin beckons hospitably.

So it is with exemplars. They by their living "cut out" a clearing in the woods of complex living. They give definition—in Day's case to poverty and food, war and peace, faith and unfaith—and provide a place on the Eberhart Avenues, in the St. Dorothy's churches, the Houses of Hospitality, and the companies of those who would counter the money-grabbers and war-makers. At these dark places, light falls, cultivation of the virtues occurs, hospitality calls, thanks to lives lived in particular ways—among others, too few others, in Day's ways.

Pedestaled saints like the original Dorothy come complete with legends that make them look nothing but saintly. Today ambiguity surrounds anyone nominated for sainthood, whether canonically or in the hearts of the people. Today the thirst for reading about scandal or seeing heroines and heroes exposed and pulled down, the taste for journalistic invasions of privacy and trial by headline and tube, leaves no one intact. Were there "good old days"?

The main difference between the good old days of sainthood and our time is that back then they had not yet invented the tape recorder and the camera. Today all the gossip gets recorded, the warts are displayed, the fallibilities revealed, the virtues tainted. That there were no good old days, however, is clear from what almost all the saints who left diaries or confessions tell about themselves. Of course, they had an impulse to exaggerate the flaws from the time before they were converted, just as authors of "born again" autobiographies invent lurid pasts to make the grace they found later look richer. But we know enough about autobiographies and confessions to know that often they reveal one set of vices to obscure from view another set more damaging.

Exemplar Dorothy Day in her autobiographies does indeed reveal how far from grace she had been. She had lived a post-conversion life so open to scrutiny that she gave evidence to others that her "clearing in the woods" was not all cultivated, all free from brambles. But for the beginnings, she can be an exemplar because she was more than ordinary like the rest of us; she was extraordinarily capable of finding trouble. She tells us, through

sequences in which we run out of commas to place between listed vices before she runs out of vices and sins
to register:

About the fact that she had affairs, lived with men to
whom she was not married, married a real loser who set
out to set records for number of marriages, had an abor-
tion, a common-law marriage, a child people of her day
would have called illegitimate, an early career of con-
sorting with bohemians and Communists who would
have shocked the Church in which she found a home—
in short, the kind of life in the woods and thickets that
would hold the most bored confessor's attention.

Find a home in the Church she did, however. Somewhere along the way, after Tamar was born, and in connection with her baptism, Miss Day recognized the
stirring of grace and pointings to a Truth that would begin to satisfy her intellectual longings and her search for
a base for community. She was baptized, thus gaining
grace and losing the father of her child, a committed
atheist.

Six years after these events she met Peter Maurin, as
disheveled a swinger of axes as one could hope to find
when it came time to create a moral "clearing in the
woods." Her exemplar was a French visitor whose ideal
was communal living in the countryside, and his farm
world tantalized her. She learned from Maurin, even
though he was a very unsystematic thinker. She also was
drawn to a school of French "personalists" led by Eman-

uel Mounier, most of whom were on the political left. They set out to revitalize Catholicism for the modern world by stressing personality as the basic principle of explanation and, as supernaturalists, focused on both the divine and the human personality.

But Day took this personalism and followed her vocation to the city. In both locales, Peter and Dorothy and their small company would exemplify the search for justice and peace and, they hoped, would spread justice and help promote peace.

Dorothy Day was an accomplished writer and journalist by then. She wrote, and then wished to forget, a novel, *The Eleventh Virgin,* which was semiautobiographical, just as most of her writings were somehow autobiographical. Exemplars may be humble, but they recognize in the events of their life and the interpretations they give these the base for helping others live theirs. Day combined her writing talents and her social passions and on May Day, 1933, in New York's Union Square, started selling *The Catholic Worker,* then as through the years for a penny a copy. If she must be canonized, it could be as much for what she did to encourage reading among workers and the unemployed, the masses and the massgoers, as for anything else. The letter, in her case, giveth life.

The Maurin and Day programs were less important than are their personalism and persons. Those who track the fashions and fads in movements for social justice between 1933 and 1980 would never find Dorothy Day "in" with the voguish or "out" with those who are beside the point. She was simply her complicated self, pragmatic enough to adjust to changes and idealistic enough to go against the trends of any time: that may be one reason she seems so "other," so "different," so likely to last after the movement people on tracks parallel to hers have lost their followings, pedestals, and places among historians' footnotes.

The program did include the founding of *The Catholic Worker* as a paper and the Catholic Worker as a movement; the invention of the Houses of Hospitality, where community and Communion, bread and Bread were available. It included sponsoring a woodland camp where conscientious objectors of many sorts could work—a camp based on a Catholic impulse, though everyone except Day knew that Catholicism did not engender or encourage pacifism. The program fostered cooperative farms that stood no more chance of altering the American economy than did the Catholic Worker of upsetting Western capitalism. No matter: the exemplar cuts a clearing in the woods so that the thicket gets defined, the light falls, and there are both cultivation and hospitality.

Now and then Day phased into the world where reporters looked in and whence headlines issued. One remembers photographs of her aging visage—a beauty, she reminded some of Garbo when young—in the tents of the farmworkers when their leader Cesar Chavez momentarily was allowed to emerge. Civil-rights workers gravitated toward her. The Catholic left found her Houses of Hospitality hospitable, good forums for refining their positions, sometimes with ideologies she did not need to accept because she found it sufficient to trust the vision and the hearts of people named Berrigan and their spiritual kin. She allowed for conversation with the likes of Robert Coles,[5] and allowed in photographers of note so long as they did not interrupt her meditation or talk or work.

Exemplar Day looks best in black-and-white photographs, and one pictures her world in black and white and gray. That world captures the shadows of the city, the bleakness that surrounds visions of human need, the darkness of the lonely heart, the brightness that falls from God into the figurative clearings in the rather literal jungles we call the city. As exemplar, here described as a misfit in her time and any time, as someone expressing "otherness" and "difference," she knew the source of that light.

One cannot turn the pages and close the books of Day biographies and autobiographies, or let memories of her photographs be imprinted as icons in the mind's eye, without seeing what exemplar Day recognized as that source of light. A worldly, eros-minded (in the good senses of what that connotes), "difficult," sinful, limited person, she did what saints do. She directed her thoughts and all inquiries past herself to the One who interrupted

The Long Loneliness with Presence. Like so many people
called activist, she was profoundly spiritual, an exemplar
who shames by contrast the airheaded "I'm-not-a-mem-
ber-or-religious-or-a-believer-but-I'm-*so*-spiritual" sorts
who write bestsellers. Her epigrams, columns, and prayers will outlast by centuries the witness of today's self-
engrossed spirituality mongers.

She *was* a church member; she *was* religious, a believer, whose "pre-Vatican II piety," as we like to tab it,
served to guide her to find company with "post-Vatican
II" sorts. She used the deeper reaches toward the deepest
particular Catholicism to reach people of other faiths and
no faith, to find communion with them. Her exemplarity
was specifically Christian. She liked to quote William
Gauchat: "There is no love without the cross, and no
cross without a victim. And whether there be on the
cross or beneath it weeping, there is Christ, and sorrow
shall be turned to joy." The Christic and Christlike both
profit from her place under that cross, and from the simple love that issued from her complex, *so* complex person
and being.

Dear child of the city of today, whose attention I
have lost by now, I leave you with this: Exemplar, then,
if not or not yet Saint Dorothy Day, also liked to quote
Leon Bloy: "There is only one unhappiness, and that is
not to be one of the Saints." Since Day came to know at
least certain kinds of happiness, she must have been one
of the saints, if not of the canonical sort. And, though I

have no right to speak for her, I have a confident hunch that she would have no difficulty at all, and would express nothing but joy, if at St. Dorothy's Church on South Eberhart you today left an apple for a teacher, a rose for a friend, and a prayer to the God of both Dorothys.

NOTES

1. Dorothy Day, *The Long Loneliness,* paperback (San Francisco: Harper and Row, 1981), 159.
2. Quoted from "Days of Action" in the Catholic Worker papers, in Mel Piehl, *Breaking Bread: The Catholic Worker and the Origin of Catholic Radicalism in America* (Philadelphia: Temple University Press, 1982), 108.
3. Quoted in Kenneth L. Woodward, *Making Saints* (New York: Simon & Schuster, 1990), 32.
4. Quoted by Woodward, *op. cit.,* 35.
5. Coles has better credentials than I to write this essay, having written a biographical reflection on Dorothy Day.

The Communion of Saints

LAWRENCE JOSEPH

I.

A TIME OF INNOCENCE. That time before I was awakened to choice. Everything about the Shrine of the Little Flower made an impression. The chapel with the alabaster statue of Saint Theresa, green and gold light fused through stained-glass windows, dozens of red roses and orchids. The side altars to Saints Mary, Sebastian, Perpetua, Jude, and Joseph. Saint Jude, Saint of the Impossible, to whom my mother prayed novenas. Saint Joseph, one of two saints whose name I have. A patron saint by historical chance. Around 1910, my grandfather emigrated from the Chouf mountains in the Ottoman province of Lebanon. When asked his name by an immigration official at Ellis Island, he replied, "Joseph," his father's first name, as he would have in Lebanon. By an act of the U.S. government, Alexander Nahed (baptized Maronite Catholic, into a rite named after a one-eyed monk who lived near the Orontes River in the sixth century) became Alexander Joseph. His family's name in America would be Joseph.

Joseph would be my father's first name, too. My father, like my mother, was born in Detroit at the end of World War I. My grandmother used to explain that she went into labor on March 19, the feast of Saint Joseph, two days before my father's birth. Because she had lost two infants, she prayed to Saint Joseph. If her child lived, she would name her Josephine, or, if a boy, Joseph. Joseph Joseph.

I was nine or ten years old when I discovered my other patron saint, Saint Lawrence. The children of the Little Flower School used to attend daily Mass. Everyone had a *Saint Joseph Daily Missal,* "The Official Prayers of the Catholic Church for Celebration of Daily Mass."(I still have it: not mine, but my mother's, which my brother and I bought for her, dated, in my mother's handwriting, "Mother's Day, May 12, 1957.") Its longest section was the "Proper of the Saints." August 10 was the feast of Saint Lawrence, Martyr. Beside a small picture, words once known by heart:

In 257 Pope Sixtus II ordained Saint Lawrence to
the diaconate. Though Saint Lawrence was still
young, the same Pope appointed him as one of
the seven deacons of the Roman Church. Summoned by the Prefect of Rome to surrender the
treasury of the Church, Saint Lawrence instead
distributed it among the poor. According to tradition, Saint Lawrence was roasted to death on a
red-hot gridiron over a slow fire.

My father and uncle, for reasons beyond them, were
owners of a failing grocery store among Detroit's poor;
Saint Lawrence's distribution of the Church's treasury
took hold of my imagination. Roasted to death on a gridiron over a slow fire—I had to know more. In my
grandparents' attic I found an answer in a small, worn
book, *Lives of the Great Saints*. (I still have this, too.)
Lawrence presented "the aged, the decrepit, the blind,
the lame, the maimed, the lepers, widows, and young
orphans"—to whom he had distributed the Church's
wealth—to the Roman Prefect, saying "Here is the
Church's treasure." "You mock me," the Prefect
shouted, insane with rage. "I'll see that you die a bitter
death." Lawrence was bound with chains on a large gridiron over a slow fire ("an angel was seen wiping his
face"). While his flesh broiled, he looked at the Prefect
and smiled: "Turn me over now, I'm done on this side."
    A sense of recognition, a common sense of irony.

That's what I felt about Saint Lawrence then, and what I feel about him now. A sense of detachment from total physical destruction, by the power of language transposed somewhere—into something—else. Not the duplicitous, hypocritical language of power which wrecks what is human, but a deeper language, forced into meaning, which reveals, you might say, the other side of our bodies and our souls.

Not long ago, after talking about Saint Lawrence over dinner one evening, I learned that he is also the patron saint of cooks. Those of us at the table baptized Catholic roared with laughter.

II.

I think of my saints.

Of Saint Augustine, born in that part of Africa now Algeria, the intensity of his language pitched to a clear and abstract fervor. *Magna vis est memoriae, nescio quid horrendum, deus meus, profunda et infinita multiplicitas; et hoc animus est, et hoc ego ipse sum:* "The force of memory, so immense, my God, an awesome thing, infinitely deep in its multiplicity; this thing that is the mind; this is who I am." The will, the spirit, like fire; memory and thought, mysterious and light, beautiful and dark.

And Saint Joan, visionary warrior of great skill and intelligence, burned alive as a heretic because—Mary Daly is right about it—she embodied an escape from patriarchy, a saint because of who she is, her being, which is the witch that burns within our true selves.

Or that other saint of fire, Ignatius of Loyola—a very important part of this puzzle—for whom God is revealed in what we sense, alive in the mind, seen through memory by the most disciplined will.

I think of Saint Thomas Aquinas, heavy and sad, who actually envisioned his *Summa Theologica*'s conflict between existence and essence, and who wrote the most beautiful poem in Latin of his time, the "Tantum Ergo," which we sang as children at the Benediction of the Blessed Sacrament.

> *Et antiquum documentum*
>
> *Novo cedat ritui;*
> *Praestet fides supplementum*
> *Sensuum defectui.*

"The ancient forms replaced by something new, and faith where the senses fail."

And, always, Saint Anne, of the church in Detroit in the shadow of the Bridge to Canada surrounded by a few wooden houses of the poor, where, at a side altar, before her statue and a statue of her daughter, Saint Mary, large candles burn in blue, white, and yellow glass consecrated with vows (a million vows), body braces, crutches, letters describing miracles in a corner, and that man over

there, who genuflects on both knees, who bows his head
to the floor and kisses it.

III.

I spoke to a good friend, a Catholic priest, who knows
his theology. I wanted to refresh my memory about the
Church's position on saints.

"So, what comes to your mind when you think about
saints?" I asked him.

"What do you mean, what comes to mind? A lot of
things come to mind."

"Theologically," I said.

"Theologically? Well, first of all, I suppose, is the
question of what a saint is. The word, of course, comes
from the Latin, *sanctus.* Holy. A saint is holy."

"But what does it mean, theologically, to be holy?"

"One can only be holy theologically. Holiness is a
religious idea. It has to do with God. 'A saint is one who
belongs to God . . .' "

"That's it?"

"No, that's not all of it. If you're Christian . . ."

"Let's stay with Catholic."

"All right, if you're Catholic—if you're Christian,
too—God is revealed through Christ. Don't forget your
Christology. Christ is of two natures, human and divine."

"So, there certainly can't be, as Camus once posited, 'a saint without God.' "

"I've been intrigued by that, too. But, no, not strictly speaking—you can't be a saint without God. If you're Christian—sorry, if you're Catholic—there's not even such a thing as a saint without Christ. Look, holiness properly belongs only to God. 'Holy, holy, holy, Lord God of Hosts,' remember? Holiness mirrors God, and, remember, God exists in Christ, who is completely human and completely God, God incarnate. The Word made flesh."

"But that only begs the question of what God is."

"Everything begs the question of what God is. Saint Irenaeus said it. I was reading Merton the other night, *Conjectures of a Guilty Bystander.* He quoted the Latin. *Gloria Dei vivens homo.* The glory of God is the human person fully alive. I know what you're going to say: It still begs the question. What does it mean, a human person fully alive? Love. God is love. That's what it means. It's irreducible. Eternal, a mystery. God is love, and love is human and divine. We don't know what it is, except what we know by the incarnation, by the Gospel."

"We're getting off track."

"Off your track, maybe."

"Let's get back to the saints. One need not be canonized to be a saint, right?"

"Well, that's an interesting history. Saint Paul in his

letters—Romans, I remember in particular—addresses the faithful as saints. In one sense, a saint is anyone alive who lives his life fully in Christ. Then, of course, anyone who dies in the state of grace is a saint."

"The state of grace?"

"If you're Catholic, there's no grace without Christ. Anyone who has lived a life according to the Gospel— life fully lived in Christ—is a saint. You don't have to be recognized by the Church; the Feast of All Saints attests to that. During the first centuries after Christ, different communities, or their bishops, canonized their own saints. After the twelfth century—the saints were probably used as a pretext for an ecclesiastical power play— permission for public veneration could be granted only by the Pope. Sometime in the sixteenth century, I think, the process we have now began. Its procedures were bureaucraticized during the Council of Trent. Now the process goes through three long stages—Venerable, Blessed, and Saint. To be declared blessed, there have to be two miracles; to be called a saint, there have to be two more. Canonization is an official declaration by the Church that a person is already in heaven and worthy of public veneration. I think canonization is considered infallible, but I'm not sure."

We paused. "Blessed Martin de Porres," I said. "My father had a statue of him, made by the husband of a woman who worked at the store. He's had it on his dresser for more than forty years. Blessed Elizabeth Seton, too, founder of the Sisters of Charity, who taught me in grade school . . ."

"She's a saint now."

"I know. We used to pray for her canonization. Somewhere in my memory I remember praying for one more miracle."

"You also remember, don't you, the difference between adoration and veneration?"

"Vaguely," I said.

"You're not supposed to worship the saints. You worship God. Toward the saints you show veneration. It's an old issue in the Church—one of the doctrinal fights during the Reformation. At the time of the Council of Trent it surfaced again. The church had gotten very defensive about saints. There was a lot of what looked like saint-worship at the time, the adoration of saints' relics, statues, and images, which was seen as an affront to Christ. The problem is that most people imagine God, even in Christ, too, as not human. Saints are human. They are close to God. So people pray to the saints, bypassing Christ. That makes the Church nervous. Christ's humanity is diminished."

"The saints act as intercessors, then."

"Yes. The Church recognizes that. But it also emphasizes the Christology of intercession. A saint is able to intercede with God—the Vulgate word is *interpellare*, to appeal to, to petition—because, to paraphrase

Irenaeus, a saint has lived a fully human life in Christ.
Saint Thomas said that prayer can be offered in different
ways. One way is by yourself, directly to God, or Christ,
alone; another is by praying to the angels and the saints
to pray to God for you."

"This is all beginning to make more sense to me," I
said. "The doctrine about the saints that has always attracted me is the communion of saints. 'I believe in the
communion of saints'—it's part of the Apostles' Creed,
isn't it?"

"You're right; it is."

"The communion of saints—the union of the faithful
on earth, the blessed in heaven, and the souls in purgatory . . ."

"Through Christ. The Council of Trent added the
notion of the Mystical Body of Christ. The faithful in
heaven, on earth, and in purgatory are one mystical
body, with Christ as their head. What affects one part
affects the others."

"But," I said, "what if you take Christ out of it—or,
at least, take out the Christological language. What do
you have then? A deep union, a common being—you
can visualize it. There are the saints on earth—'saint' in
the sense Saint Paul used it—who, to use your Saint
Irenaeus again, live fully human lives, who know love.
Technically, they're saints, right?"

"Right."

"Then there are those who have died, whose souls

are eternally alive, in purgatory or in heaven, because they lived lives fully human, that is to say, they lived lives of love. Clearly saints, right?"

"Right."

"And what affects one part of this common being, this union, this communion of saints, affects another. And what binds them together? Love, yes. But how? 'The Word made flesh,' if you want a Christology. But, Christology aside, what is 'the Word made flesh?' Language. A form of love. And when you have the language of love between the living and the dead you have that form of language called prayer."

IV.

My mother's father was a Melkite Catholic, another small Eastern rite of the Church, Orthodox until the eighteenth century, when it joined with Rome. When we were children, we went to the Melkite church, Our Lady of Redemption, in an old part of Detroit, each Palm Sunday. The Melkites stayed close to the Orthodox; the vestments, the liturgy, the Palm Sunday procession in which we held candles in one hand, palms in the other, were Byzantine. So was the church. While Father Riashi swung the censer, chanting a language I had never heard before, incense smoke piercing the musty, shadowy air, I remember, behind the altar, the faces of each of the twelve apostles painted around the apse. Saints. But these icons, bright with color, slightly abstracted, I recognized. They resembled the people around me. The presence of God, in that Melkite church, I don't remember. God and Christ were somewhere else. The saints were close and real. You could look into their eyes.

After Joseph's Market could no longer support two families, Joseph Joseph went to work as a meat cutter for the Great Atlantic & Pacific Tea Company. Around the time the international oil cartel forced Detroit's economy into depression, he was told he would be laid off unless he worked at a store in Port Huron, a two-hour drive away. So, close to sixty years old, he woke every morning at five, and my mother did, too. She took three buses crosstown to the Middle East Gourmet Shop on the city's east side, where she cooked with her aunt and two cousins. One late Saturday afternoon—what was I doing there? did my brother tell me she might be there?—I saw her by herself, kneeling before the side altar of Saint Jude in the Shrine. I watched her. Small and alone in the brown and gold shadows, praying to the saint of impossible desires. Now I realize what she prayed for that afternoon (I've never told anyone, not even now).

My grandpa Joseph died of arteriosclerosis when I was four. Before he died his legs were amputated. My grandma used to take me to the cemetery with her—a long drive into the city, past the factories, the small tool-and-die shops. There, she'd take my hand and we would walk to the grave. "Pray to Grandpa," she said. Not for

this wasn't love
then as now it was always
veneration.

Clizia, Montale's Beatrice—what is the nature of that
beauty? You can build an entire world on a memory. But
how do you say something to someone who is no longer
here, but whose presence is imminent? "The lives of
half-unheard-of saints"—yet one half is still heard of,
still known. "This wasn't love," the poet says, but look
again at the repercussions of his language, refracted and
deepening—ironic. Then, as now, veneration is always
love.

  Two years before my mother died of her terrible illness, my father asked me to make a pilgrimage to Carey,
Ohio, to the Shrine of Our Lady of Consolation. Our
family used to visit it when we were children, but I had
not been there in over thirty years. My recollections were
immediate, almost everything was the same—the side
altar with its statue of Our Lady of Consolation, where
I prayed as a child, and, where, I remembered, we would
kiss the statue's feet. I prayed for my mother before the
statue of Our Lady of Consolation, as my father had
asked me to do. I was alone in the church that February
afternoon, except for a man in the back, weeping. Downstairs, in the old church, I read letters of those seeking the intercession of miracles. Outside, there was the

holy-water font where, when I was six, my mother washed my fingers, crushed in an accident, so that they would heal, as they did.

"One may really indeed say that that is the essence of genius, of being most intensely alive, that is being one who is at the same time talking and listening," Gertrude Stein said. (Did you know she wrote about Saint Ignatius of Loyola?) "Of being most intensely alive"—*Gloria Dei vivens homo.* One who is at the same time talking and listening—is that that pure silence I remember from those times with Grandma when I prayed to Grandpa to pray for me?

Shortly before my mother died, when, because of her illness, she could not know it, my father placed beside her bed a picture of a Capuchin priest, Father Solanus Casey, who devoted his life to the poor in Detroit. The picture, shaped like a scapular, enclosed in plastic, included a scrap from a piece of clothing worn by the priest when he was alive. There is in Detroit a Cause of Father Solanus, a petition to initiate the process of beatification and canonization. The church in which Father Solanus is buried, Saint Bonaventure's, has since the Great Depression been a place in Detroit where the hungry come to receive food. But not only the poor come to Saint Bonaventure's; there are pilgrims, too, who come to this place where a holy man, who many believe is a saint, lies in the church's north transept.

"Let me show you this picture," my father said one time after we visited my mother. "It's a photograph of the dinner celebrating the opening of Our Lady of Redemption in 1927. Look closely. Here's Grandma and Grandpa Francis at one table, Grandpa and Grandma Joseph at another. And, at the head table, is Father Solanus Casey."

"What's he there for?" I asked.

"Our Lady of Redemption was located only a mile or so from Saint Bonaventure's. Father Solanus was close to the Maronites and Melkites. I've had a copy of this made, and presented it to the Capuchins. It's one of the few photographs of Father Solanus from that time."

When my mother died, the heaviness of her absence all around us, my sister said—I think she was crying—"Now, at least, I'll be able to talk with her again."

"And ask her help," I said.

"Yes, and ask her help, and listen to her, too." The resurrection of the body, I thought. And, I thought, the communion of saints.

Notes on Contributors

PAUL BAUMANN   is the associate editor of *Commonweal* magazine. A graduate of Wesleyan University and the Yale Divinity School, he is a columnist for the Religious News Service and has written for the *New York Times* and *Newsday,* among other publications. He lives in Noank, Connecticut, with his wife and their three children.

RICHARD BAUSCH   is the author of six novels, most recently *Rebel Powers,* and three volumes of short stories, including *Rare and Endangered Species.* His stories have appeared in the *Atlantic Monthly, Esquire, Harper's,* and the *New Yorker,* and in the *O. Henry Prize* and *Best American Stories* annual collections.

BRUCE BAWER is an Episcopalian and lives in New York. He is the author of several books of criticism, most recently *The Aspect of Eternity;* of a collection of poems, *Coast to Coast;* and of *A Place at the Table: The Gay Individual in American Society.*

SUSAN BERGMAN'S memoir, *Anonymity,* was published in 1994. Her essays and poetry have appeared in *Antaeus, North American Review, Ploughshares,* and other magazines. She lives outside Chicago with her husband and their children.

ROBERT COLES is the author of more than fifty books, including the Children of Crisis series, for which he won the Pulitzer Prize, and the Inner Life of Children series, which concluded with the best-selling *The Spiritual Life of Children.* A child psychiatrist who teaches at Harvard University, he lives in Concord, Massachusetts.

REV. AVERY DULLES, S.J. is the Laurence J. McGinley Professor of Religion and Society at Fordham University and Professor Emeritus at the Catholic University of America, and has written seventeen books and more than 600 articles on theological topics. Past president of both the Catholic Theological Society of America and the American Theological Society, Father Dulles serves on the International Theological Commission and as a consultor to the Committee on Doctrine of the National Conference of Catholic Bishops, and is a member of the United States Lutheran–Catholic dialogue.

PAUL ELIE, an editor with Farrar, Straus and Giroux in New York, has written for *Lingua Franca,* the *New Republic,* and *Commonweal,* to which he is a regular contributor. He was born in upstate New York and now lives in Manhattan.

ENRIQUE FERNANDEZ, a columnist for the *New York Daily News,* is writing a book about Latino culture.

RON HANSEN'S books include *Mariette in Ecstasy, Desperadoes, The Assassination of Jesse James by the Coward Robert Ford,* and the short-story collection *Nebraska,* for which he received an award in Literature from the American Academy and Institute of Arts and Letters. He teaches at the University of California, Santa Cruz, from which he is on leave on a Lyndhurst Foundation fellowship.

KATHRYN HARRISON attended Stanford University and the University of Iowa Writers' Workshop, and in 1983 was awarded a James Michener Fellowship. She is the author of two novels, *Thicker Than Water* and *Expo-*

sure; her third, *Poison,* is forthcoming. She lives in Brooklyn, New York, with her husband, writer Colin Harrison, and their two children.

LAWRENCE JOSEPH is the author of three books of poetry, *Shouting at No One, Curriculum Vitae,* and *Before Our Eyes.* He is married to the painter Nancy Van Goethem and lives in New York, where he is professor of Law at St. John's University School of Law.

NANCY MAIRS is the author of a spiritual autobiography, *Ordinary Time;* a memoir, *Remembering the Bone House: An Erotics of Place and Space;* two collections of essays, *Plaintext* and *Carnal Acts;* and a volume of poetry, *In All the Rooms of the Yellow House.* Her most recent book is *Voice Lessons: On Becoming a (Woman) Writer.* She and her husband, George, live in Tucson, Arizona, where they are active in the peace and justice community.

MARTIN E. MARTY is the Fairfax M. Cone Distinguished Service Professor at the University of Chicago, senior editor of *The Christian Century,* the George B. Caldwell senior scholar-in-residence at the Park Ridge Center for the Study of Health, Faith, and Ethics, and the author of many books on American religion. He is one of the few Christian writer-activists of his generation who never claims to have met Dorothy Day.

KATHLEEN NORRIS   is the author of *Dakota: A Spiritual Geography,* and several books of poetry, including *Little Girls in Church.* She serves on the editorial boards of the *American Benedictine Review* and *Hungry Mind Review,* and has lived since 1984 in western South Dakota.

DAVID PLANTE   was born in Rhode Island and is the author of fourteen books, most recently the novel *Annunciation.* He is also a frequent contributor to the *New Yorker.* He has received a Guggenheim fellowship and awards from the American Academy and Institute of Arts and Letters, and is the first Westerner to have taught at the Gorky Institute of Literature in Moscow. He lives in London.

FRANCINE PROSE   is the author of eight novels, including *Primitive People* and *Household Saints,* and two volumes of short stories, *Women and Children First* and *The Peaceable Kingdom.* Her essays, reviews, and stories have appeared in many magazines and journals, including the *Atlantic Monthly,* the *Yale Review,* and the *New York Times.* She lives near Woodstock, New York.

PAUL WATKINS   is the author of the novels *Night Over Day Over Night, Calm at Sunset, Calm at Dawn* (winner of the Encore Prize), *In the Blue Light of African Dreams,* and *The Promise of Light,* and the memoir *Stand Before Your*

God, a bestseller in England. He was born in California and now lives in New Jersey, where he is writer-in-residence at the Peddie School as well as visiting scholar at the Lawrenceville School.

TOBIAS WOLFF   is the author of the memoir *This Boy's Life* and the story collections *In the Garden of the North American Martyrs*, *The Barracks Thief*, and *Back in the World*. He is the editor of the *Vintage Book of Contemporary American Short Stories* and *Best American Short Stories 1994*. *In Pharaoh's Army*, a memoir of his time in Vietnam, is forthcoming. He lives in upstate New York and teaches at Syracuse University.

Permissions and Credits

THE
WORLD'S
BEST
INDOOR
GAMES

Other Pantheon books of games and
recreations that you might enjoy:

The Cooperative Sports & Games Book
The Second Cooperative Sports & Games Book
both by Terry Orlick
Original and challenging active games based on
the fun of cooperation, not competition.

_____

Solitaire: Aces Up & 399 Other Card Games
by David Parlett
Enough solitaire card games to keep you occupied
for decades of rainy days.

_____

The Great Maze Book
The Second Great Maze Book
The Hole Maze Book
all by Greg Bright
Three cunning collections to fascinate and challenge
the most ardent of puzzle solvers.

THE
WORLD'S
BEST
INDOOR
GAMES

GYLES
BRANDRETH

Pantheon Books, New York

Library of Congress Cataloging in Publication Data

Brandreth, Gyles Daubeney, 1948–
  The world's best indoor games.

  1. Games.   I. Title.
GV1229.B67   794   81-18929
ISBN 0-394-52477-2   AACR2
ISBN 0-394-71001-0 (pbk.)

Manufactured in the United States of America
First American Edition

9876543

About the Author

Gyles Brandreth was educated at Oxford and, at present, lives and works
in England. He is the author of many game books, including *Games
for Rains, Planes, and Trains; Brain-Teasers and Mind-Benders*; and *Great
Puzzle Mountain*. He is also, at thirty-two, a past president of the Oxford
Union and former European Monopoly champion.

CONTENTS

8 Contents

INTRODUCTION

You may not have noticed, but over the past decade or so a quiet revolution has been sweeping the Western world. It is a social revolution which gradually has been gathering momentum and, though no-one has yet paid much attention to it, before long everyone will be talking about it, television producers will be devoting prize-winning documentary films to it, and earnest post-graduate students will be exploring its ramifications in heavy doctoral theses.

I refer, of course, to the Indoor Games Revolution. People – of all ages, of all classes and of most nationalities – are playing games now as never before. And the games they are playing – parlour games, card games, board games, games of chance – are assuming an increasingly important part in the leisure pattern of their lives.

I am not asserting this simply because I have written this book, nor even because I happen to be an unrepentant Snakes and Ladders fanatic who is never happier than when sitting in a festive party hat making a small fortune at Tiddlywinks – or losing one at Bridge. It's a fact. While the European and American toy industries have been going through hard financial times of late, the sale of *games* of all kinds continues to show a steady increase. And, according to Dr Gallup, while watching television remains our number one pastime, games-playing in all its manifestations has moved from eighth place to fourth place in the league table of our leisure activities. It appears that in the austere 1980s we are falling back on our own resources, staying at home and doing our best to entertain ourselves.

In my own family we have been indoor games enthusiasts for generations. A century ago, in New York, my great-great-grandfather published *Brandreth's Puzzle Book*, a compendium of his favourite games, pastimes and brainteasers. The book was really intended to promote the sales of Brandreth's Pills – 'a medicine that acts directly on the stomach, bowels and liver, and through them purifies the blood: they cure rheumatism, headache, biliousness, constipation, dyspepsia and liver complaint' – but having been to Sing Sing, the bizarre location of the Brandreth Pill Factory, and both tasted the medicine and read the book, I am inclined to think my ancestors were better games players than they were pharmacists.

My own parents met over the Monopoly board. In the winter of 1936 my father bought the then very novel board game and took the box back to his lodgings where he asked his landlady if she fancied a game. She didn't, but she said that the Canadian lady and her daughter on the top floor might – and they did. Forty years later when that Monopoly tyro and the Canadian lady's daughter were celebrating their ruby wedding anniversary, I was in New York doing my best to uphold the family honour by coming third in the World Monopoly Championships. (I love games, but I am not very good at winning them. That is why I founded and now organise the British National Scrabble Championships. I am happy presiding over the competition: were I to take part I would never reach even the semi-finals!)

Naturally there is nothing new in man playing games. Many of the games which are enjoying a vogue at the moment have been popular for thousands of years. Take, as an example, a particular favourite of mine, Blind Man's Buff, perhaps the oldest party game of all. A blindfolded player rushes about the room trying to catch hold of the other sighted players who dodge out of his way. When the blindfolded player catches his victim he has to guess who it is, and if he is right to change places. In its origins the game is almost certainly connected with the early rites of human sacrifice and undoubtedly dates back to the time of the blind god Odin, chief deity of Norse mythology. Through the centuries it has been known as Billie Blind, Hoodle-cum-Blind and Blind Harrie, but it's an entertaining romp for all its gruesome history.

Some games, like Blind Man's Buff and Grandmother's Footsteps (which originally involved children daring one another to run up and touch an old lady on the back without her noticing!), spring from cruel beginnings, but most seem to me to be a mark of civilisation. After all, it was the eighteenth-century German poet Schiller who took time off from *Wilhelm Tell* to observe: 'Man only plays when in the full meaning of the word he is a man, and he is only completely a man when he plays.'

Someone who was without doubt 'completely a man' (and highly civilised with it) was Samuel Pepys. He thoroughly approved of games-playing. Just over three hundred years ago he noted in his diary, 'from thence to the Hague, again playing at Crambo in the wagon.' Crambo is played still and you will find the modern rules on page 37. A game which pre-dates Pepys, but which he never recalls having had the good fortune to enjoy, is Postman's Knock. It is an engaging domestic entertainment that is at least as historic as the first postman (1529) and, if you don't already know how to play the game, turn to page 20 and you will find you are in for a real treat.

My own favourite parlour game recently celebrated its bicentenary. The name Charades is derived from the Spanish *charrada*, meaning the chatter of clowns, but it came to England and was transformed into an after-dinner amusement in 1776. As a parlour game it really came into its own in the late nineteenth century, during the Victorian heyday of home entertainment when no house party was complete without a session of Charades or Sardines – or Apple Ducking, a particular royal favourite. When you play the latter game today (page 16) you set apples bobbing in a washing-up bowl of water and attempt to remove them with your mouth without losing either your teeth or your dignity. King Edward VII, as Prince of Wales, played the game but he had his apples bobbing in an ice-bucket filled to the brim with champagne!

Nowadays, alas, there are very few house parties and most contemporary homes don't have the size or number of rooms which made rambling Victorian country manors the perfect setting for party games. After a hard day's huntin', shootin', or fishin', the company would recharge themselves with a huge tea, then assemble in one of the downstairs living rooms and play games – word games in the library, card games in the billiards room, play-acting games in the drawing room – until it was time to change for dinner. In its way, it was an idyllic existence, but difficult to recapture or recreate in modern, urban surroundings. Difficult, but not impossible, for, as you'll know if you have ever played the game called Proverbs (page 39), where there's a will there's a way.

As I see it, the real revolution is not so much the extent to which people of all ages are now playing games, as the extent to which games playing has now become socially acceptable again. If you want to suggest a session of Beetle (page 199) or a round of Battleships (page 56) or even a hand of Brag (page 114), you no longer have to apologise first. But you do have to know the rules.

That's why I have written this book.

Almost everyone knows the rules of a handful of their favourite games, but there are scores of others equally entertaining that are rarely played today simply because no-one knows how. In producing this international games compendium, what I have tried to do is introduce in as straightforward a way as possible the rules of the world's best indoor games: from the simple (such as the parlour games I have just been discussing) to the sophisticated (such as some of the card games that appear in Chapter 4), from the obvious (Tiddlywinks, Darts) to the obscure (Gioul, Mu-Torere, Plakato), from the classic (Chess, Draughts, Backgammon) to the juvenile (Pass the Parcel, Hunt the Slipper, Musical Chairs), from games with curious names borrowed from the famous (Moriarty, Guggenheim, Botticelli) to games that don't come from the West and with which you may be unfamiliar (Achi, Four Field Kono, Wari), from paper and pencil games to gambling games, from games involving dice and dominoes and matchsticks to games you can play on your own or with the children.

Curiously, while no-one disputes that play is vital to children, a lot of people are reluctant to admit that it can also be of immense value to adults. The importance of games-playing was powerfully underlined by the German historian and philosopher, Johan Huizinga, in his book *Homo Ludens*, which is one of the few serious studies of the place of play in culture. 'Play', according to Professor Huizinga, 'adorns life, amplifies it and is to that extent a necessity, both for the individual – as a life function – and for society by reason of the meaning it contains, its significance, its expressive value, its spiritual and social associations, in short, as a cultural function. The expression of it satisfies all kinds of cultural needs.'

To say that 'play adorns life' does sound absurdly grandiose, yet having played – though by no means mastered – every one of the games you will find here, I think it is true. And by the time you finish the book I hope you will agree.

1 PARLOUR GAMES

Yes and No
Odd or Even
Shopping List
Pan Tapping
Apple Ducking
Execution
Moriarty
Mummies
Dead-Pan
Going Through the Motions
Matchbox Race
Pass the Orange
Postman's Knock
Winking
Feeding the Baby
Dumb Crambo
Zoo Quest
Sardines
The Picture Frame Game
Newspaper Fancy Dress
Taste
Find the Leader
Kim's Game
Up Jenkins
Murder in the Dark
Charades
Drama School

Yes and No

No. of players: Any number
Equipment: Five coins for each player
Complexity: ★★

This is an excellent game for getting people to talk to one another at parties. Each player is given five coins (or if that proves to be too costly, they may be given five matches). The players have to pair off and engage each other in conversation. The aim is to trick the other player into using the words 'Yes' or 'No'. The first player of the pair to say 'Yes' or 'No' is presented with a penny by the other player. The two players then split up and move on to new partners. The first player to get rid of his five coins is the winner.

Odd or Even

No. of players: Any number
Equipment: Ten coins (or matchsticks) for each player
Complexity: ★

This game bears some resemblance to *Yes and No* but places fewer demands on the conversational abilities of the players.

Each player is given ten coins. Putting any number of them in one hand, he holds out his clenched fist to any other player whom he might choose as an opponent and demands 'Odd or even?' The opponent, if he guesses wrongly, receives a coin – if he guesses correctly, he hands over a coin. The two players then reverse roles, the opponent going through the same rigmarole with some of his coins. The two players then split up and seek new opponents.

The first player to succeed in getting rid of all his coins is the winner. The player who finishes with most coins may be allowed to keep them to compensate for his terrible luck.

Shopping List

No. of players: Any large number
Equipment: None
Complexity: ✫

One of the players is the shopper. The other players, in teams of four to six, represent rival department stores. The shopper calls out items from his shopping list, which may be prepared beforehand or may be made up on the spur of the moment. The items on the list should be objects which some, at least, of the players might reasonably be expected to have about their persons: a blue comb, a safety pin, a bus ticket, a pair of braces, a theatre or cinema ticket, a key-ring with five keys on it, a matchbox containing twenty-three matches, an eyebrow pencil, a pair of socks etc. A point is awarded to the first 'store' to supply the shopper with each item, and the store with most points at the end of the game is the winner.

Pan Tapping

No of players: Any number
Equipment: A saucepan and a spoon
Complexity: ✫

One player is sent out of the room while the others decide on some task they want him to perform when he returns. The task may be anything – switching on the radio, perhaps, or sitting on a particular chair, or tearing up a newspaper, or kissing the earlobe of one of the female players.

The outsider is summoned back into the room and he is guided towards the task he has to perform by one of the other players equipped with the saucepan and spoon. This player taps the pan with the spoon, faster and louder as the outsider approaches the object he has to touch – the radio, chair, newspaper, earlobe or whatever – and slower and softer as he moves away from it. In this manner the pan-tapper guides the outsider towards the appointed object and helps him to realise what action he has to perform with it.

When the required task has been performed it becomes the pan-tapper's turn to go out of the room while a new task is chosen for him to perform.

Apple Ducking

No. of players: Any number
Equipment: Apples and a bowl of water
Complexity: ☆

This game is a traditional favourite for Hallowe'en, but it can provide fun at any time of the year.

Fill a large bowl with water and float in it half a dozen apples. Place it on the floor and surround it with towels or newspaper in case of splashes. Each player must then kneel by the bowl, with his hands behind his back, and extract an apple from the water, using only his mouth and teeth.

The more sedate version of this game involves one player ducking at a time with, say, a two-minute time limit. The more rumbustious version is in the form of a race, with several or all of the players ducking for apples at the same time, the first player to lift an apple from the water being the winner. When playing this version, the fun (which may embrace bumped heads and spilled water) may be enhanced by using apples which have been coated liberally with honey or syrup.

A closely related game is *Bob Apple*, in which one apple for each player is suspended on a string. Each player is then required to eat his apple down to the core without using his hands. The first player to succeed in this is the winner.

Execution

No of players: 4, 5 or 6
Equipment: A length of string
Complexity: ✫

This gruesome little game originated in Britain in the days before the abolition of capital punishment, when convicted murderers were still sent to the scaffold.

One player is chosen to be the executioner. The other players sit or stand in a circle with the tips of their raised forefingers pressed together in the centre of the circle. The executioner, standing outside the circle, slips a running noose over the fingers and holds the ends of the string. He cries 'Death!' and jerks up the string. The players, if their reflexes are quick enough, whip their fingers away. Any player whose finger is caught in the noose is suspended from the game and hangs about while the others continue playing.

Moriarty

No. of players: 2 (plus audience)
Equipment: Two blindfolds and two rolled-up newspapers
Complexity: ✫

As Sherlock Holmes might have said, this game is elementary. The two players are blindfolded and lie flat on the floor, face down, with their heads about a foot apart. Each player grasps the other's left wrist with his left hand and holds a rolled-up newspaper in his right hand. One player calls out 'Are you there, Moriarty?' The other player replies 'Yes' (or words to that effect) and promptly rolls out of the way while the inquirer attempts to smack him on the head with a single well-aimed blow from his rolled-up newspaper. Each player has an equal number of turns to be the assailant, and the player who scores the greater number of direct hits is the winner.

The better Sunday newspapers (complete with supplements and colour magazines) are to be preferred for this game as their prose is weightier than that of the popular tabloids. Real devotees of the game, of course, use bound volumes of *Strand Magazine*.

Mummies

No. of players: 4 or more
Equipment: A roll of toilet paper for each couple
Complexity: ☆

The players pair off into mixed couples, and the female member of each couple is given a roll of toilet paper. A three-minute time limit is set, within which each female has to use the toilet paper to swathe her male partner from head to foot so that he resembles an Egyptian mummy. The couple who are judged to have made the best mummy are the winners.

Dead-Pan

No. of players: Any number
Equipment: None
Complexity: ☆

The players sit or stand in a circle, and one of them is chosen to be the leader. The leader nudges the player on his left, who nudges the player on his left, who nudges the player on his left, and so on round the circle back to the leader. The leader now tweaks the ear of the player on his left, who tweaks the ear of the player on his left, and so on round the circle once more. For the third and subsequent rounds the leader shakes his neighbour's hand, or tickles him under the chin, or blows in his ear, or pulls his nose, or whatever turns him on, and the other players do the same around the circle.

The idea is that the players should perform all these actions without displaying any sign of amusement. A player drops out of the game if he laughs or smiles. The last player left in is the winner.

Going Through the Motions

No. of players: Any number
Equipment: None
Complexity: ✮

The players form a circle. The first player performs any action he chooses
– tapping his foot, twitching his nose, winking, bobbing up and down, or
whatever. The second player must copy the action of the first player and
at the same time perform an additional action of his choice. The third
player must copy the actions of the second player and at the same time
perform some other action. And so on round the circle, each player
copying the actions of the previous player and adding another
simultaneous action. Any player who fails to do so or who falls over,
suffering from exhaustion, is out of the game. The last player left
winking, nodding, bobbing and jerking is the winner.

Matchbox Race

No. of players: 8 or more
Equipment: Two matchboxes
Complexity: ✮

The players divide into two teams, each team forming a straight line, and
the player at the head of each line is given a matchbox cover. On the
word of command, the leader of each team pushes the matchbox cover
over his nose and has to transfer it from his own nose to the nose of the
next player in the line. Neither player may touch the matchbox cover
with his hands. The second player transfers the matchbox cover in the
same manner to the nose of the third player, and so on to the end of the
line. If any player touches the matchbox cover with his hands or lets it
drop on the floor, it must be returned to the leader of the team, who puts
it on his nose and starts all over again. The first team to transfer the
matchbox cover successfully to the end of the line wins the game.

Pass the Orange

No. of players: 8 or more
Equipment: Two oranges
Complexity: ✩

The players are divided into two teams, and the members of each team stand in a straight line. The player at the head of each line is given an orange, which he tucks under his chin. On the word 'Go!' he turns to the next player in the line and attempts to transfer the orange to the next player's chin. The second player then passes the orange to the third player, and so on down the line. At no time may the orange be touched by hand, and if it falls to the ground it must be returned to the player at the head of the line, who starts all over again. The first team to succeed in passing the orange down the line wins.

It has been found that when the lines are arranged so that males alternate with females this game usually lasts much longer. For some reason, it appears that the game is so much fun this way that players will sometimes prolong it quite unnecessarily.

Postman's Knock

No. of players: 8 or more
Equipment: None
Complexity: ✩

Postman's Knock, for some strange reason, is usually considered to be a childish game, and this source of innocent pleasure is quite unjustly neglected. Medical evidence shows that frequent applications of *Postman's Knock* makes people healthier and happier.

A male player leaves the room while all the other players are given numbers – odd numbers for the men, even numbers for the women. The outsider knocks, rat-a-tat, on the door, and the assembled players call out 'Who's there?' 'It's the postman,' replies the outsider, 'and I have something for Number 6.' (or Number 2 or Number 14 or any other even number). Out goes Number 6 to join the postman who gives her a long, lingering kiss. She remains outside to be the next postwoman while the former postman returns to the assembled players. When the players have chosen new numbers, she knocks on the door and announces that she has something for Number 9 (or any other odd number). The lucky fellow goes out to claim his kiss, and then has a turn at being the postman. And so the game continues until every player has been thoroughly kissed.

Winking

No. of players: 15 or more
Equipment: Chairs for half the players
Complexity: ★

A circle of chairs is formed, facing inwards. A woman sits in each chair, except for one chair which is left empty. Behind each chair, including the empty one, stands a man with his hands resting on the back of the chair, but not actually touching the woman sitting there.

The man standing behind the empty chair has to wink at one of the women. The women who is winked at must immediately attempt to leave her chair and dash to the empty one, while the man standing behind *her* chair attempts to restrain her by placing his hands on her shoulders. If he succeeds in putting his hands on her shoulders before she escapes, she must stay where she is and wait for another wink, he replaces his hands on the back of the chair, and the man standing behind the empty chair has to choose another woman to wink at. If the woman who is winked at does manage to get away to the empty chair, it becomes the turn of the man who let her escape to entice some other woman to his now empty chair.

After a while, when all the women have received their fair share of winks, the players change over – the men sit in the chairs and the women stand behind them and do the winking.

Feeding the Baby

No. of players: 6 or more
Equipment: A baby's bottle and a bib for each couple
Complexity: ✫

The women sit at one end of the room, each woman holding a bib and a half-filled baby's bottle. The men stand opposite their partners at the other end of the room. When the word of command is given each man dashes to his partner and sits on her knee. She fastens the bib around his neck, and feeds him from the bottle as quickly as possible. He may cling to her if he wishes (and if she permits) but he may not touch the bottle with his hands. As soon as the bottle is emptied, she removes his bib and the couple dash back to the other end of the room where the men started. The first couple to finish win the game.

The contents of the bottles – milk, gin, lemonade, champagne, or whatever – depend, of course on the type of party.

Dumb Crambo

No. of players: Any number
Equipment: None
Complexity: ✫

The players divide into teams. Team A goes out of the room while the members of team B confer among themselves to choose a word. When team A returns, team B announce a word that rhymes with the word they have chosen. Team B then are allowed three guesses in which to discover the word chosen by team A. The only restriction is that they are not allowed to speak – they must present their guesses in mime. Any player who speaks loses the game for his team. Incorrect guesses are greeted with boos and hisses. A correct guess is rewarded with applause and a point for the successful team.

The teams alternate roles, and the team with the most points when no one wants to play any longer is the winner.

Zoo Quest

No. of players: 6 or more
Equipment: A box of chocolates
Complexity: ☆

The players are split into teams, with three, four or five players in each team. One member of each team is chosen to be the leader and the other players assume the identities of various animals. They should be discouraged from being obvious animals like dogs, cats and cows – instead they should be urged (or coerced) into being, for example, a coyote, a rhinoceros, a hyena, a gorilla, a three-toed sloth and so forth.

The chocolates are scattered in various locations about the house. The team members then go off in search of the chocolates, leaving their leaders to have a few moments rest. When a player finds a chocolate he makes a noise appropriate to the animal he is impersonating, and the leader, on hearing one of his animals, goes and collects the chocolate.

After ten minutes, the team whose leader has collected the most chocolates is the winning team. Greedy players who eat the chocolates they find instead of calling their leader deserve to lose.

Sardines

No. of players: 6 or more
Equipment: None
Complexity: ☆

Sardines is best played in a large house with lots of possible hiding-places. All the players assemble in one room. The first player leaves the room and hides himself away somewhere in the house. The remaining players follow after, one at a time, at one-minute intervals. The second player has to find the first player's hiding-place and join him there. The third player has to find the first two and join them. The fourth player . . . and so on. The game ends when all the players are packed together in the larder or under the bed or wherever the hiding-place happens to be.

The Picture Frame Game

No. of players: Any number
Equipment: An empty picture frame
Complexity: ✩

This is a simple, silly game which nevertheless calls for great self-control. Each player in turn holds up in front of his face the empty picture frame, through which he regards the other players. For sixty seconds he has to keep his face absolutely immobile (apart from the occasional blink) while the other players cavort and caper and grimace and call out ribald remarks. Any player who lasts out the full minute as a picture of still life should receive a suitable reward.

Newspaper Fancy Dress

No. of players: Any number
Equipment: A newspaper for each player, and a supply of pins
Complexity: ✩✩

Each player is given a newspaper and some pins, from which he has to make himself a fancy-dress costume. The players have ten minutes in which to do this. When the ten minutes have elapsed, the players parade around the room, and the winner is the player who is judged to have made the cleverest, most amusing or most original costume.

Taste

No. of players: Any number
Equipment: Various (see text)
Complexity: ★★

Before the game begins a number of cups or glasses are set out and filled with an assortment of beverages – water, cold tea, lemonade, ginger ale, tonic water, beer, vinegar etc. The players are led in one at a time and blindfolded. Then (having been assured that they will come to no harm) they are given a sip of each liquid, which they then have to identify. The player who identifies correctly the greatest number is the winner.

Find the Leader

No. of players: 6 or more
Equipment: None
Complexity: ★★

This game, while it may appear to be silly (and there's no harm in that), can actually be quite a challenging test of observation.

One player is sent out of the room, and the other players select a leader. The leader performs some repetitive action, such as rubbing his nose (or scratching his head, or tapping his foot, or whatever) which the other players all copy. The outsider is summoned back into the room, where he finds all the players busily rubbing or tapping or scratching. Suddenly the leader switches to some different action and the other players immediately follow his lead. The leader initiates different actions at frequent intervals. The outsider, by observing closely all the players, has to determine which of them is the leader.

Each player takes a turn at being the outsider.

Kim's Game

No. of players: Any number
Equipment: a collection of miscellaneous objects; paper and a pencil for each player
Complexity: ✩✩

Kim's Game is a fine test of observation and memory which, for that reason, was a favourite game of Baden Powell, the founder of the Scout movement. It is also a lot of fun.

Before the party guests arrive or while the players are in another room, a collection of twenty or thirty objects – as varied as possible – is assembled on a tray or on a table and is covered with a cloth. The players are gathered round, the cloth is removed for thirty seconds and is then replaced. Each player is given a pencil and paper and has to list as many objects as he can remember. A player scores one point for every object he remembers, but a point is deducted for any object listed that was not actually there. The player who scores most points is the winner.

Up Jenkins

No. of players: 6, 8 or 10
Equipment: A coin (or ring or thimble or other small object)
Complexity: ✩✩

Up Jenkins is a light-hearted game of observation and deduction which offers plenty of scope for bluffing and general merriment.

The players are divided into two equal teams, seated on opposite sides of a table. If the table is small and the players are squashed together this only adds to the fun. The members of one team pass the coin from hand to hand below the table. When the leader of the opposing team calls 'Up Jenkins', the players on the team with the coin raise their hands, with fists clenched, well above the table. One fist, of course, will be concealing the coin. The leader of the opposing team then calls 'Down Jenkins' and the raised hands must be slapped down on the table with palms flat.

The opposing team now have to guess which hand the coin is under. The leader confers with his team-mates and then taps the hand that they think conceals the coin. That hand is raised, and if the coin is revealed the guessing team scores a point, otherwise the team with the coin scores a point.

The team then change roles for the next round. The winners are the team with the most points when an agreed number of rounds have been played.

The game may be played so that the guessing team is allowed three guesses to discover the hand concealing the coin, scoring three points if their first guess is correct, two points if their second guess is correct, and one point if their third guess is correct.

Murder in the Dark

No. of players: 8 or more
Equipment: Slips of paper
Complexity: ★★

A number of slips of paper are prepared, one for each player. One slip is marked with a circle, another is marked with a cross, and the rest are blank. The slips are folded and mixed up and each player picks one at random. The player who picks the circle is the detective, and he identifies himself. The player who picks the cross is the murderer and says nothing.

All the lights in the house are turned off, and all the players, apart from the detective, disperse throughout the house. The murderer prowls about until he chances upon a suitable victim in a lonely spot. Creeping up on his victim, the murderer whispers in his ear 'You're dead'. The victim screams frenziedly and falls to the floor as the murderer slinks away. As soon as the scream is heard the other players must remain where they are, while the detective makes his way as quickly as possible to the scene of the crime, switching on all the lights on his way.

The detective inspects the scene of the crime; notes the whereabouts of all the suspects; and then summons everyone into the drawing-room to be questioned in true Agatha Christie fashion. By questioning the suspects as to their movements and their location at the time of the murder, and by looking for inconsistencies in their stories, as well as by watching for signs of guilt in their faces, the detective has to identify the murderer. Each player must answer all questions with the truth and nothing but the truth – except, of course, for the murderer, who can lie as much as he likes until asked the direct question 'Are you the murderer?' when he must break down and confess all. The detective is allowed two guesses at the identity of the murderer.

Charades

No. of players: Any number
Equipment: None
Complexity: ★★

Charades is a deservedly popular game in which one team of players has to guess a word of several syllables presented in dramatic form by the other team.

The players are divided into two teams, and the first team goes into another room to choose a suitable word. The chosen word must contain several syllables, each of which may be presented in the form of a dramatic sketch, as must the word as a whole. Only the sound of the syllables is considered, not the spelling, and syllables may be grouped together. For example, the word 'trampoline' may be chosen and split into 'tramp', 'pole' and 'lean'. Or the chosen word may be 'illuminate', split up as 'ill', 'human' and 'ate'.

Having decided on the word and on the sketches they are going to perform, the members of the team return to the other room for their performance. The leader declares the number of syllables, and the players perform their sketches for the edification of the opposing team, acting out first the syllables and then the whole word. They may use speech in their sketches but it is more conventional for the sketches to be presented entirely in mime.

When the opposing team have guessed the word being presented it becomes their turn to leave the room and decide on a charade.

Another popular form of *Charades* involves acting the titles of books, films, TV programmes, songs etc. In this form of the game the titles are usually broken down into individual words rather than syllables. Another variation is *Solo Charades*, in which individual players take it in turn to perform the words or titles they choose.

Drama School

No. of players: 3 to 8
Equipment: None
Complexity: ★★

One player is chosen (or elects himself) to be the judge, and the other players sit or stand in a row facing him. The judge commands them to express various moods or emotions – anger, despair, panic, delight, boredom, pride, fear, enthusiasm, benevolence, lust, incomprehension, smugness, guilt, and so on – and awards a point to the best actor of each mood or emotion. The winner is the player who amasses the most points.

The players may be allowed full scope to use speech, gesture and facial expression or, to make it more difficult, they may be restricted to facial expression only.

2   WORD GAMES

I Spy
Spelling Bee
Backward Spelling
Action Spelling
I Love my Love
I Went to Market
A Was an Apple Pie
Traveller's Alphabet
Buzz, Fizz, Buzz-Fizz
Crambo
Initial Answers
Sausages
Word Associations
Proverbs
Last and First
I Packed my Bag
Tennis, Elbow, Foot
Number Associations
Coffee Pot
Taboo
Twenty Questions
Leading Lights
Donkey
Botticelli
What Nonsense!
Stepping Stones

I Spy

No. of players: 2 or more
Equipment: None
Complexity: ☆

One of the players thinks of some object that is visible in the room – a spoon, let us say, for example – and announces to the other players its initial letter, saying 'I spy with my little eye something beginning with S'. The other players then have to guess what the object is:

'Sofa?' 'No'
'Sugar?' 'No'
'Slippers?' 'No'
'Ceiling?' '???'
'Shoelace?' 'No'
etc. etc.

The first player to guess correctly is allowed to 'spy' the next object.

Spelling Bee

No. of players: 3 or more
Equipment: None
Complexity: ☆

One players acts as question-master and calls out a word to each of the other players in turn, who must then give the correct spelling of the word. If the player spells the word correctly he scores one point.

The question-master may call the words from a prepared list or he may make up the list as he goes along. It is, of course, most important that the words used should be matched to the abilities of the players taking part. It would be just as silly to ask a group of six-year-olds to spell words like Parallel, Psychological, Committee and Furlough as it would be to ask an average group of teenagers or adults to spell the words like Door, School, Yellow and Horse.

When a predetermined number of rounds have been played, the player with the most points is the winner.

Variation 1
The game is played as described above, except that a player who fails to spell a word correctly drops out of the game. The winner is the last player left in.

Variation 2
A player who spells a word correctly is given another word to spell. If he spells that correctly he is given another, and so on. He scores a point for each correct spelling and his turn ends only when he fails to spell a word correctly. The player with the most points at the end of the game is the winner.

Variation 3
The players are divided into two teams, sitting opposite each other. The question-master calls out a word to each player in turn, selecting the two teams alternately. A player who spells a word correctly scores a point for his team. If a player fails to spell a word correctly, the same word is offered to his opposite number in the other team who, if he can spell the word correctly, may score a bonus point for his team.

Backward Spelling

No. of players: 3 or more
Equipment: None
Complexity: ★

This is a form of *Spelling Bee* which is made a little more difficult for the players since the words called out have to be spelled backwards. This game may be played in any of the ways described for *Spelling Bee*.

Action Spelling

No. of players: 3 or more
Equipment: None
Complexity: ✫

Action Spelling is a form of *Spelling Bee* that is played strictly for
laughs. It can be organised in any of the ways described for *Spelling Bee*
but, usually, words less difficult to spell will be used.

The point of the game is that certain letters must not be spoken by
the players when spelling the words – actions must be substituted
instead. For example, the rule may be that no vowels may be spelled out
– instead of saying 'A' a player must raise his left hand; instead of saying
'E' he must raise his right hand; instead of saying 'I' he must point to his
eye; instead of saying 'O' he must point to his mouth; instead of saying
'U' he must point to any other player.

Alternatively, actions may be substituted for other letters – a growl
for a 'G', a whistle for an 'S', shading one's eyes for a 'C', a buzz for a 'B',
and so on. The game can be made as silly and as complicated as one
wants it to be.

I Love my Love

No. of players: 3 or more
Equipment: None
Complexity: ✫

This is a popular game with young children, especially little girls. The
players have to complete the sentence 'I love my love because he/she is
————' with adjectives beginning with each letter of the alphabet in
turn. The first player has to find an adjective beginning with A, the
second with B, the third with C, and so on. Thus:

Judith: 'I love my love because he is adorable.'
Roy: 'I love my love because she is beautiful.'
Josie: 'I love my love because he is charming.' etc.

It is not usually a requirement that the adjectives should be flattering – instead of being adorable, beautiful and charming, my love might be awkward, bald and careless.

Any player unable to think of an adjective beginning with the next letter of the alphabet drops out of the game, and the next player starts again using the letter A. The last player left in is the winner.

A variation of this game is to require each player to complete the longer refrain 'I love my love because he/she is —————. His/her name is ————— and he/she lives in —————', using three words beginning with the same letter, e.g. 'I love my love because she is zealous. Her name is Zoe and she lives in Zanzibar.'

I Went to Market

No. of players: 3 or more
Equipment: None
Complexity: ☆

This game is similar to *I Love My Love*, the difference being that the players have to think of nouns beginning with each letter of the alphabet in turn to complete the sentence 'I went to market and I bought —————.' For example: 'I went to market and I bought apples.'
'I went to market and I bought books.' 'I went to market and I bought cheese'. etc.

A Was an Apple Pie

No. of players: 3 or more
Equipment: None
Complexity: ☆

This game, again, is similar to *I Love My Love*, the players having to supply verbs beginning with each letter of the alphabet in turn. For example, 'A was an apple pie. A ate it', 'B bought it', 'C cut it', 'D delivered it' and so on.

Traveller's Alphabet

No. of players: 3 or more
Equipment: None
Complexity: ☆

Traveller's Alphabet is a slightly more demanding form of alphabet
sequence game. The players sit in a circle. Each player in turn asks the
player on his left two questions: 'Where are you going?' and 'What will
you do there?'. The replies consist of the name of a country and the
description of an activity, using verb, adjective and noun, all beginning
with the same letter. The first player's replies must beginning with the
letter A, the second player's with B, the third player's with C, and so on.
    For example, the conversation might go like this:

Mary: 'Where are you going?'
David: 'Australia.'
Mary: 'What will you do there?'
David: 'Assist aged Aborigines.'
David: 'Where are you going?'
Edward: 'Belgium.'
David: 'What will you do there?'
Edward: 'Buy big boots.'
Edward: 'Where are you going?'
Mary: 'China.'
Edward: 'What will you do there?'
Mary: 'Carve cheap chopsticks.' etc. etc.

    Any player who fails to reply within a reasonable time limit drops
out of the game. The winner is the last player left in.

Buzz, Fizz, Buzz-Fizz

No. of players: 3 or more
Equipment: None
Complexity: ☆

Buzz, *Fizz* and *Buzz-Fizz* are three closely-related games, and are very silly. For any of the three games the players sit or stand in a circle and call out numbers, one after the other – the first player calling 'One', the second player 'Two', the third player 'Three' and so on, round and round the circle, as quickly as possible.

If *Buzz* is being played, then the word 'Buzz' must be substituted for every multiple of 5, and substituted for the digit 5 whenever it occurs in a number. Thus 5, 10 and 15 should all be pronounced 'Buzz' and 50 and 51 should be pronounced 'Buzzty' and 'Buzzty-one'.

Fizz is similar except that 7 is the forbidden number, not 5, and the word 'Fizz' is substituted.

Buzz-Fizz (believe it or not) is a combination of *Buzz* and *Fizz*. 57, for example, becomes 'Buzzty Fizz' and 75 becomes 'Fizzty Buzz'.

You may, if you wish, switch from *Fizz* to *Buzz* to *Buzz-Fizz* in the course of a game, just to make it more confusing.

Any player who says a number instead of fizzing (or vice versa) or who fizzes when he should buzz (or verse vica) drops out of the game. The last player left is the winner.

Crambo

No. of players: 2 or more
Equipment: None
Complexity: ☆

Crambo, although it is a very unsophisticated game, has been popular for several centuries. One of the players thinks of a word and then announces to the other players a word that rhymes with the word he has chosen. For example, he might think of the word 'dull' and announce the word 'hull'. The other players are then each allowed three guesses to discover the word thought of by the first player. If a player guesses the word correctly he has the honour of choosing the word for the next round. If none of the other players can guess the word or if they have all fallen asleep then the original player has another turn.

Initial Answers

No. of players: 3 or more
Equipment: None
Complexity: ✶

One of the players is chosen to be the questioner for the first round. He asks any appropriate question, which must be answered by each of the other players in turn. Each player's answer must consist of words beginning with his own initials. For example, to the question 'What kind of food do you like?', Bob Hope might reply 'Boiled ham', Liza Minelli might reply 'Lemon meringue', Frank Sinatra might reply 'French snails', and Zsa Zsa Gabor might decide that she did not want to play such a silly game. A player who fails to give a satisfactory answer within five seconds becomes the questioner for the next round.

Sausages

No. of players: 3 or more
Equipment: None
Complexity: ✶

One of the players is chosen to be the questioner. He may ask any of the other players whatever personal questions he might choose – 'What do you think your legs look like?' – 'What are your shoes made from?' – 'To what do you attribute your beauty and vitality?' Whatever the question, the player being asked must reply 'Sausages!'. The first player who smiles or laughs or giggles or smirks or titters or grins or chortles or simpers or guffaws or sniggers or otherwise betrays any emotion other than deadly seriousness is out, and he takes the next turn at being the questioner.

Instead of using the word 'Sausages', the game may be played with any other word which the particular group of players consider to be inherently mirth-provoking.

Word Associations

No. of players: Any number
Equipment: None
Complexity: ☆

The players sit or stand in a circle. The first player says the first word that comes into his mind. The second player immediately says the first word that comes into *his* mind in response to the first player's word. The third player responds likewise to the second player's word, and so on round and round the circle. If a player hesitates before saying his word he is out. The last player left in is the winner.

This game is sometimes called Psychotherapy, and psychiatrists may charge very high fees for playing it with you.

Proverbs

No. of players: 2 or more
Equipment: None
Complexity: ☆

If more than two are playing, one player leaves the room while the others decide on a proverb. When he returns he has to guess the proverb chosen by the other players. He does this by asking each of them in turn a question, which may be about any subject under the sun. The first answer must contain the first word of the proverb, the second answer must contain the second word, and so on. When all the words of the proverb have been used, the players begin again with the first word.

For example, if the chosen proverb were 'Look before you leap' the dialogue might proceed as follows:

'How old are you?'
'I'm older than I *look* but not as old as I feel.'
'What is your favourite colour?'
'White was my favourite *before* I married, but I'm not so sure now.'
'What time is it?'
'It is time *you* bought yourself a watch.'
'What do you think of the Government?'
'I think that their forward-looking policies are a great *leap*
backwards.'
'Where are you going for your holiday next year?'
'I don't know until I've had a chance to *look* through the brochures.'

The questioner is allowed to ask as many questions as he wishes within a time limit of, say, five minutes. An incorrect guess or failure to find the proverb within the time limit means that the questioner must take another turn, otherwise the player who answered the last question becomes the next questioner.

To avoid making the answers too obvious it is necessary to choose proverbs without 'awkward' words. If the chosen proverb were 'A rolling stone gathers no moss' it might be difficult to contrive an answer in which the word 'moss', for example, did not stick out like a sore thumb. This problem, however, may be overcome to some extent by making the answers fairly inconsequential (but not too long-winded, as this rather spoils the fun) and by attempting to include in the answers plenty of red herrings, such as 'cloud', 'lining', 'eggs', 'basket' etc.

Last and First

No. of players: 2 or more
Equipment: None
Complexity: ☆

A category is chosen – Birds, Towns, Rivers, TV Programmes, Marxist Historians, or whatever. The first player calls out any word belonging to the chosen category. The second player calls out another, beginning with the last letter of the first word. The next player calls out another, beginning with the last letter of the previous word, and so on. For example, if the chosen category were Animals, the words called out might be: 'Elephant', 'Tiger', 'Rat', 'Toad', 'Dromedary', 'Yak', etc.

All the words called out must belong to the chosen category and no word may be repeated. If a player fails to think of a word or calls out a word which does not belong to the category or which has already been used then he drops out of the game. The last player left in is the winner.

I Packed My Bag

No. of players: 3 or more
Equipment: None
Complexity: ★★

This game is a test of memory and concentration, in which the players attempt to remember and repeat an increasing list of objects. For example, the first player might say 'I packed my bag with a pair of pyjamas'. The second player might say 'I packed my bag with a pair of pyjamas . . . and a silver snuff-box'. The third player might say 'I packed my bag with a pair of pyjamas, a silver snuff-box . . . and a pocket calculator'. The game continues with each player in turn repeating the list and adding one more item of his own choice. Any player who forgets an item or who gets them in the wrong order drops out of the game. The last player left in the game is the winner.

Tennis, Elbow, Foot

No. of players: 3 or more
Equipment: None
Complexity: ★★

Each player in turn calls out a word which is either directly associated with the word previously called out or which rhymes with it. For example, 'Tennis', 'Elbow', Foot', 'Ball', 'Wall', 'Paper', 'Tiger', 'Stripe', 'Ripe', 'Fruit', 'Apple', 'Core', 'Door', Key', 'Note', 'Boat', and so on. Players are out if they hesitate, if they repeat a word already called out, or if they call out a word which neither relates to the previous word nor rhymes with it. The last player left in is the winner.

Number Associations

No. of players: 3 or more
Equipment: None
Complexity: ★☆

Each player in turn calls out any number between 1 and 12. Whoever is first among the other players to respond with an appropriate association scores a point. For example, the number 2 might prompt the associations 'Two turtle doves', 'Two lovely black eyes', 'Two-way stretch', 'Tea for Two', 'A Tale of Two Cities', 'Two heads are better than one' etc. The number 7 might prompt 'Seven Pillars of Wisdom', 'Seven seas', 'Seven dwarfs', 'Seven deadly sins', 'The Magnificent Seven' etc. No association may be repeated. The player with the most points when everyone has had enough of the game is the winner.

Coffee Pot

No. of players: 3 to 8
Equipment: None
Complexity: ★☆

One player thinks of a word which has two meanings (e.g. duck) or a pair of words which have different meanings but which sound the same (e.g. bored and board). He then says aloud a sentence using both meanings but substituting the words 'coffee pot' for both of them – for example 'If you see a low flying coffee pot you'd better coffee pot,' or 'I was on the coffee pot but I quit because I was so coffee pot'.

Each of the other players may then ask one question, and the first player's answer must include one or other of his words, again disguised as 'coffee pot'. If one of the players manages to identify the 'coffee pot' word he scores a point, otherwise the first player scores the point. Each player in turn has a go at being a 'coffee potter', and the player who finishes with most points is the winner.

Taboo

No. of players: 3 *or more*
Equipment: None
Complexity: ★★

One of the players is selected to be the umpire for the first round. The umpire chooses any commonly used word – such as 'yes', 'no', 'and', 'is', 'you', 'the' – and declares that word to be taboo. He then asks questions of each of the other players in turn, and each player must reply immediately with a sensible and relevant sentence. If the player hesitates or uses the forbidden word he is out. The last player to stay in the game is the winner of that round and becomes the umpire for the next round.

In a somewhat more taxing version of this game the umpire declares a certain letter of the alphabet to be taboo and the players must then reply with a sentence that does not contain the forbidden letter.

Twenty Questions

(*Alternative name:* Animal, Vegetable, Mineral)

No. of players: 2 *or more*
Equipment: None
Complexity: ★★

One player thinks of an object and announces to the other players whether it is animal, vegetable or mineral or any combination thereof. The other players, in turn, ask any questions they like, provided that they can be answered by a simple Yes or No, the aim being to narrow down the field and eventually identify the mystery object. Twenty questions are allowed.

If the object has not been identified when twenty questions have been asked, the player who thought of the object in question reveals to the other players what it is. He then selects another object for the other players to identify. If any player correctly identifies the mystery object then that player is given the privilege of selecting the next object.

Leading Lights

No. of players: Any number
Equipment: None
Complexity: ★★

The name of a well-known person is proposed. Each player has to think of an appropriate phrase which begins with the same initials as the name in question. For example, Wolfgang Amadeus Mozart might prompt the phrases 'Was Austrian Musician' or 'Wrote Appealing Melodies'; Sigmund Freud might give rise to 'Subconscious Fantasies' or 'Sychic Fenomena' (???) or 'Sex Fiend'; Brigitte Bardot might make players think of 'Beautiful Body' and so forth.

Donkey

No. of players: 2 or more
Equipment: A dictionary (optional)
Complexity: ★★

In this game words are built up by each player in turn adding a letter while trying to avoid being the player who completes a word.

The players sit in a circle. The first player thinks of any word of four or more letters and calls out its first letter. The second player then thinks of a word beginning with that letter and calls out the second letter of the word he has thought of. The third player thinks of a word beginning with the two letters already called out and calls out its third letter. And so on, each player trying to keep the chain of letters going without calling out the last letter of a word. The player who completes a word loses a life.

For example, suppose there are three players.

Ann thinks of DANGER and calls out 'D'.
Bob thinks of DIVIDE and calls out 'I'.
Chris thinks of DISTANT and calls out 'S'.
Ann thinks of DISORDER and calls out 'O'.
Bob thinks of DISOWN and calls out 'W'.
Chris now has no option and has to call out 'N', thus completing a word and losing a life.

A player must have a valid word in mind when he adds a letter. He may be challenged by any other player who suspects that the letter called out does not help to form a word. The challenged player must then declare the word he has in mind. If he cannot do so or if his word is not a valid one then he loses a life. If he can declare a valid word then the challenger loses a life. A dictionary may be needed at this point to resolve disputes.

A player may also lose a life if he hesitates for too long before calling out a letter.

When a player has lost three lives he becomes a donkey and drops out of the game. The last player to be left in wins the game.

For a longer game the number of lives may be increased.

Botticelli

No. of players: Any number
Equipment: None
Complexity: ★★

Why this game should be named after a fifteenth-century Florentine painter is a moot point. Perhaps it is so named because people could not agree on the correct pronunciation for 'Breughel'. Whatever its origin, *Botticelli* is a fascinating guessing game, requiring a fairly good standard of general knowledge.

One player thinks of the name of a famous person or fictitious character – one who should be known to the other players – and tells the other players the initial letter of his subject's surname. The other players now have to identify the mystery person, and they do this by asking two types of question – direct questions and indirect questions. Direct questions may be asked only if the first player fails to provide a satisfactory answer to an indirect question.

For example, suppose the first player had thought of Lewis Carroll and had declared the initial letter to be 'C'. The other players might ask indirect questions such as 'Are you a famous scientist?' or 'Are you a film star?' or 'Are you a Dickens character?' The first player might reply to these questions 'No, I am not Marie Curie,' or 'No, I am not Charlie Chaplin', or 'No, I am not David Copperfield'.

If the first player, however, cannot give a satisfactory answer to a question of this type – if, for example, he can't remember the names of any Dickens characters beginning with 'C' – then the questioner may ask a direct question. A direct question should be framed so as to elicit more information about the mystery person – e.g. 'Are you living?' or 'Are you female?' or 'Are you American' – and the first player must answer, truthfully, either Yes or No.

Since truthful answers must be given to direct questions it is important that the first player should choose a character about whom he has some knowledge.

The other players should do their best to ask awkward indirect questions in the hope that the first player will not be able to answer them satisfactorily and will thus give them the opportunity to ask as many direct questions as possible, thus narrowing down the field. But a player may not ask an indirect question for which he himself has not in mind a satisfactory answer. For example, he may not ask 'Are you a Swedish film star?' unless he knows the name of a Swedish film star beginning with the given initial letter.

The mystery person may finally be revealed either by means of an indirect question which is so specific that the first player must identify himself – 'Are you an Oxford don who wrote about a Mad Hatter's tea party?' – or by means of a direct question – 'Are you Lewis Carroll?' The player who asks the question that unmasks the mystery person is the winner of that round, and he chooses a character for the next round.

What Nonsense!

No. of players: 3 or more
Equipment: Slips of paper and a pencil
Complexity: ★★

This game requires each player to talk a lot of nonsense about a particular topic for two minutes.

A list of topics is devised – as many topics as there are players – and each topic is written on a slip of paper which is then folded. The topics may be fairly straightforward, like these examples:

1 New uses for old toothpaste tubes.
2 Are chocolate sweets a health hazard?
3 Teaching goldfish to talk.
4 Who *did* kill Cock Robin?
5 Was Hiawatha really a Martian?
6 Why is a raven like a writing-desk?

Or they may be just a little more rarefied, like these examples:

7   Is it Wednesday in Bolivia?
8   The answer that cannot be questioned.
9   If not, why not?
10 The functionalism of inverse dichotomy.

Each player in turn chooses a slip at random and then has to speak for two minutes on the topic he has chosen. The player who attains the highest peaks of lunacy is the winner.

Stepping Stones

No. of players: 2 to 8
Equipment: None
Complexity: ★★☆

Stepping Stones is a mentally stimulating game of word associations, which may be played on any level from the banal to the esoteric. Each player in turn is given five themes by the other players. For example, a player may be told to get from 'Music' to 'Astronomy' via 'Cookery', 'Finance' and 'Cars'. He may use up to nine statements or phrases as stepping stones and must touch on each of the themes in the order given. The other players, acting collectively as umpires, must satisfy themselves that all the themes have been touched upon, that the sequence of associations is valid, and that any puns, jokes, allusions and the like are not too far-fetched.
Here are two ways in which the example quoted might work out:

1   Dame Nellie Melba was an opera singer. (*Music*)
2   Peach Melba was named in her honour. (*Cookery*)
3   Every peach contains a stone.
4   A stone is fourteen pounds.
5   Pounds are Sterling. (*Finance*)
6   Stirling Moss was a British racing driver. (*Cars*)
7   Moss, so they say, is not gathered by rolling stones.
8   The Rolling Stones are rock stars.
9   Stars, in fact, are formed from gas not from rock. (*Astronomy*)

1   Musicians usually begin by learning scales. (*Music*)
2   Scales are found on fish.
3   Salmon is the fish most often served with salads. (*Cookery*)
4   Salmon may be caught from river banks.
5   Banks are financial institutions. (*Finance*)
6   Bank managers usually play golf.
7   The Golf is an imported car, unlike the Mini. (*Cars*)
8   Mini-skirts should only be worn by women with heavenly bodies.
9   Stars and planets are heavenly bodies. (*Astronomy*)

3

PAPER AND PENCIL GAMES

Noughts and Crosses
Hangman
The Worm
Boxes
Sprouts
Battleships
Salvo
Aggression
Wordpower
Bulls and Cows
Categories
Guggenheim
Wordbuilder
Combinations
Anagrams
Scaffold
Alpha
Arena
Vowels
Stairway
Acrostics
Advertisements
Crossword
Crosswords
Consequences
Picture Consequences
Telegrams
Short Story

Noughts and Crosses

(*Alternative names*: Oxo or Tic-Tac-Toe)

No. of players: 2
Equipment: Paper and two pencils
Complexity: ☆

Noughts and Crosses is a tremendously popular children's game which, for generations of schoolchildren, has been one of the principal means of relieving the tedium of boring lessons. Before play begins a framework is drawn, consisting of two pairs of parallel lines crossing at right angles.

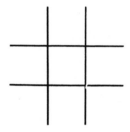

The players play alternately, the first player drawing a nought, and the second player drawing a cross, in any one of the nine spaces which is vacant. The aim of the first player is to complete a row of three noughts, and the aim of the second player is to complete a row of three crosses, while at the same time each player tries to block his opponent. The winner is the first player to complete a row, horizontally, vertically or diagonally.

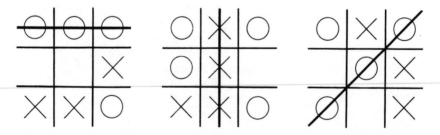

Once one learns the simple strategy required for this game it is impossible to lose unless one makes an absolutely appalling blunder. Between two experienced players every game will end in a draw, with neither player being able to complete a row.

Hangman

No. of players: 2
Equipment: Paper and two pencils
Complexity: ☆

In this popular game one player thinks of a word, preferably of six or more letters, which the other player has to discover by guessing letters. The first player writes down a series of dashes to indicate the number of letters in the word, thus: – – – – – – – –. The second player then starts guessing the letters in the word, calling out one letter at a time. If the letter occurs in the word the first player writes that letter above the appropriate dash (or dashes) wherever the letter occurs.

For each letter called out which does not occur in the word the first player draws a part of the Hangman picture, in the order shown here:

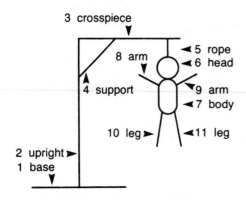

The incorrectly guessed letters are also recorded underneath the dashes so that the second player can see which letters he has already tried.

The second player wins if he correctly guesses all the letters in the word before the picture is completed. He then chooses the word in the next game for the other player to guess.

If the picture is completed before the second player has identified all the letters he is 'hanged' and loses, and the first player selects another word for him to guess.

Sometimes the game is played using agreed themes, such as Book Titles or Pop Stars, in which case the name or title to be guessed may consist of more than one word. In this case the first player will draw the dashes to show the number of letters in each word with spaces between the words.

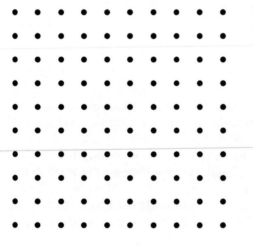

_ **A N G** _ **A N**

E R S I T O U L C D P

The Worm

No. of players: 2
Equipment: Paper and two pencils
Complexity: ☆

To begin, ten rows of ten dots each are marked on a sheet of paper, like this:

```
• • • • • • • • • •
• • • • • • • • • •
• • • • • • • • • •
• • • • • • • • • •
• • • • • • • • • •
• • • • • • • • • •
• • • • • • • • • •
• • • • • • • • • •
• • • • • • • • • •
• • • • • • • • • •
```

The first player draws a horizontal or vertical line to join any two adjacent dots. Diagonal lines are not allowed. The second player then draws another line, connecting either end of the existing line horizontally or vertically to any adjacent dot. The players then continue playing alternately in this manner, drawing a line from either end of the existing line ('the worm') to an adjacent dot. The objective is to force one's opponent into a position in which he has to draw a line which will join either end of the worm back on to itself, thus losing the game.

For example, in the game illustrated below the player whose turn it is to move is bound to lose since, no matter which end he plays, he has to join the worm back on to itself.

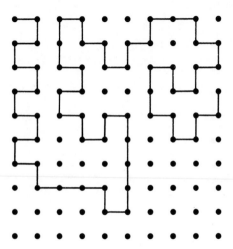

Boxes

No. of players: 2
Equipment: Paper and two pencils
Complexity: ✶✶

To begin, ten rows of ten dots are marked on a sheet of paper, as shown for the previous game. The players take it in turn to draw a straight line connecting any two dots which are next to each other, either horizontally or vertically. Diagonal lines are not allowed. The objective is to complete as many 'boxes' as possible. A box is completed by drawing the fourth side of a square when the other three sides have already been drawn. Therefore, as a matter of strategy, a player generally tries to avoid drawing the third side of any square as this would give his opponent a chance to complete a box.

Whenever a player completes a box he writes his initial inside it, and he has to draw another line. Thus a player's turn does not end until he draws a line which does not complete a box.

The game ends when all the boxes have been completed. The player who has completed the highest number of boxes is the winner.

In the game illustrated here (in which neither player has played very skilfully!) the player who has the next turn will be able to complete three boxes in the lower right-hand corner.

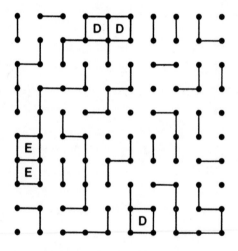

The game may begin with fewer dots if a quick game is required or with more dots if a longer game is wanted.

Another version of the game is played so that the winner is the player who completes fewer boxes than his opponent. In this version players try to avoid having to draw the fourth side of a box.

Sprouts

No. of players: 2
Equipment: Paper and two pencils
Complexity: ★★

This game originated in the early 1960s. Since then it has spread around the world and has become a firm favourite among pencil and paper games. It looks very simple but a lot of concentration is required if one is to play it really well.

To begin, 3, 4 or 5 dots are marked at random on a sheet of paper. Each player in turn draws a line beginning and ending on any of the dots (so a line may join two dots together or may loop round and end on the dot it started from) and then draws a new dot on the line he has just drawn. So, starting with 4 dots, after both players have had one turn the position might look like this:

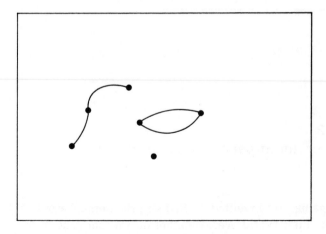

In drawing the lines, two simple rules must be observed:
(a) No line may cross any other line or pass through a dot.
(b) No dot may have more than three lines leading from it.

The players continue playing alternately until no more lines can be drawn, and the player who draws the last line is the winner.

For example, in the position illustrated below, the player with the next turn must win. The only line that can be drawn will connect the top and bottom dots and, even though a new dot will be created on that line, it will be impossible to draw any further lines.

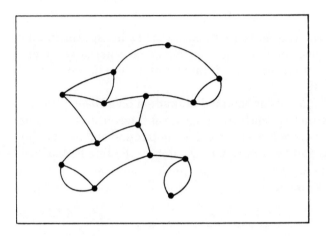

Battleships

No. of players: 2
Equipment: Paper and a pencil for each player
Complexity: ★★

It is said that this game was invented by British prisoners-of-war in Germany during the First World War. Whether or not that is so, it is certainly true that this is a very popular game, one in which skill and luck are equally blended.

Before the game begins each player marks out on his sheet of paper two identical playing areas, each area consisting of a large square divided into 100 smaller squares, ten squares across by ten squares down. This preparation may be made less of a chore if one uses printed graph paper with squares of a suitable size. Each playing area should have the letters A to J across the top and the numbers 1 to 10 down one side, so that each square may be identified by its letter and number. Thus the squares in the top row are A1, B1, C1 and so on; the squares in the bottom row are A10, B10, C10 etc. One area is marked Home Fleet and the other area Enemy Fleet.

Each player now places his fleet in the Home Fleet area. From this point until the end of the game each player must take care that his sheet cannot be seen by the other player.

A fleet consists of the following ships:

1 battleship   (4 squares)
2 cruisers   (3 squares each)
3 destroyers   (2 squares each)
4 submarines   (1 square each)

A player may place his ships where he likes in the Home Fleet area, subject to the following rules:

(a) The squares forming each ship must be in a straight line, across or down.
(b) There must be at least one empty square between ships – in other words, no two ships may touch, even at a corner.

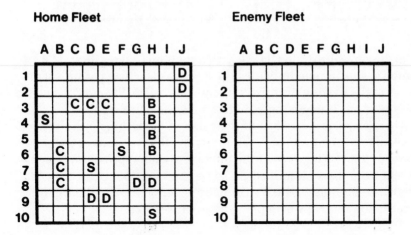

When both players have drawn their fleets then battle can commence. The objective, of course, is to sink the enemy fleet. To sink each ship all the squares forming the ship must be hit.

Each player in turn fires a shot at the Enemy Fleet by naming out loud a square, for example A7 or D3. The opponent then examines his Home Fleet area to see whether that square is occupied by a ship. He must declare whether the shot was a hit or a miss, and if it was a hit he must identify the type of ship. The player firing the shot records a miss by marking the appropriate square in the Enemy Fleet area with a dot, or records a hit by marking the square with a letter identifying the type of ship.

The players continue firing alternately until one of the players wins the game by completely destroying the enemy fleet.

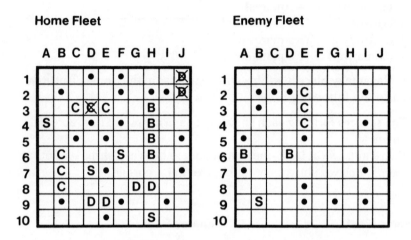

In the game illustrated it is clear that shots on squares B6 and C6 are required to sink the enemy battleship. It is also clear that, because of the rules as to the placing of ships, squares such as D5, F2 and C9 must be unoccupied, so it would be pointless to waste shots on them.

There are many versions of the game of battleships – the version described here being one of the simplest. In other versions of the game the size of the playing area or the number of each type of ship may be different from those described. In some versions, too, ships may be placed diagonally as well as horizontally or vertically, and there may be no restriction on ships occupying adjacent squares.

Salvo

No. of players: 2
Equipment: Paper and pencil for each player
Complexity: ✩✩✩

This game is similar to *Battleships* but with one difference which makes *Salvo* a considerably more skilful game. The difference is that instead of firing one shot in his turn a player fires a 'salvo' of three shots. The opponent then declares whether any of the shots were direct hits and what types of ship were hit by the salvo, but not the results of any individual shot. For example, the first player may call out 'C7, D12 and H2' and the second player may reply 'Two hits, one on a submarine and one on a battleship'.

The fact that a player does not know exactly which of his shots were hits makes this a more complex game than *Battleships*.

Aggression

No. of players: 2
Equipment: Paper and two pencils
Complexity: ✩✩✩

Aggression is a pencil-and-paper wargame in which the players attack and conquer each other's countries. The objective is to reduce as far as possible the number of countries occupied by the opponent's armies while trying to retain as many as possible of the countries occupied by one's own armies. Players can cast themselves in the role of Napoleon versus Wellington, or Montgomery versus Rommel, or America versus Russia – or even, if they prefer, Julius Caesar with his legions versus Genghis Khan with his Tartar hordes!

It is also a good example of a simple-but-complex game, in that it can easily be learned and played at a basic level by children or it can be played by professors of mathematics with considerable in-depth analysis of strategy and tactics.

The first stage of the game is the drawing of the battle area, which is a map of a number of imaginary countries with common boundaries. Any number of countries may be drawn, but twenty is the usual number. They may be any size and shape, but should not be too small. The players take it in turn when drawing the map, each adding one country in his turn. The countries are then marked with letters for identification.

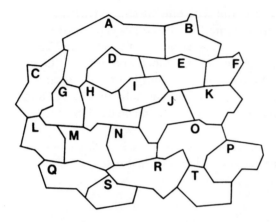

The second stage of the game is to occupy the countries with armies. Each player has 100 armies. The players take it in turn to allocate any number of their armies to an unoccupied country, writing the number of armies in the appropriate area. For example the first player may decide to occupy country D with 20 of his armies, then the second player may decide to occupy J with 22 armies, then the first player may put 3 armies in A, and so on. Preferably, pencils of two different colours should be used to distinguish one player's armies from those of his opponent; alternatively, one player may underline his numbers.

It is for each player to decide whether he occupies a few countries with large numbers of armies or whether he places a few armies in each of a large number of countries.

This stage of the game finishes when both players have allocated all their armies or when all the countries have been occupied.

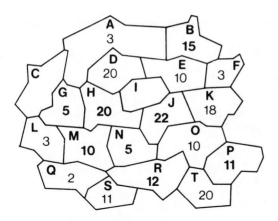

The third and final stage of the game is the aggressive part. Each player in turn uses the armies in one or more of the countries occupied by him to conquer an adjacent country occupied by his opponent, thus wiping out the opponent's armies stationed in that country. Adjacent countries are those with a common boundary. For example, in the game illustrated here, A, E and F are adjacent to B, and E, F, J and O are all adjacent to K.

A player may conquer one of his opponent's countries only if he has more armies in adjacent countries than the opponent has in the country being attacked. The number of armies in the conquered country is crossed out, playing no further part in the game. The conquering armies, however, remain intact.

It should be noted that conquering a country does not increase the number of countries that a player occupies – it simply decreases the number of countries occupied by the opponent. It should also be noted that countries not occupied by either player take no part in this stage of the game except as 'neutral zones'.

The game ends when neither player can conquer any more of his opponent's countries. The player left occupying the highest number of countries is the winner.

The game that we have illustrated might proceed in this way:

Player 1	*Player 2*
A, E, F conquer B	P, R conquer T
A, D conquer H	J conquers K
O conquers N	R conquers S
A, L conquer G	J conquers O
(Player 1 passes	J conquers E
as he cannot conquer	M conquers L
any more countries)	M conquers Q

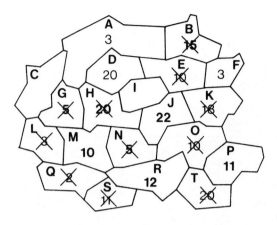

The second player wins, since he has four countries left while the first player is left with only three.

Wordpower

No. of players: 2
Equipment: Paper and a pencil
Complexity: ★★★

The first player thinks of a 5-letter word which has to be guessed by the second player.

Guessing the mystery word involves logical deduction and a process of elimination. The second player proposes any 5-letter word and the first player indicates how close this word is to the mystery word by awarding points – one point for each letter in the proposed word that corresponds with a letter in the mystery word. Note that the second player is not told which letters are correct, only how many. The second player carries on making guesses until he has enough information to identify the mystery word. The paper and pencil are needed for the second player to record his guesses, the points they scored, and the letters that can be eliminated.

The players then change roles for the second round, and the first player has to guess a 5-letter word thought of by the second player. The winner of the game is the player who identifies the mystery word in the fewer number of guesses.

Here is a sample round, showing the sort of reasoning that is required:

1	**DANCE**	1 point	
2	**SANDY**	2 points	
3	**HANDY**	1 point	(There must be an **S** and no **H**)
4	**SOUND**	1 point	(That eliminates **O, U, N, D** – from guess 2 there must be an **A** or **Y**)
5	**SUNNY**	1 point	(That eliminates **Y**. The word contains **S, A** – from guess 1, that eliminates **C, E**)
6	**FAILS**	2 points	(That eliminates **F, I, L**)
7	**STRAP**	4 points	(The word contains two of the letters from **T, R, P**)
8	**GRASP**	3 points	(So the word contains **T** and no **G** – we now have **S, A, T** plus either **R** or **P** and one other or a repeated letter)
9	**STAMP**	3 points	(So it's **S, T, A, R** and another – no **M** or **P**)
10	**STRAW**	That's it!	

A̶B̶C̶D̶E̶F̶G̶H̶I̶J̶K̶L̶M̶N̶O̶P̶Q̶R̶S̶T̶U̶V̶W̶X̶Y̶Z̶

Bulls and Cows

No. of players: 2
Equipment: Paper and a pencil
Complexity: ✰✰✰

Bulls and Cows is another game of logical deduction that is similar to *Wordpower* except that numbers not words are to be guessed and the scoring of guesses is rather different.

The first player thinks of a 4-digit number (e.g. 4711 or 9362). The second player guesses by proposing any 4-digit number. The first player tells him how close his guess is by saying how many 'bulls' and 'cows' he has scored. A bull means that the guess contains a correct digit in the correct position; a cow means that the guess contains a correct digit but that it is in the wrong position. The second player continues guessing until he has enough information to identify the mystery number. For example, if the number thought by the first player was 9362 then the guesses and responses might proceed like this:

'1234'	'2 cows'
'2468'	'1 bull, 1 cow'
'1580'	'Nothing'
'2346'	'1 bull, 2 cows'
'4367'	'2 bulls'
'9362'	'4 bulls. That's it!'

The paper and pencil will be needed by the second player to record his guesses and their scores, and possibly to work out which digits can be eliminated and what possibilities remain.

When the mystery number has been guessed, the players change roles and the first player has to guess the number thought of by the second player. The player who requires the fewer number of guesses to identify the mystery number is the winner.

Categories

No. of players: 2 or more
Equipment: Paper and a pencil for each player
Complexity: ★★

The players decide on a list of categories (preferably twelve or more). The fairest way is for each player to propose an equal number of categories. These may be simple and straightforward (e.g. Animals, Countries, TV Programmes, Indoor Games) or more specialised (e.g. Peruvian Footballers, Hydrocarbons, People And Places Named In Proust's *A La Recherche Du Temps Perdu*) depending on the composition of the group that is playing.

Each player writes down the list of categories on his sheet of paper, and then a letter of the alphabet is chosen at random. A time limit of, say, ten or fifteen minutes is agreed. The players then have to write down as many words as they can beginning with the chosen letter for each of the categories.

When the time is up each player in turn reads out his list of words. A word which has not been thought of by any other player scores two points. A word which one or more other players have also listed scores one point. The player with the most points is the winner.

For subsequent rounds a new initial letter is chosen. The same categories may be used again or a new list of categories may be selected.

Guggenheim

No. of players: 2 or more
Equipment: Paper and a pencil for each player
Complexity: ★★

Guggenheim is basically a variation of the previous game, *Categories*. A list of categories is chosen and each player writes the list down the left-hand margin of his sheet of paper. A keyword of five or more letters is then chosen and each player writes the keyword, spaced out, along the top of his sheet of paper. A time limit of ten or fifteen minutes is agreed, and each player must then write down one word beginning with each letter of the keyword for each category. For example, with a keyword of **MAYBE** a completed list might look something like this:

	M	**A**	**Y**	**B**	**E**
Colours	Mauve	Amber	Yellow	Bistre	Ebony
Items of clothing	Mitten	Apron	Yashmak	Blouse	?
Birds	Mallard	Albatross	Yellow-hammer	Bantam	Egret
Indoor Games	Muggins	Aggression	Yacht	Back-gammon	Euchre
Countries	Malaysia	Andorra	Yemen	Burundi	Ethiopia
Poets	Milton	Arnold	Yeats	Burns	Eliot

Wordbuilder

No. of players: 2 or more
Equipment: Paper and a pencil for each player
Complexity: ★★

The players are all given the same starter word, which should be a moderately long word such as HIPPOPOTAMUS or CONTRABAND.

Each player then has to write down a list of words using the letters contained in the starter word. A time limit of ten minutes is set, and the player who lists the most words within this time limit is the winner.

The following rules are usually applied:

(a) Each word must contain at least four letters.
(b) Proper nouns (names of people, places etc.) are not allowed.
(c) Foreign words, abbreviations and plurals are not allowed.
(d) A letter may be used in any word no more than the number of times it occurs in the starter word.

It might be a good idea to have a dictionary available to check disputed words.

As an example the following list shows some of the words that might be made from CONTRABAND:

Band	Crab	Cord	Carton	Brand
Bard	Drab	Cobra	Brat	Bacon
Dart	Drat	Cart	Adorn	Road
Baron	Acorn	Card	Abandon	Broad
Barn	Corn	Cant	Trod	Toad

Combinations

No. of players: 2 or more
Equipment: Paper and a pencil for each player
Complexity: ★★

A list of ten or more 2-letter or 3-letter combinations which could occur within words is prepared. Such a list might contain letter combinations such as the following:

–BL–	–RF–	–IX–	–GTH–	–MON–
–QU–	–MN–	–SU–	–BUL–	–TOG–

Each of the players writes down the list on his sheet of paper. A time limit of five minutes is set, in which each player has to find as long a word as possible containing each of the letter combinations. The scoring is one point per letter for each word, and the player with the highest total score is the winner.

For example, using the combinations shown above, a player might achieve this result:

Troublesome	=	11
Perfection	=	10
Sixteenth	=	9
Strengthen	=	10
Commonwealth	=	12
Prerequisite	=	12
Condemned	=	9
Persuasively	=	12
Ebullience	=	10
Photographic	=	12
Total score	=	**107**

Anagrams

No. of players: 2 or more (plus a question-master)
Equipment: Paper and a pencil for each player
Complexity: ☆☆

The question-master chooses a category such as Countries, Birds, Garden Flowers or Rivers, and prepares a list of words belonging to that category. He then prepares another list of the same words but with the letters of each word jumbled up. The list of jumbled words is placed in a position where all the players can see it, or alternatively each player is given his own copy. A time limit of five or ten minutes is set, in which each player has to discover the original words by unscrambling the jumbled versions. The winner is the first player to unscramble all the words correctly or the player with the most correct words when the time limit has expired
    For example:

Jumbled Countries

1	Neaky	5	Nomoac	9	Regalia
2	Rumba	6	Bedraum	10	Agalamute
3	Courade	7	Waliam	11	Englander
4	Wednes	8	Presagion	12	Netsetinchile

Solution

1	Kenya	5	Monaco	9	Algeria
2	Burma	6	Bermuda	10	Guatemala
3	Ecuador	7	Malawi	11	Greenland
4	Sweden	8	Singapore	12	Liechtenstein

Scaffold

No. of players: 2 or more
Equipment: Paper and a pencil for each player
Complexity: ★★

The players are all given the same three letters – R, D, T, for example –
and they have ten minutes in which to form a list of words which contain
those three letters in the order given. Such a list might contain the
following words if R, D, T were the letters given:

CORDITE	**PRODUCT**
CORDIALITY	**CREDIT**
RADIOLOGIST	**ARIDITY**
RADIATOR	**GRADUATE**
PREDATOR	**INTRODUCTION**

Players score one point for each word listed, and the player with the
highest score is the winner.

The three letters should be chosen carefully so that it is possible to
find a good number of words which use them. Thus L, M, E or R, F, N or
M, I, T, for example, would be satisfactory, but Z, Q, N or W, X, F could
just possibly result in scores of zero all round (unless you are playing
with a group of Serbian lexicographers).

Alpha

No. of players: 2 or more
Equipment: Paper and a pencil for each player
Complexity: ★★

This is a word-listing game in which the players have a time limit of ten minutes in which to list words beginning and ending with the same letter of the alphabet. There are two different versions of the game.

In the first version the players simply have to list as many words as they can that end with the same letter with which they begin. The winner is the player who produces the longest list of such words.

In the second version, which is a more demanding test of vocabulary, each player first writes the letter of the alphabet down the left-hand margin of his sheet of paper. Then for each letter he has to find the longest possible word which begins and ends with that letter. When the time limit has expired, the players score one point for each letter of each word they have listed and the player with the highest total score is the winner. One player's completed list might look something like this:

A	AMNESIA	=	7	**N**	NATIONAL-ISATION	=	15
B	BEDAUB	=	6	**O**	OVERDO	=	6
C	CYCLONIC	=	8	**P**	PARTNERSHIP	=	11
D	DEDICATED	=	9	**Q**			
E	EVERYONE	=	8	**R**	REGULATOR	=	9
F	FLUFF	=	5	**S**	SUCCINCTNESS	=	12
G	GRADUATING	=	10	**T**	TOURNAMENT	=	9
H	HUNCH	=	5	**U**			
I				**V**			
J				**W**	WINDOW	=	6
K	KAYAK	=	5	**X**			
L	LONGITUDINAL	=	12	**Y**	YELLOWY	=	7
M	METAMORPHISM	=	12	**Z**			

Arena

No. of players: 2 or more
Equipment: Paper and a pencil for each player
Complexity: ☆☆

The players have ten minutes in which to form as long a list as possible of 5-letter words which have a vowel as the first letter, a consonant as the second, a vowel as the third, a consonant as the fourth, and a vowel as the last letter. Such a list might include words such as these:

ARENA	OPERA	UNITE
AROMA	ABODE	AMUSE
ELOPE	AWAKE	OKAPI
EVADE	IMAGE	AGATE

The player who produces the longest list will be the winner.

Vowels

No. of players: 2 or more
Equipment: Paper and a pencil for each player
Complexity: ☆☆

This is another word-listing game which is a good test of vocabulary. A particular vowel is chosen, and the players have ten minutes in which to produce a list of words which must conform to the following simple rules:

(a) Each word must contain at least five letters.
(b) Each word must contain the chosen vowel twice or more, and must contain no other vowel.
(c) Proper nouns, foreign words and hyphenated words are not allowed.

Here are typical words which might be listed for each chosen vowel:

A   CATAMARAN, KAYAK, BALLAD, ANAGRAM, SALAD,
       BANTAM . . .
E   REBEL, PRECEDE, REDEEMER, REFEREE, BEETLE, FEEBLE . . .
I   MINIM, CIVIL, PIPPIN, RIPPING, ILLICIT, IMPLICIT . . .
O   ROBOT, MORON, COMMON, DOCTOR, CORDON,
       MONSOON . . .
U   SUBURB, HUMDRUM, UPTURN, SUNBURN, RUMPUS,
       SUCCUBUS . . .

Players score one point for each time the chosen vowel occurs in each of their words. The player with the highest total score is the winner.

Stairway

No. of players: 2 or more
Equipment: Paper and a pencil for each player
Complexity: ☆☆

A letter of the alphabet is called out and the players have ten minutes in which to form a 'Stairway' of words beginning with that letter. The stairway consists of a 2-letter word, then a 3-letter word, then a 4-letter word, and so on. Here is an example for the letter M:

M
ME
MAN
MINT
MELON
MEADOW
MISSION
MATERNAL
MORTALITY
MISFORTUNE
MAGNIFICENT
MATHEMATICAL
MISCELLANEOUS
MULTIPLICATION
MISAPPREHENSION

The winner is the player who forms the longest stairway.

Acrostics

No. of players: 2 or more
Equipment: Paper and a pencil for each player
Complexity: ☆☆

A word of six or seven letters is chosen, and each player writes the word down in a column on the left side of his sheet of paper. He then writes the same word in another column to the right of the first one, but this time with the letters in reverse order. Let us say the chosen word is CARAMEL, then each player's sheet of paper should look something like this:

```
C            L
A            E
R            M
A            A
M            R
E            A
L            C
```

The players are then given five minutes in which they have to write the longest word they can think of, beginning and ending with each pair of letters provided by the two columns.

The players score one point per letter for each of their words, and the player with the highest total score is the winner.

```
C  hape   L = 6          C  ontractua   L  = 11
A  pple   E = 5          A  dministrativ E  = 14
R  hyth   M = 6          R  egionalis   M  = 11
A  lgebr  A = 7          A  spidistr    A  = 10
M  othe   R = 6          M  usketee     R  =  9
E  xtr    A = 5          E  uthanasi    A  = 10
L  ogi    C = 5          L  inguisti    C  = 10
                 40                             75
```

Advertisements

No. of players: 3 or more
Equipment: Old magazines; paper and a pencil
for each player
Complexity: ✩✩

This game is a test of observation (and of the power of advertising). It relies on the fact that much magazine and newspaper advertising places less emphasis on pictures of the product than on 'images' – sun-drenched beaches, pretty girls, laughing family groups, cartoon characters etc.

Some preparation is required beforehand. You need to sort through a number of old magazines and newspapers, cutting out suitable pictures from advertisements for well-known products. The advertisements should be neither too familiar nor too obscure. You may need to cut out of the pictures the name of the product or any other tell-tale indications. Any number of pictures between twelve and twenty should be sufficient. The pictures must be numbered, and may either be pasted on to a board or simply laid out on a table where all the players can see them.

Each of the players is given a pencil and paper, and they have ten minutes in which to write down the names of the products being advertised. The player with the highest number of correct answers is the winner.

Crossword

No. of players: 2
Equipment: Paper and two pencils
Complexity: ✩✩

Before the game begins a square grid is drawn, with nine squares across and nine squares down. A larger grid may be drawn if a longer game is required. The first player writes a word anywhere in the grid, either across or down, and scores one point for each letter in the word. The players then play alternately, each player forming another word which must interlock with one or more of the previously entered letters in crossword fashion, and scoring one point for each new letter written. For example, if a player writes in the word CROSSWORD, linking with the C and W of previously completed words, he would score 7 points – he cannot claim for the C and W. Proper nouns, abbreviations and foreign words are not allowed.

Play continues until neither player can find further letters that can be inserted to form new words. The player with the highest score is the winner.

D	I	S	C	U	S	S		P
I		H		T				O
S	T	R	E	N	U	O	U	S
T		C		M				T
U	S	K		B	O	O	M	
R	O	O	M		L			A
B		A		I		A	N	
E		S	T	O	N	E	D	
D	O		E		G		O	X

Mary	Michael
9	8
8	8
6	4
2	4
2	2
1	1
1	
29	27

Crosswords

No. of players: 2 or more
Equipment: Paper and a pencil for each player
Complexity: ★★

Although this and the previous game have similar names they are in fact quite different. (An interesting, though irrelevant, point to note is that the completed grid in the previous game resembles the type of crossword that is popular in Britain, whereas the completed grid in this game resembles the type of crossword that is more popular in France.)

Before the game begins each player draws on his sheet of paper a grid with five squares across and five squares down. If a longer game is required or if there are more than five players a larger grid may be used. Each player in turn then calls out any letter of his choice. All the players must then enter that letter in their own grids, in any position they choose. Once a letter has been entered it may not be moved. The aim is to form words either across or down.

The game ends when all the squares have been filled. The scores are then worked out according to the number of letters in the words each player has formed. One point is scored for each letter contained in a valid word – one-letter words, proper nouns, foreign words and abbreviations do not count. A letter may not be shared by two or more words in the same row or column. (Thus if a player has a row that reads **CONET** the most he can score is 4 points for **CONE** – he cannot also score points for **ON**, **ONE** or **NET**.) One bonus point is scored for each word that completely fills a row or column.

The player with the highest total score is the winner.

Player 1   Player 2

D	O	G	M	I	3
A	T	B	E	T	5
R	O	L	I	S	2
T	O	U	G	H	6
F	X	T	O	E	3

4 3 0 4 5

F	O	E	A	T	5
O	R	X	G	M	2
O	B	I	T	H	3
D	O	T	L	I	3
G	U	E	S	T	6

4 3 4 0 3

Score: 35 points   Score: 33 points

Consequences

No. of players: Any large number
Equipment: Paper and a pencil for each player
Complexity: ☆

Consequences is a party game which is very popular with children (particularly grown-up children). It can be marvellously silly, and is played purely for amusement – there are no winners or losers.

Each player is provided with a pencil and a sheet of paper. The idea is to write little stories to which each player contributes a part without knowing what any of the other players has written. This random composition can produce ludicrous results.

For each part of the story the players are told what sort of information is required, e.g. a female character, a male character, where they met, and so on. After writing each part of the story the player folds over the sheet to conceal what he has written and passes the folded sheet to the next player on his left. At the same time he will receive from the player on his right a different folded sheet, on which he will write the next part of the story. This process is repeated until each player has written all the required parts of the story, all on different sheets of paper. The papers are then unfolded and the results read out.

The parts that make up the story may vary, but the traditional *Consequences* story goes something like this:

1	A female character	e.g. Little Bo-Peep
2	Met a male character	e.g. Met Mao Tse-Tung
3	Where they met	e.g. Behind the Bicycle Shed
4	What he did	e.g. He Pinched Her Bottom
5	What she did	e.g. She Smoked A Big Cigar
6	What he said	e.g. He said 'The End Of The World Is Nigh'
7	What she said	e.g. She said 'We Are Not Amused'
8	What the consequence was	e.g. The Consequence Was a Rise In World Oil Prices
9	And what the world said	e.g. And the World said 'All's Fair in Love and War'

Picture Consequences

No. of players: 3 or more
Equipment: Paper and a pencil for each player
Complexity: ☆

This is another popular party game, for children or for sophisticated adults. Each player is given a pencil and a sheet of paper which has two lines drawn across it to divide the paper into three equal sections. The lines are not absolutely necessary but they do make the game easier for young children (or for the sophisticated adults who may have imbibed too much of the party spirit).

In the top section of the paper the player draws a head – which may be the head of a person, a bird, an animal or whatever he chooses. The neck should be drawn to go just over the line into the middle section. He then folds the top of the paper down to the first line to conceal what he has drawn, and passes the sheet of paper to the next player on his left.

Using the sheet of paper passed to him by his neighbour he draws a body and legs – again either human or otherwise – in the centre section, joining it on to the neck drawn by his neighbour. The legs should be drawn to go just over the line into the lower section. Again the sheet of paper is folded to conceal what has been drawn and is passed on.

Using the next sheet of paper passed to him, he then draws some feet – once more either human or otherwise – in the lower section, to join on to the legs already drawn.

Each player will have contributed parts to three different drawings. It is important that at each stage no player lets any of the other players see what he is drawing. When the pictures are all completed the players unfold the sheets of paper to see what has been drawn, and then laugh themselves silly.

Telegrams

No. of players: 3 or more
Equipment: Paper and a pencil for each player
Complexity: ★★

Each player in turn calls out a letter of the alphabet at random, and all the players write down the letters as they are called out. A list of about 15 letters should be formed in this way. The players then have five minutes in which each of them has to compose a telegram, the words of which must begin with the listed letters in the order given. Stops (full stops) may be inserted where required and the last word of the telegram may, if the player so desires, be the name of the imaginary sender.

For example, if the letters called out were H,A,I,B,B,A,U,T,L,D,H,S,A,O,C one player might write:

> **HAVE ARRIVED IN BLACKPOOL BUT AM UNABLE TO LOCATE DECKCHAIRS HENCE SAND ALL OVER CYNTHIA**

whereas another player might write:

> **HURRY AND IMMEDIATELY BRING BACK ALL UNUSED TEA LEAVES STOP DADDY HATES SUPPING ALE OR COCOA**

When the five minutes are up each player reads out his telegram, and the winner is the player whose telegram is judged to be the most sensible, the cleverest, the wittiest or the silliest.

Short Story

No. of players: 2 or more
Equipment: Paper and a pencil for each player
Complexity: ✫✫

A time limit of five or ten minutes is set. Within that time limit each player has to compose a short story. The only restriction is that no word used may contain more than three letters. When the time limit has expired all the stories are read out. The player whose composition is judged to be the cleverest or most amusing is the winner.

Here is an example of the sort of story that could be produced:'A man had a pig in a sty. It ate all he fed it. But one day the pig bit the man. By gum, was the man mad! Now the pig is ham in a can.'

4 CARD GAMES

Whist
Solo Whist
Bridge
Hearts
Black Maria
Slobberhannes
Polignac
Nap
Ecarte
Four-handed Euchre
Three-handed Euchre
Two-handed Euchre
Call-ace Euchre
Rummy
Gin Rummy
Cribbage
Bézique
Cassino
Pontoon
Poker
Draw Poker
Spit in the Ocean
Five Card Stud
Six Card Stud
Seven Card Stud
Brag

Whist

No. of players: 4
Equipment: Standard pack of 52 cards
Complexity: ☆☆☆

Whist, the fore-runner of *Bridge*, is a four-handed partnership game in which points are scored for tricks and honours. The cards rank from ace high to 2 low.

Partners sit opposite each other. The pack is cut to decide first deal, and thereafter each player deals in turn. Thirteen face-down cards are dealt, one at a time, to each player, except that the last card (the dealer's) is dealt face up to establish the trump suit.

Each player picks up the cards dealt to him and arranges them into suits. The player to the left of the dealer leads to the first trick. The other players in turn must follow suit if they can, otherwise they may play a trump or discard a card of another suit as they wish. The trick is won by the highest ranking card of the suit that was led or by the highest trump if any were played. The winner of each trick leads to the next. And so on until all the tricks have been played.

A game is won by the first side to score 5 points. The side winning the majority of tricks (i.e. seven or more) scores 1 point for each trick won in excess of six. Points are also scored for honours – the ace, king, queen and jack of trumps. A side dealt all four honours scores 4 points; or 3 points if dealt any three of them. However, points for honours cannot be scored by a side already holding 4 points towards game at the beginning of the deal. Nor can a side score honours points if the opposing side has already scored sufficient points from tricks to give them the game.

If a player revokes (i.e. fails to follow suit when he could have done so) the penalty is 3 points, which his opponents may either add to their own score or deduct from the score of the revoking side.

A rubber is the best of three games, and the value of a rubber is determined by game points (not to be confused with points from tricks and honours). The side winning a game scores 1 game point if the opposing side has 3 or 4 points, 2 game points if the opposing side has 1 or 2 points, or 3 game points if the opposing side has not scored at all in this game. In addition, the winners of a rubber get 2 extra game points. The value of the rubber is the difference between the game points scored by the winners and the losers, and thus may range from 1 to 8 game points.

Solo Whist

No. of players: 4
Equipment: Standard pack of 52 cards
Complexity: ★★★★

Solo Whist is a gambling game for four players, each playing for himself though temporary partnerships are possible, and is one of the most popular card games. It is considered by many to be the equal of *Bridge* in terms of skill and complexity and to be superior in terms of enjoyment. Whereas thousands of books have been written about all aspects of *Bridge*, very little has been written about *Solo Whist* – and some players claim this as an advantage, pointing out that *Solo Whist* remains flexible while *Bridge* has become over-systematised.

The cards rank from ace high to 2 low, as normal. The players cut for first deal and the player with the lowest card deals. The cards are dealt three at a time, face downwards, for four rounds and the last four cards are then dealt singly. The last card – the dealer's – is dealt face up to indicate the trump suit.

When all the players have picked up and examined their cards the bidding commences. A bid is a declaration by a player that he will attempt to win a certain number of tricks. Each player in turn, beginning with the player to the left of the dealer, may either pass or make a higher bid than any previous bid. A player whose bid is overcalled by another player may subsequently make an even higher bid, but a player who has passed once is not allowed to make a subsequent bid. A player whose bid is followed by three subsequent passes then has to win the declared number of tricks. If he is successful the other players pay him, otherwise he has to pay them – the stakes depending on the value of the bid.

The bids, in ascending order, are as follows:

(a) **Proposal and Acceptance (Prop and Cop)**
A player calling 'I propose' (or more commonly 'Prop') declares that in partnership with any other player who accepts he will win at least eight tricks with the trump suit indicated by the deal. Unless there has been an intervening higher bid, any subsequent player may become the partner by calling 'I accept' (or more commonly 'Cop'). These two players play in partnership if there is no subsequent higher bid.

(b) **Solo**
A bid to win at least five tricks playing alone against the other three players, with the trump suit indicated by the deal.

(c) **Misère**
A bid to lose every trick, playing with no trump suit.

(d) **Abundance**
A bid to win at least nine tricks, with the trump suit to be declared by the bidder himself. The trump suit is not named at the time of the bid. In some schools the player, if this is the highest bid, declares the trump suit after the other players have passed and before the first trick is played. In other schools the first trick is played with the trump suit indicated by the deal, and the Abundance bidder's choice of trump only takes effect for the second and subsequent tricks.

(e) **Royal Abundance**
A bid to win at least nine tricks, with the trump suit indicated by the deal.

(f) **Misère Ouverte (or Spread)**
A bid to lose every trick, playing with no trump suit, and with the bidder's cards exposed face upwards on the table after the first trick.

(g) **Abundance Declared**
A bid to win all thirteen tricks, playing with no trump suit, but with the bidder having the privilege of leading to the first trick.

If all the players pass without making a bid the hands are thrown in and the deal passes to the next player. If a player makes a Prop bid and the other players all pass he may, if he wishes, make a higher bid – otherwise the hands are thrown in. The one exception to the rule that a player may not bid after having passed is that the player to the left of the dealer (but no other player) may, after passing initially, accept a Prop bid from another player.

The normal rules of trick-taking apply (as in Whist), with the lead to the first trick being made by the player to the left of the dealer (except in the case of an Abundance Declared bid) and the winner of each trick leading to the next.

Each deal counts as a separate game. Stakes are paid individually by the other players to the highest bidder if he succeeds in winning the requisite number of tricks; otherwise, he pays each of them individually. The actual stakes, of course, are a matter of agreement by the players but the relative values of the bids are normally as follows:

Prop and Cop	2 units (1 for each partner)
Solo	2 units
Misère	3 units
Abundance	4 units
Royal Abundance	4 units
Misère Ouverte	6 units
Abundance Declared	8 units

The usual practice is for the stakes to depend solely on whether or not the bid is successful, but some players also include bonuses overtricks and penalties for overtricks (often ¼ or ½ unit per trick).

Bridge

No. of players: 4
Equipment: Standard pack of 52 cards
Complexity: ★★★☆

The game we call *Bridge* (or to give it its full, formal name, *Contract Bridge*) evolved from *Whist* over a number of years. The game of *Biritch* or *Russian Whist*, introduced in about 1880, was a version of *Whist* in which the dealer could nominate the trump suit. *Bridge-Whist*, introduced in 1896, gave the dealer the option of letting his partner nominate the trump suit. *Auction Bridge*, introduced in 1904, had many of the features of the current game but had a much less refined scoring system. *Contract Bridge* was given its present form in 1925 by an American millionaire Harold S. Vanderbilt, and was given its present pre-eminence among card games by the indefatigable promotional activities of Ely Culbertson, who also introduced the first standard bidding system.

Bridge has the pre-eminence among card games that *Chess* has among board games. It is a complex game, and it is said that to learn how to play *Bridge* requires a minimum of six months' study and practice. But there are thousands of dedicated players to claim that the satisfaction to be derived from the game justifies this effort.

Bridge is a partnership game for four players. Partners sit opposite each other, and are usually referred to as North-South and East-West.

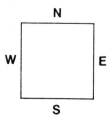

The cards rank from ace high to 2 low. For the purposes of bidding (though not in play) the suits are also ranked in the order: spades (highest), hearts, diamonds, clubs (lowest). Spades and hearts are referred to as major suits, diamonds and clubs as minor suits.

At the beginning of the game there is a draw for partners and first deal. The pack is spread out face down and each player draws a card. The players drawing the two highest cards are partners against the other two, and the player drawing the highest card has first deal.

The normal etiquette observed when dealing is for the player to the left of the dealer to shuffle the pack and for the player to the right of the dealer to cut the pack. The cards are then dealt out, one at a time and face down, to give each player 13 cards.

The game consists of two parts – the bidding (or auction) and the play. The play consists of 13 tricks, and in the bidding each side tries to estimate the number of tricks they think they can win with their combined hands. A bid is a declaration by one side that they will attempt to win a certain number of tricks with a certain nominated trump suit. The highest bid becomes the contract. In the subsequent play the side making the highest bid will attempt to fulfil this contract winning at least the declared number of tricks, while the opposing side will try to stop them.

The bidding begins when every player has had an opportunity to study the cards in his hand. Beginning with the dealer, each player in turn may pass, bid, double or redouble.

To pass a player says 'No bid'. This does not prevent him from making a subsequent bid when his turn comes round again in the bidding.

A bid is a declaration that a player's side will win a certain number of tricks with a nominated trump suit (or with no trumps). Since there are 13 tricks to be taken, the side winning the majority of tricks must win

7 or more. The first 6 tricks won are known as 'the book' and tricks won in excess of 6 are known as 'odd tricks'. Bids are made in terms of odd tricks. Thus, for example, a bid of One Club is a bid to win 7 tricks with clubs as the trump suit, and Two No Trumps is a bid to win 8 tricks with no trump suit.

Each bid must be higher than the previous one. That is, it must be for a higher number of tricks or for the same number of tricks but with a higher ranking suit as trumps. A No Trump bid ranks above a bid in any suit. Thus the possible bids in ascending order are: One Club, One Diamond, One Heart, One Spade, One No Trump, Two Clubs, Two Diamonds, Two Hearts, Two Spades, Two No Trumps, and so on.

Instead of making a bid a player may make a call of 'Double' or 'Redouble'. A call of 'Double', which can only be made after an opponent's bid, signifies that a player is confident of being able to prevent the opposing side from winning the number of tricks bid. A call of 'Redouble', which can only be made if the previous call was a 'Double' from an opponent, signifies that a player is confident that his partner's last bid which has been doubled *can* be successful. Doubling or redoubling doubles or quadruples the points or penalties for success or failure if the bid becomes the contract. A bid that has been doubled or redoubled can be overcalled by a higher bid in the normal way – e.g. the bidding might proceed: Two Clubs, Double, Redouble, Two Hearts – and the double or redouble is thus cancelled.

The contract is established when the last and highest bid (whether undoubled, doubled or redoubled) has been followed by three consecutive Passes. The player on the contracting side who first nominated the trump suit of the contract is the 'declarer', and he will play both his own and his partner's hand.

The opening lead is made by the player to the left of the declarer. As soon as the opening lead has been made, declarer's partner lays all his cards face upwards on the table, with each suit in a separate column of overlapping cards in order of rank. Declarer's partner takes no further part in the play. His hand – known as the 'dummy' – is played for him by the declarer.

The cards are played to each trick in clockwise order, and normal rules of trick-taking apply. A player must follow suit if he can, otherwise he may play a trump or discard a card of any other suit as he pleases. A trick is won by the highest ranking card of the suit that was led, or by the highest ranking trump if any were played. The winner of each trick leads to the next. If the declarer wins a trick from his own hand he must lead to the next trick from his own hand; if he wins a hand from the dummy he must lead to the next trick from the dummy. All the tricks won by one side must be kept in one place and arranged to show clearly the number of tricks won so far.

Scoring is done on a sheet divided into two columns. It is customary for both sides to keep score – to provide a double check – and to record their own score in one column headed WE and their opponents' score in the other column, headed THEY. A horizontal line divides the columns into an upper half and a lower half, and points may be scored 'above the line' or 'below the line'. Only points scored below the line count towards game.

A game is won by the first side to reach or exceed 100 points below the line. A rubber is won by the first side to win two games. A side with one game won is said to be 'vulnerable'.

Details of the scoring are shown in the accompanying table. Trick points can only be scored by the declarer's side, if the contract succeeds. Only the odd tricks contracted for can be scored below the line. Overtricks – those won in excess of the contract – are scored above the line.

A successful contract to win 12 tricks is called a Little Slam. A successful contract to win all 13 tricks is called a Grand Slam. There are bonus points for winning a Slam, and for winning a doubled or redoubled contract. These bonus points are scored above the line.

If the declarer 'goes down' (i.e. if the contract does not succeed) the opposing side score points above the line for each 'undertrick' (i.e. each trick by which declarer falls short of the contract).

Regardless of whether the contract fails or succeeds, either side may score points above the line for 'honours'. Honours are the five highest-ranking cards in the trump suit – A to 10 – or, in a No Trumps contract, the four aces. Points are scored for having been dealt honours in one's hand, and thus represent a pure chance element.

When a game is won, a line is drawn below the trick scores for both sides. Trick points for the next game, starting again from zero, are scored below this line. At the end of a rubber the winning side scores a bonus above the line of 700 points if the opposing side has not won a game, or 500 points if the opposing side has won a game. All the points above and below the line are then totalled for each side. The difference between the two scores represents the value of the rubber.

Bridge Scoring Table

Contract succeeds: Points scored below the line for each odd trick bid and won

	Undoubled	*Doubled*	*Redoubled*
In minor suit (clubs or diamonds)	20	40	80
In major suit (hearts or spades)	30	60	120
No trumps – first odd trick	40	80	160
No trumps – subsequent tricks	30	60	120

Contract succeeds: Points scored above the line by Declarer

	Not Vulnerable	*Vulnerable*
Per overtrick, if undoubled	(Trick value–as above)	
Per overtrick, if doubled	100	200
Per overtrick, if redoubled	200	400
Bonus for doubled or redoubled contract	50	50
Little Slam	500	750
Grand Slam	1000	1500

Contract fails: Points scored above the line by Defenders

	Not Vulnerable	*Vulnerable*
If undoubled, for each undertrick	50	100
If doubled, for 1st undertrick	100	200
If doubled, for subsequent undertricks	200	300
If redoubled, for 1st undertrick	200	400
If redoubled, for subsequent undertricks	400	600

Honours: Points scored above the line

For all 5 trump honours in one hand	150
For any 4 trump honours in one hand	100
For 4 aces in one hand in No Trump contract	150

Rubber and Game Points

For winning rubber, if opponents have won no game	700
For winning rubber, if opponents have won one game	500
Unfinished rubber: for having won one game	300
Unfinished rubber: for having part score in unfinished game	50

Hearts

No. of players: 3 to 7
Equipment: Standard pack of 52 cards
Complexity: ★★☆

Hearts is one of a number of games in which the aim is to avoid winning tricks that contain certain penalty cards. The penalty cards in *Hearts* (as one might reasonably anticipate) are hearts, each of which counts one point. Thus there are 13 penalty points to be distributed among the players.

Before the game begins it may be necessary to remove some cards from the pack, according to the number of players, so that the pack may be dealt out fully with each player receiving an equal number of cards. With three players the 2 of clubs is removed; with five players the 2 of clubs and 2 of diamonds are removed; with six players all the 2s are removed; with seven players the 2 of clubs, 2 of diamonds and 2 of spades are removed.

The cards are cut to select the dealer, and the dealer deals out the cards, one at a time and face down.

The player to the left of the dealer leads to the first trick, and thereafter the winner of each trick leads to the next. Players must follow suit if they can, otherwise they may play any card. There are no trumps and a trick is always won by the highest card of the suit that was led.

At the end of the hand each player counts the number of hearts in the tricks he has won and scores that number of penalty points. The winner is the player with the lowest number of points after an agreed number of hands, or the player with the lowest number of points when any player's score reaches a set number such as 50.

An alternative method, when the game is played for stakes, is for each hand to be considered a separate game. Each player pays into a pool one unit for each heart he has taken and the pool is shared by any players with no hearts. If all the players have taken one or more hearts the pool is carried forward to the next game.

Black Maria

No. of players: 3 to 7
Equipment: Standard pack of 52 cards
Complexity: ✫✫✫

Black Maria is similar to *Hearts*, except for the following differences:

(a) The queen of spades ('Black Maria') is an extra penalty card which counts a hefty 13 penalty points.
(b) After the deal, but before the first lead, there is an exchange of cards. Each player, after examining the cards in his hand, passes any three cards face down to the player on his right. A player may not look at the cards he has received until he has passed on the cards he has discarded from his own hand.

Slobberhannes

No. of players: 3 to 6
Equipment: Short pack of 32 cards
Complexity: ✫✫

Slobberhannes is played with a pack from which all cards below seven have been removed. If there are three, five of six players the two black 7s are also removed. Cards rank from ace high to 7 low. The objective is to avoid taking the first trick, the last trick, and the trick containing the queen of clubs.

The cards are dealt out one at a time and face down so that each player receives an equal number of cards and there are none left over. The player to the left of the dealer leads to the first trick. A player must follow suit if he can, otherwise he may play any card of his choice. There are no trumps and a trick is won by the highest card of the suit that was led. The winner of each trick leads to the next.

A player taking the first trick, the last trick or a trick containing the queen of clubs is penalised one point. A player unfortunate enough to win all three of these tricks scores an extra penalty point, making four in all.

Polignac

No. of players: 3 to 6
Equipment: Short pack of 32 cards
Complexity: ★★

Polignac is similar to *Slobberhannes* except that the penalties are for taking tricks containing jacks – two penalty points for the jack of spades and one penalty point for each of the other jacks.

Nap

No. of players: 2 to 6 (best with 4 or 5)
Equipment: Standard pack of 52 cards
Complexity: ★★★

Each player is dealt five face-down cards, one at a time. There is then a round of bidding, in which the player who bids to take the highest number of tricks chooses trumps and has to make the number of tricks he has bid in order to win. The bidding begins with the player to the left of the dealer and ends with the dealer, each player having only one opportunity to bid. A player may pass or make a bid higher than any previous bids.

   Nap is usually played for stakes. The possible bids, in ascending order, and their stake value if won or lost are as follows:

One	(bid to win one trick)	1 unit
Two	(bid to win two tricks)	2 units
Three	(bid to win three tricks)	3 units
Misery	(bid to win no tricks, with no trumps)	3 units
Four	(bid to win four tricks)	4 units
Nap	(bid to win five tricks)	10 units if won, 5 if lost
Wellington	(bid to win five tricks)	20 units if won, 10 if lost

Wellington may only be bid to overcall a previous bid of Nap and is a declaration to win all five tricks at double stakes.

The player making the highest bid leads to the first trick and, except when the bid is Misery, the card that is led determines the trump suit. Normal rules of trick-taking apply, as in *Whist*.

If the bidder wins his contract each of the other players pays him the appropriate stake. If he fails to win his contract he pays each of the other players the appropriate stake. Stakes are paid only according to the number of tricks that were bid. No account is taken of any excess tricks or of the number of tricks by which a bidder fails to make his contract.

Ecarte

No. of players: 2
Equipment: Short pack of 32 cards
Complexity: ★★☆

Ecarte is an old game of French origin, which is derived from the even older French game of *Triomphe*. It is played with a 32-card pack – a standard pack from which all cards below 7 have been removed. The cards in descending order of rank are K, Q, J, A, 10, 9, 8, 7 – note the unusual position of the ace. The objective of the game is to score points by winning tricks.

Each player deals in turn, and five cards are dealt face down to each player. The cards are dealt either as a batch of two followed by a batch of three or vice versa (but whichever method is chosen should be applied throughout the game). The remainder of the pack is placed face down to form a stock, and the top card of the stock is turned over and placed face up alongside the stock to establish the trump suit. If this card happens to be a king the dealer scores 1 point.

The non-dealer always leads to the first trick but before doing this he may propose an exchange of cards. To do this he says 'cards' and the dealer may either accept or refuse. If the dealer accepts, the non-dealer discards any number of cards (from one to five) face down and draws an equal number from the top of the stock; the dealer then does likewise. The non-dealer may then, if he wishes, propose another exchange of cards and again the dealer may accept or refuse. This continues until the non-dealer chooses to lead, or until the dealer refuses a proposal or until the stock is exhausted.

The non-dealer leads to the first trick, and thereafter the winner of each trick leads to the next. The second player to a trick must follow suit if he can; if he cannot follow suit he must play a trump if he has one; he must also win the trick if he can do so.

The scoring is as follows:

(a) If any cards were exchanged, the winner of the hand scores 1 point for winning 3 or 4 tricks or 2 points if he wins all 5 tricks.

(b) If the non-dealer loses after failing to propose or if the dealer loses after refusing the first proposal then the winner scores 2 points regardless of the number of tricks won.

(c) A player holding the king of trumps scores 1 point if he declares it immediately before playing to the first trick.

The game is won by the first player to score 5 points.

Four-Handed Euchre

No. of players: 4
Equipment: Short pack of 32 cards
Complexity: ✩✩✩

Euchre, like *Ecarte*, is a descendant of the old game of *Triomphe*. It originated in the United States and remains most popular in the north-eastern United States and Canada.

There are several variations of *Euchre*, for any number from two to seven players. The most popular version is the four-handed partnership game described here.

From a standard 52-card pack all cards below 7 are removed to leave a 32-card pack. The highest trump is the jack, called the 'right bower'. The other jack of the same colour as the trump suit, called 'left bower', is also regarded as a trump and ranks second. For example, if hearts are trumps the jack of hearts is right bower and the jack of diamonds is left bower. Thus in the trump suit there are nine cards, ranking right bower, left bower, A, K, Q, 10, 9, 8, 7; in the other suit of the same colour as trumps there are seven cards, ranking A, K, Q, 10, 9, 8, 7; and in each of the remaining suits there are eight cards, ranking A, K, Q, J, 10, 9, 8, 7.

Partners sit opposite each other. Players draw to decide first deal, and thereafter the deal passes to the left.

Each player is dealt five cards, in batches of two and then three (or three and then two). The next card is turned face up to propose the trump suit – but this only becomes the trump suit if accepted by one of the players. Beginning with the player to the left of the dealer each player may either pass or accept the trump suit. To pass, a player says 'Pass'. To accept, an opponent of the dealer says 'I order it up', the dealer's partner says 'I assist' or the dealer says 'I call it up'. Once one player has accepted, the dealer has the option to taking the turned-up card into his hand and discarding any other card or of retaining his existing hand. Play then begins.

If all four players pass, the turned-up card is turned face down. There is then a second round in which each player in turn may either pass or nominate a trump suit of his own choice. Once one player has nominated a trump suit play may begin. If all four players pass, the hands are thrown in and the next player deals.

The player who decides the trump suit, whether by accepting or nominating, becomes the 'maker'. He has the option of playing the hand without his partner (to aim for a higher score), in which case he says 'I play alone'. His partner then lays his cards face down on the table and remains out of the game (although he still shares in the stakes).

If the maker is playing alone, the opening lead is made by the player to his left. Otherwise, the opening lead is made by the player to the left of the dealer. The usual rules of trick-taking apply, as in Whist.

Points are scored by the partnership winning three or more tricks. Winning three or four tricks is called 'the point'; winning all five tricks is called 'the march'. If the maker and his partner win less than three tricks they are said to be 'euchred'. The maker and his partner score 1 for the point and 2 for the march, but a maker playing alone scores 4 for the march. If they are euchred, the opponents score 2.

The first partnership to score a previously agreed number of points (usually 5, 7 or 10) wins the game.

Three-Handed Euchre

No. of players: 3
Equipment: Short pack of 32 cards
Complexity: ★★☆

In this version of the game the maker always plays alone and the other two players form a temporary partnership against him. The maker scores 1 for the point and 3 for the march; his opponents score 2 points if he is euchred. Otherwise, the rules of the four-handed game apply.

Two-Handed Euchre

No. of players: 2
Equipment: Short pack of 32 cards
Complexity: ★★☆

This is similar to the four-handed game except that (of course!) there are no partnerships and the maker always plays alone. Scoring is 1 for the point, 2 for the march and 2 for euchre. The game may also be played with a 24-card pack (that is, with all cards below 9 removed).

Call-Ace Euchre

No. of players: 4, 5 or 6
Equipment: Short pack of 32 cards
Complexity: ★★☆

Trumps are chosen in any of the ways described for the four-handed game. The maker may then opt to play alone, or he may select a partner by naming any suit. The player holding the highest card of that suit in play becomes the maker's partner.

Thus, at the start of play the maker does not know the identity of his partner. Nor can any of the other players be sure whether or not he is the maker's partner – unless he happens to hold the ace of the nominated suit. Even then he does not announce the fact. The identity of the maker's partner only becomes revealed as the cards are played. It may indeed turn out to be the case that the maker is playing alone, if he himself holds the highest card of the nominated suit.

Scoring is as in the four-handed game, except that each player individually scores for point, march or euchre.

Rummy

No. of players: 2 to 6
Equipment: Standard pack of 52 cards
Complexity: ★★☆

Rummy is one of the most popular card games – and like almost all popular card games it has given rise to a host of variations. The standard version is described here.

The objective of the game is to be the first player to 'go out' (i.e. get rid of all the cards in one's hand) by 'melding'. Melding consists of forming groups or sequences of cards. A group is three or more cards of the same rank (e.g. three kings). A sequence is three or more cards of the same suit in sequence (e.g. 5, 6, 7 of clubs). Normally the ace ranks low, so A, 2, 3 is a sequence, but Q, K, A is not. A secondary objective is to reduce as far as possible the total face value of the unmelded cards left in one's hand.

The dealer is chosen in the customary way, by cutting or drawing. The players are dealt their cards one at a time and face down. The number of cards each player receives depends upon the number of players in the game – ten cards each for two players; seven cards each for three or four players; six cards each for five or six players. After the deal the remainder of the pack is placed face down in the centre of the table to form the stock, and the top card of the stock is turned face up beside it to form the first card of the discard pile.

Each player in turn draws either the top card of the stock or the top card of the discard pile, and adds it to his hand. He may then, if he so desires, place any melds he has been able to form on the table in front of him. He may also 'lay off' any individual cards that extend existing melds on the table – he may add cards on his opponents' melds as well as on his own. Finally he discards one card, placing it face up on top of the discard pile.

A player goes out, and thereby wins the hand, when he plays the last card from his hand, whether as part of a meld, a lay off or a discard. The face value of the cards left in the hands of his opponents is totalled to give his score for the round. For the purposes of scoring, an ace counts as 1 and a court card counts as 10.

A player 'goes rummy' if he goes out by melding his entire hand in one turn without previously having melded or laid off any cards. In this case his score is doubled.

If no player has gone out by the time the stock is exhausted, the discard pile is simply turned over to form a new stock and the game continues as normal.

The first player whose score reaches a predetermined number of points wins the game.

Gin Rummy

No. of players: 2
Equipment: Standard pack of 52 cards
Complexity: ★★★

As in Rummy, the objective of the game is to meld the cards in one's hand into groups or sequences. There are, however, certain important differences in the way the game is played.

The players cut the pack to determine the lead. The player who cuts the higher card may choose to deal first or may require his opponent to do so. Thereafter the deal alternates. Ten cards are dealt, one at a time, to each player. The remainder of the pack is placed face down on the table to form the stock, the top card of the stock being turned over and placed face up alongside it as the first card of the discard pile.

The non-dealer may begin play by taking the face-up card. If he does not want to take it, the dealer may take it. If both players refuse it, the non-dealer draws the top card of the stock. As in Rummy, each player in turn takes the top card from either the stock or the discard pile and discards one card from his hand.

Melds are not laid down on the table in the course of play. Instead a player keeps his melds in his hand and goes out by 'knocking' when his 'deadwood' (that is, the cards in his hand that do not form part of a group or sequence) total ten points or less. A player may knock only when it is his turn. After drawing from the stock or discard pile the usual practice is for the player to knock on the table and then discard face down. The player then lays his hand face up on the table, sorted clearly into melds and deadwood. His opponent similarly lays down his hand, but is then allowed to 'lay off' – that is, to add odd cards from his own hand to melds in the knocker's hand. If, however, the knocker has laid down a 'gin hand' – one with no deadwood – his opponent may not lay off any cards.

If the knocker's deadwood count is lower than that of his opponent he scores the difference. If a player lays down a gin hand he scores the total value of his opponent's deadwood plus a 25 point bonus. However, if a player knocks and his opponent has an equal or lower deadwood count, then the opponent wins the hand, scoring the difference plus a 25 point bonus for 'undercut'. A gin hand cannot be undercut.

The score is kept with pencil and paper. A player's score for a hand is added to his previous score and a line is drawn under it. A game ends when one player's score reaches 100. He then scores a bonus of 100 points for game. If his opponent has failed to win a single hand the winner's total score is doubled for 'shut-out'. Finally, to each player's score is added 25 points (called a 'line bonus' or 'box bonus') for each hand he has won.

Roy	Nigel
24	17
55	39
68	86
87	
	161
115	
100	
100	
315	

Roy wins by 154 points (315 – 161)

The last two cards in the stock may not be drawn. If there are only two cards left in the stock and neither player has knocked, then the hand is a tie and no points are scored. The same dealer deals again for the next hand.

Cribbage

No. of players: 2
Equipment: Standard pack of 52 cards; cribbage board for scoring
Complexity: ★★

The game of *Cribbage* is said to have been invented by Sir John Suckling, the seventeenth-century poet, soldier and courtier. There are three main variations of the game – five-card, six-card and seven-card *Cribbage* – plus other versions for three or four players. The original five-card game for two players – still the most popular version of the game – is described here.

 Cribbage is all about scoring points in the course of play. A cribbage board is therefore really essential for recording each player's score. A game is usually played to 61 points.

 The players cut to decide first deal, and thereafter the deal alternates. The generally observed etiquette is that the dealer shuffles the pack and places it in front of his opponent who cuts it. The dealer then deals five cards face down to each player and places the remainder of the pack face down on the table. On the first deal of the game the non-dealer immediately pegs three points – '3 for last' – to offset his opponent's advantage of first deal.

 Each player discards two of his five cards face down, to form a 'crib' of four cards. The crib belongs to the dealer and, as will be described shortly, will be used by him later to score points. Therefore the dealer will discard cards which should help to form scoring combinations, whereas the non-dealer will discard cards which he thinks will be least useful to the dealer.

 The remainder of the pack is cut once more by the non-dealer and the dealer turns up the top card of the lower half. This card is the 'start' and remains face up during play. If the start is a jack the dealer pegs two points – '2 for his heels'.

 The play consists of each player in turn laying one of his three cards face up on the table before him and announcing the cumulative total of the cards played so far. This continues until all six cards have been played or until the total face value of the cards played reaches 31. All court cards count as 10, aces count as 1, and other cards count their pip value.

 A player who plays a card to bring the total to exactly 15 scores 2 points. The total of the cards played may not go over 31 – if a player cannot lay down a card without going over this total he says 'Go'. His opponent then continues playing if he can. Whoever plays the last card scores 2 points if he brings the total to exactly 31, otherwise he scores '1 for last'.

Points are also scored in the course of play for pairs and runs. A player laying down a card of the same rank as the card just played by his opponent scores '2 for a pair'. Note that although court cards count as 10 they can only be scored as pairs if they are of the same rank – e.g. two kings but not king and queen. If the first player follows with a third card of the rank he scores 6 for a 'pair royal'. If the second player can then play a fourth card of the same rank – a rare occurrence – he scores 12 for a 'double pair royal'.

A run is a sequence of three or more cards of consecutive rank, which do not have to be of the same suit. Runs count 1 point for each card in the run. The cards do not need to be played in order – for example, if the first player plays a 3 and the second player a 5, the first player might then play a 4 and peg 3 points for a run. The second player could then score 4 points for a run of four by playing either a 2 or a 6.

After the hands have been played in this way we come to the 'show'. Both players gather up their own cards. The non-dealer shows and scores for his hand first. For this purpose the start, though it is not removed, is considered part of his hand, and he scores for all combinations in the four cards.

Two points are scored for each combination of cards totalling fifteen. The same card may be counted several times in different combinations. Thus a hand of 3, 6, 6, 9 would yield 6 points for fifteens (for 6–6–3, for 6–9, and for another 6–9). Points are scored in the same way for pairs and for runs (with scoring similar to that in the play) and for flushes. A player scores 3 points for a flush if the three cards in his hand are of the same suit or 4 points if the start is also of the same suit. Finally he scores '1 for his nob' if his hand contains the jack of the same suit as the start.

The dealer then shows his hand and scores in the same way for any combinations in his three cards together with the start. He then turns over the four cards of his crib. The dealer scores for the crib, again in conjunction with the start, in exactly the same way except that a flush is scored only if all five cards are of the same suit and is worth 5 points.

The Cribbage Board

The Cribbage board is a very convenient device for recording scores in the game of *Cribbage*, where points are scored throughout the course of play. It may also be used for scoring in some domino games such as *Fives and Threes*.

In its traditional form it is an oblong piece of wood, about 10 in by 3 in.

There are two rows of 30 holes (arranged in groups of 5) plus an end hole for each player, and is designed for scoring games to 61 or 121 points.

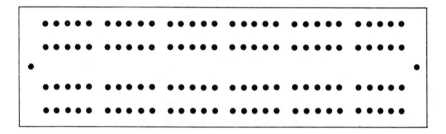

Normally each player marks his score with two pegs, which are moved up the outer row and down the inner row to the end hole, according to the number of points scored. When a game is played to 121 points the pegs travel round twice before reaching the end hole.

The first score made by a player is marked by placing one peg that number of holes from the start. His next score is marked by placing his second peg that number of holes in front of his first peg. Subsequent scores are marked by moving the rearmost peg the appropriate number of holes in front of the leading peg. This leap-frogging method provides a check on accuracy.

Bézique

No. of players: 2
Equipment: 2 32-card packs (Bézique packs)
Complexity: ★★

Bézique is an excellent card game for two players, being quite easy to learn and not too demanding to play. It is a trick-taking game but the scoring, in the main, is based on declaring combinations of cards from one's hand. Points are scored for taking tricks containing certain point-scoring cards, which are known as 'Brisques', but the principal purpose of taking tricks is to enable one to declare one's combinations – and to prevent one's opponent from doing so.

Bézique is played with two 32-card packs – normal packs from which all cards below seven have been removed. The order in which cards rank for the purpose of taking tricks is: ace, 10, king, queen, jack, 9, 8, 7 – note the position of the 10.

The two packs are thoroughly shuffled together and the players cut for deal. The dealer gives eight cards to each player, dealing three cards, then two cards, then three cards at a time. The remaining cards are placed face down on the table to form a stock. The top card is turned over and placed face up beside the stock – the suit of this card determines the trumps for this deal. If this card happens to be a 7 the dealer scores 10 points.

The play is in two stages and the first stage consists of 24 tricks. The non-dealer leads to the first trick, and thereafter the winner of each trick leads to the next. After each trick the winner may declare any one of a number of combinations, and then both players replenish their hands by drawing a card from the stock, the winner drawing first. In this stage of the game it is not necessary to follow suit – the second player to a trick may follow suit, trump or discard just as he pleases. A trick is won by the highest card of the suit led, unless it is trumped, and if two cards of the same value are played then the leader wins the trick.

The combinations that may be declared and scored by the winner of a trick are as follows:

(a) **Common Marriage** – K and Q of the same suit (not trumps) – scoring 20 points.
(b) **Royal Marriage** – K and Q of the trump suit – scoring 40 points.
(c) **Bézique** – Q of spades with J of diamonds – scoring 40 points.

(d) **Double Bézique** – both **Q** of spades and both **J** of diamonds – scoring 500 points.
(e) **Four Jacks** – 40 points.
(f) **Four Queens** – 60 points.
(g) **Four Kings** – 80 points.
(h) **Four Aces** – 100 points.
(i) **Sequence** – A, **10**, **K**, **Q**, **J** of trumps – scoring 250 points.

A player declares a combination by laying the appropriate cards face up on the table in front of him and marking the score. Cards declared in combinations stay on the table until played – they still form part of the player's hand and may be played to tricks as and when required.

The same cards may also be used in later declarations, provided the declarations are of different kinds. For example, a king could be used for a Marriage and then later for Four Kings, but not for another Marriage. A king and queen of the trump suit may be used for a Royal Marriage, and may subsequently be used for a sequence with the addition of the A, 10, J. It is also permissible to use the two cards forming a Bézique as part of a subsequent Double Bézique, though neither card could be used as part of another single Bézique.

A player who holds the 7 of trumps may declare it and exchange it for the exposed trump card, scoring 10 points. The player holding the second 7 of trumps also scores 10 points when he plays it.

After the twenty-fourth trick has been taken there will be only one card left in the stock, plus the exposed trump card. The winner of that trick draws the stock card and the loser takes the exposed trump card. This is the last trick which allows the winner to make a declaration.

The second stage of the game now begins. The players gather any face-up cards in front of them into their hands, and play the last eight tricks. The rules for this stage are different. A player must, if he can, play a higher card of the suit that was led; if he cannot do so, he must nevertheless follow suit if he can; if he cannot follow suit he must play a trump if he has one; otherwise he may discard. No declarations may be made at this stage of the game, but the winner of the last trick scores 10 points.

When the last trick has been won, each player examines the cards in the tricks he has taken, to determine how many Brisques he has won. Brisques are every ace and every 10 included in a trick, and they each score 10 points.

A game is usually played to 1000 or 2000 points.

Cassino

No. of players: 2, 3 or 4
Equipment: Standard pack of 52 cards
Complexity: ★★

Cassino may be played by two players, by three players, or by four players playing either individually or in partnerships. It is, however, best with two players and this is the version described here.

The objective of the game is to score points by capturing cards, in accordance with the following scoring system:

For capturing the 10 of diamonds ('Big cassino')	2 points
For capturing the 2 of spades ('Little cassino')	1 point
For capturing more cards than one's opponent	3 points
For capturing more spades than one's opponent	1 point
For each ace that is captured	1 point

In addition, 1 point is scored each time a player makes a 'sweep', which means taking in any one turn all the face-up cards in the layout.

Apart from the scoring values shown above, the suits are disregarded. Court cards have no numerical value, being used only for matching, but other cards count their face value, aces counting as one.

The dealer deals two cards to his opponent, two cards face up on the table (the 'layout'), then two cards to himself. He then repeats this process, so that each player has four cards and there are four in the layout. When both players have played all the cards in their hands, each is dealt another four cards in two lots of two – but no more cards are dealt to the layout. This continues until all the cards have been dealt.

Each player in turn, commencing with the non-dealer, plays one card from his hand. In his turn a player may perform one of four actions – taking, building, calling and trailing.

Taking

A player may 'take' face-up cards in the layout if he has a card of the same value in his hand. He does this by placing his card on top of the layout card and then placing both cards face down in front of him. With a court card a player may take only one card of the same face value in the layout. For example, if there are two kings in the layout he may take only one of them with a king from his hand. But with a card other than a court card he may capture two or more cards of the same face value with one card from his hand. A player may also take cards which in combination add up to the same value as a card in his hand. For example, if the layout contains a 2, 3, 5 and 10 then a player with a 10 in his hand could take all of them – the 10 (being of the same face value) and the 2, 3 and 5 as a group (totalling 10).

Building

In 'building' a player places a card on one of the cards in the layout if the sum of the face values is equal to the face value of another card in his hand. For example, if he holds a 2 and a 7 and there is a 5 in the layout, he may place the 2 on the 5 and announce 'Sevens'. Then on his next turn he may take the 2 and 5 with the 7 – unless his opponent forestalls him by taking the 2 and 5 with a 7 of his own. Cards which have been built on may not be taken separately, only as a group – so in this example the 5 in the layout could no longer be taken on its own. However, a build may be 'raised' – so the opponent could, for example, place another 2 on top of the 2 and 5 and announce 'Nines'.

If the build is not taken or raised a player may be able to make another build of 7. He would then place this second build on top of the first build of 7 and announce 'Building sevens'. This forms a multiple build. Multiple builds may not be raised – the two builds in this example may now only be taken by a 7.

Calling

If a player has two cards in his hand of the same face value as a combination of cards in the layout he may claim the layout cards for his next turn by playing one of the cards from his hand. For example, if the layout contains a 3 and a 6 and he has two 9s in his hand he may play a 9 to the layout, announcing 'Nines', with the intention of taking all these cards on his next turn. But of course his opponent, if he has a 9 of his own, may capture the cards for himself.

Trailing

If a player is unable to take, build or call he must 'trail' by adding a card from his hand to the layout..

The game ends when all the cards have been played. Any cards left in the layout are collected by the last player to 'take'. This does not count as a sweep.

The players then add up their scores for the cards they have taken – and for any sweeps they may have made in the course of the play. Each deal may be reckoned as a separate game – the player with the greater number of points being the winner – or play may be to a previously agreed number of points such as 21.

Pontoon

No. of players: 4 or more
Equipment: Standard pack of 52 cards
Complexity: ☆

Pontoon (also known as *Vingt-et-Un* or, as they say in France, *Twenty-one*) is a gambling game which, in its own way, is every bit as skilful and exciting as *Bingo*.

The players draw cards to decide who will be the banker, and the object of the game is for the other players (the 'punters') to obtain hands better than that of the banker. The suits of the cards are disregarded – all that matters is their numerical value. Court cards count 10; aces count either 1 or 11 at the option of the holder; other cards count their pip value.

A hand in which the cards add up to a total greater than 21 is 'bust' and loses. A hand in which the total value of the cards is between 16 and 21 beats the banker if the value of his hand is lower or if it is bust. A 'pontoon' is a hand totalling 21 in two cards – an ace and a ten or court card – and this beats the banker unless he also has a pontoon. A 'five card trick' is a hand containing five cards totalling 21 or less, and beats the banker unless he also has a five card trick. 'A 'royal pontoon' is a hand consisting of three 7s and beats the banker whatever cards he holds. The banker may not count a royal pontoon – if his hand consists of three 7s it counts only as a normal 21.

Stakes are won from or paid to the banker, and for this purpose coins, counters or other suitable means of exchange are usually employed.

The banker deals one card face downwards to each punter and then one to himself. Each punter (but not the banker) looks at his card, and then stakes any amount up to an agreed maximum. The banker then deals a second card to each punter and one to himself. Each player looks at his second card. At this point the banker may look at his cards.

If any player has a pontoon he declares it. If the banker has a pontoon the deal ends and he collects from any punter who also has a pontoon the stake he has wagered and from any other punter double the stake he has wagered. Otherwise the banker offers extra cards to each of the punters in turn, beginning with the player on his left. A punter has three options:

(a)   to 'stand' (or 'stick') – that is, to take no more cards from the banker.
      A player may stand only if the total value of his hand is 16 or more.

(b) to 'buy' a card – that is, to lay an additional stake (not less than the amount for which he bought any previous card and not greater than his existing stake) and to obtain an extra card face down from the banker.

(c) to 'twist' – that is, to be dealt an extra card face upwards without increasing the stake.

The banker finishes dealing with one player before proceeding to the next. Five cards is the maximum that a player can hold, and a player's fifth card, even if it is bought, is always dealt face upwards. A player who has bought a card may subsequently twist – but not vice versa. A player who goes bust or who gets a royal pontoon must declare the fact.

When all the punters have been given the cards they have asked for, it is the banker's turn to play. He turns his cards face up and deals himself as many extra cards as he wishes.

Settlement is then made, with the banker paying those players with better hands than he has and collecting from the others. The following table summarises the normal scale of payments. Positive numbers represent payment from banker to punter; negative numbers represent payment from punter to banker. 1, 2 and 3 represent single, double and treble stakes.

Banker's Hand	Bust	16	17	18	19	20	21	Five Card	Pontoon	Royal Pontoon
Bust	−1	+1	+1	+1	+1	+1	+1	+2	+2	+3
16	−1	−1	+1	+1	+1	+1	+1	+2	+2	+3
17	−1	−1	−1	+1	+1	+1	+1	+2	+2	+3
18	−1	−1	−1	−1	+1	+1	+1	+2	+2	+3
19	−1	−1	−1	−1	−1	+1	+1	+2	+2	+3
20	−1	−1	−1	−1	−1	−1	+1	+2	+2	+3
21	−1	−1	−1	−1	−1	−1	−1	+2	+2	+3
Five Card	−2	−2	−2	−2	−2	−2	−2	−1	+2	+3
Pontoon	−2	−2	−2	−2	−2	−2	−2		−1	

A change of banker occurs when a punter wins with a pontoon, the winning punter becoming the next banker. If two or more punters win with a pontoon then the player nearest to the left of the banker becomes the new banker.

An additional rule sometimes encountered is that when a punter is dealt a pair as his first two cards (e.g. two queens) he may 'split' the hand to form two separate hands, staking on each card the amount he originally staked on his first card. The banker then deals a second card face down to each of the two hands, which are thereafter dealt with independently.

Poker

No. of players: 2 to 10
Equipment: Standard pack of 52 cards; betting chips
Complexity: ☆☆☆

Poker originated and developed in the United States in the nineteenth century, and is now one of the most popular games in the world. It is, of course, very much a gambling game – and must be played for real stakes. But a gambling game is not necessarily the same thing as a game of chance – Poker is a game requiring a great deal of skill.

There are countless hundreds of variations of the game of Poker and it would be impossible to describe them all here. These variations differ, however, only in detail and all share certain basic principles. A player familiar with these basic principles should have no difficulty in playing any of the variations when he comes across them. The basic principles will be described briefly in this section and some of the most common variations will be presented in the following sections.

A standard pack of 52 cards is used for Poker – though sometimes with a joker added. The cards rank from ace high to 2 low, but the ace also ranks low in the sequence 5, 4, 3, 2, A. There is no ranking of suits.

When Poker is played seriously, counters or betting chips are used rather than cash, and chips of different colours are used to represent different values – e.g. white, 1 unit; red, 5 units; blue, 10 units; yellow, 25 units. It is customary for each player to buy chips from the banker (i.e. the person organising the game). During the game each player must keep all his chips on the table in front of him, in full view of the other players. The chips are then cashed in at the end of the game.

The first dealer of the game is chosen as follows. One player takes the shuffled pack and deals one card face up to each player until a jack is dealt. The player receiving the jack becomes the first dealer for the game itself, and thereafter the deal always passes to the next player to the left.

In all variations of *Poker* the cards are dealt one at a time in a clockwise direction, beginning with the player to the left of the dealer. Usually each player receives five cards, but in some variations each player may receive more than five cards, some face up – 'upcards' – and some face down – 'hole cards' – from which he selects five to be his playing hand. In other variations each player may receive fewer cards and some cards may be dealt in the middle to be shared by all the players. A playing hand, however, always consists of five cards.

The objective of the game is to win the highest possible stakes by betting as to which player holds the best hand. This involves calculation and bluff – the winner is not necessarily the player holding the best hand. All bets are made by players putting chips into a pile – the 'pot' – in the middle of the table, and the pot may be won in one of two ways. The game may proceed to a 'showdown' in which all the players left in the game show their hands – in this case the player with the best hand does win. Alternatively one player may make a bet that none of the other players is willing to meet – that player automatically wins, without having to show his hand, and this is where bluffing plays a part.

The card combinations that determine which player has the best hand are common to all the variations of *Poker*. These combinations are as follows:

(a) **Straight Flush**

Five cards in sequence in the same suit. An ace may be considered high as in A-K-Q-J-10 (which is known as a Royal Flush) or low as in 5-4-3-2-A. If two or more players have a straight flush, the one with the highest-ranking top card wins – e.g. K-Q-J-10-9 beats J-10-9-8-7. A tie is possible.

(b) **Four of a Kind**

Four cards of the same rank (the fifth card being unmatched). If two or more players have Four of a Kind, the highest-ranking hand wins – e.g. four aces will beat four kings.

(c) **Full House**

Three cards of one rank and two of another. As between two hands of this type, the one with the higher-ranking three of a kind wins – e.g. K-K-K-2-2 beats Q-Q-Q-J-J.

(d) **Flush**

Five cards all of the same suit but not in sequence. As between two hands of this type, the one with the higher ranking top card wins, or if the top cards are equal the one with the higher-ranking second card, and so on – e.g. K-J-10-9-4 beats K-J-10-8-6. A tie is possible.

(e) **Straight**
Five cards in sequence though not all belonging to the same suit. An ace may be either high or low. As between two hands of this type the hand with the higher-ranking top card wins. A tie is possible.

(f) **Three of a Kind**
Three cards of the same rank (the other two cards being unmatched). As between two hands of this type the higher-ranking three of a kind wins – e.g. K-K-K-7-2 beats Q-Q-Q-J-9.

(g) **Two Pairs**
Two cards of one rank and two cards of another rank (the fifth card being unmatched). As between two hands of this type, the hand with the higher-ranking pair wins, or if they are equal the hand with the higher-ranking second pair, or if both pairs are equal the hand with the higher-ranking unmatched card – e.g. J-J-10-10-3 beats J-J-9-9-K and J-J-10-10-4 beats J-J-10-10-3. A tie is possible.

(h) **One Pair**
Any two cards of the same rank (the other three cards being unmatched). As between two such hands, the hand with the higher-ranking pair wins, or if they are equal the hand with the highest-ranking unmatched card – e.g. 10-10-Q-5-3 beats 10-10-9-8-6.

(i) **High Card**
Five unmatched cards. As between two such hands, the hand with the higher-ranking top card wins, or if they are equal the higher-ranking second card, and so on – e.g. A-Q-J-5-4 beats A-Q-10-6-5.

The players may agree to designate certain cards to be 'wild'. A wild card is one that may represent any card that the player holding the wild card wants it to represent. Sometimes a joker (or two jokers) can be added to the pack as wild cards, but more often cards of a particular rank are designated wild cards – usually 2s ('deuces wild'). With wild cards two additional poker hands are possible:

(j) **Five of a Kind**
Four cards of the same rank plus a wild card. This hand beats all the other hands.

(k) **Double Ace Flush**
An ace-high flush plus a wild card. This hand ranks higher than a flush but lower than a full house.

In all variations of the game there will be at least one round of betting (known as a 'betting interval') and usually there will be two or more. The number of betting intervals and when they take place will depend on the variation being played, as will the method for deciding which player starts the betting. After one player has started or 'opened' the betting, each of the other players in turn has three options:

(a) to drop out (or 'fold' or 'pass'). This means that he discards his hand and takes no further part in the play. A player may drop out at any stage and he forfeits any stakes that he may already have paid into the pot.

(b) to stay in (or 'call' or 'see'). This means that he pays into the pot just enough to make his total stake exactly equal to the greatest total stake put into the pot by any other player.

(c) to raise (or 'up' or 'go better'). This means that he puts into the pot enough to stay in plus an extra amount – the 'raise'. The other players, to stay in, must then put into the pot enough to make their total stakes equal to his, or drop out, or raise again

In some *Poker* games, players may be allowed to 'check'. This means that, at the beginning of a betting interval, a player may stay in but bet nothing. But once any player makes a bet, the betting interval continues as normal and checking is not allowed.

A betting interval ends when all the players have checked, or when all but one of the players have dropped out – the player left in being, of course, the winner – or when all the bets have been equalised – that is, all the players have bet the same amount and the turn has come round again to the last player to raise.

For example:

Player	Action	Bet	Total bet
A	checks	0	0
B	checks	0	0
C	checks	0	0
D	opens for 5	5	5
E	stays in	5	5
F	drops out	0	0
A	stays in	5	5
B	raises 5	10	10
C	stays in	10	10
D	stays in	5	10
E	raises 10	15	20

A	drops out	0	5
B	stays in	10	20
C	stays in	10	20
D	drops out	0	10

B, C and E remain in and the betting has been equalised.

There may be various limits placed on the size and number of raises allowed, and these are always agreed before the game begins.

As mentioned previously, there are innumerable variations of *Poker*, but the two main forms are *Draw Poker* and *Stud Poker* (each of which has its own numerous variations).

In *Draw Poker*, a player is dealt all his cards face down and they are not seen by his opponents. There is a betting interval, after which the players left in discard any cards they do not want and are dealt replacements from the pack. This is followed by a second betting interval, after which – if more than one player is left in – there is a showdown and the player with the best hand wins.

In *Stud Poker* a player is dealt some of his cards face up and some face down. Normally the first deal is a face-down card and a face-up card. There follows a betting interval. Then each player is dealt one more card, there is a betting interval, each player is dealt another card, there is a betting interval, and so on. The last betting interval is followed by a showdown if more than one player is left in. Because this form requires more skill than *Draw Poker* and because the pot is usually larger (since there are more betting intervals) this is the form of the game preferred by the really expert gamblers.

Another way in which *Poker* is often played is *Dealer's Choice*, in which the dealer specifies the variation to be played. This may be a standard form, any known variation – or any variation he cares to devise, provided the other players agree.

Draw Poker

No. of players: Preferably 5 to 7
Equipment: Standard pack of 52 cards
Complexity: ✩✩✩

Before each deal an agreed stake – the 'ante', usually a chip of the lowest value – is put into the pot by each player. The dealer then deals five cards to each player, one card at a time and face down.

The deal is followed by the first betting interval, which starts with the player to the left of the dealer. He may either check or bet. If he checks, each player in turn after him has the same two options until one player opens by making the first bet. Thereafter players must call, raise or fold until the betting interval is completed. In one popular form of *Draw Poker* called *Jackpots* a player may not open unless he has a pair of jacks or a better hand.

When the first betting interval is over the draw takes place. The dealer takes the pack of cards left over from the original deal and asks each active player in turn (i.e. each player who is still in the game, not having folded) whether he wants to exchange any of his cards. A player may 'stand pat' – retain all the cards he was dealt originally – or may discard from one to three cards from his hand, placing them face down on the table and receiving the same number dealt from the top of the pack. Three cards is usually the maximum number of cards that may be discarded, but in some variations a player may discard any number, even all five.

The second betting interval then takes place, starting with the player who opened the first.

If, after the second betting interval, all the players but one have folded, that player takes the pot without being required to show his hand. Otherwise there is a showdown and each player 'in on the call' must place all five of his cards face up on the table. The player with the best hand wins the pot.

Spit in the Ocean

No. of players: Preferably 5 to 7
Equipment: Standard pack of 52 cards
Complexity: ★★☆

This is normally played in the same way as *Draw Poker* except that each player is dealt four cards and an extra card (the 'spit') is dealt face up in the centre of the table. This card is considered to be the fifth card in every player's hand.

Five Card Stud

No. of players: Preferably 7 to 10
Equipment: Standard pack of 52 cards
Complexity: ★★☆

The dealer deals each player a face-down card (the 'hole card') and then deals each player a face-up card. Each player then examines his hole card without revealing it. There is then a betting interval, which begins with the player who has the highest face-up card – if two or more players tie for highest face-up card the betting begins with the first to the left of the dealer. In this first betting interval players may stay, raise or fold, but no checking is permitted.

Each active player is then dealt another face-up card. There is another betting interval, beginning with the player whose face-up cards form the highest-ranking *Poker* combination. In this and the subsequent intervals players may check until one of the players opens the betting. A fourth, and then a fifth card is dealt in the same way, each being followed by a betting interval which is begun by the player whose face-up cards show the best *Poker* combination.

If, at any stage of the game, there is only one active player left, all the others having folded, then that player wins the pot. Otherwise the final betting interval is followed by a showdown, in which each active player turns up his hole card, and the player with the best hand wins the pot.

Six Card Stud

No. of players: 5 to 8
Equipment: Standard pack of 52 cards
Complexity: ★★☆

This is very similar to *Five Card Stud* except that each active player is dealt a sixth card, face down, and this is followed by one more betting interval. Each player selects any five of his six cards to be his final hand for the showdown.

Seven Card Stud

No. of players: 5 to 7
Equipment: Standard pack of 52 cards
Complexity: ★★☆

This, again, is very similar to *Five Card Stud*. Each player is dealt two face-down cards and one face-up. There is a betting interval. There are three more rounds of dealing in which each active player receives a face-up card, each round being followed by a betting interval. Then each player is dealt another face-down card and there is a final betting interval, followed by the showdown.

Brag

No. of players: 3 or more
Equipment: Standard pack of 52 cards
Complexity: ★★☆

The game of Brag has a very long history and it is a forerunner of *Poker* with which it shares many general features.

Brag hands, in descending order of value, are as follows:

(a) **Prial**
Three cards of the same rank (e.g. 9-9-9).

(b) **Running Flush**
Three cards of the same suit in sequence (e.g. 10-J-Q of hearts).

(c) **Run**
Any three cards in sequence (e.g. 5-6-7).

(d) **Flush**
Any three cards of the same suit (e.g. 2-6-J of diamonds).

(e) **Pair**
Two cards of the same rank, the third card being unmatched.

(f) **High Card**
Three unmatched cards. As between two hands of this type, the hand containing the highest card wins.

Cards rank from ace high to 2 low, but an ace may also count low in the run A-2-3.

Before the game, limits for stakes and raises are agreed, as in *Poker*. To begin the game the dealer antes (i.e. puts an initial stake into the pot). Three cards are then dealt, one at a time and face down, to each player. Thereafter each player in turn has the option of calling, raising or folding. As in *Poker*, there can be an element of bluff. If all but one of the players fold the remaining player wins automatically, otherwise there is a showdown and the player with the best hand wins.

Suits

Everyone is familiar with the modern card suits of clubs, diamonds, hearts and spades. But in the evolution of the playing card there have been several different packs with various other suits.

The oldest surviving playing cards are believed to be a set in the Bibliothèque Nationale in Paris. These cards, dating from the fourteenth or early fifteenth century, have suits of Chalices, Swords, Coins and Staves which are thought to represent the four classes of mediaeval society – the clergy, the aristocracy, merchants and peasants. These same suits were used for playing cards in Spain and Northern Italy as well as in Southern France. In the north and centre of France the suits were usually Hearts, Pikes, Clover leaves and Paving tiles, while in Germany the usual suits were Hearts, Acorns, Bells and Leaves.

Incidentally, the 'spades' on our modern packs are not digging implements but spears (*spade* being Italian for spears).

5   BOARD GAMES

Horseshoe
Madelinette
Nine Holes
Achi
Four Field Kono
Alquerque
Nine Men's Morris
Mu-Torere
Hex
Fox and Geese (1)
Fox and Geese (2)
Fox and Geese (3)
Wolf and Goats
Halma
Chinese Checkers
Backgammon
Dutch Backgammon
Plakato
Gioul
Acey Deucey
Russian Backgammon
Wari
Draughts
Losing Draughts
Diagonal Draughts (1)
Diagonal Draughts (2)
Italian Draughts
Spanish Draughts
German Draughts
Russian Draughts
Polish Draughts
Canadian Draughts
Turkish Draughts
Lasca
Reversi
Chess

Losing Chess
Randomised Chess
Refusal Chess
Pocket Knight Chess
Two Move Chess
Progressive Chess
Kriegspiel
Go
Go-Moku

Horseshoe

No. of players: 2
Equipment: Board and 4 counters
Complexity: ★

Horseshoe is a very simple game which is played in many parts of the world (in China it is known as Pong Hau K'i). It is played on a board which may easily be drawn on a piece of paper, and each player starts with two counters positioned as shown in the illustration. For an impromptu game coins serve very well as counters, with one player's coins placed heads up and other player's placed tails up.

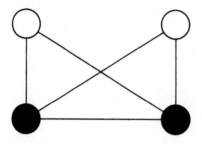

The first player starts by moving one of his counters along a line to the empty point in the centre. The second player then moves one of his counters along a line to the new vacant point. The play continues alternately, each player in turn moving one of his counters along a line to the vacant point. The objective is to block one's opponent so that he cannot move either of his counters.

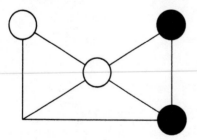

White can now move into a winning position

Madelinette

No. of players: 2
Equipment: Board and 6 counters
Complexity: ★★

Madelinette is played in exactly the same way as *Horseshoe*, and the objective is the same – to block the counters of one's opponent so that they cannot be moved. The game is slightly more challenging than *Horseshoe* since the board contains more lines, and each player starts the game with three counters which are positioned as shown in the diagram.

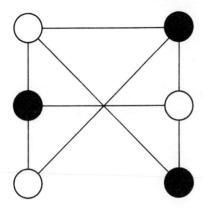

Nine Holes

No. of players: 2
Equipment: Board and 6 counters
Complexity: ★★

Nine Holes is played on a simple board which looks like this:

The counters are played on the points formed where the lines intersect. Each player starts with three counters, and they take it in turn to place a counter on any one of the nine points that is vacant, until all six counters are on the board. Then each player in turn may move one of his counters to an adjacent empty point. The first player to get his three counters in a straight line is the winner.

Achi

No. of players: 2
Equipment: Board and 8 counters
Complexity: ★★

Achi, a game which is played by Ghanaian schoolchildren, is very similar to *Nine Holes*, but each player starts with four counters and the board has diagonal lines added.

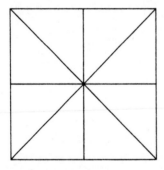

The players take it in turn to place one of their counters on an empty point. When the eight counters are on the board, each player in turn may move one of his counters along a line to an empty point in an attempt to get three counters in a row. The first player to do so is the winner.

Four Field Kono

No. of players: 2
Equipment: Board and 16 counters
Complexity: ★★

Each player starts with eight counters, set out on the board as shown in the illustration.

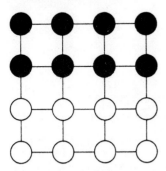

The object of the game is to capture all the counters of one's opponent or to block them so that they cannot move. The players take it in turn to move. To capture one of the opponent's counters, a counter has to jump over another counter of the same colour as itself and land directly on the opponent's counter. The captured counter is then removed from the board. When such a capturing move is not possible, a counter may only be moved along one of the lines one point at a time.

Alquerque

No. of players: 2
Equipment: Board and 24 pieces
Complexity: ★★

Alquerque is a very old game which was a forerunner of the game of *Draughts*. Each player starts the game with twelve pieces which are set out on the board like this:

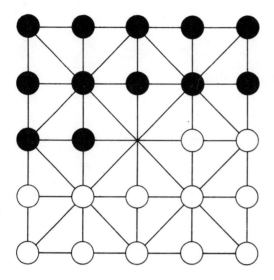

The players have alternate moves. A piece may be moved along a line in any direction to any adjacent point that is empty, or if an adjacent point is occupied by an enemy piece and the point beyond it is empty then the enemy piece may be captured by being jumped over and removed from the board. Two or more captures may be made in this way in one move, changes of direction being permitted. A player who may make a capture must do so, and he must capture all the pieces possible in that move, otherwise he is 'huffed' and the offending piece is removed from the board.

The game is won by capturing all the opponent's pieces.

Nine Men's Morris

No. of players: 2
Equipment: Board and 18 counters
Complexity: ★★

Nine Men's Morris is played on a board that looks like this:

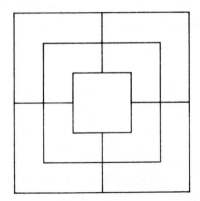

At the start of the game each player has nine pieces or 'men'. Each player in turn places one of his men on any vacant point on the board. The objective is to get three men in a row along any line, thus forming a 'mill' – and to prevent one's opponent from doing so. Each time a player forms a mill he is able to remove from the board any one of his opponent's men that he chooses – but not one which forms part of a mill unless there are none other available. After both players have placed all their men on the board they continue playing alternately, now moving one man at a time along a line to any adjacent point that is empty in an attempt to form further mills.

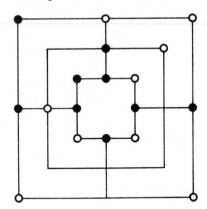

As before, forming a mill entitles a player to remove one of his opponent's men from the board.

The game is won when one's opponent is left with only two men or when his men are blocked so that they cannot be moved.

Mu-Torere

No. of players: 2
Equipment: Board and 8 counters
Complexity: ✫✫

Mu-Torere is a game from New Zealand – it is the only known board game of Maori origin. The board consists of an eight-pointed star with a circle in the middle. The eight points are known as the 'kewai' and the circle in the middle is called the 'putahi'. Each player starts with four counters, placed on four adjacent kewai.

The players move alternately, with Black having the first move. There are three types of move:

(a) A counter may be moved from one of the kewai to the putahi, but only if there is one of the opponent's counters on one (or both) of the kewai on either side of it.
(b) A counter may be moved from the putahi to any of the kewai.
(c) A counter may be moved from any of the kewai to the next on either side.

All of the moves are, of course, subject to the rule that the point being moved to must be unoccupied – only one counter is allowed on each point.

The objective of the game is the block one's opponent so that he cannot move, and the first player to succeed in this objective is the winner.

The scope for strategy might seem rather limited – a player's move is often forced and he has at other times a choice of only two moves – yet this is still quite a challenging and fascinating game.

Hex

No. of players: 2
Equipment: Board and 122 counters
Complexity: ★★

The game of *Hex* was invented in the 1940s by the Danish mathematician, inventor and poet, Piet Hein. It is a game which is very simple in principle but which is really intriguing.

The board is diamond-shaped and is made up of adjoining hexagons. The standard board has eleven hexagons along each edge, but boards with a greater or lesser number of hexagons may be used. The two opposite sides of the board belong to Black and the other two belong to White. The four corner hexagons belong to both players.

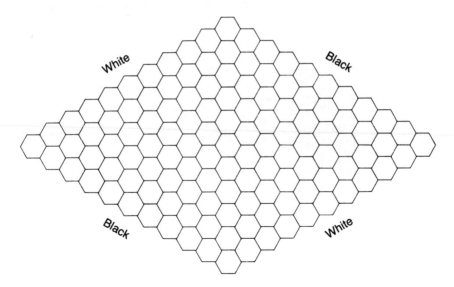

Two sets of counters are required, one black and one white. Using the standard board, the highest number of counters a player will need is 61 but usually he will not need to use all of them.

The game begins with the board completely empty, and the players take turns to place one of their counters in any vacant hexagon, with Black playing first. The objective for each player is to form a continuous line of counters connecting his two sides. The winning line does not have to be straight – provided it has no gaps it may twist and turn and may be any length.

Although the game is simple in principle, analysis of strategy can be quite complex. For example, though it is clear that Black, having the first move, has an advantage – especially if he places his first counter in the centre hexagon – no one has yet been able to work out how he should use this advantage to ensure a win. Nevertheless some players insist that Black should be handicapped by not being allowed to place his first counter in the centre hexagon.

Instead of a board composed of hexagons, a board may be used which is composed of equilateral triangles. The counters are then placed on the intersections – not in the spaces. This is the exact equivalent of the original game. The advantage is that it is much simpler to produce a home-made board of this type. Here is an illustration of such a board, showing the final position in a game that has been won by Black.

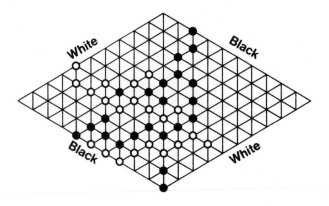

Fox and Geese (1)

No. of players: 2
Equipment: Board and 14 pieces
Complexity: ★★

The game of *Fox and Geese* originated in Scandinavia in the Viking era. Since then it has spread all over the world and there are countless variations. The distinctive features of the game in all its variations are that (unlike most other board games) the two players have unequal numbers of pieces, with different powers of movement, and they have different objectives.

The most common variation today is played on a board like the one illustrated here. One player has thirteen pieces – the 'Geese' – and the other player has one piece – the 'Fox'. At the beginning of the game the pieces are placed on the board like this:

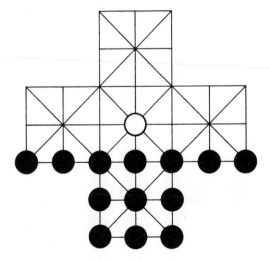

The players take it in turn to move, with the Fox having the first move. Fox and Geese move in the same way – one step in any direction along a line to an adjacent empty point. But the Fox may also capture Geese – if a Goose is on the next point to the Fox and the point immediately beyond is empty, the Fox may jump over the Goose and remove it from the board. The Fox may make several such jumps in one move, capturing a Goose with each jump. The Geese, however, are not allowed to jump over the Fox or over one another.

The Geese win the game if – by surrounding him or forcing him into a corner – they block the Fox so that he cannot move. The Fox wins the game if he captures so many Geese that there are not enough of them left to block him.

Fox and Geese (2)

No. of players: 2
Equipment: Board and 13 pieces
Complexity: ★☆

A slightly different (and earlier) variation of the game of *Fox and Geese* is played on a board resembling that for the previous game, but without the diagonals. At the beginning of the game the Fox and twelve Geese are placed on the board as illustrated.

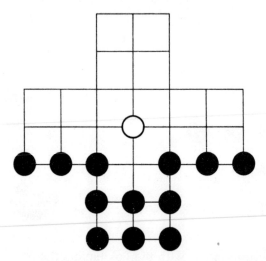

The Fox may move one step forwards, backwards or sideways to an empty point. He may also capture a Goose by jumping over it on to an empty square immediately beyond. The Geese may move one step forwards or sideways only – they are not allowed to move backwards. The Geese win the game if they block the Fox so that he cannot move. The Fox wins if he can break through the Geese to the bottom end of the board – where, of course, the Geese may not pursue him.

Fox and Geese (3)

No. of players: 2
Equipment: Board and 5 pieces
Complexity: ★★

This version of the game is played on an ordinary checkerboard as used for *Chess* or *Draughts*. At the beginning of the game the four Geese are placed on the black squares at one end of the board. The player with the Fox positions him on any other black square that he might choose.

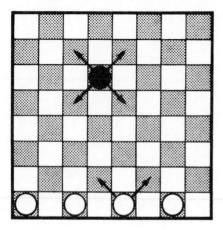

The players move alternately. The Geese may only move diagonally forwards, one square at a time, keeping to the black squares. The Fox also moves only one square at a time, on the black squares, but he may move diagonally forwards or diagonally backwards. There is no jumping and capturing in this version of the game. The Geese win if they block the Fox so that he cannot move. The Fox wins if he can break through the line of Geese to the bottom end of the board.

Wolf and Goats

No. of players: 2
Equipment: Board and 13 pieces
Complexity: ✭✭

Don't let the name fool you – *Wolf and Goats* is really yet another variation of *Fox and Geese* masquerading (like a wolf in sheep's clothing?) under a change of style.

An ordinary checkerboard is used for the game. The twelve Goats are initially placed on the black squares of the first three rows, and the Wolf is placed on either of the black corner squares at the other end of the board.

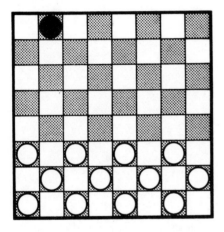

The Goats may move diagonally forwards one square at a time. The Wolf may move diagonally forwards or backwards and may capture Goats by jumping over them. The aim of the Goats is to block the Wolf so that he cannot move, while the Wolf aims to break through them, wreaking havoc on the way, to the other end of the board.

Halma

No. of players: 2 or 4
Equipment: Board and 64 pieces
Complexity: ☆☆☆

Halma was invented in the 1880s. It is played on a chequered board with sixteen squares on each side. Each corner has a section bounded with heavy lines, containing thirteen squares. Two opposite corners have an additional heavy line bounding an area with nineteen squares. These areas are the starting and finishing positions.

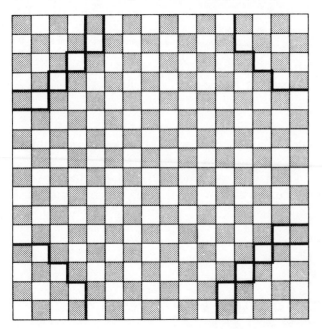

There are four sets of pieces, each set being of a different colour. Two sets contain 13 pieces and the other two sets contain 19 pieces.

If there are four players, each starts with thirteen pieces, placed in the marked-off section in his corner of the board. If there are two players, each starts with nineteen pieces in one of the corners with the larger marked-off sections. The aim is to transfer one's pieces to the corner which is diagonally opposite, and the first player to do so is the winner.

Each player in turn is allowed to move one of his pieces. There are two types of move – steps and hops. A piece may step one square in any direction to a vacant square. Alternatively, a piece may hop over any other piece (whether or not it is of the same colour) if there is a vacant square immediately beyond it. In one move a piece may make several such hops, provided that each hop is over one piece into a vacant square. Steps and hop may not be combined in one move. There is no capturing and no pieces are removed from the board.

Successful play consists of forming 'ladders', thus providing a series of hops for one's own pieces to take them a good distance across the board in one move – and blocking ladders formed by one's opponents.

Chinese Checkers

No. of players: 2 to 6
Equipment: Board and 90 pieces
Complexity: ✩✩✩

Chinese Checkers (which is neither Chinese nor Checkers) is a modern game based on the same principles as *Halma*.

The board is in the form of a six-pointed star, each point being of a different colour. The pieces are usually plastic pegs which fit into holes

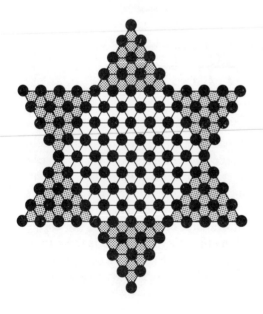

on the board, and there are six sets of 15 pieces – each set being of the same colour as one of the points of the star.

If there are two players, each starts with 15 pieces in the appropriately coloured point. If there are more than two players, each player starts with 10 pieces. The aim is to transfer all one's pieces to the opposite point, the first player to do so being the winner. The moves consist of steps and hops as in *Halma*.

Backgammon

No. of players: 2
Equipment: Board and 30 men; four dice; doubling die (optional)
Complexity: ★★☆

Backgammon is one of the great games of the world. It is also claimed sometimes that it is one of the oldest games in the world and that its history may be traced back thousands of years – but this is not strictly true. *Backgammon*, as we know it, first appeared in England in the seventeenth century (though the use of the doubling die was not introduced until the 1920s, in the USA). It had some features in common with a variety of earlier games, all of which shared the same name of *Tables*, and which had reached Europe from the Middle East in the eleventh century. Earlier games – played by the Romans or by the ancient Egyptians – which are claimed to be the ancestors of *Backgammon* had little in common with the game that we know apart from the fact that they were race games using counters and dice.

Although backgammon does not have the depth and complexity of *Chess* or *Go*, it makes up for this in being exciting and fast-moving. It is a paradox that although the moves in *Backgammon* are dependent on the throw of the dice it is a game of almost pure skill. This is because, although the outcome of a single game may to some extent be determined by luck, over a number of games the element of luck will 'cancel out', so to speak, and the more skilful player will triumph.

Each player has fifteen men, and the players are conventionally called Black and White (though their sets of men may be any two contrasting colours). Each player also has two dice.

The board is divided into four sections, known as 'tables'. Each table contains six long, tapering points which are coloured alternately red and white. There is no particular significance to this alternate colouring – it merely serves as an aid to visualising moves. The two inner tables are separated from the two outer tables by a strip which is known as the 'bar'.

Backgammon is a race game and the objective is to be the first player to move all one's men round the board into one's inner table and from there to remove them from the board. The diagram below shows how the men are set out on the board at the beginning of the game. The points are numbered here for reference only – they are not normally printed on the board.

White's outer table   White's inner table

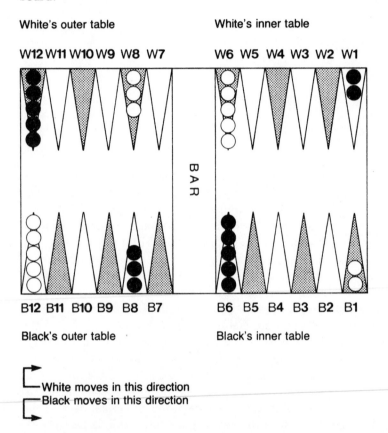

White moves in this direction
Black moves in this direction

To decide who moves first, each player rolls one of his dice. If both players throw the same number they roll again until two different numbers are thrown. The player throwing the higher number has the first move, and he moves his men according to the numbers on the two dice. For example, if White throws a 6 and Black throws a 1, then White has the first move and his throw is considered to be 6-1. After that the players move alternately, each player rolling his own two dice to determine his move. As a matter of etiquette, each player, after throwing, lets his dice stand until the other player has thrown his dice and made his move.

Each player advances his men a number of points – towards his own inner table – according to the numbers thrown with the dice. The numbers shown by the two dice are not added together but are taken separately. For example, if a player throws a 6-1 he may advance one man six points and advance another man one point, or he may advance one man six points and then advance the same man another one point (or advance the same man one point and then six points).

If a player can use only the number shown by one of his dice (because of closed points, as described further on) then the other numbered is disregarded. If it is possible for him to use one number or the other but not both, then he must use the higher number.

When a double is thrown, a player moves twice the values shown. For example, a double 6 gives a player four moves of six points each.

If a point is unoccupied it is said to be 'open' and either player may play a piece on to that point. If a player has two or more men on a point that point is said to be 'made' or 'closed'. A player may play further men on to a point that he has made but he may not play any pieces on to a point that has been made by his opponent.

If a point is occupied by a single man that man is known as a 'blot'. A player may play one of his men on to a point occupied by an enemy blot. The blot is then said to be 'hit' – it is removed from the point and placed on the bar.

A player who has a man on the bar must 'enter' it into the opponent's inner table by throwing a number corresponding to an open point or a blot. While he has a man on the bar he may not move any other of his men. If, for example, White has a man on the bar and he throws a 2-3 and the points B2 and B3 have been made by Black then White's throw is void and he may not move. But if Black had a blot on B2, White could enter on that point, hitting the Black blot and sending it to the bar, and he could then use the 3 to move the same man or another man. Both players may have any number of men on the bar at the same time.

When a player has moved all his men into his own inner table – but not before – he may begin 'bearing off' (that is, removing his men from the board). A man may be borne off each point indicated by the number on either of the dice. For example, if White throws a 4-2 he may bear off a man from W4 and another from W2. He may, alternatively, use all or part of the throw to move men inside his inner table. On a throw of 4-4, for example, White might move a man from W6 to W2, move another from W5 to W1 and bear off two men from W4.

It is not always necessary to throw the exact number to bear off a piece from a point. If a number is thrown that is higher than any point on which the player has men left, then he may bear off from the highest occupied point. For example, if Black is left with men only on the points B4, B2 and B1 and he throws a 6-2 he may bear off from B4 and B2.

If a player has a blot that is hit while he is bearing off, that man must be re-entered from the bar into his opponent's inner table and be moved round the board into his own inner table before he can continue bearing off.

The winner is the first player to bear off all his men. If the loser has borne off one or more of his men he loses a single game. If he has not borne off any men he loses a 'gammon' or double game. If he has not borne off any men and in addition he has one or more men left on the bar or in the winner's inner table then he loses a 'backgammon' or triple game.

The doubling die is a modern introduction to increase further the value of a game and is used when the game is played for stakes. Its faces show the numbers 2, 4, 8, 16, 32 and 64. Either player, at any stage in the game when it is his turn to play, and if he thinks that he has an advantageous position, may propose the first double by saying 'I double'. His opponent then has the option of declining the double – thereby conceding the game and paying the original stake – or accepting the double, in which case the game proceeds for double stakes. If he accepts the double the doubling die is placed, with the 2 uppermost, at his side of the board and he is said to be in control of the die. As long as he has control of the doubling die his opponent may not double again, but he may redouble if the balance of the game shifts (as it often does) and he thinks that he now has the better chance of winning. If the redouble is accepted the die is turned to show the 4 and passed to the first player, otherwise the game is conceded by the first player who pays double stakes. The doubling die may be passed back and forth in this way several times in the course of the game, each player alternately having the right to double.

The result of the game – whether it is a single win, gammon or backgammon – acts as a multiplier of the value of the doubling die. Thus if the basic stake is £100, the doubling die shows 32 and you win a backgammon, your opponent has to hand over £9600. Though many players play without using the doubling die there is no doubt that its use adds extra zest to the game.

Some players also allow automatic doubling of the stake each time the same number is thrown by both players at the start of the game when throwing for first play. The number of automatic doubles is usually limited by agreement to one or two.

Dutch Backgammon

No. of players: 2
Equipment: Board and 30 men; four dice
Complexity: ★★★

Dutch Backgammon is the same as the standard game, except for the following differences:

(a)   At the start of the game all the men are placed on the bar. A player must enter all 15 of his men before making any other move.
(b)   A player is not allowed to hit a blot until he has moved at least one man around the board into his own inner table.

Plakato

No of players: 2
Equipment: Board and 30 men; four dice
Complexity: ★★★

Plakato is a form of *Backgammon* which is very popular in Greece. It is played in the same way as *Backgammon* except for the following differences:

(a)   At the start of the game each player has all his men positioned on the number 1 point in his opponent's inner table.
(b)   There is no bearing off. Instead, each player has to move all his men right round the board to his own number 1 point.
(c)   Blots are not hit and sent to the bar. Instead, they are blocked, and may not be moved while one of the opponent's men is on the same point.

Gioul

No. of players: 2
Equipment: Board and 30 men; four dice
Complexity: ✮✩✩

Gioul is another form of *Backgammon*, that is popular in the Middle East. It differs from *Backgammon* in the following respects:

(a) At the start of the game each player has all his men positioned on the number 1 point in his opponent's inner table.

(b) Blots are not hit and sent to the bar. Instead, they are blocked, and may not be moved while one of the opponent's men is on the same point.

(c) When a double is thrown, a player is allowed to move according to that double – and then for each subsequent double up to double 6. For example, if he throws a double 3, he has moves for double 3, double 4, double 5 and double 6.

(d) If a player is unable to use any of the moves resulting from the throw of a double, these moves may be claimed by his opponent.

Acey Deucey

No. of players: 2
Equipment: Board and 30 men; four dice
Complexity: ✮✩✩

Acey Deucey is a variant of *Backgammon* that is popular in the US Navy. It differs from the standard game in the following respects:

(a) The game starts with no men on the board.

(b) The players throw single dice, as usual, to decide who will play first, but the first player then throws both his dice for his first throw.

(c) Throws may be used to enter additional men on to the board or to move those already entered. Blots are hit and sent to the bar in the normal manner. Men may be moved before all 15 men have been placed on the board but – as in the normal game – may not be moved while a man that has been hit remains on the bar.

(d) A throw of 1-2 (Acey Deucey) has special status. Having moved a 1 and a 2, the player throwing 1-2 may then name any double he chooses and move his men accordingly. He then has an extra turn and is allowed to throw both dice again. However, if he cannot use any part of the throw, he forfeits the rest. If, for example, he can use the 1 but not the 2, he forgoes the double and the extra throw.

(e) There are a number of sub-variations (no pun intended – these apply on battleships and cruisers as well as on submarines) concerning doubles and scoring. Some allow automatic doubles every time a 1-2 is thrown. Some replace the standard doubling and tripling for gammon and backgammon by a system whereby the loser pays one unit of the stake for each man left on the board or for the number of points needed to bear it off.

Russian Backgammon

No. of players: 2
Equipment: Board and 30 men; four dice
Complexity: ★★★

Whereas in all other variations of *Backgammon* the players move their men in opposite directions around the board, in *Russian Backgammon* (owing, no doubt, to their collectivist philosophy) both players move in the same direction.

The game starts with no men on the board. Both players enter their men on to the same inner table, and once a player has entered two men he may use his throws to enter further men or to move those already on the board.

Blots may be hit and must be re-entered before any other man may be moved, as in the standard game.

When a double is thrown a player moves as normal according to that double but then moves also according to the complement of that double – the complement of a number being its difference from 7. For example, a player throwing a double 2 may move four 2s and then four 5s – but he may use the 5s only if he can use all four 2s. Provided that he can use all the eight moves he has an extra turn and is allowed to throw both dice again.

Wari

No. of players: 2
Equipment: Board and 48 counters
Complexity: ★★★

Wari is one of a group of basically similar games known as *Mancala* games, which are played all over Asia and Africa and also in America where they were introduced by slaves from Africa.

The 'board' may be a wooden dish with two rows of six shallow depressions carved in it, or two similar rows of depressions scooped out of the earth, or two rows of six saucers, or (more simply) a piece of paper or card with two rows of six 'holes' drawn on it. The 'counters', to be authentic, should be seeds or small stones, but coins, buttons or any other small objects may be used.

At the start of the game four counters are placed in each hole.

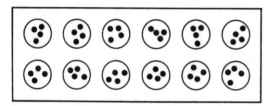

The players sit on either side of the board, and the six holes nearest to each player form his row. The first player begins by picking up the four counters from any hole in his row and 'sowing' them one by one, in an anti-clockwise direction, in the next four holes. For example:

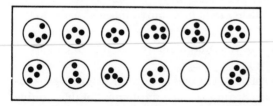

The other player then takes the counters from any hole in his row and sows them one by one in an anti-clockwise direction. And so the game continues, each player in turn sowing the counters from any one of the holes in his row.

If in any player's turn the last counter to be sown goes into one of the opponent's holes and that hole now contains either two or three counters, then he wins all the counters in that hole, and he removes them from the board. He also wins the counters in any adjacent holes that contain either two or three counters.

If, after a while, a hole contains twelve or more counters then a sowing from that hole will take more than one complete circuit of the board. When this happens, the original hole from which the twelve or more counters were taken is left empty and it stays empty for the remainder of the game.

If a player has no counters left in his row when it is his turn then the game is over. However, when an opponent's row is empty a player must, if possible, making a sowing which will leave at least one counter in his opponent's row. If he cannot do so the game is finished and he takes all the counters left on the board and adds them to those he has already won.

The game may also end by agreement if there are only a few counters left on the board and they are just being moved round the board with neither player being able to win any more counters. In that case each players takes the counters from his own row and adds them to the counters he has already won.

Each player then counts the number of counters he has won, and the player with the greatest number is the winner.

Draughts

No. of players: 2
Equipment: Board and 24 pieces
Complexity: ★★☆

Draughts, or *Checkers* as it is known in America, is a game of skill for two players. There are a large number of national variations, of which the game as played in Britain and America is but one. For obvious reasons, however, we will consider the British and American game as the standard version, and the other variations will be described later in this chapter in terms of their differences from this game.

Draughts is played on a square board which is divided into 64 smaller squares. The squares are alternately black and white. The pieces or 'men' are thick flat discs, normally made of wood. One player has twelve white pieces, and the other has twelve black pieces. (Actually the squares and the pieces may be of any light and dark colours – red and white or green and buff, for example – but whatever the actual colours they are always referred to as 'black' and 'white').

The player with the black pieces always has the first move. To determine which player should have the black pieces the usual procedure is for one player to pick up a black piece and a white piece and, holding his hands under the table or behind his back, to conceal a piece in each hand. He then holds out his fists to the other player, who chooses one or the other. The colour of the piece in the fist he chooses determines the colour of the pieces he will play with.

At the start of the game the board is positioned so that each player has a black square at his left-hand corner, and each player's pieces are set out on the black squares of the three rows nearest to him.

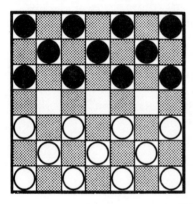

The player with the black pieces makes the first move and thereafter the players move alternately. The objective is to remove all the opponent's pieces from the board by capturing them, or to block them so that they cannot be moved.

The pieces are moved only on the black squares, so they must move diagonally, and they may be moved only to an empty square.

When not capturing an opposing piece, a piece can move only one square at a time. A capture consists of a piece jumping over an opposing piece on an adjoining square into an empty square beyond. The piece that is captured is then removed from the board. Several pieces may be captured in this way in one move, so long as each piece that is captured has an empty square beyond it.

(a)   (b)

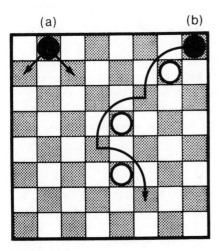

(a) Non-capturing move
(b) Capturing move

Initially the pieces may only be moved forwards – that is, away from the player making the move. However, when a piece reaches one of the four squares at the far edge of the board it is promoted to a 'king'. It may then move either forwards or backwards. A king is recognised by being 'crowned' – that is, it has another piece of the same colour (from among those previously captured and removed from the board) placed on top of it to form a sort of double-decker piece. A player's turn always ends when a piece is crowned, even though the newly-made king may then be in a position to capture opposing pieces.

If a player can make a capturing move then he must do so, even if it is to his disadvantage. Where he has a choice of moves which will capture opposing pieces – a move which will capture two pieces, for example, or another which will capture three pieces – then he may choose which move to take, but he must make all the captures that are possible on that move.

If a player fails to capture a piece when he could do so, then his opponent has three options before making his own move:

(a)   He can accept the offending move and do nothing.
(b)   He can insist that the move be taken back and replayed to make the possible capture.
(c)   He can 'huff' the other player by removing from the board the piece which made the offending move.

As stated previously, a game is won by capturing all the opponent's pieces or by blocking them so that they cannot move. A tied game results when neither player is able to force a win. If one player is in a stronger position he may be required to win the game within his next 40 moves or else be able to demonstrate a clear advantage over his opponent. If he fails to do so the game is declared a draw.

There are a number of other rules which are mainly matters of etiquette:

(a) **Time Limits**

A play is only allowed five minutes in which to make a move. If he takes longer than this the other player (or the referee, in tournament play) may call 'Time'. If the player does not complete his move within one minute after that he loses the game.

(b) **Adjusting Pieces on the Board**

If a player wishes to adjust any pieces properly on the squares he must announce his intention before doing so. The first time a player breaks this rule he may be cautioned, and if he does it again he forfeits the game.

(c) **Touch and Move**

If a player, when it is his turn to move, touches one of his pieces then he must move that piece if it can make a legal move. If it cannot make a legal move, the same penalties apply as for the previous rule.

(d) **False and Improper Moves**

A player making any false or improper move immediately forfeits the game. If a piece is moved so that any part of it goes over one of the corners of the square on which it is positioned then the move must be completed in that direction – playing it in any other direction constitutes an improper move.

Although *Draughts*, in contast to *Chess*, might be regarded by very many people as literally 'child's play', there are many players who take it very seriously indeed and who consider it to be the equal of *Chess* (if not superior) in terms of skill and complexity. The openings, traps and combinations, the end-game, general strategy and tactics are all analysed in great detail. *Draughts* problems are composed and studied in the same way as *Chess* problems. National and International tournaments are organised, as well as National and World Championships.

Losing Draughts

No. of players: 2
Equipment: Board and 24 pieces.
Complexity: ★★★

As the name might lead you to expect, in *Losing Draughts* the winner is the first player to get rid of all his pieces. The rules are the same as those for the normal game of *Draughts* except that huffing is not allowed. A player must always capture all the pieces that he possibly can. If he fails to do so, his opponent may insist that he take the move back and play it again to capture the pieces that he missed.

Diagonal Draughts (1)

No. of players: 2
Equipment: Board and 24 pieces
Complexity: ★★★

This is an interesting and enjoyable variation of *Draughts*. The rules are almost exactly the same as for the standard game. The only differences are the way the pieces are positioned at the start of the game – they are lined up across the corners as shown in the diagram – and the squares on which kings are made are the four squares nearest to the opponent's corner of the board.

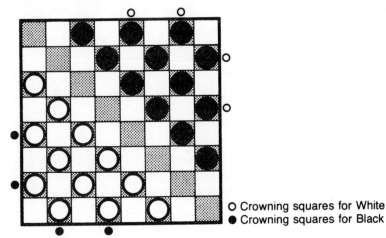

O Crowning squares for White
● Crowning squares for Black

Diagonal Draughts (2)

No. of players: 2
Equipment: Board and 18 pieces
Complexity: ★★☆

This is very similar to the previous game, except that each player starts with only nine pieces, which are set out as shown in the diagram. The squares on which kings are made are the three squares nearest to the opponent's corner.

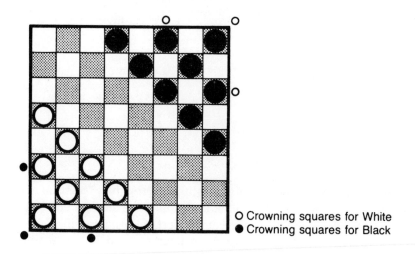

○ Crowning squares for White
● Crowning squares for Black

Italian Draughts

No. of players: 2
Equipment: Board and 24 pieces
Complexity: ★★☆

Italian Draughts is similar to the standard game of Draughts played in Britain and America, except that the board is usually positioned so that each player has a white square at his left-hand corner, and the rules relating to captures are rather different.

(a) A king may not be captured by an uncrowned piece.

(b) A player who is able to make a capturing move must do so.

(c) If a player has a choice of capturing moves he must choose the move which captures the greatest number of pieces. If a king may capture either another king or an uncrowned piece, then it must capture the other king.

Spanish Draughts

No. of players: 2
Equipment: Board and 24 pieces
Complexity: ★★☆

Spanish Draughts is in most respects similar to *Italian Draughts*. The difference is that kings are much more powerful, having what is known as the 'long move'. This means that a king may be moved any number of squares along a diagonal, as long as it is unobstructed (in much the same way as a Bishop moves in *Chess*).

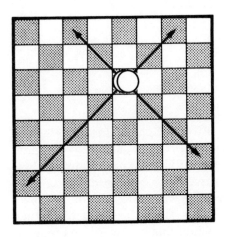

A king may capture an opposing piece anywhere on the same diagonal provided that there are no pieces in between and there are one or more empty squares immediately beyond it. The jump may end in any of the empty squares beyond the captured piece. If the king, having made a capture, can then capture another piece on a different diagonal he must do so. The move continues until the king has captured all the pieces that it can. Only when the move is complete are the captured pieces removed from the board, but they may not be jumped over more than once.

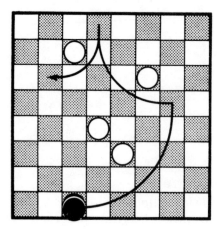

German Draughts

No. of players: 2
Equipment: Board and 24 pieces
Complexity: ✫✫✫

German Draughts is played in the same way as *Spanish Draughts* but has two additional features. First, in *German Draughts*, although ordinary (uncrowned) pieces may only move forwards when not capturing, they may make capturing moves either forwards or backwards. Second, a piece may only be crowned if its move *ends* when it reaches the last row on the far side of the board. If its move takes it to the last row and it is then in a position to capture other pieces by jumping backwards in the same move, it must do so. It does not become a king on that move.

Russian Draughts

No. of players: 2
Equipment: Board and 24 pieces
Complexity ★★☆

Russian Draughts is very similar to *German Draughts*, i.e. when a piece reaches the last row at the far side of the board it must jump backwards to capture other pieces, if it may do so. In *Russian Draughts*, however, it does become a king on that move. The other difference is that when a player has a choice of capturing moves there is no compulsion to make the move that captures the highest number of pieces.

Polish Draughts

No. of players: 2
Equipment: Board and 40 pieces
Complexity: ★★☆

Polish Draughts is played with the same rules as *German Draughts*. It is, however, played on a larger board consisting of 100 squares. Each player starts the game with 20 pieces set out on the first four rows.

Canadian Draughts

No. of players: 2
Equipment: Board and 60 pieces
Complexity: ★★☆

Canadian Draughts is another game that is played with the same rules as *German Draughts*. It is played on an even larger board consisting of 144 squares, and each player starts the game with 30 pieces set out on the first five rows.

Turkish Draughts

No. of players: 2
Equipment: Board and 32 pieces
Complexity: ★★★

Turkish Draughts is played on a standard chess board. Each player starts the game with 16 pieces which are set out on *both* black *and* white squares of each player's *second* and *third* rows. The distinctive features of *Turkish Draughts* are that the pieces move forwards or sideways but *not* diagonally and thus they move on both black and white squares.

A piece becomes a king when it reaches the last row at the far end of the board. It may then move any number of squares forwards, backwards or sideways.

The method by which a king captures other pieces is similar to that in *Spanish Draughts* except, of course, that the jumps are not diagonal. The captured pieces are removed from the board immediately after each capture – they are not left on the board until the end of the move, and thus do not block further captures.

A player who is able to make a capturing move must do so. If he has a choice of capturing moves, he must choose the move that captures the greatest number of pieces.

The game is won by capturing all the opponent's pieces or by blocking them so that they cannot be moved. The game is also won by a player with a king if his opponent is left with just a single uncrowned piece.

Lasca

No. of players: 2
Equipment: Board and 22 pieces
Complexity: ★★

Lasca was invented by Edward Lasker, an American chess master. It is played on a square board which is divided into 49 smaller squares, alternately black and white, with a white square in each corner. Play is on the white squares only.

One player has eleven white pieces and the other player has eleven black pieces. The pieces are flat discs, like *Draughts* pieces – but each piece is marked with a spot on one side. When the unmarked side is uppermost the piece is known as a 'soldier'. When the piece is turned over so that the marked side is uppermost the piece is known as an 'officer'.

At the beginning of the game each player sets up his pieces on the white squares of the three rows nearest to him. All the pieces start as soldiers.

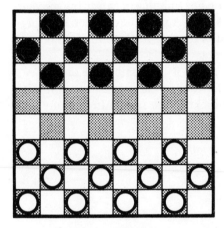

White has the first move and after that the players move alternately.

The manner in which the pieces move and capture other pieces is similar to the manner in which they move and capture in *Draughts*. The distinctive features of *Lasca*, however, are 'columns' and 'guides'. A column may be a single piece or it may be a pile of pieces, one on top of another. The top piece of the column is the guide. The colour of the guide determines to which player the column belongs. The rank of the guide – soldier or officer – determines the way in which the column moves.

At the beginning the the game each piece is a single column with a soldier as a guide. A column guided by a soldier may move diagonally forward, one square at a time (just like an ordinary piece in *Draughts*). When the column reaches the far end of the board, the guide is turned over to become an officer. A column guided by an officer may move one square in any direction (just like a king in *Draughts*).

Pieces are captured by one column jumping over an enemy column into an empty square beyond (just like a capture in *Draughts*). In *Lasca*, however, no pieces are removed from the board, and only the guide is captured, not the whole column. The captured guide is added to the bottom of the column that captured it.

For example, suppose a column of two white pieces jumps over a column of two black pieces. The guide of the black column is added to the bottom of the white column. The other black piece that was on the bottom of its column remains on its original square. If the white column in this example was guided by an officer then it could jump back over the remaining black piece, adding it to the bottom of its column and ending up on its original square.

A player who is in a position to capture an enemy piece must do so, and if he can capture several enemy pieces one after the other in the same move, he must capture all of them. If he has a choice of capturing moves he can choose which one he wants to take. A move ends when no more pieces can be captured or when a soldier reaches the far end of the board and becomes an officer.

The objective of the game is to make it impossible for one's opponent to move. This is achieved either by having all the columns guided by one's own pieces or by blocking the remaining enemy columns so that they cannot move.

Reversi

No of players: 2
Equipment: Board and 64 pieces
Complexity: ★★☆

Reversi – like *Halma* – was invented in the 1880s. It is played using all the squares of an ordinary chessboard. The pieces are coloured white on one side and black on the other. Each player has thirty-two pieces, one player playing them with the black side uppermost and the other playing them with the white side uppermost.

Black always begins the game, and the first four moves are taken up by each player in turn placing one of his pieces on one of the four central squares of the board.

After the four central squares have been filled, the players continue playing alternately, but each move has to be a taking move – a player who cannot make a taking move has to pass until he can do so.

A taking move consists of a player trapping one or more enemy pieces between two of his own. To do this a piece must be placed on the board next to an enemy piece and it must trap one or more enemy pieces between itself and another of the player's own pieces in a straight line – horizontally, vertically or diagonally – with no empty spaces in between. It is often possible in one move to take several pieces in different lines simultaneously.

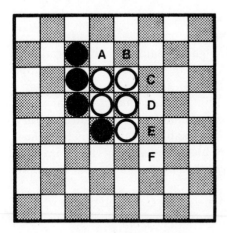

For example, in the position illustrated here Black may play a piece in any of the lettered squares. Playing in square B he will take one white piece, playing in squares A, D or F he will take two white pieces, but playing in squares C or E he will capture three white pieces.

Pieces that are taken are turned over to displayed the colour of the player that took them. Thus pieces once played are never removed from the board or moved from their original squares, but they may be turned over to transfer ownership several times in the course of the game.

The game ends when all sixty-four pieces have been played or when neither player can move. The winner is the player with the greater number of pieces of his colour on the board at the end of the game.

Chess

No. of players: 2
Equipment: Board and 32 pieces
Complexity: ★★★★

The first recorded description of the game of *Chess* comes from eighth-century India. From India the game seems to have spread to Persia and then to the Arabs, and to have been introduced into Europe during the Moorish occupation of Spain. During this period of the game's history it was gradually evolving, and the features of the game that we know today were finally determined in the sixteenth century.

Chess, like *Draughts*, is played on a square board consisting of 64 smaller squares coloured alternately black and white. The board is always positioned so that each player has a white square at his right hand side.

At the beginning of the game the pieces are set out on the board like this:

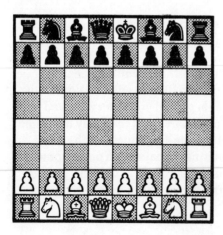

Each player has sixteen pieces, consisting of:

1 king   ♚   2 knights   ♞

1 queen   ♛   2 rooks   ♜

2 bishops   ♝   8 pawns   ♟

Note that the white queen always starts the game on a white square, and the black queen on a black square.

The player with the white pieces always make the first move, after which the players move alternately. A piece may be moved to an empty square or may capture an enemy piece by occupying the square on which that piece stood – the captured piece being removed from the board. At no time may a square be occupied by more than one piece.

The objective of the game is to checkmate the opponent's king. If the king is threatened with capture on the next move it is said to be 'in check'. When a player makes a move that threatens the opposing king with capture it is customary for that player to say 'Check'. The player whose king is in check must on the next move rescue it in one of these three ways:

(a)   by moving the king to another square where it is not threatened,
(b)   by capturing the piece that is giving check,
(c)   by interposing another piece between the king and the piece that is giving check.

If the king cannot be rescued from check then the situation is called 'checkmate' (or simply 'mate') and the player whose king is checkmated loses the game.

Each of the different chess pieces has different powers of movement.

The king may move only one square at a time, in any direction. Of course, it may not move to a square that is threatened by an enemy piece – in other words, the king is not allowed to move into check.

A bishop moves diagonally, and may move any number of squares as long as it is unobstructed. Thus a bishop which starts the game on a black square is restricted to the black squares for the rest of the game. Each player starts the game with one bishop on a black square and another on a white square.

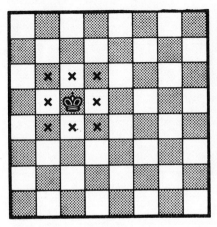 

A rook (sometimes called a castle) may move any number of squares along a row (usually called a 'rank') or column (usually called a 'file') so long as it is unobstructed.

The queen may move any number of squares along a rank, file or diagonal – that is, it combines the powers of movement of a rook and a bishop. The queen is the most powerful piece on the board.

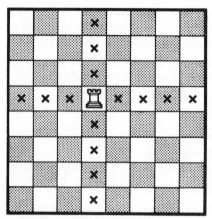 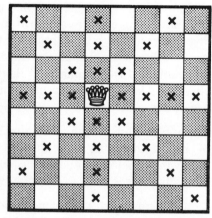

The knight's move differs from that of the other pieces in that it does not move in a straight line and it may jump over other pieces. The knight in a single move moves one square along a rank or file and then one square diagonally – if necessary jumping over any intervening pieces.

The normal move for a pawn, except when capturing, is one square forward along a file. On its first move, however, a pawn may move either one square or two squares. When a pawn reaches the opposite side of the board (the eighth rank) it is promoted and becomes a queen, rook, bishop or knight. Naturally, players usually choose to promote pawns to queens but there may be circumstances in which it is preferable to promote a pawn to a rook, bishop or knight.

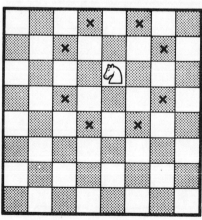 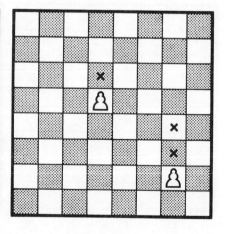

All the pieces, with the exception of the pawn, capture in the same way as they move normally. A pawn captures by moving one square diagonally forward.

There is, in addition, one special type of pawn capture: the capture *en passant* (in passing). If a pawn moves two squares on its initial move, and there is an enemy pawn on an adjacent file which could have captured it had it moved only one square, then it can be captured exactly as if it had only moved one square – the capturing pawn moves one square diagonally forward and the captured pawn is removed from the board. The *en passant* capture, if it is to be made, must be made *immediately* after the opposing pawn has made its two-square move.

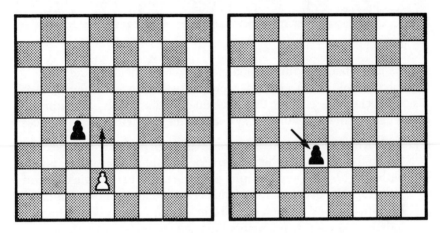

There is one more special type of move to be described, and that is *castling*. This differs from every other move in that two pieces are moved at the same time – the king and a rook. Castling consists of moving the king two squares to the right or left from its starting position and moving the rook to the square the king has just passed over. Castling may not be performed in any of the following circumstances:

(a) if there are any pieces between the king and the rook,
(b) if the king is in check,
(c) If the square that the king passes over or moves to is threatened by an enemy piece,
(d) if either the rook or the king has previously been moved.

Castling has two main purposes – to tuck the king safely in the corner where it is more easily protected, and to bring the rook more quickly into play.

As described previously, a game is won by checkmating the opponent's king. Often a game is won before that stage – when a player resigns because he can see that checkmate is inevitable. Sometimes, also, a game is drawn. A draw may occur in the following circumstances:

(a) Lack of material – when there are not enough pieces left on the board to win the game for either player. For example, if one player is left with only his king and the other player is left with only his king and a bishop, the game is drawn since checkmate cannot be forced.

(b) Perpetual check – when one player can continue giving check indefinitely to his opponent's king but cannot checkmate it.

(c) Stalemate – when one player, it being his turn to move, can make no legal move, but his king is not in check.

(d) Repetition – when exactly the same position occurs three times with the same player having the next move. Either player may then claim a draw.

(e) Fifty-move rule – when no capture or pawn move has been made by either player during his past fifty moves.

(f) Agreement – when both players agree to a draw.

Learning the moves of the different pieces is, of course, only the first step in learning how to play the game. Obviously a thorough description of strategy and tactics is beyond the scope of this book, but the following general principles should be helpful to the beginner and the occasional player.

Successful play often hinges on control of the centre squares. It is therefore advisable to begin by moving at least one of the centre pawns forward two squares. As many pieces as possible should then be brought into play as quickly as possible. A common mistake made by beginners is to bring out the queen very early and to move it aimlessly around the board, attempting attacks that are easily countered, meanwhile leaving the other pieces on their original squares. In general, the knights and bishops should be brought into play before the queen, and the knights, if possible, should be placed on safe squares near the centre of the board rather than at the edges where they are less effective. It is also usually good policy to castle fairly early in the game.

Before making any move you should check whether your opponent's previous move poses any threats that you have to counter, whether his previous move has left any weaknesses in his position that you can exploit, and whether your proposed move leaves any of your own pieces in a vulnerable position. If there are no immediate threats and you are not sure which move to make, decide which of your pieces is least usefully placed and move that piece to a square where it is more useful.

The best and quickest way of improving one's game is to play as often as possible against an opponent slightly better than yourself. If you always play inferior players or players who are very much better than you are, then you will learn little if anything from them. It also helps to play as many different opponents as possible.

For recording games there are two systems of notation in general use – the Descriptive, or English, system and the Algebraic, or Continental, system.

In the Descriptive system, the pieces are represented by their initial letters (Kt or N being used to represent a knight) and the squares are numbered according to the pieces which stand at the end of the files at the start of the game. For example, the square on which the queen stands is Q1 and the squares in front of it are Q2, Q3 and so on to Q8. Pieces are differentiated according to whether they are on the king's side of the board or on the queen's side – for example QR (queen's rook) and KR (king's rook). Each square has two names – depending on whether it is being regarded from White's point of view or from Black's point of view. For example, White's king's rook starts the game on his square KR1, which is Black's KR8.

A move is described by writing the piece which is moved and the square it is moved to. If, for example, White's first move is to move the pawn in front of his queen two squares forward, this would be written P-Q4 (read as 'Pawn to queen four'). Captures are shown by an 'x' – e.g. QRxP (read as 'Queen's rook takes pawn'). Other symbols used are: ch (check) e.p. (en passant) 0-0 (castles, king's side) 0-0-0 (castles, queen's side) !(good move) ?(dubious move).

BLACK

QR8	QN8	QB8	Q8	K8	KB8	KN8	KR8
QR7	QN7	QB7	Q7	K7	KB7	KN7	KR7
QR6	QN6	QB6	Q6	K6	KB6	KN6	KR6
QR5	QN5	QB5	Q5	K5	KB5	KN5	KR5
QR4	QN4	QB4	Q4	K4	KB4	KN4	KR4
QR3	QN3	QB3	Q3	K3	KB3	KN3	KR3
QR2	QN2	QB2	Q2	K2	KB2	KN2	KR2
QR1	QN1	QB1	Q1	K1	KB1	KN1	KR1

WHITE

BLACK

QR1	QN1	QB1	Q1	K1	KB1	KN1	KR1
QR2	QN2	QB2	Q2	K2	KB2	KN2	KR2
QR3	QN3	QB3	Q3	K3	KB3	KN3	KR3
QR4	QN4	QB4	Q4	K4	KB4	KN4	KR4
QR5	QN5	QB5	Q5	K5	KB5	KN5	KR5
QR6	QN6	QB6	Q6	K6	KB6	KN6	KR6
QR7	QN7	QB7	Q7	K7	KB7	KN7	KR7
QR8	QN8	QB8	Q8	K8	KB8	KN8	KR8

WHITE

White's point of view   Black's point of view

The moves are conventionally recorded in two columns, White's moves in the first column and Black's in the second column. Here, as an example, is a famous game played in 1854 between G. A. Anderssen and J. Dufresne:

	Anderssen	**Dufresne**			White	Black
	White	*Black*				
1	P-K4	P-K4		13	Q-R4	B-N3
2	N-KB3	N-QB3		14	QN-Q2	B-N2
3	B-B4	B-B4		15	N-K4	Q-B4
4	P-QN4	BxNP		16	BxQP	Q-R4
5	P-B3	B-R4		17	N-B6 ch	PxN
6	P-Q4	PxP		18	PxP	R-N1
7	0-0	P-Q6		19	QR-Q1	QxN
8	Q-N3	Q-B3		20	RxN ch	NxR
9	P-K5	Q-N3		21	QxP ch	KxQ
10	R-K1	KN-K2		22	B-B5 ch	K-K1
11	B-R3	P-N4		23	B-Q7 ch	K-Q1
12	QxP	R-QN1		24	BxN mate	

In the Algebraic system each square is represented according to the rank and file it is on – the eight files being represented by the letters a to h, and the eight ranks by the numbers 1 to 8. The squares are always described as from White's point of view.

a8	b8	c8	d8	e8	f8	g8	h8
a7	b7	c7	d7	e7	f7	g7	h7
a6	b6	c6	d6	e6	f6	g6	h6
a5	b5	c5	d5	e5	f5	g5	h5
a4	b4	c4	d4	e4	f4	g4	h4
a3	b3	c3	d3	e3	f3	g3	h3
a2	b2	c2	d2	e2	f2	g2	h2
a1	b1	c1	d1	e1	f1	g1	h1

Moves are recorded by writing the piece which is moved and the square it is moved to, thus Be4. Other abbreviations are generally the same as for the Descriptive notation.

Losing Chess

No. of players: 2
Equipment: Board and 32 pieces
Complexity: ★★★★

This game is one of a number of unorthodox variations of Chess. In Losing Chess the objective is to lose all one's pieces. The king has no special status and can be taken like any other piece. A player who is able to capture an opposing piece must do so. The first player to get rid of all his pieces is the winner.

Randomised Chess

No. of players: 2
Equipment: Board and 32 pieces
Complexity: ✰✰✰✰

Randomised Chess is played in the same way as conventional *Chess* except that at the beginning of the game the pieces on the first rank are arranged in a random manner (provided that it is the same for both players), e.g. king, knight, rook, bishop, rook, knight, bishop, queen. Thus the result is like a game of *Chess* without conventional Opening theory.

Refusal Chess

No. of players: 2
Equipment: Board and 32 pieces
Complexity: ✰✰✰✰

Refusal Chess is played in the same way as normal *Chess* except that at each move a player has the right to refuse his opponent's choice of move and to insist that he play some other move instead. The right of refusal may be exercised as often as one likes during the game – but only one refusal per move.

Pocket Knight Chess

No. of players: 2
Equipment: Board and 32 pieces plus 2 extra knights
Complexity: ✰✰✰✰

This is played in the same way as normal *Chess* except that each player starts the game with an extra knight in his pocket. At any stage of the game, when it is his turn to move, a player may place his extra knight on any vacant square on the board. This counts as his move, and thereafter the extra knight functions as a normal piece.

Two Move Chess

No. of players: 2
Equipment: Board and 32 pieces
Complexity: ★★★☆

In this variation of *Chess* the normal rules apply except that each player has two moves at a time instead of one. A player giving check on his first move forfeits his second move. A player who is in check must get out of check on his first move.

Progressive Chess

No. of players: 2
Equipment: Board and 32 pieces
Complexity: ★★★☆

This is a tremendously challenging *Chess* variation and it requires great ability to think ahead. White has one move, then Black has two moves, White then has three moves, then Black has four moves, and so on. When a player gives check this ends his turn and he forfeits the rest of his moves. A player who is in check must get out of check on his first move.

Kriegspiel

No. of players: 2 plus referee
Equipment: 3 boards and 3 sets of chess pieces
Complexity: ★★★★☆

Kriegspiel is a very challenging variation of *Chess* in which neither player sees the pieces of his opponent or knows exactly what moves his opponent is making.

Each player has his own board, as does the referee. Neither player is allowed to see the board of his opponent – normally the two players sit back to back. The referee's board must also be concealed from both players though he must be able to see their boards.

At the start of the game White sets out the white pieces on his board in the normal way, and Black does the same with the black pieces on his board. The referee sets up his own board with both black and white pieces and he duplicates the moves on this board throughout the game.

The players move alternately. If no capture or check is involved and the move is legal, the referee will announce 'White has moved' or 'Black has moved' as appropriate. No information is given about the piece that has moved or the square it has gone to.

If a player – White, let us say – moves a piece to a square that is occupied by one of his opponent's pieces (other than the king) the referee announces 'White captures' and he removes the captured piece from Black's board. Thus Black knows that there is now a white piece on that square but he does not know what piece it is or which square it was moved from. White, on the other hand, knows that he has captured a black piece but does not know which piece he has captured.

A move that gives check is announced as such, identifying the line of attack – rank, file, long diagonal or short diagonal – e.g. 'White has moved, giving check on the seventh rank', or 'Black has moved, giving check on the short diagonal', or 'White has moved, giving check with a knight'.

Of course, since each player can see only his own pieces, many of the moves he tries will be illegal. When this happens the referee announces 'Illegal' and the player must withdraw that move and try another.

A player, at any time when it is his turn to move, may ask the referee if he has any possible captures *with a pawn*. The referee answers either 'Yes' or 'No'. If the reply is 'Yes', the player must attempt at least one pawn capture before trying another move.

Kriegspiel obviously requires a very high level of *Chess* skill, since the referee is the only person who really knows what the position is on the board. A player, however, may gather information about the disposition of his opponent's forces by attempting moves which he knows are quite likely to be illegal, and by attempting long-ranging moves with bishops, rooks and queen. Information may also be provided by announcements concerning checks and pawn captures.

Go

No. of players: 2
Equipment: Board and 361 pieces
Complexity: ★★★★

The game of Go is believed to have originated in China about 2000 BC. It was later introduced into Japan, and the Japanese are now the world's foremost exponents of the game.

Go is just as complex and demanding a game as *Chess*, and as with *Chess* whole books can be, and have been, written which are devoted to just a single aspect of the game. Obviously only the basic principles can be presented here.

The board is ruled with 19 horizontal lines and 19 vertical lines, forming a total of 361 points where the lines intersect. The pieces are called 'stones' – one player starts with 181 black stones and the other player starts with 180 white stones.

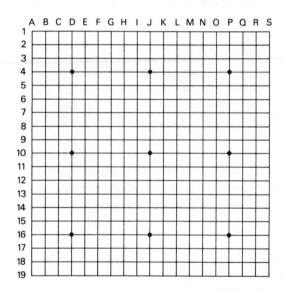

At the beginning of the game the board is empty. Each player in turn places one of his stones on a vacant point, the objective of the game being to surround vacant territory. Points are also scored for capturing enemy stones. Stones once placed on the board are not moved unless they are captured – in which case they are removed from the board. The board is thus gradually filled up with stones until the game ends when all vacant territory has been surrounded by one player or the other. Each player then counts the number of points he has surrounded and the number of enemy stones he has captured – the player with the higher total being the winner.

The player with the black stones normally has the first turn. Since this confers an advantage the weaker player is usually allowed to play with the black stones. There is a further handicapping system, whereby if one player is markedly weaker than the other he may be allowed, on his first move, to place two or more stones on the board – on the marked handicap points.

Handicap	Handicap points used
2	P4,D16
3	P4,D16,P16
4	D4,P4,D16,P16
5	D4,P4,J10,D16,P16
6	D4,P4,D10,P10,D16,P16
7	D4,P4,D10,J10,P,10,D16,P16
8	D4,J4,P4,D10,P10,D16,J16,P16
9	D4,J4,P4,D10,J10,P10,D16,J16,P16

Vacant points that are adjacent – horizontally or vertically – to a stone are known as its 'liberties'. When all of a stone's liberties are occupied by enemy stones it is captured and removed from the board. A group of stones of the same colour connected horizontally or vertically is known as an 'army'. Armies may be captured in the same way as single stones. In the diagram below, white stones played on any of the points marked with a cross will capture black stones. Stones such as the black stones in this diagram which are liable to be captured on the next move are said to be in 'atari'. It should be noted that it is not necessary for the attacking stones to be connected horizontally or vertically.

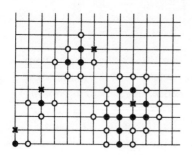

Note that in the fourth example above the black army is captured by playing a white stone in an internal liberty – such as internal space is known as an 'eye'. If the external liberties of the black army had not previously been completely occupied by white stones, a white stone could not be played in the eye – as it would itself immediately be captured. Such a move is illegal. Therefore, when capturing an army which has an eye, the final move which captures the army must be within the eye.

An important principle, which follows from this, is that whenever an army has two or more separate eyes it can never be captured.

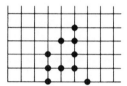

The next diagram illustrates what is known as a 'ko' situation. If White were to play on the point indicated in the first position this would lead to the second position, and if Black were then to play on the point indicated in the second position this would lead back to the first position. Obviously this could continue indefinitely. To prevent this happening there is a rule that the second player may not recapture in a ko situation until he has made at least one other move elsewhere on the board.

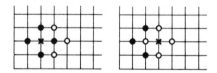

It is important to understand how captures may be made but it is more important to realise that surrounding vacant points is the primary objective and capturing enemy stones is secondary to this. A general principle to follow is that stones should not be played inside territory which is securely held by the opponent as they are sure to be captured eventually. Another general principle is that, since the scoring is based on the *vacant* points that one has surrounded, stones should not be played unnecessarily within one's own territory, as they merely reduce one's score.

The game ends when both players agree that there are no more points to be gained. If only one player considers the game to be ended he says 'Pass' and is not allowed to make any further moves. The other player may then continue playing until he, too, judges that he can secure no further points.

Each player counts the number of vacant points in his territory and adds to this the number of enemy stones he has captured in the course of the game. The player with the higher total is the winner.

Go-Moku

No. of players: 2
Equipment: Go board and 200 pieces
Complexity: ★★★

One player has 100 white pieces (or 'stones') and the other player has 100 black pieces. Each player in turn places one of his stones on any vacant point on a *Go* board, the objective being to get five pieces of one's own colour in a row, horizontally, vertically or diagonally – while at the same time, of course, trying to prevent one's opponent from doing so. The first player to get five in a row is the winner.

If both players have played all their stones without getting five in a row, the game continues with each player in turn moving one of his stones horizontally or vertically to an adjacent vacant point until one player succeeds in forming a row of five.

6 DOMINO GAMES

Introduction: History, General Principles and Terminology

It is generally agreed by the experts that dominoes originated in China, perhaps as many as 2000 years ago, and that they were introduced into Europe by Venetian traders in the fourteenth or fifteenth century. From Italy they were subsequently introduced into France, and it is believed that the English may first have learned about dominoes from French prisoners-of-war during the Napoleonic Wars.

Dominoes, for nearly all their history, have been especially popular among working men. In the days when paper was an expensive commodity, dominoes, carved from bone, were more easily made and more durable then the playing cards which were popular among the upper classes.

Dominoes are rectangular tiles, made usually from bone, ivory, wood or plastic. A standard European set consists of 28 tiles. The face of each tile is divided by a central line into two equal squares, each of which is either blank or marked with pips from one to six in number. This set is also known as the Double-6 set, as the double-6 is the top domino in the set. All the games described in this chapter are played with this set.

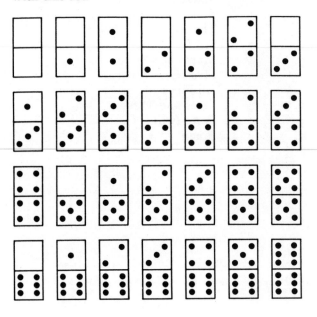

In some games reference is made to the 'suit' of a domino. The domino suits are as follows:

Blank suit:	Double-blank, 6-blank, 5-blank, 4-blank, 3-blank, 2-blank, 1-blank.
1 suit:	Double-1, 6-1, 5-1, 4-1, 3-1, 2-1, 1-blank.
2 suit:	Double-2, 6-2, 5-2, 4-2, 3-2, 2-1, 2-blank.
3 suit:	Double-3, 6-3, 5-3, 4-3, 3-2, 3-1, 3-blank.
4 suit:	Double-4, 6-4, 5-4, 4-3, 4-2, 4-1, 4-blank.
5 suit:	Double-5, 6-5, 5-4, 5-3, 5-2, 5-1, 5-blank.
6 suit:	Double-6, 6-5, 6-4, 6-3, 6-2, 6-1, 6-blank.
Double suit:	Double-6, Double-5, Double-4, Double-3, Double-2, Double-1, Double-blank.

It may be noted that every domino belongs to two suits – for example, the 6-5 belongs to the 6 suit and the 5 suit, and the double-3 belongs to the 3 suit and to the double suit.

There are larger sets of dominoes than the Double-6 set. There is a Double-9 set, consisting of 55 dominoes up to double-9, and a Double-12 set, consisting of 91 dominoes up to double-12. These sets are not very common, but almost all the games for a double-6 set may be played with these larger sets, with in some cases a slight modification of the rules.

Dominoes offer hours of fun and fascination. Most of the games are quite easy to learn, and a novice can quickly reach an acceptable level of play, though real expertise, of course, is only acquired after much practice.

Although there is a tremendous range and variety of domino games, certain general principles apply. These principles are described here to avoid constant repetition in the descriptions of the games that follow. Domino novices are urged to acquaint themselves thoroughly with the information in this section before studying the descriptions of the individual games.

The Players
Some of the games are for two players, some for four, and some for any number from two to five. Where there are four players they may play individually or two may play in partnership against the other two. Partners should sit on opposite sides of the table, as for bridge or whist.

Shuffling
Before each game or each hand, the dominoes are all placed face down on the table and are moved around until they are thoroughly mixed. It is customary for all players to take part in the shuffle.

Drawing a Hand

After the dominoes have been shuffled, each player selects the number of dominoes required for the game being played. Except in games such as *Blind Hughie*, in which the players are not allowed to look at the dominoes they have drawn, the player may hold his dominoes in his hand, place them in a rack, or stand them on edge before him on the table, so that they are visible to him but concealed from the other players. The dominoes that are left when all the players have drawn their hands are known as 'the boneyard'. The dominoes in the boneyard are usually moved to one side of the table, still face down, and depending on the game being played they may remain out of play for that hand or they may form a pool from which later draws may be made.

Leading

In some games the lead (i.e. the first turn) goes to the player who has drawn the double-6. If no player holds this domino then the lead goes to the player holding the next highest double. In other games the lead is decided by lot before the hands are drawn. Each player picks up one domino, and the lead goes to the player picking up the domino with the highest number of pips – in the event of two players tying those players select again. The dominoes are shuffled before and after this draw for lead.

Direction of Play

After the first player has led, play always proceeds to the left (in a clockwise direction) around the table.

The Play

In a few games – those based on card games – the dominoes are played so that tricks may be taken.

The basic characteristic of most domino games, however, is that the dominoes are played so that matching ends are adjacent.

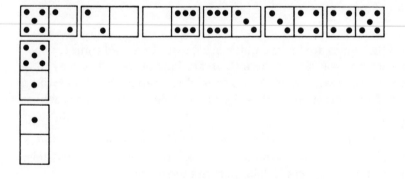

In most games the players may build on either end of such a row, which is known as 'the line of play'. Note that the row may bend at right angles (particularly when nearing the edge of the table!).

Doubles are usually played *across* the line of play, whereas the other dominoes are played *with* the line of play.

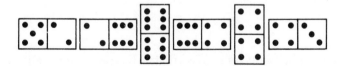

Usually one can play only against the sides of the doubles, as in the illustration above, but in a few games one may play against the ends as well, like this:

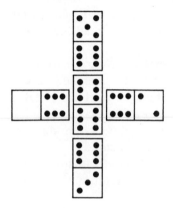

Passing
In some games, if a player cannot match a domino from his hand with either end of the line, he is said 'to pass' or to be 'knocking', and it is customary for the player to knock on the table when this happens. Play immediately passes to the next player.

In some games the player who is unable to play a matching domino must draw a domino from the boneyard.

End of Play
A hand ends when one player has played all his dominoes (this is known as 'going out') or when all the players are unable to play from their hands and have all passed in turn (this is known as a 'blocked game').

Scoring
There are various scoring systems, depending on the particular game

being played. Most games, however, consist of a number of 'hands' or rounds, and are played until one player attains an agreed number of points such as 100. The scoring is usually based on the number of pips on the dominoes remaining in the players' hands. A cribbage board may be used to record the score, in which case the game is usually played to 61 points or 121 points.

General Rules
(a) If, in the course of play, a player realises that he has drawn too many dominoes, one of his dominoes must be chosen at random by another player and returned to the boneyard.
(b) If, in the course of play, a player realises that he has drawn too few dominoes, he must draw from the boneyard to make up the right number.
(c) If a player accidentally exposes one of his dominoes so that it is seen by one of the other players then it must be shown to all the other players.
(d) If a player misplays (for example, if he joins a 5 on to a 6, or if he plays out of turn) then he must take the domino back and play correctly if the misplay is discovered before the next player takes his turn. If the misplay is not discovered before the next player takes his turn then the misplay must be accepted and if any points were scored on the misplay they, too, are allowed to stand.
(e) Once a domino has been played, provided it is not a misplay, the player may not change his mind and take the domino back.

Variations
Many of the games described in this chapter have a tremendous number of variations. Ask a number of *Block* players, for example, what rules they play by and the likelihood is that you will be given several slightly different versions.

While the basic formula of any game will be agreed on by (almost) everyone, versions of the game may differ in the following respects:

(a) The number of dominoes drawn by each player.
(b) The lead player – he may be chosen by lot or he may be the player holding the highest double.
(c) The domino played by the lead player – it may be the highest double in his hand or it may be any domino he chooses.
(d) Whether dominoes are drawn from the boneyard if a player cannot play a domino from his hand.

(e) Whether the boneyard is drawn upon till only two dominoes remain or whether it is drawn upon until it is empty.
(f) The way in which points are scored at the end of a hand, and the number of points a game is played to.

It would be an impossible task to describe all the possible variations of each game. The best method – the one adapted here – is to describe one generally accepted version of each game, and to advise readers that, although they might encounter other variations, the basic principles remain the same.

Fours

No. of players: 3, 4 or 5
Equipment: Set of dominoes
Complexity: ⋆

Fours is a simple domino game which is eminently suitable for young players, and is usually the first domino game they learn to play.
    The lead player is chosen by lot, and each player then draws his dominoes. If three are playing each draws nine dominoes, if four are playing each draws seven dominoes, if five are playing each draws five dominoes. Any dominoes left over are put to one side and are not used in the game.
    The object of the game is to be the first player to get rid of all his dominoes. Each player in his turn is allowed to continue playing dominoes from his hand for as long as he can match either end of the line of dominoes already played, after which the turn passes to the next player on the left.
    The first player leads with any domino that he chooses from his hand. Naturally he will take care to choose the domino that allows him to get rid of as many other dominoes as possible. He will continue playing his dominoes until he can no longer do so. If he is very lucky he will be able to play all his dominoes in one turn and will win the game.
    This does not happen very often, however – it usually takes at least two turns to get rid of all one's dominoes. Each player plays in turn until one player wins the game by getting rid of all his dominoes. In some cases it may happen that the game becomes blocked and all the

players are left with dominoes that cannot be played. When this happens, each player adds up the number of pips on the dominoes left in his hand, and the winner is the player with the lowest total.

Ends

No. of players: 4
Equipment: Set of dominoes
Complexity: ★

Ends is a simple but fascinating domino game, which can be enjoyed equally by children and adults.

Each player draws seven dominoes, and the game is started by the player with the double-6 placing it face upwards in the centre of the table. Each player in his turn is now allowed to play one domino that matches either end of the line of dominoes already played, the turn always passing to the next player on the left around the table. If a player cannot go when it is his turn, he must ask the player on his left for a suitable domino. If that player has a domino that can be played he gives it to the player who asked for it, who then plays it. The player on the left then has his turn as usual.

If the player on the left does not have a playable domino, he must ask the next player on *his* left. If that player does not have a playable domino, he again must ask the player on *his* left. The first player in this chain who *does* have a playable domino gives it to the player who first requested it. The player who asked for the domino plays it and the game proceeds as normal.

If the request passes right round the table and no player has a playable domino, then the player who first asked for it is allowed to play *any* domino from his hand on either end of the line, without making a match.

The winner is the first player to get rid of all his dominoes.

Blind Hughie

No. of players: 2 to 5
Equipment: Set of dominoes
Complexity: ★

This is purely a game of chance, and is popular with children. The lead player is chosen by lot. With two or three players, each draws seven dominoes; with four or five players, each draws five dominoes. A player is not allowed to look at the dominoes he has drawn – they must remain face down on the table in a row in front of him.

The lead player begins by turning over the leftmost domino of his row and placing it in the centre of the table. Each player in his turn then looks at the leftmost domino of his row. If he can match it to either end of the line of play then he plays it, otherwise he replaces it, face down, at the rightmost end of his own row.

Play continues around the table until one player wins by playing all his dominoes, or until the game is blocked because none of the players can play their remaining dominoes, in which case nobody is the winner.

Round the Clock

No. of players: 2 to 5
Equipment: Set of dominoes
Complexity: ★★

A leader is chosen by lot and the players then draw their hands – seven dominoes each for two players, six dominoes each for three players, five dominoes each for four or five players.

Play begins with the player who has the double-6 in his hand laying it face up in the centre of the table. If none of the players has the double-6 then the leader must draw a domino from the boneyard. If it is the double-6 he plays it, otherwise the next player must draw from the boneyard. This continues around the table until the double-6 is drawn and played or until there are only two dominoes left in the boneyard. If the double-6 happens to be one of these two dominoes left in the boneyard then the game is abandoned and new hands are drawn for a fresh game.

Once the double-6 has been played, the next four dominoes must be played against the sides and ends of double-6. If a player cannot play from his hand and there are more than two dominoes in the boneyard he may draw one of them. If he still cannot play then he must pass.

When these dominoes have been played, the next four dominoes played must be the doubles for the four ends.

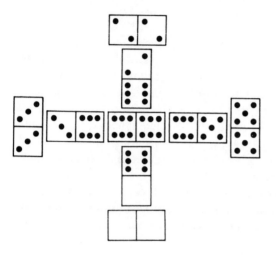

The next four dominoes must be played against the doubles on the ends, and so on.

The winner is the first player to get rid of all his dominoes or, if the game is blocked, the player left with the lowest number of pips in his hand.

Maltese Cross

No. of players: 4
Equipment: Set of dominoes
Complexity: ★★

Maltese Cross is somewhat similar to *Round the Clock*. Each of the four players draws seven dominoes, and the player with the double-6 leads. Dominoes may be played to both ends and both sides of the double-6 so that a four-ended line of play results. However, there is one rule that gives *Maltese Cross* its distinctive character. This rule is that, until a double has been played, all ends with that number are blocked.

Take this situation as a example:

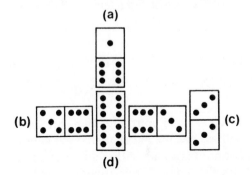

The player whose turn it is may play any matching domino at (c) or (d) since the double-6 and double-3 have been played. But only the double-1 may be played at (a) and only the double-5 at (b).

If a player in his turn is unable to play a domino from his hand then he must pass.

The first player to get rid of all his dominoes is the winner. If the game is blocked, then the winner is the player who has the lowest number of pips left in his hand.

Block

No. of players: 2, 3 or 4
Equipment: Set of dominoes
Complexity: ★★

Block is probably the most popular of all domino games. If there are two players each draws seven dominoes. If there are three or four players each draws five dominoes. The lead player, who is chosen by lot, plays any domino from his hand. The next player must play a domino which matches either end of the starter, or if he does not have a matching domino he must pass. Play progresses round the table in this way with each player adding a domino to either end of the line or passing. Doubles are placed across the line of play.

The aim is to be the first player to play all the dominoes in your hand, and to do this you should to attempt to play dominoes that will block your opponents and force them to pass. Therefore a good hand is one which contains a preponderance of one suit. For example, if the line looks like this:

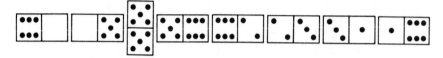

and you hold the double-6, 6-3 and 6-4, then your opponents are fully blocked since all the sixes have either been played or are in your hand. You may play the double-6 and your opponents will still be knocking. You can then play either the 6-3 or the 6-4 and your opponents will be restricted to playing on that one end – you still hold a block on the other.

Play continues until one player has played all his dominoes – in which case he is the winner and he scores one point for each pip in his opponents' hands – or until all the players are blocked – in which case the winner is the player with the lowest number of pips in his hand and his score is the total number of pips in his opponents' hands minus the number of pips in his own hand.

The winner of one hand is given the lead in the next hand, and the game is played to an agreed number of points.

Partnership Block

No. of players: 4
Equipment: Set of dominoes
Complexity: ★★

This is the same as the previous game, except for the following differences:

(a) Two players play as partners against the other two and score jointly.
(b) When one player has played all his dominoes, the partnership scores the number of pips in the hands of the opposing partnership.
(c) When the game is blocked, the partnership with the lowest total of pips in their two hands scores the difference between the number of pips in their opponents' hands and the number of pips in their own.

Tiddly-Wink

No. of players: 2, 3 or 4
Equipment: Set of dominoes
Complexity: ★★

Tiddly-Wink is a variation of *Block* with the following differences:

(a) The dominoes are shared equally between the players, any left-over dominoes remaining in the boneyard.
(b) The player with the highest double always leads.
(c) Any player who plays a double may, if he wishes, play another matching domino on the free side of that double within the same turn.

Sebastopol

No. of players: 4
Equipment: Set of dominoes
Complexity: ★★

Each player draws seven dominoes, and the player who holds the double-6 leads. The next four dominoes must be played against the sides and ends of the double-6 to form 'the star' as in this example:

If a player does not have a 6 in his hand, he must pass until the star has been completed. Thereafter play proceeds as for *Block* except that

there are four ends to play on instead of two. Scoring is the same as for *Block*.

Cyprus

No. of players: 4
Equipment: Set of dominoes
Complexity: ☆☆

Cyprus is similar to *Sebastopol* except that after the double-6 has been led the next six dominoes must be played against it to form a star with six ends like this:

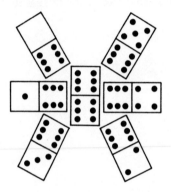

If a player does not have a 6 in his hand, he must pass until the star has been completed. Therafter play proceeds as for *Block* except that there are now six ends to play on.

Cyprus is sometimes played with a double-9 set of dominoes, and in that version the double-9 is led and the star is formed with eight ends.

French Draw

No. of players: 2, 3 or 4
Equipment: Set of dominoes
Complexity: ★★

This is basically the same game as *Block* except that dominoes may be drawn from the boneyard in the course of play.

With two or three players each draws seven dominoes; with four players each draws six dominoes. The lead player, who is chosen by lot, plays any domino he chooses from his hand. Subsequently any player, if he is unable to play a matching domino from his hand or if he simply does not wish to do so, must draw a domino from the boneyard and continue doing so until he draws one that he is able and willing to play or until only two dominoes are left in the boneyard. A player who cannot play a domino from his hand when only two dominoes remain in the boneyard must pass.

Play continues until one player goes out (in which case he is the winner) or until the game is blocked (in which case the winner is the player with the lowest number of pips left in his hand).

The winner, as in *Block*, scores points equal to the total number of pips left in his opponents' hands minus the number of pips (if any) left in his own hand. The game is played to an agreed number of points.

Draw or Pass

No. of players: 2, 3 or 4
Equipment: Set of dominoes
Complexity: ★★

The lead player is chosen by lot and the players then draw their dominoes – seven dominoes each if there are two players, and five dominoes each if there are three or four players.

The lead player plays any domino he chooses from his hand. After that each player in his turn can choose to do one of three things:

(a) He can play a domino from his hand to match either end of the line of play.

(b) He can draw as many dominoes as he likes from the boneyard (provided that two always remain there). If he chooses to draw he cannot also play a domino in that turn.

(c) He can pass – and is allowed to do this even though he may have a domino that he could play if he wished.

Play continues round the table in the normal way, each player in turn choosing one of these three options. Play ends when one player goes out or when all the players pass in succession.

The winner is the player who goes out or who has the lowest number of pips left in his hand. He scores points equal to the number of pips left in his opponents' hand minus the number of pips (if any) left in his own hand. The game is played to an agreed number of points (usually 100).

Bergen

No. of players: 2, 3 or 4
Equipment: Set of dominoes
Complexity: ★★

If there are two or three players each draws six dominoes; if there are four players each draws five dominoes. The objectives are to be the first player to play all one's dominoes, to block one's opponents, and to score special points by playing so that the same number appears at both ends of the line of play. When the same number does appear at both ends of the line, as in this example, this is known as a 'double-header'.

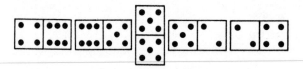

When the same number appears three times at the ends (i.e. when one end is a double) this is known as a 'triple-header'.

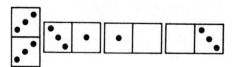

The player with the highest double leads and immediately scores two points for a double-header, or if none of the players has drawn a double the player with the lowest domino leads that but does not score. Play proceeds as for *French Draw* except that whenever a player plays a domino to form a double-header he scores two points and whenever he forms a triple-header he scores three points.

The winner of a hand, who also scores two points, may be the player who first plays all his dominoes or, in a blocked game, the player left with no doubles, the fewest doubles or the lowest number of pips in his hand.

A game is usually played for ten or fifteen points.

Matador

No. of players: 2, 3 or 4
Equipment: Set of dominoes
Complexity: ★★

Matador is an intriguing game in which dominoes are played not so that joined ends match, but so that joined ends add up to seven. Doubles (except the double-blank) are not played across the line of play but are treated as ordinary dominoes.

There are, however, four dominoes – the 'matadors' – which have special features. The matadors are the double-blank and the three dominoes which have pips adding up to seven – the 6-1, the 5-2 and the 4-3. A matador is a sort of joker or wild card that can be played anywhere on the line of play. When they are played the join does not have to add up to seven. Matadors are placed across the line of play.

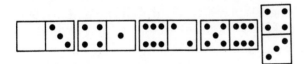

Against the 4-3 matador one could play a four (making a join of seven with the 3 of the matador) or a three (making a join of seven with the 4) or, of course, another matador.

Note the blank at the end of the line illustrated above. Only a matador may be played next to a blank, since so other domino can make a join adding up to seven.

When the first player has been chosen by lot, the players draw their dominoes. If there are two players each draws seven dominoes; if there are three players each draws six dominoes; if there are four players each draws five dominoes.

The first player leads with any domino he chooses from his hand, and play proceeds to the left around the table in the usual fashion. Any player, in his turn, who is unable to play a domino from his hand or simply does not wish to do so must draw a domino from the boneyard – and continue doing so until he draws one that he is able and willing to play, or until only two dominoes remain in the boneyard. When there are only two dominoes left in the boneyard a player must play a domino if he can, and must pass if he has no playable domino.

Play continues until one player has played all his dominoes – in which case he is the winner, scoring one point for each pip in his opponents' hands – or until none of the players can play any more dominoes – in which case the player with the lowest number of pips in his hand is the winner, and his score is the total number of pips in his opponents' hands minus the number of pips in his own.

A game is played to an agreed number of points.

Fives

No. of players: 2, 3 or 4
Equipment: Set of dominoes
Complexity: ✩✩

Fives is the simplest of a group of domino games in which the object of the game is not only to be the first player to get rid of all his dominoes but also to score points by making the ends of the line of play add up to certain numbers.

In *Fives* dominoes are played so that joined ends match. If the pips at the ends of the line of play then total five the player scores one point; if they total ten he scores two points; if fifteen he scores three points; if twenty he scores four points. If the ends do not add up to the multiple of five no points are scored. Doubles are always played across the line of play and both halves of the double are counted in the number of pips. For example, the last player in the game shown here would have scored two points, since the ends add up to ten.

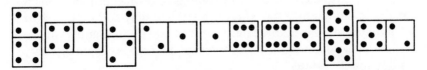

The first player is chosen by lot, and the players then draw their dominoes. If there are two players each draws seven dominoes; if there are three players each draws six dominoes; if there are four players each draws five dominoes.

The first player leads with any domino he chooses from his hand. Each player then follows on in his turn, trying, of course, to score as many points as possible and to prevent his opponents from scoring points.

If a player, in his turn, is able to play a matching domino then he must do so. If he cannot play any of his dominoes then he must draw from the boneyard until he is able to play, or if there are no dominoes left in the boneyard he must pass.

Play continues in this way until one of the players has played all his dominoes, in which case he is the winner, or until the game is blocked, in which case the winner is the player left with the lowest number of pips in his hand. The winner adds together the number of pips left in his opponents' hands, subtracts the number of pips (if any) left in his own hand, and scores one point for every five pips in this total.

A game is usually played to 61 points.

Threes

No. of players: 2, 3 or 4
Equipment: Set of dominoes
Complexity: ★★

Threes is played in exactly the same way as *Fives* except that the scoring is based on multiples of three instead of on multiples of five. Thus a player scores one point if the ends of the line of play add up to 3, two points if they add up to 6, three points if they add up to 9, and so on. At the end of the hand, the winner scores one point for every three pips left in his opponents' hands.

Sniff

No. of players: 2, 3 or 4
Equipment: Set of dominoes
Complexity: ★★

The playing and scoring in *Sniff* is like that in *Fives*, being based on scoring points for ends that add up to multiples of five. In *Sniff*, however, the line of play may have up to four ends, so higher scores may be achieved.

The first player is chosen by lot, and the players then draw their dominoes. If there are two players each draws seven dominoes; if three players each draws six dominoes; if four players each draws five dominoes. The first player leads with any domino he chooses from his hand, and the turn passes round the table in the usual way.

Until the first double is played, the line of play has two ends, as in *Fives*. The first double to be played is called 'the Sniff' and it may be placed *across* the line of play or *with* the line of play, as the player chooses. If the Sniff is played with the line of play, dominoes can be played on the sides of the Sniff, but only after the open end has been played on. If the Sniff is played across the line of play, dominoes can be played on the ends of the Sniff, but only after the open side has been played on. The subsequent doubles are always played across the line of play, and only their sides can be played on.

As in *Fives*, a player must play a domino if he can. If he cannot, he must continue drawing from the boneyard until he draws a domino that he can play. If the boneyard is empty he must pass.

Play continues until one player goes out or until the game is blocked. The points scored at the end of play are the same as in *Fives*, with the winner scoring one point for every five pips left in his opponents' hands. The game is played to an agreed number of points, usually 61.

Muggins

No. of players: 2, 3 or 4
Equipment: Set of dominoes
Complexity: ★★

Muggins is another game, like *Fives* and Sniff, in which the aim is to play so that the ends of the line of play add up to multiples of five. In *Fives* there are only two ends to be counted, in *Sniff* there may be up to four – in *Muggins* there may be even more – but in other respects the method of scoring is exactly the same as for the other two games.

Each player draws his dominoes – seven dominoes if there are two players; six dominoes if there are three players; five dominoes if there are four players.

The player who has the highest double in his hand leads with that domino (and if it happens to be the double-5 – because the double-6 is in the boneyard – he will immediately score two points). Play then proceeds around the table in the usual way, with each player playing matching dominoes on the ends of the line of play. A player must play a domino if he can, otherwise he must draw from the boneyard until he draws a playable domino. If the boneyard is empty then he must pass.

Doubles are always played across the line of play. The ends of any double may be played on once the open side has been played on.

As for *Fives* and *Sniff*, the winner at the end of a hand scores one point for every five pips left in the hands of his opponents.

Five up

No. of players: 2, 3 or 4 `*`
Equipment: Set of dominoes
Complexity: ★★

Five Up is a variant of *Muggins* and is played in the same way except for the following differences: (a) The lead player for the first hand is chosen by lot, and he may play any domino he chooses from his hand. The lead passes to the next player on the left for each subsequent hand. (b) Regardless of the number of players, each draws only five dominoes.

All Fives

No. of players: 2, 3 or 4
Equipment: Set of dominoes
Complexity: ★★

All Fives is another variant of *Muggins*, with the following differences:

(a) The lead player for the first hand is chosen by lot, and he may play any domino he chooses from his hand. The lead passes to the next player on the left for each subsequent hand.
(b) Regardless of the number of players, each draws only five dominoes.
(c) When a player plays a double or a domino from which he scores points he immediately has an extra turn. If he does not have a playable domino for his extra turn he must draw from the boneyard until he draws a playable domino or until the boneyard is empty.
(d) A player may not go out by playing a double or a domino that scores points. When such a domino is the last one in his hand he must play it and then draw from the boneyard until he draws a domino that he can play or until the boneyard is empty. If the boneyard is already empty when it is his turn to play his last domino he may not play it and must pass.

Fives and Threes

No. of players: 2, 3 or 4
Equipment: Set of dominoes
Complexity: ★★

Fives and *Threes* is a very popular domino game. As its name suggests, it is a combination of the game of *Fives* and the game of *Threes*. In the version usually played, however, the rules of *Fives* and *Threes* are slightly different from the rules of the other two games.

The lead player is chosen by lot and the players then draw their dominoes. The draw is seven dominoes for two players, six dominoes for three players, and five dominoes for four players. The lead player plays any domino he chooses from his hand, and the other players follow on in their turn as usual. If a player does not have a domino he can play then he knocks and the turn passes to the next player on his left. There is no drawing of extra dominoes from the boneyard.

Points are scored when the number of pips at the ends of the line of play add up to a multiple of three or a multiple of five thus:

Pip Total	Score
3 or 5	1
6 or 10	2
9	3
12 or 20	4
18	6
15	8 (5 threes and 3 fives)

As you can see, the best score is when the pips add up to 15 – that is, when the ends are a 5 and the double-5 or a 3 and the double-6. The next best score is when the pips add up to 18 – that is, when the ends are a 6 and the double-6. Therefore, if you have the double-6 or double-5 in your hand, it should be played with care so that you, and not your opponents, get the high scores.

Play continues until one player has played all his dominoes or until the game is blocked. If a player has played all his dominoes he scores one extra point. No extra points are scored if the game is blocked.

A cribbage board is often used to record the scores, and a game is played to 61 points.

Forty-Two

No. of players: 4
Equipment: Set of dominoes
Complexity: ★★

Forty-two could be described as a card game that is played with dominoes. Two players play in partnership against the other two, they bid for the number of tricks they think they can win, score points for winning tricks, and can score bonus points. From this you can see that there is some resemblance to the game of *Bridge* – but rest assured, *Forty-two* is a good deal less complicated than that noble game.

There are five points-scoring dominoes, known as 'honours', in *Forty-two*. The three dominoes which have five pips – the 5-blank, the 4-1, and the 3-2 – are worth five points each. The two dominoes which have ten pips – the double-5 and the 6-4 – are worth ten points each.

The maximum number of points that can be scored in a round is 42 (hence the name of the game), made up as follows:

(a) One point for each trick taken (7 points altogether).
(b) Bonus points for tricks containing the honours (35 points altogether).

To begin a game the players draw for partners and to see who will lead the bidding. Each player draws one domino. The player who draws the highest domino will lead the bidding, and his partner is the player who draws the next highest domino. The players arrange themselves around the table so that partners sit opposite each other.

Each player then draws seven dominoes, and examines his hand in an attempt to guess how many points he and his partner will be able to score.

The player who won the draw to lead the bidding makes the first bid and the other players then bid in turn, the bidding going round the table only once. A bid must be for 30 points or more and must be higher than any previous bids. If a player does not wish to bid then he may pass.

The player who makes the highest bid has then, together with his partner, to attempt to take tricks to the value of the bid (or more).

The player who made the highest bid leads with any domino he chooses from his hand, and this domino determines which suit is trumps for the round. Since every domino belongs to two suits, he declares which of the two is the trump suit. For example, if he leads the 5-4 he may declare either fives or fours as trumps. The other players each play one domino in turn, and the player who plays the highest trump wins the trick.

For subsequent tricks, unless a trump is led, the suit is determined by the highest number on the domino that is led. Thus if threes are trumps and the 5-2 is led, the suit being led is fives.

Players must follow suit if they can. If they cannot, they may play any suit they choose, including trumps. A trick is won by the highest domino of the suit that was led or, if a trump was played, by the highest trump.

The player who wins a trick puts the four dominoes face down in front of him, and he leads the first domino for the next trick.

When all seven tricks have been taken, the scores for the round are worked out. If the partnership who made the highest bid were successful in winning tricks equal to or greater in value than their bid they score the number of points bid plus the value of their tricks. If they were unsuccessful, however, then their opponents score the number of points bid plus the value of the tricks that they have won.

Further rounds are played until the score of one partnership reaches some agreed figure such as 150 or 250.

Bingo

No. of players: 2
Equipment: Set of dominoes
Complexity: ★★★

Bingo is another domino game that bears some resemblance to a card game – in this case the resemblance is to *Bézique*. The scoring system in Bingo is quite complicated, but you should not let this deter you from playing what many consider to be the best of all domino games.

Points are scored in two ways – by winning tricks that contain certain dominoes, and by having doubles in one's hand.

The dominoes that score points in a trick are as follows:

(a) The double of the trump suit, which scores 28 points.
(b) The double-blank (called 'bingo') which scores 14 points – except, of course, when blanks are trumps and it scores 28.
(c) The other doubles, which score their pip value.
(d) The dominoes of the trump suit (other than the double) which score their pip value, with a blank counting as seven.
(e) The 6-4 and the 3-blank, which each score 10 points.

A player, when it is his turn to lead, may claim points if he has two or more doubles in his hand. To claim these points a player must lead one of the doubles and show the others to his opponent. The calls and the points claimed are as follows:

(a) For two doubles, the player calls 'Double', claiming 20 points.
(b) For three doubles, the player calls 'Triplets', claiming 40 points.
(c) For four doubles, the player calls 'Double doubles', claiming 50 points.
(d) For five doubles, the player calls 'King', claiming 60 points.
(e) For six doubles, the player calls 'Emperor', claiming 70 points.
(f) For all seven doubles, the player calls 'Invincible', claiming 210 points.

The player must win the trick in order to gain the points he has claimed.

Each player should record the points he has gained from tricks and doubles at the time the tricks are taken.

There is a bit more than this to the scoring system, but the rest is better left until we have looked at the way in which the game proceeds.

The first player is chosen by lot. Each player then draws seven dominoes, the remaining fourteen forming the boneyard. The second player determines trumps by turning over one domino in the boneyard so that it is face upwards. The higher pip value on that domino is the trump suit (a blank, being worth seven, is higher than any other pip value).

The initial phase of play begins with the first player leading any domino he chooses from his hand. The higher pip value of this domino determines the suit being led.

The second player then plays any domino he chooses from his hand – he does not have to follow suit. If he plays a higher domino of the suit that was led, or a trump (when a trump was not led), or the double-blank ('bingo', which wins any trick in which it is played) then he wins the trick. Otherwise the first player wins the trick.

The winner of the trick leads the next domino, but before that both players draw a domino from the boneyard (the winner of the trick drawing first).

The first phase proceeds in this way until all the dominoes have been drawn from the boneyard. The last domino to be drawn must always be the domino that was turned up to establish trumps.

In the second phase the remaining tricks are played with a change in the rule about the dominoes the second player may play. From this point the second player must always follow suit if he can. If he cannot follow suit he must play a trump or 'bingo' if he can. Only if he does not have a domino of the suit being led, a trump or 'bingo', may he play any other domino.

It is possible to go from the first phase into the second phase before all the dominoes have been drawn from the boneyard. If a player, after he has won a trick, thinks that his hand is good enough to score at least 70 points from tricks and doubles without drawing any more from the boneyard, then instead of drawing from the boneyard he turns the trump domino face down. This is known as 'closing' and, from that point on, the rules of the second phase apply – there is no further drawing from the boneyard, and the second player must follow suit if he can.

The object of the game is to score seven 'sets', and the first player to do so is the winner. Sets are scored as follows:

(a)   One set is scored for every 70 points gained from tricks and doubles.
(b)   One set is scored by the first player to score 70 points – if his opponent has scored 30 points or more.
(c)   Two sets are scored by the first player to score 70 points – if his opponent has won a trick but has scored less than 30 points.
(d)   Three sets are scored by the first player to score 70 points – if his opponent has not yet won a trick.
(d)   Two sets are scored by the opponent of a player who 'closes' and then fails to score 70 points.
(f)   One set is scored for taking the double of the trump suit with 'bingo'.

7   DICE GAMES

Going to Boston
Fifty
Chicago
Beetle
Pig
Twenty-one
Round the Clock
Centennial
Everest
Hearts
Drop Dead
Craps
Shut the Box
Crag
Yacht
Poker Dice
Liar Dice

Going to Boston

No. of players: 2 or more
Equipment: 3 dice
Complexity: ★★

The first player rolls all three dice at once. He then leaves the die which shows the highest number (if two are equally high, he leaves only one of them) and he rolls the other two again. Of these two he again leaves the die showing the higher number and rolls the other die again. This completes his turn, and his score is the total shown by the three dice. When all the players have done the same in their turn, the player with the highest score is the winner of that round.

An agreed number of rounds are usually played, and the player who has won the most rounds is the winner of the game.

Fifty

No. of players: 2 or more
Equipment: 2 dice
Complexity: ★★

Fifty is a very simple dice game, in which the objective is to be the first player to score (would you believe it?) fifty points. Each player in turn throws the two dice once and he scores only if a double is thrown. A double 6 scores 25 points. A double 5, double 4, double 2 or double 1 scores 5 points. But when a player throws a double 3 he loses all the points he has scored so far and has to start all over again.

Chicago

No. of players: 2 or more
Equipment: 2 dice
Complexity: ☆

This simple game, which is all luck and no skill, is based on the eleven possible totals which can be obtained from throwing two dice – that is, totals from 2 to 12.

The dice pass around the table eleven times, and each player in his turn throws the two dice once. On the first round each player who throws the dice to make a total of 2 scores two points, the others scoring nothing. On the second round each player who throws the dice to make a total of 3 scores three points, the others scoring nothing. The game proceeds in this way, on successive rounds the players having to throw a total of 4, 5 and so on up to 12, and scoring accordingly. The player who obtains the highest total score is the winner.

Beetle

No. of players: 2 to 6
Equipment: One die; paper and a pencil for each player
Complexity: ☆

Beetle is the most popular family dice game. The objective is to be the first player to complete the drawing of a beetle. Artistic talent, however, is not absolutely necessary, as you may see from this example:

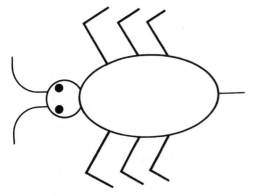

The beetle consists of thirteen parts: body, head, tail, two eyes, two feelers and six legs. The right value must be thrown with the die before each part may be drawn.

Special 'beetle dice' are obtainable for playing this game, with the faces marked B (body), H (head), T (tail), E (eye), F (feeler) and L (leg). A standard die, however, serves just as well, with the numbers corresponding to the parts of the beetle as follows:

1 for the body
2 for the head
3 for each leg
4 for each eye
5 for each feeler
6 for the tail

Thus, to complete his beetle, a player must throw a 1, a 2, six 3s, two 4s, two 5s and a 6.

Player take it in turn to throw the die, each player throwing it only once in each round.

Before a player can start drawing his beetle he must throw a 1. This permits him to draw the body. Once the body is drawn, he may start adding the head, legs and tail when he throws the appropriate numbers with the die. The feelers and eyes, however, cannot be added until after he has thrown a 2, enabling him to draw the head.

The game is sometimes played for points. A round ends when one player has completed his beetle. He scores 13 points, and each of the other players scores one point for each part he has drawn. Further rounds are played and the game is won by the first player to score 51 points.

Pig

No. of players: 2 or more
Equipment: One die
Complexity: ☆

Before the game begins a preliminary round is played in which each player throws the die once. The player who throws the lowest number begins the game. He then throws the die and scores the value shown by the die. He throws again and adds this score to his previous score. He may continue doing this as many times as he likes, on each throw adding to his previous score, until he decides to stop. However, if at any time he throws a 1 his turn ends and he loses his whole score for that turn. The play passes around the table, each player in his turn throwing the die until he decides to stop or until he throws a 1.

The scores are recorded for each turn and the first player to attain a total score of 101 is the winner.

Twenty-One

No. of players: 2 or more
Equipment: One die; a supply of counters (or coins or whatever)
Complexity: ★

This is a version of the card game *Pontoon* that is played with dice. The 'stakes' may be counters, buttons, matchsticks, pennies, £10 notes or whatever you wish. We will assume that counters are being used.

The players each put one counter into the kitty. Each player in turn then throws the die as many times as he likes, adding up the numbers thrown, in an attempt to get a total of twenty-one or near as possible to it. A player whose total goes over twenty-one is 'bust' and is out of the game.

When all the players have had a turn the player whose total is nearest to twenty-one collects the kitty. If two or more players get equally high totals they may share the kitty or there may be a play-off between them.

Play may continue until one player has won all the counters, or for an agreed number of games after which the player with the highest number of counters is the winner.

Round the Clock

No. of players: 2 or more
Equipment: 2 dice
Complexity: ☆

The object of the game is to roll, in the correct sequence, a 1, then a 2, then a 3, and so on up to 12. Each player in turn rolls the two dice. For the numbers up to 6 either of the individual dice values or the total value of the two dice may be counted. For instance, if a player needs a 4 he will be successful if either of the dice shows a 4 or if the dice show a 3 and a 1. For the numbers from 7 to 12 obviously only the total value of the two dice is counted. The first player to reach 12 is the winner.

Centennial

No. of players: 2 or more
Equipment: 3 dice; paper and a pencil;
a counter for each player
Complexity: ☆

Centennial is essentially an extended version of Round the Clock. The players' positions are recorded on a simple board which may be drawn on a piece of paper. It consists of a row of twelve numbered squares, which should be large enough to place the counters on.

1	2	3	4	5	6	7	8	9	10	11	12

The objective is to move one's counter, according to the numbers thrown with the dice, from 1 to 12 and then back to 1 again. The first player to do so is the winner.

Each player in his turn throws the three dice. His throw must contain a 1 before he can place his counter on square 1, then he will need a 2 or two 1s in order to move to square 2, and so on. In each throw the value of any individual die, or the combined values of any two dice, or the total value of all three dice may be counted.

In one turn a player may be able to move his counter several places. If a player, for example, on his first turn is lucky enough to throw a 1, a 2, and a 4, then the 1 will take him to square 1, the 2 to square 2, the 2 plus 1 to square 3, the 4 to square 4, the 4 plus 1 to square 5, the 4 plus 2 to square 6, and finally the 4 plus 2 plus 1 to square 7. Not bad for one throw!

The players continue throwing the dice in turn until one player wins by completing the round trip from square 1 to square 12 and back down to square 1 again.

There is one extra rule which makes it worthwhile for a player to watch his opponents' throws carefully. This rule is that if a player throws a number that he needs but overlooks it and does not use it then that number may be claimed by any other player who needs it. The number must be claimed as soon as the dice are passed on and the player claiming it must be able to use it immediately.

Everest

No. of players: 2 or more
Equipment: Paper and a pencil for each player; 3 dice
Complexity: ☆

Everest is similar to *Centennial*, but whereas in *Centennial* the numbers from 1 to 12 and back to 1 have to be scored in the right sequence, in *Everest* they may be scored in any sequence. Because of this difference, each player needs his own sheet of paper marked with two rows of 12 squares, one numbered from 1 to 12 and the other numbered from 12 to 1.

1	2	3	4	5	6	7	8	9	10	11	12

12	11	10	9	8	7	6	5	4	3	2	1

Each player in turn throws the three dice. He may then cross off any numbers on his chart, in any order and using either row, according to the values of the dice.

The values of the dice may be used singly or in any combination, but (unlike the scoring in *Centennial*) each value may be counted only once. Thus if a player throws a 1, a 2 and a 4 he has the choice of crossing off the following numbers on his chart:

(a) a 1, a 2 and a 4, or (b) a 1 and a 6, or (c) a 2 and a 5, or (d) a 3 and a 4, or (e) a 7. The first player to be able to cross off all his twenty-four numbers is the winner.

Hearts

No. of players: 2 or more
Equipment: 6 dice
Complexity: ☆

This game in its original form is played with six special dice, each of which has its faces marked with the letters H, E, A, R, T, S. These 'hearts dice' may be bought, but the game may be played just as well with ordinary dice.

There is a preliminary round to select the first player (usually the player who obtains the highest score from throwing the six dice). Then each player in his turn throws the six dice. Points are scored for throwing the following combinations of numbers:

1,2	= five points
1,2,3	= ten points
1,2,3,4	= fifteen points
1,2,3,4,5	= twenty points
1,2,3,4,5,6	= twenty-five points

If two dice of the same value are thrown, only one of them counts. However, if the throw contains three 1s then the unfortunate player loses all the points he has scored so far. The winner is the first player to score 100 points.

Drop Dead

No. of players: 2 or more
Equipment: 5 dice
Complexity: ☆

Each player in turn throws the five dice. If any of the five dice show a 2 or a 5 he scores nothing, otherwise his score is the total of the numbers shown by the five dice. Any dice showing a 2 or a 5 are put to one side and he throws the remaining dice again. Again, if any of the dice show a 2 or a 5 they are put aside and he scores nothing, otherwise the total of the dice is added to his previous score. He continues in his way, throwing with an ever-decreasing number of dice, and increasing his score whenever a throw does not include a 2 or a 5. His turn ends when his last die shows a 2 or a 5 and he is said to have 'dropped dead'.

When all the players have had their turn the player with the highest score is the winner.

Player 1		**Player 2**		**Player 3**	
Throw	*Total Score*	*Throw*	*Total Score*	*Throw*	*Total Score*
1,1,3,4,5	0	1,1,3,6,6	17	2,2,3,5,5	0
3,3,4,6	16	1,2,2,4,6	17	2	0
2,4,4,5	16	1,3,6	27		
1,6	23	2,3,4	27		
2,3	23	1,4	32		
1	24	2,5	32		
6	30				
5	30				

Craps

No. of players: 2 or more
Equipment: 2 dice; a supply of counters (or buttons or whatever) for use as stakes
Complexity: ★

Craps is of course a gambling game and is often played with great earnestness for considerable stakes. Each player takes a turn to be the 'shooter' (that is, the person who throws the dice). He places on the table whatever stake he is prepared to wager. All or part of this stake may be matched (or 'covered') by the other players.

The shooter throws the two dice. If the total value is 7 or 11 this is known as 'a natural', and the shooter immediately wins all the stakes that have been wagered. If the total of the two dice is 2, 3 or 12 this is known as 'craps' and the shooter immediately loses.

If the shooter throws any other total on his first throw (that is, 4, 5, 6, 8, 9 or 10) this number is known as his 'point'. He continues throwing until he either throws his point again or until he throws a 7 (any other totals thrown being disregarded). If his point comes up first then he wins. If a 7 comes up first then he loses.

As long as the shooter wins, he retains the dice, places a new stake and shoots again. As soon as he loses he passes the dice to the next player who then becomes the shooter.

Shut the Box

No. of players: 2 or more
Equipment: 2 dice; paper and pencil; 9 counters
Complexity: ✩✩

This is a traditional dice game from the North of France, where it is played on a special wooden board consisting of a tray in which the dice are thrown and a row of nine numbered boxes with sliding lids which can cover or disclose the numbers.

To play the game at home you will need a sheet of paper on which is drawn a row of nine squares, numbered from 1 to 9, and nine counters (or coins or buttons or whatever) with which you can cover the numbers.

| 1 | 2 | 3 | 4 | 5 | 6 | 7 | 8 | 9 |

The objective is to cover as many numbers as possible.

At the beginning of each player's turn all the numbers are uncovered. He throws the two dice and adds together their values. He must then choose numbered squares which add up to the same total and cover them. For example if he threw a 6 and a 4, the total would be 10 and he could choose to cover squares 6 and 4, or 7 and 3, or 8 and 2, or 9 and 1, or 6 and 3 and 1, and so on. He then throws the dice again. Again he must choose numbers to cover that will add up to the same total as the dice. Of course, they must be numbers that have not already been covered.

A player is allowed to throw with only one die, if he wishes, once the three top numbers (7, 8 and 9) have been covered. He continues throwing until he fails to find a combination of numbers to cover that will match the dice total. The numbers that remain uncovered are added together to form the player's score.

When all the players have had their turn the winner is the player with the lowest score.

Crag

No. of players: 2 or more
Equipment: 3 dice; score sheet and pencil
Complexity: ☆☆

To play Crag you will need a score sheet drawn like this:

	Player 1	Player 2	Player 3
Ones			
Twos			
Threes			
Fours			
Fives			
Sixes			
Odd Straight			
Even Straight			
Low Straight			
High Straight			
Three of a kind			
Thirteen			
Crag			
Totals			

There is a preliminary round to determine who will be the first player. Each player throws the dice once, and the player with the highest score will start the game.

The game itself starts with the first player throwing the three dice. He may then, if he wishes, throw one, two or all three dice again. His objective is to obtain one of the following scoring patterns:

1 **Ones** (scoring one point for each 1 thrown – maximum 3 points)
2 **Twos** (scoring two points for each 2 thrown – maximum 6 points)
3 **Threes** (scoring three points for each 3 thrown – maximum 9 points)
4 **Fours** (scoring four points for each 4 thrown – maximum 12 points)
5 **Fives** (scoring five points for each 5 thrown – maximum 15 points)
6 **Sixes** (scoring six points for each 6 thrown – maximum 18 points)
7 **Odd Straight** (the 1, 3 and 5 – scoring 20 points)
8 **Even Straight** (the 2, 4 and 6 – scoring 20 points)
9 **Low straight** (the 1, 2 and 3 – scoring 20 points)
10 **High Straight** (the 4, 5 and 6 – scoring 20 points)
11 **Three of a kind** (all three dice showing the same value – scoring 25 points)
12 **Thirteen** (a total of thirteen without a double – 2, 5 and 6, or 3, 4 and 6 – scoring 26 points)
13 **Crag** (a total of thirteen including a double – 1, 6, 6 or 3, 5, 5 or 5, 4, 4 – scoring 50 points)

His score is recorded on the chart and the dice are passed to the next player. Each player in his turn throws the three dice and may decide to score with the dice as thrown or to throw one or more again in an attempt to obtain a better score. His score is then recorded and the play passes round the table.

A player may or may not have a choice as to which pattern he scores. Let us say, for example, he has thrown two 4s and a 6. He may choose to score 8 points for Fours or 6 points for Sixes if he has not already scored for either of these patterns. If he has already scored for one of them then he is obliged, this time, to score for the other. If he has already scored for both of these patterns then he must choose some other pattern for which to score nought.

When the dice have passed thirteen times around the table the players will have filled in all thirteen spaces on the score sheet. The player with the highest total score is the winner.

Yacht

No. of players: 2 or more
Equipment: 5 dice; score sheet and pencil
Complexity: ★★

To play *Yacht* you will need a score sheet drawn like this:

	Player 1	*Player 2*	*Player 3*
Ones			
Twos			
Threes			
Fours			
Fives			
Sixes			
Little Straight			
Big Straight			
Full House			
Four of a Kind			
Choice			
Yacht			
Totals			

A preliminary round is played to select the first player. Each player throws the dice once, and the player with the highest score will start the game. The dice pass around the table twelve times, and each player in his turn will be attempting to obtain one of these twelve patterns:

1 **Ones** (scoring one point for each 1 thrown – maximum 5 points)
2 **Twos** (scoring two points for each 2 thrown – maximum 10 points)
3 **Threes** (scoring three points for each 3 thrown – maximum 15 points)

4   **Fours** (scoring four points for each 4 thrown – maximum 20 points)
5   **Fives** (scoring five points for each 5 thrown – maximum 25 points)
6   **Sixes** (scoring six points for each 6 thrown – maximum 30 points)
7   **Little Straight** (1,2,3,4,5 – scoring 15 points)
8   **Big Straight** (2,3,4,5,6 – scoring 20 points)
9   **Full House** (three of any number and two of another – scoring pip value – for example, 1,1,1,2,2 would score 7 points and 6,6,6,5,5 would score 28 points)
10 **Four of a Kind** (four of any number – scoring the pip value of the four dice – for example, 1,1,1,1,6 would score 4 points and 6,6,6,6,1 would score 24 points)
11 **Choice** (no pattern is required and the score is the total pip value of the five dice – the aim is to obtain as high a total as possible – for example, 3,5,5,6,6 would score 25 points)
12 **Yacht** (all five dice showing the same number – scoring 50 points)

Each player in his turn throws the five dice. He must then declare which one of the twelve patterns he is going to aim for. This must be a different pattern for each of his turns. Having declared the pattern he is trying to achieve, he is then allowed two further throws, each time throwing any or all of the five dice again (but he is not obliged to use all three throws if he obtains the required pattern on his first or second throw). If he achieves the pattern he has declared then his score is entered on the score sheet, otherwise a score of nought is entered.

Although luck plays a large part in the game, if high scores are to be achieved good judgement and calculation of probabilities are also required.

When the dice have passed around the table twelve times the players will have filled in all twelve spaces on the score sheet. The totals are calculated and the player with the highest total score is the winner.

Poker Dice

No. of players: 2 or more
Equipment: Set of 5 poker dice (or 5 standard dice)
Complexity: ★★

This game is usually played with a set of five special poker dice, each of which has its faces marked (rather like miniature playing cards) with

Ace, King, Queen, Jack, 10, 9. It may be played, using the same rules, with standard dice, but then the game loses something of its flavour.

Each player in turn throws the five dice. His objective is to get the best possible poker 'hand'. The hands, in descending order of value, are:

1   **Five of a Kind** (five aces ranking highest and five 9s lowest)
2   **Four of a Kind** (ranking as for Five Of a Kind)
3   **Full House** (three of a kind and a pair – ranking according to the three of a kind – for example, K, K, K,9,9 ranks higher than Q,Q,Q,J,J)
4   **Straight** (five consecutive values – A,K,Q,J,10 ranking higher than K,Q,J,10,9)
5   **Three of a Kind** (three aces ranking highest and three 9s lowest)
6   **Two Pairs** (the higher pair determines the value – for instance A,A,10,10,0 beats K,K,Q,Q,10)
7   **One Pair** (a pair of aces ranking highest and a pair of 9s lowest)
8   **Ace High** (ranking according to the value of the highest 'backers' – for example, A,K,J,10,9 beats A,Q,J,10,9)

If a player is not satisfied with his hand on the first throw he may throw any number of the dice a second time (and, in some versions of the game, a third time) in an attempt to improve his hand.

When all the players have had their turn, the player who obtained the best hand is the winner.

Liar Dice

No. of players: 3 or more
Equipment: Set of 5 poker dice (or 5 standard dice);
dice cup (optional); 3 counters for each player.
Complexity: ★★★

Liar Dice is a fascinating game of deceit, deception, bluff and counter-bluff, and is considered by many to be by far the best of all dice games. Like *Poker Dice* the game is best played with a set of special poker dice but may be played with ordinary dice. The hands and their relative values are the same as described for the game of *Poker Dice*.

Each player starts the game with three counters – these are his 'lives' and when he loses all three he is out of the game.

A preliminary round is played to determine who will be the first player. Each player throws the five dice, and the player who obtains the highest hand starts the game.

The game starts with the first player throwing the five dice, concealing them with the dice cup or with his hands so that he, but none of the other players, may see what he has thrown. He then declares his hand (e.g. 'Pair of Queens' or 'Full House, Nines and Jacks'). This call may actually be the hand he has thrown or it may be a complete and utter lie. If he lies, he may declare a hand higher than or lower than the hand he has really thrown.

The next player on the left may either accept or challenge the call. If he accepts the call, the first player passes the dice to him, taking care that they remain concealed from the other players and that none of the dice get turned over accidentally. This is more easily performed if a dice cup (or other container) is used to cover the dice.

The second player examines the dice. He may then decide to throw none, some or all of the dice again. He must declare truthfully how many dice he is throwing. At all times the dice must remain concealed from the other players. He then has to declare a hand better than the hand declared by the previous player. This may be either a higher type of hand or a higher-ranking hand of the same type. If the first player had declared 'Pair of Queens' then he could, for example, declare 'Three Tens' or 'Pair of Aces'. Again, this may be true or bluff – equal to, higher than or lower than the actual hand.

The next player then has the choice of accepting the hand or challenging it. If he accepts it, he may throw any number of the dice again and must then declare a higher hand.

The play continues around the table in this way until a challenge is issued. The player being challenged exposes the dice. If the declarer can refute the challenger by showing that his declaration was equal to or less than the actual hand, then the challenger must pay one counter into the pool. If, on the other hand, the declarer has called a hand that was better than the actual hand then it is the declarer who must pay a counter into the pool.

After a challenge a new round is started by the challenger (or by the next player if the challenger has lost his last life).

The game continues until all but one of the players have lost their three lives and have been eliminated. The last player left in is the winner.

8 MATCHSTICK GAMES

Match Tower
Take the Last
Garden Path
Nim
One Line Nim
Odd or Even
Kayles
Tac Tix
Matchboxes
Maxey

Match Tower

No. of players: 2 or more
Equipment: An empty bottle and a good supply of matches
Complexity: ⋆

The empty bottle should be one with a narrow neck, such as a wine bottle. If the only available wine bottle is full, it is *not* a good idea to drink the contents merely to provide an empty bottle for this game – a steady hand is required.

The number of matches required depends upon the dexterity of the players. For clumsy players only a few dozen matches will be needed while expert players may need several hundred. The aim is to build up layer after layer of matches over the mouth of the bottle, each player in turn adding one match. The first four matches are laid across the mouth of the bottle, the next four are laid across the first four, the next four across the previous four, and so on.

There are no winners, but the loser is the player who first dislodges the structure and sends it tumbling down. He must pay whatever penalty is decided by the other players.

Take the Last

No. of players: 2 or more
Equipment: 50 matches
Complexity: ⋆

Place the fifty matches in a heap on the table. Each player in turn has to take matches from the heap, and may take any number he pleases between one and six. The player who takes the last match is the winner.

Alternatively the game may be played·as follows. Each player has three lives. As before, each player in his turn takes up to six matches from the heap. But this time the player who takes the last match loses a life. When a player loses all his lives he drops out of the game. The winner is the last player left when all the others have dropped out.

Garden Path

No. of players: 2
Equipment: Board, and about 15 matches for each player
Complexity: ✫✫

Each player's matches should be clearly distinguishable from those of
his opponent. You could use matches with heads of two different
colours or else use ink, paint or crayon to colour them. You also need a
board, which can be drawn on card or paper. The board consists of a grid
of 25 squares as in the diagram. The sides of the squares should be just a
fraction greater than the length of the matches being used. The sides of
the grid should be labelled North, South, East and West as shown.

   Each player in turn puts one of his matches on any vacant line on the
board. One player's objective is to form a continuous path from North to
South, and the other player's objective is to form a continuous path from
East to West. Each player, of course, will attempt to block his opponent
while at the same time trying to complete his own path. The first player
to complete his path is the winner.

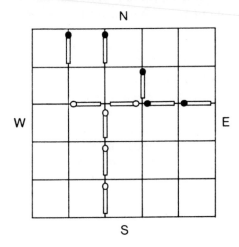

Nim

No. of players: 2
Equipment: 15 matches (or possibly more)
Complexity: ★☆

Nim is a very old game and is believed to have originated in China. The basic version of the game starts with three rows of matches – three matches in the first row, five in the second row, and seven in the third row.

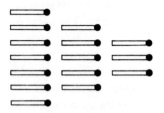

Each player in turn has to pick up any number of matches from any one of the rows. He may pick up only one match or the whole row or any number in between – but only from one row at a time. The player who picks up the last match is the winner.

Variation 1
The game is played exactly as described above, but the winner is the player who forces his opponent to pick up the last match.

Variation 2
The game may start with any number of rows, containing any number of matches. Try it, for example, with five rows containing 4, 5, 6, 7 and 8 matches.

One Line Nim

No. of players: 2
Equipment: 15 matches
Complexity: ★☆

The fifteen matches are laid out in a line.

Each player in turn has to pick up one, two or three matches. The winner is the player who forces his opponent to pick up the last match. You may also try playing *One Line Nim* with 21 or 25 matches instead of 15.

Odd or Even

No. of players: 2
Equipment: 25 matches
Complexity: ★★

Place the matches in a line on the table, as for *One Line Nim*. Each player in turn has to pick up one, two or three matches. When all the matches have been picked up the winner is the player with an even number of matches in his hand. Alternatively, the game may be played so that the winner is the player who has picked up an odd number of matches.

Kayles

No. of players: 2
Equipment: About 20 matches
Complexity: ★★

Kayles, in fact, can be played with any number of matches from 5 upwards, but 20 is a reasonable number. You may play with fewer matches than this if you want a shorter game or with more if a longer game is required.

The matches are laid end to end in a long line. Each player in turn takes either one match or two matches which are touching each other. The player who takes the last match is the winner. Alternatively, the game may be played so that the winner is the player who forces his opponent to take the last match.

Tac Tix

No. of players: 2
Equipment: 16 matches
Complexity: ★★☆

The game of *Tac Tix* was invented by Piet Hein, a remarkable Danish mathematician, inventor and poet (among other things) who also invented the board game of *Hex*. The matches are arranged in a square formation, like this:

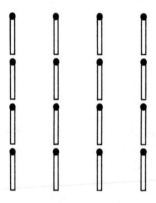

Each player in turn takes one or more matches from any one row or column, but the matches he takes must be adjacent, with no gaps in between.

For example, suppose the first player takes all four matches from the second row. The second player may then take any number of adjacent matches from one of the other rows, but he is now unable to take the three remaining matches from any of the columns, because of the gap — he may only take any one match or the lower two. The winner of the game is the player who forces his opponent to take the last match.

(There is not much point in playing so that the winner is the player who *takes* the last match, because then the second player can always win by playing symmetrically opposite his opponent.) Advanced players might like to try the game using a 5 × 5 or 6 × 6 square instead of the 4 × 4 square shown here.

Matchboxes

No. of players: 2
Equipment: 220 matches
Complexity: ★★

The matches are laid out in a square grid as in the diagram. Each player in turn may remove any one match or he may remove any two matches that are touching (either in a straight line or at right angles). The player who removes the last match is the winner.

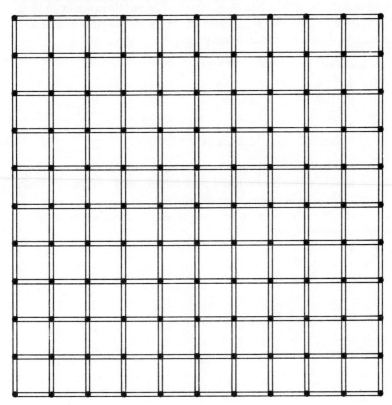

Maxey

No. of players: 2
Equipment: Pencil and paper; 10 matches
Complexity: ★★

The playing area is a piece of paper on which seven parallel lines have been drawn. The lines should be about the same length as a match and a little less than a match-length apart. The players start with five matches each, and each player in turn plays one match. A player may place his match on to one of the parallel lines or, if two adjacent lines are occupied by matches, he may 'bridge' those two matches by playing a match across them. Any pair of matches may only be bridged once.

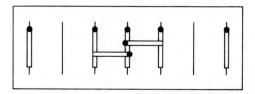

A player scores one point each time he plays a match on to a line next to a line that is already occupied by a match, and two points each time he forms a bridge between two matches.

The player with the most points when all the matches have been played is the winner.

9

GAMES OF CHANCE

Scissors, Paper, Stone
Fingers
Spoof
Crown and Anchor
Put and Take
Fan Tan
Lotto

Scissors, Paper, Stone

No. of players: 2
Equipment: None
Complexity: ⋆

Variations of this game are known in many parts of the world. 'Scissors', 'paper' and 'stone' are represented by extending a hand to form different shapes – a hand with two fingers extended (in a sort of horizontal V-sign) represents scissors; a flat hand extended horizontally represents paper; a clenched fist represents stone.

Each player conceals one hand behind his back. Simultaneously both players show their hands, forming whichever of the three shapes they have chosen. The winner is decided by the rule 'Scissors cut paper; paper wraps stone; stone blunts scissors'. Thus scissors wins against paper, paper wins against stone, and stone wins against scissors. If both players choose the same shape, the round is a draw. Any number of rounds may be played to determine the overall winner.

Fingers

No. of players: 2
Equipment: None
Complexity: ⋆

This is a guessing game, in which the aim is to guess the total number of fingers (from nought to ten) that will be displayed by the two players.

Each player conceals one hand behind his back. Simultaneously both players show their hands with any number of fingers extended. For the purposes of this game thumbs count as fingers, and a clenched fist represents nought. At the same time as revealing his hand each player calls out a number from nought to ten, which is his guess at the total number of fingers which will be displayed by the two players. If both players guess correctly, or if neither guesses correctly, the round is a draw. Any previously agreed number of rounds may be played.

Spoof

No. of players: 3 or more
Equipment: Three small objects (such as coins or matches)
for each player
Complexity: ✫

Spoof is a game of bluff, in which the objective is to guess the total number of objects concealed in the hands of the players.

Each player has three small objects – coins, matches, paperclips or anything small enough to be enclosed in a clenched fist. He chooses any number of them to conceal in his fist, and holds his fist out in front of him. When all the players are holding out their fists, each player in turn, proceeding in a clockwise direction, has a guess at the total number of objects concealed. Each player's guess must be different. The players then open their fists and the objects are counted. The player guessing correctly or whose guess is nearest to the correct number wins the round.

The player guessing first has the advantage that he can guess any number he likes, but the players guessing subsequently have the compensating advantage that they can deduce information from the guesses already made – if they can tell when another player is bluffing.

Crown and Anchor

No. of players: 7
Equipment: Board; set of 3 dice
Complexity: ✫

Crown and Anchor is a simple gambling game that was at one time popular in the British Navy.

The faces of each of the three dice are marked with a crown, an anchor and four aces. The board is also marked with these symbols. One player is the banker, and the other players place stakes on the board to bet on the symbols of their choice. The banker rolls the dice, and a player may win one, two or three times his stake according to the number of times his chosen symbol appears on the uppermost faces of the dice. The banker, of course, has the odds in his favour, pocketing on average half the stakes. Each player has a session as a banker.

Put and Take

No. of players: Any number
Equipment: Put and Take top
Complexity: ☆

Put and Take is played with a special eight-sided top, of which the faces are marked as follows:

PUT 1	PUT 4
TAKE 1	TAKE 4
PUT 3	PUT ALL
TAKE 3	TAKE ALL

Each player puts an agreed stake into the pot. Then each player in turn spins the top and, according to the face that is uppermost when the top comes to rest, puts the indicated amount into the pot or takes the indicated amount from the pot. PUT ALL means that the player must put into the pot a sum equal the amount already there; TAKE ALL means that he wins the entire pot.

Put and Take tops may be bought in some toyshops, but some searching may be required to find one. A simple home-made substitute may be produced by cutting out an eight-sided shape from stiff card and marking it as in the illustration. A nail is pushed through the centre so that the top can be spun, and the edge on which the top settles determines the action to be taken.

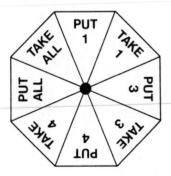

Fan Tan

No. of players: Any number
Equipment: A board, a bowl of beans, and a stick
Complexity: ⋆

Fan Tan is a Chinese gambling game, and is incredibly popular not only in Asia but also in Chinese communities throughout the world. Many Chinese people have a passion for gambling, and indeed they must to be so addicted to this game, which is often played in all-night sessions and for very high stakes.

The board, usually improvised, is simply a flat playing surface with the corners marked 1, 2, 3 and 4. Each player places a stake on one of these four numbers. The banker has a bowl of beans (dried beans, that is, not the baked-in-tomato-sauce variety) from which he takes a random handful and places them in the centre of the board. With a stick he counts off the beans in groups of four. It is only the number of beans – from 1 to 4 – in the last group that is important. This is the number that the players have wagered on and that determines whether they win or lose.

Lotto

No. of players: 2 to 6
Equipment: Lotto cards; 90 numbered discs
Complexity: ⋆

Lotto (alias *Housey Housey* or *Tombola*), at one time a popular family game in many countries – in the days before television – is the forerunner of modern, commercialised *Bingo*.

Each player has a special card marked with fifteen numbers between 1 and 90. None of the numbers is duplicated on other cards.

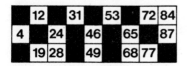

One of the players is the caller, and he has a set of 90 numbered discs which he draws at random, one at a time, from a bag or other suitable container. Each number is called out as it is drawn, and the disc is given to the player on whose card it appears. That player covers the number on his card with the disc. When all the numbers on a player's card have been covered he calls 'Lotto' and wins the game.

10 ALLSORTS

Marbles

No. of players: Any small number
Equipment: Marbles
Complexity: ☆

Marbles (also called taws or alleys or bools) are small, hard balls which are usually made from glass but may also be made of clay, stone, wood or other materials.

There are several schools of thought as to the optimal technique of marble propulsion. Some players merely roll them, but dedicated players usually prefer to flick (or 'knuckle') them. To do this, the back of the hand is placed on the ground with the side of the forefinger at right-angles to the required line of flight. A marble is poised in the crease of the top joint of the forefinger and is flicked smartly with the thumb.

There are many different games which can be played with marbles. With a few exceptions they all share the common principle of shooting a marble to hit another target marble, thus winning it. Some of the more popular games are described here.

Captures

A game for two players. The first player shoots his marble. The second player then shoots his marble in an attempt to hit the first player's marble. If he hits it he keeps it, otherwise the first player shoots his marble again, from its last position, in an attempt to hit the second player's marble. The players continue playing alternately in this way until one hits and wins the other's marble.

Spanners

This is the same as *Captures*, with the additional rule that when a player's marble is less than a hand's span from that of his opponent he may attempt a 'span'. This consists of flicking the two marbles together with finger and thumb. A hit means that he wins his opponent's marble, but a miss means that he loses his own marble to his opponent.

Alleys

This game may be played by any small number of players. The first player places a marble any agreed distance from the throwing-line. The other players in turn shoot their marbles in an attempt to hit this target. Any marbles that miss the target are pocketed by the first player. When a player succeeds in hitting the target he takes the place of the first player and he wins any marbles missing the target.

Dobblers

Another game for any small number of players. A row of marbles is formed, using one or two marbles from each player. The players, each using one throwing marble, shoot in turn and win any marbles they displace from the row. A successful shot entitles a player to an extra shot. A player's throwing marble is always left lying after his turn, and if it is hit by another player's marble he must put an extra marble in the row.

One Step

This game is played in the same manner as *Dobblers* except that each player's first shot is made by taking one step forward and then throwing from an upright position. Subsequent shots must also be made from an upright position but without the step forward.

Spangy

This is a game for 5 players. A square is drawn on the floor and each player places a marble in the square – one in the centre and one at each corner. The players shoot in turn, from a throwing-line about 10 yards from the square. A player wins any marbles that he succeeds in knocking out of the square. If his marble comes to rest within a hand's span of one of the target marbles he may win that marble if he makes a successful span (as in *Spanners*). A player always picks up his marble at the end of his turn, starting his next turn from the throwing-line.

Ring Taw

This game may be played by any small number of players. A circle of about one foot in diameter is drawn on the floor, with an outer circle of about seven feet in diameter. Each player puts one or two marbles in the inner circle.

Shooting from any point outside the outer circle, each player in turn attempts to knock one or more marbles out of the inner circle. If he is successful he wins any that he dislodges and has another shot from the point where his marble came to rest. After a player's turn has finished his marble is left where it is until his turn comes round again. If it is hit by another player's shot he has to give another marble to the player who hit it.

Increase Pound

This is similar to *Ring Taw*, but with the following differences:
(a) Knocking a marble out of the inner circle does not entitle a player to an extra shot.
(b) A player whose marble comes to rest inside the inner circle forfeits it. On his next turn he must shoot with a fresh marble from any point outside the outer circle.
(c) A player whose marble is hit when it lies within the outer circle must hand over to the shooter all the marbles he has won so far.

Fortifications

Four concentric circles are drawn on the floor. Each player places one marble in the outer circle, two in the next circle, three in the next, and four in the inner circle. Each player in turn shoots in an attempt to knock a marble from the outer circle. If he succeeds he wins the marble that he dislodges. If he fails he must place an extra marble in that circle. When, and only when, the outer circle has been cleared, the players may aim for marbles in the next circle – but any player who failed to win a marble from the outer circle is out of the game. When the second circle has been cleared the players proceed to the next circle, and so on. When attacking the second circle a hit entitles a player to an extra shot; when attacking the third circle two consecutive hits entitle a player to an extra shot; when attacking the inner circle three consecutive hits entitle a player to an extra shot.

Hundreds

This is a game for two players. A small circle is drawn on the floor. Each player shoots one marble in an attempt to get it in the circle. If both players get their marbles in the circle they both shoot again. When only one of the players gets his marble in the circle he scores 10 points and shoots again. He continues shooting and scoring 10 points each time he is successful, until he misses or until he has scored 100 points. If he misses before scoring 100 points, his opponent starts shooting, in the same way, until he misses or scores 100. Play alternates in this way and the first player to score 100 points wins the game.

Bounce Eye

A circle of about one foot in diameter is drawn on the floor. Each player puts one or more marbles in the circle to form a cluster in the centre. Each player in turn, from a standing position, drops a marble on the cluster, winning any marbles that are knocked out of the circle. If none are knocked out, the unsuccessful player has to add an extra marble to the group in the circle.

Spillikins

No. of players: 4 to 6
Equipment: Set of spillikins
Complexity: ★★

Spillikins (also known as *Jackstraws*) may be played with a set of about fifty straws or strips of plastic, wood, bamboo, ivory or bone. The most common form, however, consists of thin, rounded sticks, 6 to 8 inches long, with points at each end and coloured to indicate various point-values.

One player picks up all the spillikins and drops them on the table or floor to form a heap. The next player then attempts to remove one spillikin from the heap without disturbing any of the others. If he is successful he keeps it and attempts to remove another. The slightest disturbance of any spillikin other than the one he is trying to remove ends his turn, and the next player takes his turn. The game ends when all the spillikins have been successfully removed from the heap. The players' scores are then added up and the player with the highest score is the winner.

A sharp eye and a steady hand are requisites for successful play. Many different techniques may be used – plucking with finger and thumb, pressing down the end of a spillikin and drawing it out gently, pressing down an end sharply to jerk a spillikin off the top of the heap, and so on. In some versions of the game once a spillikin of a particular value has been removed it may be used as a tool to help remove others.

Fivestones

No. of players: 1 *or more*
Equipment: Five stones
Complexity: ✮✮

To play *Fivestones* you may use the knucklebones of a sheep, or small pebbles, but in this age of sophistication the 'stones' are more usually a set of small wooden or plastic cubes.

The game consists of a series of lesser games to be played with the stones, in which they are thrown into the air and caught again in various ways. There is an almost infinite variety of these lesser games and they may be played in any order. The players should agree beforehand the games to be played and the sequence (usually in order of increasing complexity). Each player in turn then goes through the sequence of games until he fails on one of them, and it then becomes the next player's turn. When a player's turn comes round again he recommences with the game in which he failed on his previous turn. The first player to complete the sequence successfully is the winner.

Many of the games start with the same basic throw. The stones are thrown up into the air from the palm of the hand, and as many as possible are caught on the back of the hand. They are then thrown from the back of the hand and as many as possible are caught in the palm.

Ones

The player performs the basic throw, as described above. If he succeeds in catching all five he immediately goes on to the next game. If he catches none, he has failed and the turn passes to the next player. Otherwise, he transfers all but one of the stones he has caught to his other hand. The single stone is thrown in the air, one of the fallen stones is gathered in the throwing hand, and the thrown stone is caught in the same hand. One of these two stones is transferred to the other hand. This process is repeated until all the stones on the floor have been gathered.

Twos

The five stones are scattered on the ground. One stone is picked up and thrown into the air, two of the stones on the ground are gathered into the throwing hand, and the thrown stone is caught in the same hand. Two stones are transferred to the other hand. The process is repeated, gathering the remaining two stones from the floor.

Threes

This is played in the same way as *Twos*, except that three stones are gathered on the first throw and the remaining stone on the second throw.

Fours

This is like *Twos* except that all four stones on the floor must be gathered in one throw.

Pecks

The basic throw is performed, and if all five stones are caught the player immediately goes on to the next game. Otherwise he keeps all the caught stones in his hand, holding one of them between thumb and forefinger. This stone is thrown into the air, one of the stones on the floor is gathered in the throwing hand and the thrown stone is caught in the same hand. This process is repeated until all five stones have been gathered into the throwing hand.

Bushels

The player performs the basic throw. If all five stones are caught he goes on to the next game; if none are caught his turn ends. Otherwise he throws in the air all the stones in his hand, one of the stones on the floor is gathered in the throwing hand, and all the thrown stones are caught in the same hand. This is repeated until all the stones have been gathered in the same hand.

Claws

The game begins with a modification of the basic throw. The player throws the five stones and attempts to catch them on the back of his hand. If none are caught his turn ends. If all five are caught the player attempts to complete the basic throw and if he is successful he goes on to the next game. If one or more, but not all five, are caught on the back of the hand they remain there while the player picks up the remaining stones on the ground between the fingers of his throwing hand – no more than one stone between any two fingers. He then throws the stones from the back of his hand and catches them in his palm. The stones held between the fingers must then be manoeuvred into the palm – without using the other hand.

Ones Under The Arch

The five stones are scattered on the floor. The player forms an arch by touching the thumb and forefinger of the non-throwing hand to the floor. One stone is picked and thrown into the air. Before it is caught again in the throwing hand one of the remaining stones must be knocked under the arch. This is repeated until all four stones have been knocked under the arch. The arch is then removed, the stone is thrown into the air and the other four stones are gathered into the throwing hand and the thrown stone is caught in the same hand.

Twos Under the Arch

This is the same as Ones Under the Arch except that two stones must be knocked under the arch on each throw.

Threes Under the Arch

Three stones must be knocked under the arch on the first throw, and the remaining stone knocked under the arch on the second throw.

Fours Under the Arch

All four stones must be knocked through the arch at the same time.

Stables

The five stones are scattered on the floor. The fingers and thumb of the non-throwing hand are spread out and placed so that the fingertips are touching the floor and the palm is raised, the spaces between the fingers forming the four stables. One stone is thrown into the air, and before it is caught one of the other stones must be knocked into one of the stables. In this manner a stone is knocked into each of the four stables in turn. The non-throwing hand is then moved away, the throwing stone is thrown into the air, the four stones are gathered into the throwing hand, and the thrown stone is caught in the same hand.

Toad in the Hole

The five stones are scattered on the floor. The non-throwing hand is placed so that the thumb lies straight on the floor with the fingers curled round to form a hole. One stone is thrown into the air and before it is caught again in the throwing hand one of the remaining stones must be picked up and dropped into the hole. This is repeated until all four stones have been dropped into the hole. The non-throwing hand is moved away, the throwing stone is thrown into the air, the four stones are gathered into the throwing hand, and the thrown stone is caught in the same hand.

Snake in the Grass

Four of the stones are placed in a straight line, about six inches apart. The fifth stone is thrown into the air and before it is caught again in the same hand one of the end stones is moved. The moved stone must follow the path shown round the other stones and back to its starting point.

As many throws as required may be taken to complete the manoeuvre, provided that on each throw the end stone is moved part of the way and provided that no other stone is touched.

Tiddlywinks

No. of players: 2, 3 or 4
Equipment: Cup; 6 winks and a squidger for each player
Complexity: ★★

Tiddlywinks may be played on the floor but is best played on a table which is covered with a thick cloth or a piece of felt. The cup, which should be about 1½ inches wide and 1 or 2 inches high, is placed in the centre of the table. Each player has six winks, which are small flat disks of plastic or bone, and a squidger, which is a larger disk. A wink is squidged by pressing the edge of one's squidger against the edge of the wink, thus making the wink jump into the air. The object of the game is to be the first player to squidge all one's winks into the cup.

Each player lines his winks up in front of him at an equal distance from the cup. To determine the order of play each player squidges one wink, and the player who gets his wink nearest to the cup is the first to play. Play proceeds from player to player in a clockwise direction around the table.

A player may squidge only his own winks and has one squidge per turn except that when he succeeds in potting a wink he is entitled to an extra squidge. Winks are always squidged from where they lie (except that, when a wink is accidentally squidged off the table, it may be replaced on the nearest point on the edge of the table).

When a wink is covered by another wink, it is said to be squopped. If a player has a wink that is squopped by an opponent's wink he may not squidge it – he must wait until the opponent removes his wink or must attempt to dislodge it by squidging another of his own winks at it.

Successful play requires not only accurate squidging but also the ability to judge when to pot and when to squop.

Golomb's Game

No. of players: 2
Equipment: Chessboard; set of pentominoes
Complexity: ★★★

This simple yet complex game was invented by Solomon W. Golomb, an American research mathematician.

Pentominoes are described in the chapter on Solo Games. This game for two players requires only a chessboard and a set of pentominoes of which the unit square is the same size as the squares of the chessboard. Each player in turn picks an unplayed pentomino and places it on the board to cover five vacant squares. The last player to be able to place a piece on the board is the winner. That's all there is to it. Try it. It's fascinating.

Calculator 21

No. of players: Any small number
Equipment: 2 dice; a pocket calculator per player
Complexity: ☆

The roll of the dice indicates a calculation to be performed on a player's calculator. The aim is to reach a displayed total of exactly 21, and the first player to do so is the winner.

Each player in turn rolls the two dice. One of the dice determines the number to be entered on his calculator. The other determines the arithmetic operation to be entered – an odd number indicating subtraction and an even number addition. The player may choose which of the dice to use as a number and which to use as an operation. For example, a throw of 5,2 may be entered on the calculator as 5 + or as 2 −.

For example:	Roll	Enter	Display
	4,5	5 +	5
	6,2	6 +	11
	6,5	5 +	16
	4,1	4 −	20
	2,2	2 +	18
	6,4	4 +	22
	3,1	1 −	23
	3,2	2 −	21

Darts

No. of players: Any number
Equipment: Dartboard; set of 3 darts per player
Complexity: ☆☆

The standard dartboard is 18 inches in diameter and is divided into twenty numbered segments, high numbers alternating with low numbers. There is a narrow outer ring, in which a dart scores double the score for the segment, and a narrow ring midway between the centre and the outer ring, in which a dart scores treble. In the centre of the circle there are two concentric rings – known as the bull – the outer bull scoring 25 and the inner bull scoring 50.

Darts may be played by individual players, by pairs or by teams. In singles games the players take alternate turns – a turn consisting of throwing three darts. In pairs or team games the pairs or teams take alternate turns, the players on each side throwing in succession. There is usually a preliminary throw to establish who has the first turn, the player throwing nearest to the bull playing first.

Only darts in the board at the end of a player's turn count in the scoring. Darts that miss the board or that hit the board outside the scoring area or that drop out from the board do not count and may not be re-thrown. The method of scoring is to subtract the score for a player's turn from a target total, which is usually 301 for singles game, 501 for doubles game, and 1001 for team games. But before beginning to score, a side must score a double (by throwing a dart into the outer doubles ring). The starting double is scored as are any darts thrown after it in that turn but not darts thrown before the double. Thus, for example, if a player on his first turn in a singles game throws a 7, a double 20 and an 11 his score for that turn is 51, so his new target is marked as 250 (301 − 51). A player must also finish with a double which brings his score exactly to nought. If the score for a player's turn would take him past nought, or to one, then he does not score at all for that turn.

David	Edward
250	284
240	220
104	159
22	101
–	

Apart from the standard game described above there are a number of other darts games which, although they might be looked down on by serious darts players, may provide a good deal of enjoyment.

Round the Clock

This game is for any number of players, playing all against all. Three darts are thrown in a turn. Starting with a double, each player has to throw a 1, then a 2 and so on up to 20, and has to finish with a treble. The first player to finish the sequence is the winner.

Shanghai

This game is somewhat similar to *Round the Clock* except that each player on his first turn aims for and scores only 1s, on his second turn aims for and scores only 2s and so on. The player with the highest total score after twenty turns is the winner.

Scram

This is a game for two players, one being the 'stopper', the other being the 'scorer'. Each player in turn throws three darts. The stopper goes first, aiming with his three darts to block the scorer. Each segment of the board that is hit by the stopper is thenceforth closed to the scorer. The scorer aims to score as many points as possible before the stopper closes all the segments on the board. The players then change roles, and the player with the higher number of points as scorer wins the game.

Darts Football

This game is for two players, each throwing three darts in turn. The first player to throw a dart in the bull 'gets control of the ball' and starts scoring one goal for each double he throws – until his opponent gets control of the ball by throwing a bull and *he* starts scoring for each double. The first player must then aim for another bull to recover the ball. The winner is the first player to score ten goals.

Darts Cricket

This is a game for two teams. A coin is tossed to decide which team bats first. The batting team and the bowling team take alternate turns, a turn consisting of three darts. Runs are scored by the batting team for each point scored in excess of 40 in a turn. For example, a member of the batting team getting 60 with his three darts would score 20 runs. The bowling team aims for bulls to take 'wickets', an outer bull taking 1 wicket and an inner bull taking 2 wickets. When 10 wickets have been taken by the bowlers, the teams change over. The game is won by the team with the higher number of runs.

Billiards

No. of players: 2
Equipment: Billiard table; balls; cues
Complexity: ★★★

Billiards has been defined as a game in which balls on a table are poked with a stick. There is, of course, much more to it than that, and it is a game which, although it can be enjoyed by a complete novice, demands great skill if it is to be played well.

The playing area of a standard billiard table measures 12 ft by 6 ft 1½ in (though scaled-down versions may be used) and is of green baize over a bed of slate, being bordered by cloth-covered rubber 'cushions'. There are six pockets – one at each corner and one midway down each of the long sides. Twenty-nine inches from the bottom cushion is the 'baulk line', the space between this line and the bottom cushion being known as 'baulk'. On the baulk line there is a semi-circle known as the 'D'. Down the centre of the table there are four 'spots' – the billiard spot, 12¾ in from the top cushion; the centre spot between the two centre pockets; the pyramid spot, midway between the centre spot and the top cushion; and the baulk spot in the centre of the baulk line.

Three balls are used – a red ball and two white cue balls, one of which is marked with a spot so that they may be distinguished. Each

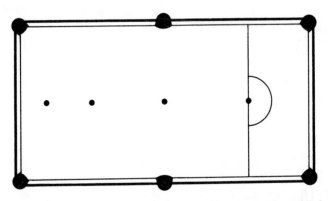

player has a cue – a long, tapered, wooden rod – which he uses to strike his cue ball. One other piece of equipment that may be used is a 'rest' – a cue-like rod with an X-shaped metal end on which the cue may be rested for shots where the cue ball would otherwise be inaccessible.

Each player may strike with the cue only his own cue ball, and points are scored as follows:

(a) Two points if the cue ball hits the opponent's cue ball and 'pots' it (i.e. sends it into a pocket).
(b) Two points if the cue ball is potted 'in off' the opponent's cue ball.
(c) Three points if the cue ball hits the red ball and pots it.
(d) Three points if the cue ball is potted in off the red ball.
(d) Two points for a 'cannon' if the cue ball hits both the other balls.

A player whose cue ball fails to hit either of the other balls forfeits one point, unless the cue ball goes into a pocket, in which case he forfeits three points.

To decide who has the first shot, the players 'string' by playing their cue balls simultaneously from the 'D' to rebound off the top cushion. The player whose ball returns nearer to the bottom cushion has the first shot.

To start the game the red ball is placed on the billiard spot, and the first player plays his cue ball from any point in the 'D'. When the first player's turn is finished, the second player brings his cue ball into play.

A player's turn, known as a 'break', may consist of any number of shots provided that he scores with each shot. Only when a shot fails to score does his turn end, and his opponent follows. When the red ball is potted it is immediately replaced on the billiard spot. When the opponent's cue ball is potted it remains out of play for the remainder of that break. When a player pots his own cue ball it is brought back into play by being placed anywhere in the 'D' before the other player starts his break. A cue ball brought back into play may not strike any other ball in the baulk unless it first strikes a cushion outside the baulk.

The game may be won by the player scoring the greater number of points in an agreed length of time or by the player whose score first reaches an agreed total.

Snooker

No. of players: 2 or more
Equipment: Billiard table; balls; cues
Complexity: ★★★

Snooker may be played by two players or by a greater number playing either in teams or all against all. Twenty-two balls are used – a white cue ball, fifteen reds and six colours. The points values of the balls are as follows: Red – 1 point, Yellow – 2 points, Green – 3 points, Brown – 4 points, Blue – 5 points, Pink – 6 points, Black – 7 points.

At the start of the game the balls are placed on the table as follows: the red balls in the form of a triangle with its apex on the pyramid spot and its base towards the top cushion; the yellow on the right-hand corner of the 'D'; the green on the left-hand corner of the 'D'; the brown on the baulk spot; the blue on the centre spot; the pink on the pyramid spot; the black on the billiard spot.

The players draw to decide who will play first, and the first player plays the cue ball from anywhere within the 'D' to strike a red. As in *Billiards*, each player's break continues until he plays a shot which fails to score. The first shot of each break must be at a red, as long as any reds remain on the table. If it is potted the player scores 1 point, and then aims to pot any one of the colours that he might choose. Having potted a colour he scores accordingly, and then aims to pot another red. The player's break continues this way, potting reds and colours alternately. Reds that are potted are not replaced on the table. While any reds remain on the table, colours are replaced on their respective spots after being potted. If a player should inadvertently pot the cue ball he forfeits four points, his break ends, and the next player brings the cue ball back into play in the 'D'.

The player who pots the last red then aims to pot any one of the colours as usual. If he is successful that colour is replaced on its spot. Thereafter the colours must be potted in strict order of ascending points value and, when potted, are not replaced on the table.

SOLO GAMES

Count Them Out

No. of players: 1
Equipment: Set of dominoes
Complexity: ☆

This is an extremely simple game, in which there is absolutely no element of skill.

The dominoes are shuffled and are all laid out in a straight line, face down. They are then turned over to be face up, without being moved from their original positions in the line. The player begins counting from 0 to 12, moving his finger along the line of dominoes and touching a domino each time he calls a number. Whenever he reaches 12 he starts counting again at 0, and whenever he reaches the end of the line of dominoes he goes back to the beginning of the line. Each time the number he calls matches the pip value of the domino he is touching (e.g. if he calls 0 when touching the double-blank or 9 when touching the 6-3) he discards the domino and pushes the remaining dominoes together to close up the gap. The objective is to discard all the dominoes.

Grace's Patience

No. of players: 1
Equipment: Set of dominoes
Complexity: ☆

The dominoes are shuffled thoroughly and are all laid out, face down and end to end, in a straight line. They are then turned face up without moving them from their original positions in the line.

The objective is to find adjacent matching pairs and discard them, and to continue doing this until all 28 dominoes have been discarded. Two adjacent dominoes may be discarded only if they have matching ends, e.g.

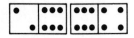

Whenever two dominoes are discarded the remaining dominoes are pushed together to close the gap. Care must be taken when deciding the order in which dominoes are to be discarded.

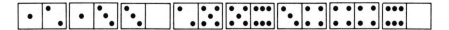

For example, in the position above, discarding the 2-5 with the 5-6 would block the game – in order to win it is necessary to discard the 3-4 and double-4 and then the 5-6 and 6-blank.

Even exercising the utmost skill, one will not win very often.

Twelves

No. of players: 1
Equipment: Set of dominoes
Complexity: ★★

The dominoes are shuffled and six are drawn to form a hand. Any two dominoes in the hand which have a combined pip value of 12 (e.g. the double-blank and double-six or the 1-3 and 6-2) may be discarded and placed in a discard heap. Each time two dominoes are discarded another two are drawn from the boneyard. The game is won if all 28 dominoes can be discarded in this way.

Five Piles

No. of players: 1
Equipment: Set of dominoes
Complexity: ★★

The dominoes are shuffled and three are drawn and turned face up to form a reserve. The remaining 25 dominoes are arranged in five piles with five dominoes in each. The piles are then turned over so that the dominoes are face up. The top dominoes of the piles are examined, and if any two of them have a combined pip value of 12 they may be removed and placed in a discard heap. The process is then repeated with the dominoes now on top of the piles. At any time, also, a domino from the reserve may be paired and discarded with a domino on top of the pile if they have a combined pip value of 12. The objective is to discard, in this manner, all 28 dominoes.

Sir Tommy

No. of players: 1
Equipment: Standard pack of 52 cards
Complexity: ⋆

Patience (in the UK) and *Solitaire* (in the USA) are generic terms for a wide range of different card games for one player. It is said that *Sir Tommy* is the original patience (or solo) game from which all the rest are derived.

The objective is to build up four ascending sequences from ace to king, regardless of suit and colour. Cards are dealt out from the stock one at a time on to any one of four face-up waste piles. The aces when they turn up are used to form four foundations next to the waste piles.

The foundations may be built on, placing any 2 on any ace, any 3 on any 2, and so on. The top card of any waste pile may be played on to a foundation, in this way, but cards may not be transferred from one waste pile to another.

The stock is dealt out only once – there is no second chance. There is a small amount of skill involved in the decision as to which waste pile a card from the stock is dealt, but it is simply a matter of avoiding the necessity of covering a low-ranking card with a high one.

Lady Betty

No. of players: 1
Equipment: Standard pack of 52 cards
Complexity: ☆

This is exactly the same as *Sir Tommy* except that six waste piles are used instead of four, and thus the patience works out more frequently. The sexist implication of the names of these two games is, of course, that the ladies require an easier game than the men.

Puss in the Corner

No. of players: 1
Equipment: Standard pack of 52 cards
Complexity: ☆

The aces are removed from the pack and placed face upwards to make four foundations, arranged in a square. The remainder of the pack forms the stock. The objective is to build up on the foundations ascending sequences of cards of the same colour (though not necessarily of the same suit) from ace to king.

The stock is dealt out, one card at a time. If a card is not playable on to a foundation it is played onto any one of four face-up waste piles which are formed in the course of play at the four corners of the foundation square.

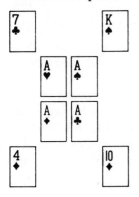

If the patience has not worked out when the last card of the stock has been dealt, one more deal is permitted. The four waste piles are gathered together in any order without shuffling to form a new stock, which is then dealt out again.

Clock Patience

No. of players: 1
Equipment: Standard pack of 52 cards
Complexity: ✶

This is a very simple patience game, requiring no skill or judgement, but it is one which seldom works out.

The pack is dealt out in thirteen piles, with four cards face down in each pile. The piles are arranged in the form of a clock face, with the thirteenth pile in the centre.

The objective is to end with four cards of the same rank in each pile in its correct place on the clock – i.e. four aces at one o'clock, four 2s at two o'clock, and so on, with four jacks at eleven o'clock, four queens at twelve o'clock and four kings in the centre.

The top card of the centre pile is turned up and is placed face upwards at the bottom of the pile that occupies the space belonging to that card (e.g. a 4 is placed at the bottom of the four o'clock pile). The top card of this pile is turned and placed under the appropriate pile. The player continues moving cards in this manner until all the cards are in the correct piles or until the game is blocked.

Monte Carlo

No. of players: 1
Equipment: Standard pack of 52 cards
Complexity: ⋆

This patience game is also known by the names of *Weddings* or *Double And Quits*. It is a simple, straightforward game, in which the cards are matched up in pairs.

The pack is shuffled and twenty cards are dealt out, face upwards, in four rows of five cards each. Any two cards of the same rank that are adjacent in the layout – horizontally, vertically or diagonally – may be discarded, but only two cards may be discarded at a time. The vacated spaces are then closed up by moving cards from right to left and by filling vacant spaces at the right end of a row with cards from the left end of the row below. The order in which the cards were originally dealt should be preserved, and the end result should be two spaces at the right end of the bottom row. Two more cards are dealt to these spaces, and the process of discarding a pair and moving up is repeated. This is continued until the game is blocked because no more pairs can be found to be discarded or until all the cards have been discarded in pairs.

Klondike

No. of players: 1
Equipment: Standard pack of 52 cards
Complexity: ⋆⋆

This is almost certainly the best known and most popular patience (or solitaire) game. In Britain it is often known as *Canfield,* which in America is the name by which *Demon* is better known.

Twenty-eight cards are dealt out in the following manner. First a row of seven, with the first card face up and the rest face down. Then a row of six, the first card face up and overlapping the second card of the first row and the rest face down and overlapping the cards of the first row. Then a row of five, a row of four and so on, each row overlapping the previous row and starting with a face-up card overlapping the second card of the previous row. Aces as they become available are placed in a row above the layout to form foundations. The aim is to build each suit in the correct sequence from ace to king.

The remainder of the pack is placed face down as the stock. Cards are turned up from the stock one at a time, and if not playable on the foundations or on the layout are placed face up on a discard pile. The top card of the discard pile is always available to be played to the foundations or the layout.

On the columns of the layout descending sequences of cards are built of alternating colour (e.g. red 10 on black J, black 9 on red 10, etc.). The bottom card of each sequence is available to be played to a foundation. A sequence as a whole may be transferred to another column to form a longer sequence. When a face-down card is exposed at the bottom of a column it is turned face up. When a complete column is cleared, the space may be filled only with a king or with a sequence built on a king.

The stock may be played through only once.

Demon

No. of players: 1
Equipment: Standard pack of 52 cards
Complexity: ★★

Thirteen cards are dealt face down to a reserve pile, which is then turned over so that only the top card is visible. The next four cards are dealt face up in a row to the right of the reserve pile, forming the 'tableau'.

The next card is dealt face up above the first card of the tableau to form the first of four foundations. As they become available, the other three cards of the same rank as this card will be placed to form the other three foundations. The objective is to build up each suit in sequence on its foundation. Thus if, for example, the foundation is the 9 of clubs the sequence to be built up will be 9,10,J,Q,K,A,2,3,4,5,6,7,8 of clubs, and similar sequences will be built up for the other suits on their foundations.

The remainder of the pack, when the reserve pile, tableau and first foundation have been dealt out, forms the stock. The stock is turned over in batches of three cards on to a waste pile. If there are less than three

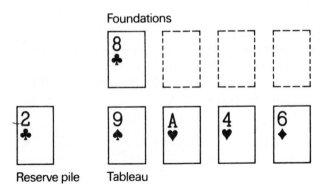

cards at the end of the stock they may be turned over singly. The only card in the waste pile that is available for play is the top card though, of course, when it is played it will make the card below available.

The foundations may be built up in suit sequence. Cards may be built on the columns of the tableau in descending sequence of alternate colour (e.g. red jack on black queen, black 10 on red jack, etc.). An entire column may be transferred on to another column, provided that this sequence is maintained. As soon as a tableau column becomes vacant it is filled with the top card of the reserve pile or, if no cards are left in the reserve pile, with the top card of the waste pile (though in this case there is no obligation to fill the space immediately).

When the end of the stock is reached, the waste pile is turned over to form a new stock which is then redealt, without shuffling. This may be performed as often as required until the game is either blocked or won.

The game is very rarely won.

Cribbage Solitaire

No. of players: 1
Equipment: Standard pack of 52 cards; cribbage board
Complexity: ★★

This is a game for the *Cribbage* enthusiast to play when he cannot find an opponent to play against.

The player deals six cards to himself and two to the crib. He then discards two cards from his hand to the crib, and turns up a start from the top of the pack.

He scores for his hand and then for the crib, as in the show when playing *Cribbage*.

The eight cards in the hand and the crib are then put to one side, and a fresh hand and crib are dealt (using the start as the first card of the new hand) and scored. In this way six hands are dealt and scored, and the objective is to score 120 points or more.

Match Words

No. of players: 1
Equipment: 28 matches
Complexity: ☆

The matches are arranged as shown in the diagram:

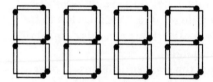

The object of the game is to see how many words can be formed by removing various numbers of matches. It will be found that not many words may be formed by removing less than 5 matches or more than 11 matches, but the numbers in between offer plenty of scope. For example:

Removing 6

SOAP   BUSH

Removing 8

POOL   CHOP

Removing 10

Elimination

No of players: 1
Equipment: Pocket calculator
Complexity: ★★

Any five-digit number is entered into the calculator. The objective is to reduce that number to zero in four steps, using only the arithmetic functions − and ÷ with two-digit numbers.
    For example:

14587   47629

− 67 = 14520	− 29 = 47600
÷ 60 = 242	÷ 40 = 1190
÷ 11 = 22	÷ 70 = 17
− 22 = 0	− 17 = 0

    A rather more demanding version of the game is to start with a six-digit number, which has to be reduced to zero in four steps in the same way.

Tangram

No. of players: 1
Equipment: Seven-piece tangram set
Complexity: ★★

Tangram is an ancient Chinese game-puzzle-recreation. The tangram set
is a set of seven pieces formed by the dissection of a square as shown in
the diagram.

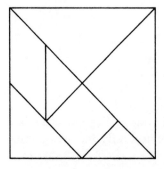

A tangram set may easily be made at home from stiff card or from
wood, or a set may be bought (they can sometimes be found in the
trendier sort of gift shop).

The object is to arrange the pieces to form various shapes. This may
be done free-style, just putting the pieces together in various ways to see
what shapes turn up. An amazing variety of aesthetically pleasing
designs can be discovered in this way. Alternatively the tangram set can
be used in puzzle mode, the objective being to put the pieces together to
make some set design, such as this parallelogram.

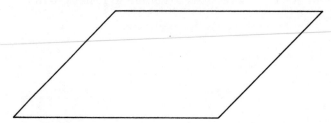

A marvellous puzzle of this type, devised by the great puzzle-setter
Henry E. Dudeney, is to use all the tangram pieces to form each of these

two figures, which appear to be identical except that one has a foot and
the other does not.

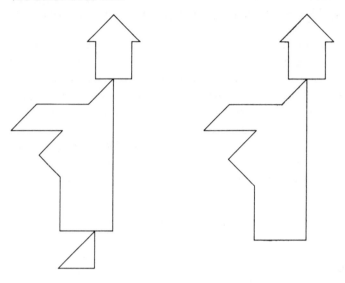

Solitaire

No. of players: 1
Equipment: Board and 33 pieces
Complexity: ✩✩

The *Solitaire* board is normally made of wood or plastic and has 33 holes
to hold the pieces (which may be small marbles or pegs).

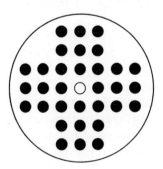

A piece may only be moved by jumping over another piece which is adjacent horizontally or vertically and landing in the next hole, which must be vacant. The piece that was jumped over is then removed from the board.

For the basic game, all the pieces are placed on the board. One piece is then removed, normally from the centre hole but optionally from any other hole. The objective is to make a series of moves that will result in only one piece being left on the board. To provide a greater challenge it may be stipulated that the last remaining piece should be in the centre hole or in any other hole that may be nominated.

Other problems may be set – for example, starting with only nine pieces arranged in the form of a cross in the centre of the board and ending with one piece in the centre hole.

Pentominoes

No. of players: 1
Equipment: Set of pentominoes
Complexity: ✩✩✩

Pentominoes were introduced to the world by a Californian mathematician, Solomon W. Golomb, in an article published in the *American Mathematical Monthly* in 1954.

Starting from the definition of a domino as two squares 'simply connected' (i.e. joined along their edges) he coined the word polyomino to describe the class of shapes formed by squares thus connected. Thus, a monomino is a single square, a domino 2 squares simply connected, a tromino 3 squares, a tetromino 4 squares, a pentomino 5 squares, a hexomino 6, and so on.

Of all this family of polyominoes, it is the pentomino which has attracted the most interest because of its suitability for games and puzzles.

There are twelve distinct ways in which five squares can be joined together to form a pentomino. These twelve shapes constitute a set of pentominoes. A set may easily be made from stiff card or from wood.

There are a number of problems which may be set, in which the objective is to put the pentominoes together to form various shapes. For

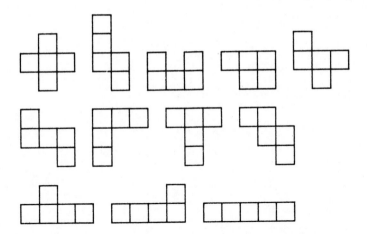

example, all 12 pieces may be used to construct a 5 × 12 rectangle, a
6 × 10 rectangle, a 4 × 15 rectangle or a 3 × 20 rectangle. Of these the
3 × 20 rectangle is by far the most difficult to construct.

Another popular problem (known as 'the triplication problem') is to
choose one of the pieces and then to use nine of the remaining eleven to
construct a large-scale replica of the chosen piece. This will be three
times the height and three times the length of the original. The
triplication problem may be solved for each of the twelve pentominoes.

12 CHILDREN'S PARTY GAMES

*Some words of caution
for parents*

Ring a Ring of Roses
The Farmer's in his Den
Three Blind Mice
Oranges and Lemons
Poor Pussy
Squeak, Piggy, Squeak
Pass the Parcel
Musical Chairs
Musical Bumps
Musical Islands
Musical Statues
Hunt the Thimble
Hot and Cold
Hunt the Slipper
Blind Man's Buff
Blind Postman
Cat and Mouse
Hide and Seek
Potato Race
Balloon Race
Blow Ball
Nose Ball
Ankle Race
Plate and Feather Race
Newspaper Race
Back-to-Back Race
Three-Legged Race
Piggy-Back Race
Tortoise Race
Two Minute Race
Pass the Balloon
Egg and Spoon Race
Simon Says

Do This, Do That
On and Off
Card Throwing
Ping-Pong Throwing
Coin on the Plate
Wool Gathering
Balloon Battle
Goodies and Baddies
Handshake
Happy Travellers
Dead Lions
Ghosts

Some Words of Caution for Parents

When organising a children's party it is the responsibility of the adults involved to set the pace. With very young children it is generally not wise to have more than two or three organised games – it is better to provide a selection of toys for the little ones to play with most of the time. With older children one must be careful not to let the fun get out of hand. Children usually love the more active running, chasing and racing games, but they should not be permitted to play too many such games or for too long at a time. Intersperse them with some of the quieter games. Otherwise, with too much excitement and hilarity, 'it will all end in tears'.

With some of the more boisterous games, close adult supervision may be necessary to make sure that nothing gets broken or damaged, that the children don't try to exceed their capabilities and that younger, smaller children don't suffer at the hands of older, bigger ones. But try not to fence the children in with too many prohibitions. Try to achieve a happy balance and the children will enjoy themselves – and so will you.

Ring a Ring of Roses

No. of players: 3 or more
Equipment: None
Complexity: ☆

The players join hands and dance round in a circle, singing:

'Ring a ring of roses,
A pocket full of posies,
A-tishoo, A-tishoo,
We all fall down.'

As the last word is sung, the players all drop down to sit on the floor.
This is repeated as often as required – young children enjoy it

immensely and seldom want to stop. The original verse may be repeated each time, or these other verses may be used as well:

'The king has sent his daughter
To fetch a pail of water,
A-tishoo, A-tishoo,
We all fall down.

The bird upon the steeple
Is singing to the people,
A-tishoo, A-tishoo,
We all fall down.

The wedding bells are ringing,
The boys and girls are singing,
A-tishoo, A-tishoo,
We all fall down.'

The Farmer's in his Den

No. of players: 8 or more
Equipment: None
Complexity: ✱

One of the players is chosen to be the Farmer. The other players form a circle and dance round him, singing:

'The farmer's in his den,
The farmer's in his den,
Heigh-ho, heigh-ho,
The farmer's in his den.

The farmer wants a wife
The farmer wants a wife,
Heigh-ho, heigh-ho,
The farmer wants a wife.'

At this point the Farmer chooses one of the other players to be his

Wife and to join him in the middle of the circle. The players continue singing:

> 'The wife wants a child,
> The wife wants a child,
> Heigh-ho, heigh-ho,
> The wife wants a child.'

The Wife chooses another player to be the Child, who also comes into the middle. The players continue singing:

> 'The child wants a nurse,
> The child wants a nurse,
> Heigh-ho, heigh-ho,
> The child wants a nurse.'

The Child picks a player to be the Nurse, who joins the group in the middle. The players continue singing:

> 'The nurse wants a dog,
> The nurse wants a dog,
> Heigh-ho, heigh ho,
> The nurse wants a dog.'

The player chosen by the Nurse goes into the middle on hands and knees. The players sing the last verse:

> 'We all pat the dog,
> We all pat the dog,
> Heigh-ho, heigh-ho,
> We all pat the dog.'

All the players pat the Dog, who then becomes the Farmer for the next round of the game.

Three Blind Mice

No. of players: 5 or more
Equipment: None
Complexity: ☆

One of the players is chosen to be the Farmer's Wife. The other players join hands to form a circle around the Farmer's Wife and dance round her, singing:

> 'Three blind mice, see how they run.
> They all run after the Farmer's Wife,
> Who cut off their tails with a carving knife.
> Did you ever see such a thing in your life
> As three blind mice?'

As the last word is sung the players scatter and run to the walls of the room, while the Farmer's Wife tries to catch one of them. A player is 'safe' once he touches a wall. The first player to be caught becomes the Farmer's Wife for the next round of the game.

Oranges and Lemons

No. of players: 6 or more
Equipment: None
Complexity: ☆

Two of the players are chosen to form an arch. To do this they stand facing each other, holding hands with their arms raised in the air. One of the players is 'Oranges' and the other is 'Lemons'.

The other players march round in a large circle, one behind another, continually passing under the arch. As they march they sing this traditional English nursery rhyme:

> 'Oranges and Lemons,
> Say the bells of St. Clement's.

You owe me five farthings,
Say the bells of St. Martin's.
When will you pay me?
Say the bells of Old Bailey.
When I grow rich,
Say the bells at Shoreditch.
Pray, when will that be?
Say the bells at Stepney.
I'm sure I don't know,
Says the great bell at Bow.
Here comes a candle to light you to bed,
Here comes a chopper to chop off your head.'

As the last line is sung the players forming the arch move their arms up and down, finally bringing them down to trap one of the players marching through the arch.

The game continues in this way until all the players have been trapped under the arch. As the players are trapped they are asked to choose Oranges or Lemons. They join a line on one side of the arch or the other, according to their choice, each player holding the waist of the player in front. The game then concludes with a tug-of-war between Oranges and Lemons.

Poor Pussy

No. of players: 4 or more
Equipment: None
Complexity: ☆

All the players sit in a circle. One player is then chosen to go into the middle to be the pussy cat. The pussy cat, on hands and knees, goes to each player in turn, purring and crying 'Meeow' as much like a cat as possible. Each player must stroke or pat pussy's head three times, each player saying 'Poor pussy, poor pussy'. The first player to smile or laugh takes the next turn at being the pussy cat.

Squeak, Piggy, Squeak

No. of players: 5 or more
Equipment: A blindfold and a cushion
Complexity: ☆

One player is chosen to be blindfolded and is given a cushion to hold. He is turned around three times and the other players sit down in a circle around him. The blindfolded player has to place the cushion on another player's lap and then sit on it. He calls out 'Squeak, Piggy, squeak' and the player he is sitting on must squeak like a little pig.

If the blindfolded player can name the player he is sitting on then they change places, otherwise the blindfolded player must find another lap to sit on.

Whenever there is a new blindfolded player the others swap seats before he tries to sit on their laps.

Pass the Parcel

No. of players: 4 or more
Equipment: A small present; gift-wrapping materials; a piano, or record-player or other source of music.
Complexity: ☆

In preparation for the game, the present is wrapped in ten layers (or thereabouts) of paper, each layer being fastened either with string or with adhesive tape.

The players sit in a circle, and while the music is playing they pass the parcel from hand to hand around the circle, as quickly as possible. The music is stopped abruptly at frequent intervals, and when this happens the player holding the parcel at that moment unwraps one layer of paper. The player who is lucky enough to unwrap the final layer wins the present.

Musical Chairs

No. of players: 4 or more
Equipment: Chairs (one fewer than the number of players); a
piano, record-player or other source of music.
Complexity: ☆

The chairs are lined up in the centre of the room, alternate chairs facing opposite walls. The music is started, and while it is playing the children march round and round the line of chairs, without touching them. When the music stops, each child has to try to sit in a chair. The one who is left without a chair is eliminated. One chair is removed and the game starts again. This is repeated until in the last round there are two players and a single chair – the first one to sit in the chair when the music stops is the winner.

Musical Bumps

No. of players: 4 or more
Equipment: A piano, record-player or other source of music
Complexity: ☆

This is similar to *Musical Chairs*, except that the chairs are not required. While the music is playing, the children skip up and down. When the music stops, the children drop down to sit cross-legged on the floor. The last one to do so is eliminated. This is repeated until only one player is left.

Musical Islands

No. of players: 8 or more
Equipment: Small mats or sheets of newspaper; a piano or
record-player or other source of music
Complexity: ☆

The mats or sheets of newspaper are placed on the floor at various points around the room to form 'islands'. The players walk around while the music plays, and when it stops they rush to get on to an island. An island may be occupied by several players, but any player who cannot squeeze on to an island or who falls off is eliminated. The number of islands is gradually reduced, and the last player left in the game is the winner.

Musical Statues

No. of players: 4 or more
Equipment: A piano or record-player or other source of music
Complexity: ★

While the music is playing the children must dance about the room moving continually. As soon as the music stops they must 'freeze' in whatever position they happen to be in at that moment and must remain as still as statues. Anyone who moves is out. The music is restarted and the children continue dancing. The game continues in this manner until only one player is left in, and that player is the winner.

Hunt the Thimble

No. of players: 3 or more
Equipment: A thimble (or other suitable small object)
Complexity: ★

One player is chosen to 'hide' the thimble while all the other players are out of the room. The thimble should not really be hidden but should be placed in some inconspicuous spot where it will be visible to all the players though not immediately noticeable. The players then come back into the room and begin to hunt the thimble. Each player, as soon as he spots the thimble, sits down without saying anything and without drawing attention to its location. The last player to spot the thimble and sit down is the loser, and he hides the thimble for the next round.

Hot and Cold

No. of players: 3 or more
Equipment: A thimble (or other suitable small object)
Complexity: ☆

One player leaves the room while the other players hide the thimble. When he is called back into the room the other players help him in his search for the thimble by calling out 'Cold' or 'Very cold' as he moves further away from it, and 'Warm', 'Hot', 'Very hot' as he moves nearer to it. Each player has a turn at being the one who has to find the thimble.

Hunt the Slipper

No. of players: 8 or more
Equipment: A slipper or shoe
Complexity: ☆

The players sit in a circle on the floor with one player sitting in the middle with the slipper. The player in the middle hands the slipper to one of the players around the circle, then covers his eyes and recites this rhyme:

> 'Cobbler, cobbler, mend my shoe,
> Have it done by half past two.
> Cobbler, cobbler, tell me true,
> Which of you has got my shoe?'

While the player in the middle is reciting, the players around the circle pass the slipper from one to another behind their backs. Whoever is holding the slipper when the last word of the rhyme is uttered holds on to it, being careful to keep it out of sight. The player in the middle has two tries to guess who is holding the slipper. If he guesses correctly, the player holding the slipper goes into the middle for the next round.

Blind Man's Buff

No. of players: 4 or more
Equipment: A blindfold
Complexity: ✫

One player is chosen to be the Blind Man and is blindfolded. The other players lead him to the middle of the room, turn him round three times in each direction, and then leave him on his own.

The Blind Man tries to catch one of the other players, while they move about the room, calling to him and taunting him, approaching as near as they dare and dodging away again. A player who is touched by the Blind Man must immediately stand still. If, by touching and feeling, the Blind Man can say who it is he has caught then the captured player becomes the Blind Man for the next round of the game. If the Blind Man guesses wrongly the name of the captured player, then he must let him go and carry on trying to catching another player.

Blind Postman

No. of players: 8 or more
Equipment: A blindfold
Complexity: ✫

One player is chosen to be the postman and is blindfolded. The other players sit in a circle with the postman standing in the middle. Each of the seated players is given the name of a town. The postman calls out the names of two towns, and those two players have to exchange seats, while the postman attempts to occupy one of the temporarily vacant seats. Whoever loses his seat becomes the postman.

Cat and Mouse

No. of players: 8 or more
Equipment: A blindfold
Complexity: ☆

One player is chosen to be the cat and is blindfolded. Another player is chosen to be the mouse. The other players form a circle, with the cat and the mouse standing in the middle. The cat has to try to catch the mouse by following the sound of his voice. At any time the cat can stand still and call 'Meeow'. The mouse must then reply 'Squeak squeak' but can immediately run, creep or tiptoe to another part of the circle. When he is caught he becomes the cat for the next round and another player is chosen to be the mouse.

Hide and Seek

No. of players: Any number
Equipment: None
Complexity: ☆

A particular spot is chosen to be 'home'. The seeker stands there, covers his eyes, and counts up to fifty while the other players scatter and hide themselves in various parts of the house. When he has counted up to fifty, the seeker calls out 'Ready!' and goes off in search of the other players. The first player to be spotted and tagged by the seeker becomes the seeker for the next round. But any player who manages to get 'home' without being tagged is safe.

Potato Race

No. of players: 2 or more
Equipment: Three potatoes for each competitor; a
cardboard box
Complexity: ✩

The cardboard box is placed at one end of the room; all the potatoes are placed in a pile at the other end. The players are lined up beside the box. They have to run to the other end of the room, pick up a potato, bring it back and drop it in the box. They repeat this procedure twice more, and the first player to drop three potatoes in the box is the winner.

Balloon Race

No. of players: 2 or more
Equipment: One balloon for each competitor
Complexity: ✩

The competitors stand at one end of the room, and each is given a balloon of a different colour. They race to the far end of the room and back again, taking their balloons with them. The only restriction is that the balloons may not be held – they must be moved along by being patted or kicked. Any player who holds his balloon is sent back to the start and has to begin all over again.

Blow Ball

No. of players: 2 or more
Equipment: One ping-pong ball and one straw for each
competitor
Complexity: ✩

Starting at one end of the room, each of the competitors, on hands and knees and using a drinking straw, has to move a ping-pong ball to the other end of the room and back again by blowing through his straw. Any competitor who touches the ping-pong ball with the straw or with any part of his body is sent back to the start. The first player to complete the course successfully is the winner.

Nose Ball

No. of players: 2 or more
Equipment: One ping-pong ball per competitor
Complexity: ☆

This is similar to *Blow Ball*, except that the players have to push the ping-pong balls with their noses.

Ankle Race

No. of players: 2 or more
Equipment: None
Complexity: ☆

The competitors line up at one end of the room, each one crouching or bending down and grasping his ankles. They must race to the other end of the room and back again in this position. Any competitor who takes his hands away from his ankles is sent back to the start.

Plate and Feather Race

No. of players: 2 or more
Equipment: A paper plate and a feather for each competitor
Complexity: ☆

The competitors line up at one end of the room, and each is given a feather on a paper plate. Carrying their plates, they have to race to the other end of the room and back again. A competitor whose feather comes off his plate must stop to put it back again, but otherwise no competitor must touch the feather on his plate – anyone who does so is sent back to the start.

Newspaper Race

No. of players: 2 or more
Equipment: Two sheets of newspaper for each competitor
Complexity: ☆

The competitors, each with two sheets of newspaper, line up at one end of the room. They have to make their way to the other end of the room and back again, using their sheets of newspaper as stepping stones. Each player stands on one sheet, lays the other on the floor in front of him, steps on to it, picks up the first sheet and lays it on the floor in front of him, steps on to that, and so on. Any player who touches the floor with any part of his body is sent back to the starting point and has to begin all over again.

Back-to-Back Race

No. of players: 4 or more
Equipment: None
Complexity: ☆

The players compete in pairs, each pair standing back to back with their arms linked at the elbows. Starting at one end of the room, the linked pairs race to the other end and back again.

Three-Legged Race

No. of players: 4 or more
Equipment: A scarf for each pair of competitors
Complexity: ☆

The players compete in pairs. Each pair of players stand side by side, and a scarf is used to tie the right leg of one player to the left leg of the other. Starting at one end of the room, the pairs race to the other end of the room and back again.

Piggy-Back Race

No. of players: 4 or more
Equipment: None
Complexity: ☆

The players compete in pairs. One member of each pair climbs on to the other's back to be carried. Starting at one end of the room, the pairs of competitors race to the other end of the room. There the rider dismounts, and he has to carry his partner back to the starting-point.

Tortoise Race

No. of players: 2 or more
Equipment: None
Complexity: ☆

This is an unusual race, in that the aim is to be the last to finish. Starting at one end of the room, the competitors 'race' to the other end as slowly as possible. They must go in a straight line towards the other end of the room, and are not allowed to stop – they must continue moving, however slowly. The last to finish is the winner.

Two Minute Race

No. of players: 2 or more
Equipment: A watch with a second hand
Complexity: ★★

Before the game begins any clocks in the room are removed or covered up, and any wristwatches are confiscated. Starting at one end of the room, the players then 'race' to the opposite wall in exactly two minutes. The competitors can move as slowly as they like but they must never stop moving, and they have to use their own sense of timing to complete the course when they think two minutes have passed. The competitors are timed by an umpire who is provided with a watch with a second hand. The winner is the player who is nearest to the wall when the two minutes have passed.

Pass the Balloon

No. of players: 6 or more
Equipment: Two balloons
Complexity: ★

The players are divided into two teams, and the members of each team stand in line, one behind another. The leader of each team is given a balloon, and when the signal is given to start, he passes it over his head to the player behind, who passes it over his head to the player behind him, and so on down to the end of the line. When the player at the end of the line receives it, he runs round to the front of the line. The balloon is then passed back as before. This continues until the original leader receives the balloon at the end of the line and returns to his place at the front. The first team to finish wins the game.

Egg and Spoon Race

No. of players: 8 or more
Equipment: A spoon for each player; two ping-pong balls
Complexity: ☆

Hard-boiled eggs are traditionally used for this game. When playing at home, however, it is advisable to substitute ping-pong balls – they cause less mess if they are trodden into the carpet.

The players are divided into two teams, forming parallel lines. Each player is given a spoon which he holds in his mouth, and a ping-pong ball is placed in the spoon of the first player in each team. The first player has to transfer the ping-pong ball from his spoon to the spoon of the second player, and so on down the line. No player may use his hands to touch the ball. If it falls to the floor the player who dropped it must go down on hands and knees and scoop up the ball with the spoon still held in his mouth. The first team to transfer the ping-pong ball successfully to the player at the end of the line wins the game.

Simon Says

No. of players: 4 or more
Equipment: None
Complexity: ☆

One of the players is chosen to be the leader, and the other players space themselves out in front of him. The leader performs various actions (such as standing on one leg, patting his head, raising his left arm, bending down) and commands the other players to do the same. If he begins the command with the words 'Simon says' – e.g. 'Simon says, touch your toes' – then the other players must obey the command. If the command does not begin with the words 'Simon says' – e.g. 'Touch your toes' – then the other players must not perform that action. A player who makes a mistake or who hesitates for too long before doing what Simon says drops out of the game. The last player left in is the winner, and he becomes the leader for the next round.

Do This, Do That

No. of players: 4 or more
Equipment: None
Complexity: ✩

This game is similar to *Simon Says*. Whenever the leader performs some action and says 'Do this', the other players must copy him. But when he performs some action and says 'Do that', the other players must remain still.

On and Off

No. of players: 4 or more
Equipment: An old blanket
Complexity: ✩

An old blanket is spread out on the floor. When the leader calls 'Everybody off the blanket' the children stand on the blanket, and when the leader calls 'Everybody on the blanket' they all get off, always doing the opposite of what the leader tells them. Any player who makes a mistake is out, and the last player left in is the winner.

Card Throwing

No. of players: Any number
Equipment: A wastepaper bin and an old pack of cards
Complexity: ✩

Each contestant is given ten playing cards, which he attempts to flick into the wastepaper bin. The players should stand about eight feet from the bin but, of course, this distance may be varied depending on the ages of the players. The player getting most cards into the bin is the winner.

Ping-Pong Throwing

No. of players: Any number
Equipment: A wastepaper bin and five ping-pong balls
Complexity: ☆

This is similar to the previous game except that each player in turn attempts to throw the five ping-pong balls into the bin. Balls that bounce out of the bin do not count in the score.

Coin on the Plate

No. of players: Any number
Equipment: A plate (preferably enamel or aluminium) and a supply of coins
Complexity: ☆

The players, each of whom is provided with five coins, stand about six feet away from the plate. The player who manages to throw most coins so that they land on the plate – and don't bounce off – is the winner.

Wool Gathering

No. of players: Any number
Equipment: A chair and a ball of wool for each player
Complexity: ☆

A ball of wool is entwined round the legs and back of each player's chair. When the word of command is given, each player has to wind his wool up into a neat ball again without rising from his seat. The first player to succeed is the winner.

Balloon Battle

No. of players: Any number
*Equipment: A rolled-up newspaper and a balloon on a
string for each player*
Complexity: ☆

Each player has his balloon tied to his ankle, and is armed with a
rolled-up newspaper. While attempting to protect his own balloon, each
player tries to burst as many of the other balloons as possible, using only
his rolled-up newspaper. No balloon may be touched by hand. A player
whose balloon is burst is eliminated, and the last player left in is the
winner.

Goodies and Baddies

No. of players: Any number
Equipment: Two balloons
Complexity: ☆

The players are divided into two teams. One team, the Goodies, attempt
to keep a balloon up in the air while the other team, the Baddies, attempt
to burst it, using only their hands and feet – pins and other suchlike
weapons of destruction are outlawed. When the balloon eventually has
been burst, the teams swap roles and play with the second balloon.

Handshake

No. of players: 8 or more
Equipment: None
Complexity: ✰

One of the players is 'it'. The others stand in a circle, facing inwards, with their hands behind their backs. The player who is 'it' runs around the outside of the circle, slaps the hands of one of the players, and carries on running. The player whose hands were slapped runs around the circle in the opposite direction. When they meet they shake hands and then race back to the vacant space in the circle. The one who gets there last is 'it' for the next round.

Happy Travellers

No. of players: 6 or more
Equipment: A newspaper for each player
Complexity: ✰

The players sit in two rows, facing one another with their knees touching, and squashed together like passengers on a very crowded train. Each player has a folded newspaper which has been thoroughly muddled up – with pages in the wrong order, some being back to front and some upside down. On the word of command each player tries to arrange the pages of his newspaper into the correct order as quickly as possible. The first to succeed is the winner.

Dead Lions

No. of players: Any number
Equipment: None
Complexity: ☆

This is a very quiet game which makes an ideal interlude when the party becomes too boisterous.

The players lie face down on the floor and pretend to be dead lions. Any player who makes the slightest movement is eliminated, and the last player left in is the winner. The players who have been eliminated may help to spot movements made by the remaining dead lions, and they may 'encourage' the lions to move by taunting them or trying to make them laugh – but no touching is allowed.

Ghosts

No. of players: 8 or more
Equipment: An old sheet
Complexity: ☆

The players are divided into two teams. The first team leaves the room, and its members come back, one at a time, to stand in the doorway draped in the sheet and moaning and groaning like a ghost. The second team has to guess the identity of each member of the first team as they appear. The teams then change roles. Thus every player has a turn at being a ghost. The game is won by the team which correctly identifies most of the other team's ghosts.

13 CHILDREN'S CARD GAMES

Snap
Speed Snap
Old Maid
Le Vieux Garçon
Beggar my Neighbour
Donkey
Snip-Snap-Snorem
Happy Families
Fish
Go Boom
Cheat
I Doubt It
Slapjack
Menagerie
Animal Noises
War
Cuckoo
Pelmanism
My Ship Sails
Rolling Stone

Snap

No. of players: 2 or more
Equipment: Normal pack of 52 cards (or two packs shuffled together if there are more than 4 players).
Complexity: ✩

Special *Snap* cards may be bought for this game but it can be played just as well with ordinary playing cards.

All the cards are dealt out to the players, one card at a time and face down. Some players may get one card more than the others but this does not really matter. Each player forms his cards into a neat pile in front of him, face down, without looking at them. The player to the left of the dealer takes the top card from his pile and puts it face up on the table to start a new pile next to his face-down pile. The player to his left does likewise, and so on around the table. The cards played on to the face-up piles should be placed tidily so that only the top card of each face-up pile can be seen.

Whenever any player sees that the cards on top of any two face-up piles have the same value (e.g. two sevens or two queens) he calls 'Snap'. The first player to do so wins both piles and adds them to the bottom of his own face-down pile. Play then starts again with the player to the left of the last player turning over a card.

A player who has played all the cards from his face-down pile can still stay in the game as long as he has a face-up pile in front of him. He passes when it is his turn to play a card, but he may still call 'Snap' when he sees two cards of the same value, and thus may get a new face-down pile. Only when a player has neither a face-up pile nor a face-down pile is he out of the game.

If a player calls 'Snap' in error when there are not two cards of the same value showing, then he is penalised by having to give each of the other players a card from his face-down pile. These cards are added to the bottom of the other players' face-down piles.

The winner is the player who wins all the cards.

Variation 1
In this variation, if two or more players call 'Snap' and it cannot be decided who called first, the matching face-up piles are put together to form a face-up pile (called the 'pool') in the middle of the table. Play continues, and when the top card of any face-up pile matches the top card of the pool the first player to call 'Snap pool' wins the pool.

Variation 2
When a player has played all the cards from his face-down pile he is allowed to turn over his face-up pile to form a new face-down pile from which he may play cards.

Variation 3
Instead of having a separate face-up pile for each player, all the players turn over their cards on to one central face-up pile. Players call 'Snap' when the two top cards are of the same value. This makes the game less interesting, but it is easier for younger children.

Speed Snap

No. of players: 2 or more
Equipment: As for Snap
Complexity: ⋆

This is the same as normal *Snap* except that all the players turn over a card at the same time, and play proceeds as briskly as possible. This makes *Speed Snap* a faster and more exciting game.

Old Maid

No. of players: 3 or more
Equipment: Normal pack of 52 cards
Complexity:

Special sets of *Old Maid* cards may be bought, but the game may equally well be played with an ordinary pack of cards from which one queen is removed. There are no winners in this game – only a loser. The object is to get rid of all one's cards by laying them on the table as matched pairs (e.g. two aces, two sevens etc.). One player will be left with an odd queen, thus losing the game.

The whole pack is dealt out to the players, one card at a time and face down. Some players may have one card more than the others, but this does not really matter. Each player picks up and examines his cards without letting them be seen by any of the other players. He discards, by placing face down on the table in front of him, any pairs of cards with the same value. If he has three cards of the same value he may only discard two of them and must keep the third, but if he has four of the same value he may discard them as two pairs.

When all the players have done this, the player to the left of the dealer fans out his cards and offers them face downwards to the next player on his left. The player to whom they are offered takes any one of them and puts it with his own cards. If it forms a pair with any card that he already holds he can then discard the pair. This player in turn then fans out his cards and offers them face downwards to the player on *his* left, who takes any one of them.

This continues around the table until all the players have managed to pair and discard all their cards – except for one player left holding the odd queen, who is the 'old maid'.

Le Vieux Garçon

No. of players: 3 or more
Equipment: Normal pack of 52 cards
Complexity: ☆

This French game is played in exactly the same manner as *Old Maid* except that it is played with a pack of cards from which the jack of hearts, jack of diamonds and jack of clubs have been removed. At the end of the game the loser is the player who is left holding the jack of spades – the *vieux garçon* or 'old boy'.

Beggar My Neighbour

No. of players: 2 to 6
Equipment: Normal pack of 52 cards
Complexity: ☆

This popular game, although it is very simple and requires no skill, can be very exciting.

The whole pack is dealt out to the players, one card at a time and face down. Some players may get one card more than the others but this does not really matter. Each player forms his cards into a neat pile, face down, without looking at them. The player to the left of the dealer begins the game by turning up the top card of his pile and placing it face up in the centre of the table. Each player in turn, going round to the left, similarly turns up the top card of his pile and places it face up on the central pile.

This continues until one player puts on the central pile an ace or a court card (king, queen or jack). When this happens the next player has to 'pay' him by playing a certain number of cards on to the central pile – four cards for an ace, three cards for a king, two cards for a queen, and one card for a jack. However, if one of the 'pay' cards happens to be an ace or a court card the payer stops paying and the next player has to pay him the appropriate number of cards. This continues around the table until a player pays the correct number of cards without turning up an ace or a court card. The player who played the last ace or court card wins the central pile and places it face down at the bottom of his own pile. The last player then starts a new round by playing the top card of his pile face up in the centre of the table and play continues as before.

A player who has played all his cards drops out of the game. The winner is the last player left in the game.

Donkey

No. of players: 3 to 13 (best with 5 or 6)
Equipment: Normal pack of 52 cards
Complexity: ∗

Donkey is a game for fast, furious fun. There are no winners, only a loser who is the 'donkey'.

From the pack of cards a number of sets are taken out, each set consisting of four cards of the same value. There should be one set for each player. The rest of the pack is put aside and is not used. For example, if there are five players the aces, twos, threes, fours and fives might be used.

The cards are shuffled thoroughly and dealt out face down to the players. The objective is to obtain four cards of the same value, or to avoid being last to react when another player has done so. Each player picks up his four cards and examines them, making sure that they are concealed from the other players. He chooses one card that he does not want and puts it face down on the table in front of him. All the players, at the same time, pass their face-down card to the next player on the left. Each player picks up the card he has been given and puts it in his hand with his other cards.

Again each player chooses a card he does not want (which may be the card he has just been given) and puts it face down on the table to be passed to the next player. The passing continues in this way, as quickly as possible, until one player has four cards of the same value in his hand. As soon as this happens he quickly places his cards face down on the table and puts his finger alongside his nose.

When the other players see what is happening they also must do the same as quickly as possible. The last player to put his finger to his nose is the 'donkey' for that round.

Further rounds are played until one player has been 'donkey' six times. He is the loser and as a penalty must 'hee haw' three times.

The best way of keeping score is to write down the names of the players on a sheet of paper and to write down one letter of the word 'donkey' by a player's name whenever he loses a round. The first player to have the word 'donkey' beside his name is the loser.

Variation
A number of counters (or buttons or matchsticks or whatever) are placed in the middle of the table. The number of counters must be one less than the number of players. When a player lays down his cards because he has a set of four he grabs a counter, and the other players must then do the same. The player who fails to grab a counter is the 'donkey' for that round.

Snip-Snap-Snorem

No. of players: 3 or more
Equipment: Normal pack of 52 cards
Complexity: ✫

The whole pack is dealt out face down to the player. Some players may get one more card than the others but this does not really matter. The players pick up their cards and look at them, without letting the other players see them.

The player to the left of the dealer starts the game by playing any card he chooses from his hand and placing it face up in the centre of the table. The next player to his left must play a card of the same value if he has one, placing it on top of the first card in the centre, and calling 'Snip'. If he has more than one card of the same value he plays only one of them. If he does not have a card of the same value he calls 'Pass'. It is then the turn of the next player on the left.

The game continues around the table in this way, each player playing a card of the same value as the first card if he can, or else calling 'Pass'. The player putting out the second card calls 'Snip', the player putting out the third card calls 'Snap', and the player putting out the fourth card calls 'Snorem'.

The player of the fourth card starts a new round by playing any card he chooses from his hand.

The winner is the first player to get rid of all his cards.

Variation 1
If a player has two or more cards of the same value then he must play them all in one turn. For example, if the first player plays a jack and the next player has two jacks he must play both of them at once, calling 'Snip Snap'.

Variation 2
Each of the players starts the game with an equal number of counters (or buttons or matchsticks or whatever). Whenever a player has to call 'Pass' he pays one counter into the kitty. The first player to get rid of all his cards wins all the counters in the kitty.

Happy Families

No. of players: 3 or more
Equipment: Normal pack of 52 cards (or 'Happy Families'
pack)
Complexity: ☆

This is a very popular game for young children. The whole pack is dealt out face down to the players. Some players may get one card more than the others but this does not really matter. Each player picks up and examines his cards and sorts them into 'families'. A family is four cards of the same value (e.g. four sixes or four queens). Throughout the game each player should take care to avoid letting other players see what cards he has in his hand.

The player to the left of the dealer begins the game by asking any other player for a particular card that he wants, to help complete a family. He may ask for any individual card he chooses provided that he already has at least one member of that family in his hand. If the player being asked has the card then it must be handed over to the player making the request, who again may ask any player for another particular card. He can go on doing this for as long as he continues to receive the cards he has asked for. When a player is asked for a card that he does not have then it becomes his turn to ask other players for the cards he wants.

Whenever a player collects all four members of a family he places the four cards face down on the table in front of him.

The game ends when all the cards have been collected into families, and the player who has collected the highest number of families is the winner.

Fish

No. of players: 2 or more
Equipment: Normal pack of 52 cards (or 'Happy Families'
pack)
Complexity: ☆

Fish is very similar to *Happy Families*, and like that game it may be played with an ordinary pack of cards or with a special 'Happy Families' pack.

Five cards are dealt out to each player, one at a time and face down. The rest of the pack is placed face down in the centre of the table and is known as the 'fish pile'. Each player picks up his cards and examines them. Throughout the game each player should take care that other players do not see what cards he has in his hand.

The player on the left of the dealer starts the game by asking any other player for any particular card he chooses – provided that he already has at least one card of the same value in his hand. If the player asked has the card then it must be handed over, and the first player may again ask any player for another card. He can continue doing this for as long as he receives the cards he has asked for.

When a player is asked for a card that he does not have then he says 'Fish' and the player making the request must take the top card from the fish pile. It then becomes the turn of the player saying 'Fish' to ask other players for the cards he wants. Whenever a player collects all four cards of a particular value he places them face down on the table in front of him.

The winner is the first player to get rid of all his cards. If two players finish at the same time, the one who has collected the most groups of four is the winner.

Go Boom

No. of players: 2 to 12
Equipment: Normal pack of 52 cards (or two packs if more than 6 players)
Complexity: ☆

The cards are shuffled and the dealer deals out the cards face down, dealing one card to each player in turn, and proceeding clockwise around the table until each player has been dealt seven cards. The remaining cards are placed face down in a neat pile (called the 'stock') in the centre of the table. Each player then picks up and examines his cards. The object of the game is to be the first player to get rid of all his cards.

The player to the left of the dealer starts the first round by choosing a card from his hand and placing it face up on the table beside the stock, thus forming the start of a new face-up pile. Then each player plays in turn, proceeding to the left around the table. Each player has to play a card of the same suit as the first card or, if he has no card of that suit in his hand, a card of the same value as the first card. For example, if the first card was the eight of hearts then he must play a heart or, if he has no hearts, an eight.

If a player has neither a card of the correct suit nor a card of the correct value in his hand then he must take a card from the top of the stock, and must carry on doing so until he picks a card that he can play. If all the cards of the stock have been taken he says 'Pass' and the turn passes to the next player.

The round ends when each player has played a card or has passed. The player who played the card of the highest value (ace counting high) starts the next round. If two or more players played equally high cards the first one to have played his card starts the next round.

The first player to get rid of all his cards is the winner. It is customary for the winner to yell 'Boom!' in as loud a voice as possible. (This might account for the name of the game.)

Variation
Go Boom may, if you like, be played for points. A series of games are played, and whenever a player 'goes boom' he scores points according to the total value of the cards left in the hands of the other players. An ace counts as one point, a two as two points and so on, court cards all counting as ten points. The first player to score 250 points, say, is the winner of the series.

Cheat

No. of players: 3 or more
Equipment: Normal pack of 52 cards
Complexity: ☆

Cheat is an entertaining game that allows plenty of scope for lying and bluffing. It is best played as quickly as possible.

The cards are shuffled and the whole pack is dealt out to the players. Some players may get one card more than the others but this does not really matter. The object of the game is to get rid of all the cards in one's hand.

The player to the left of the dealer starts the game by choosing any card from his hand and placing it face down in the centre of the table. At the same time he announces its value. The next player on his left then plays a card face down on top of the first, announcing the next higher value. For example, if the first player said 'Nine', the second player must say 'Ten'. The card he plays may be a ten – he may be telling the truth. But on the other hand he may 'cheat' by playing a card of any other value.

So the game continues, each player in turn playing a card face down on to the centre pile and announcing the next value, the following calls being 'Jack', 'Queen', 'King', 'Ace', 'Two' etc. It is important that each player should make sure that none of the other players can see the value of the card he is playing.

Whenever a player has played his card any other player may challenge him by calling 'Cheat'. The card is then turned over so that all the players may see it. If the card actually is what the player announced it to be (i.e. he was telling the truth) then the challenger has to take all the cards from the centre of the table and add them to his hand. If the player *had* cheated, however, and the card is not what he had declared it to be then *he* has to add the cards from the centre of the table to *his* hand.

If several players all call 'Cheat' at more or less the same time, you may need an umpire to decide who called first and therefore has the right to be the challenger. But probably the best way to decide is to play by the rule that if two or more players call 'Cheat' at the same time the challenger is the one nearest to the left-hand side of the player being challenged.

After a challenge a new round starts with the player to the left of the challenged player playing and announcing any card he chooses from his hand.

The game ends when one player gets rid of all his cards, and that player is the winner.

The players who are most successful are usually those who can bluff by looking innocent when they are cheating and by looking guilty when they are playing truthfully.

I Doubt It

No. of players: 3 or more
Equipment: Normal pack of 52 cards
Complexity: ★

I Doubt It is played in the same way as *Cheat*, except for the following differences:

(a) Instead of playing only one card at a time each player may play up to four cards at a time.
(b) The players announce the number of cards they are playing as well as their value (e.g. 'Three aces' or 'One three' or 'Four jacks' etc.).
(c) A player may 'cheat' not only by playing cards that are not of the value that he announces, but also by playing more cards than he announces.
(d) A challenge is issued by calling 'I doubt it'.

Slapjack

No. of players: 2 or more
Equipment: Normal pack of 52 cards (or two packs if there are more than 4 players)
Complexity: ★

Slapjack is a simple game that may be enjoyed by very young children. It is most fun when played as quickly as possible.

The object of the game is to win all the cards by slapping the jacks when they appear. All the cards are dealt out to the players. It does not matter if some players get one card more than the others. Each player forms his cards into a neat pile face down in front of him without looking at them. The player to the left of the dealer starts the game by taking the top card of his pile and placing it face upwards in the centre of the table. The player on his left then takes the top card from his own pile and places it face upwards on top of the first player's card. Each player in turn around the table does the same, playing a card face up on top of the previous player's card.

Whenever a jack appears as the top card of the pile, the first player to slap his hand on top of it wins all the cards in the pile. He turns over the cards he has won and shuffles them into his own face-down pile. The player to his left then starts a new round by playing the top card of his pile face up in the centre. When more than one player slaps the jack the player whose hand is underneath wins the pile. If a player slaps a card that is not a jack he must give the top card of his pile to the player whose card he slapped.

A player who is left with no cards may stay in the game until the next jack is played. If he is the first to slap it he wins the pile and can carry on playing, otherwise he drops out of the game.

The winner is the player who wins all of the cards.

Menagerie

No. of players: 3 or more
Equipment: Normal pack of 52 cards (or preferably two packs if more than 4 are playing)
Complexity: ★

This game, which is similar to *Snap*, is a great favourite with children. Before the game begins each player must be given the name of an animal – the longer the name the better. The fairest way to do this is to write some animal names on small pieces of paper which are then folded and mixed up, and to let each player pick one at random. Some suitable animal names are

RHINOCEROS	ANT-EATER	ORANG-UTANG
HIPPOPOTAMUS	CHIMPANZEE	FLITTERMOUSE
DROMEDARY	ARMADILLO	GRIZZLY BEAR
PORCUPINE	BUSHBABY	PLATYPUS

Each player must try to remember the animal names of the other players.

The cards are shuffled and are all dealt out to the players, one card at a time and face down. It does not matter if some players get one card more than the others. Each player forms his cards into a neat pile face down in front of him without looking at them. The player to the left of the dealer takes the top card from his pile and puts it face up on the table to start a new pile next to his face-down pile. The player on his left does the same, and so on around the table. The cards played on to the face-up piles should be placed neatly so that only the top card of each face-up pile can be seen. Whenever the top card of any player's face-up pile has the same value as the top card of another player's face-up pile, then each of these two players should, as quickly as possible, call out the other's animal name three times. The first to do so correctly wins the other's face-up pile and, turning it over, adds it to the bottom of his own face-down pile. The player to the left of the winner then starts a new round by turning up the top card of his pile, and so the game goes on.

A player who calls out an animal name by mistake (when there are no matching cards) must give his face-up pile to the player whose animal name he called out.

If a player has used all the cards in his face-down pile he turns over his face-up pile when it is his turn to play and continues playing from that. A player who has no cards left drops out of the game.

The winner is the player who wins all the cards.

Animal Noises

No. of players: 3 or more
Equipment: As for Menagerie
Complexity: ✶

Animal Noises is the same as *Menagerie* except that the players are given the names of animals (cat, dog, sheep, duck, donkey, cow etc.) whose noises may easily be imitated. When matching cards are seen the two players must each make the noise of the other's animal three times (e.g. 'Woof woof woof' or 'Baa baa baa').

War

No. of players: 2
Equipment: Normal pack of 52 cards
Complexity: ☆

War is a simple but satisfying game for which no skill whatever is required – the outcome is decided purely by chance.

One player deals out all the cards, one at a time and face down. Each player forms his cards into a neat pile face down in front of him, without looking at them. Each player then picks up the top card from his pile and the two cards are placed face upwards and side by side in the centre of the table.

If one card is of higher value than the other, the player who put out the higher card wins both of them and puts them, face down, at the bottom of his pile. Suits are not important – an ace is the highest value, followed by king, queen, jack, ten and so on down to two which is the lowest.

If both cards are of the same value, each player takes a card from the top of his pile and places it *face down* on top of his original card. He then plays one more card *face up* on top of that. If the two top cards are again equal, each player again plays a face-down card followed by a face-up card on top of the cards he has played previously. This goes on until one of the two top cards is higher than the other, and the player of the higher card wins all the cards in the centre of the table.

The game may be played until one player wins all the cards. But because the game may go on for a very long time when played this way, it may be decided that the winner is the player with the higher number of cards after the game has been played for some agreed length of time.

Cuckoo

No. of players: 3 or more
Equipment: Normal pack of 52 cards; 3 counters per player
Complexity: ☆

The object of this game (which also goes by the name of

Ranter-Go-Round) is to avoid being left with the lowest card. The cards rank in value from king (highest) to ace (lowest), suits being ignored. Each player is given three counters before the game begins. These are his 'lives' and when he has lost all three of them he is out of the game.

One card, face down, is dealt to each player. Each player picks up his card and looks at it, without letting it be seen by any of the other players. The player to the left of the dealer then decides whether he wants to keep his card or to exchange it. Naturally, if it is a high card he will want to keep it, but otherwise he puts it face down on the table and offers it to the next player on his left, saying 'Change'.

The player being offered the exchange may refuse it if his card is a king – he says 'King' and the first player must keep his own card. But if his card is not a king then he has no choice – he must accept the exchange. He puts his card face down on the table and each player picks up the other's card. But now it is his turn to decide whether to keep the card he has been given or to exchange it. If he so chooses he offers to exchange his card, in the manner just described, with the next player on his left. So the game goes on, once round the table, each player holding on to his card or offering to exchange it with the next player.

The dealer's turn comes last, and if he wants to exchange his card he does so by cutting the pack and taking the top card from the lower half. If the card the dealer takes from the pack is a king, he is the loser of the round and he loses a life. Otherwise the players all reveal their cards and the player with the lowest card loses a life. If two or more players tie for lowest card they all lose a life.

More rounds are played and each player drops out of the game when he has lost his last life. The winner is the last player left in the game.

Pelmanism

No. of players: 2 or more
Equipment: Normal pack of 52 cards
Complexity: ★

This game (also known as *Concentration*) is an excellent test of memory and of concentration. It can be enjoyed both by children and adults – and the younger players may often prove to be more skilful than their elders.

The pack is shuffled thoroughly and then all the cards are laid out, singly, face down on a large table (or on the floor). The cards may be laid out in rows or higgledy-piggledy, as long as no card is touching any other card.

Then each player in turn turns over any two cards so that all the players may see them. If the cards are of different values (e.g. a king and a seven) then he turns them face down again in their original positions and it is the next player's turn. But if the two cards are of the same value (e.g. two sixes) then the player wins them and puts them in a pile in front of him. He then has another turn and may continue as long as he turns over matching pairs. His turn ends when he turns over two cards that do not match.

Successful play depends on watching all the cards that are turned over and then replaced, and memorising their values and positions. For example, suppose the first player turned over a three and a seven and the second player turned over a king and a seven. The third player should immediately be able to turn over and win the pair of sevens – provided that he remembers where they are.

The game continues until all the cards have been won, and the player who has collected the highest number of cards is the winner.

My Ship Sails

No. of players: 4 to 7
Equipment: Normal pack of 52 cards
Complexity: ☆

My Ship Sails is a simple game but can be very exciting when played as quickly as possible.

The pack is shuffled and seven cards are dealt to each player, one card at a time and face down. The remaining cards are put to one side and are not used. Each player picks up his cards and sorts them into suits. Throughout the game each player should take care not to let any of the other players see the cards he has in his hand. The object of the game is to be the first player to collect seven cards of the same suit (i.e. seven hearts, seven diamonds, seven clubs or seven spades).

Each player selects from his hand one card that he does not want and places it face down on the table in front of him. All the players, at the same time, pass their face-down card to the next player on the left. Each player then picks up the card he has been passed and puts it in his hand with his other cards.

Again each player chooses a card to get rid of and the cards are passed on in the same way. This goes on until one player has managed to collect seven cards of the same suit. He calls out 'My ship sails' and wins the game.

Rolling Stone

No. of players: 4, 5 or 6
Equipment: Normal pack of 52 cards
Complexity: ☆

The object of the game is to be the first player to get rid of all his cards. Before the game starts, some cards must be removed from the pack so that there are just eight cards for each player. If there are six players all the twos should be removed; if there are five players all the twos, threes and fours should be removed; if there are four players all the twos, threes, fours, fives and sixes should be removed. The remaining cards are shuffled thoroughly and then dealt out one at a time, face down, so that each player receives eight cards. Each player picks up his hand and sorts it into suits.

The player to the left of the dealer chooses a card from his hand and plays it face up in the centre of the table. Each player in turn, proceeding round the table to the left, must place on top of it a card of the same suit if he can. If all the players put out a card of the same suit the pile of cards is put to one side and is not used for the rest of the game. The player who played the highest card (ace being high) then starts the next round by playing any card from his hand.

If at any time a player is unable to play a card of the suit that was led he must pick up all the cards that have already been played in that round and add them to his hand. He then starts a new round by playing a card of any other suit (he is not allowed to start with one of the cards he has just picked up).

The first player to get rid of all his cards is the winner.

INDEX